No Killer Instinct

R. E. Rothermich

Published by **Rogue Phoenix Press**
Copyright © 2015

ISBN: **978-1-62420-130-1**

Credits
Cover Artist: Amanda Kelsey
Editor: Sherry Derr-Wille

Dedication

To my beautiful wife Linda and the rest of our wonderful family; a labor of love, dedicated to you. To Carolyn; a true patriot and the best sister one could ever hope for.

Acknowledgements

Linda, thank you for your patience and encouragement throughout this endeavor. Tom Byrnes, life long friend and fellow author, thank you for your guidance from the very start. Dianna Graveman, who made thousands of corrections to my manuscript and added so many great suggestions to make this a better novel; thank you. Lieutenant Colonel Robert Wangen, U.S. Army (Retired); thank you, Bob, for your professional contribution that added authenticity and captured the genuine patriotic spirit of your 425th, Company 'F', Rangers. Dave Singer of Peregrine Manufacturing Inc., thank you for the much needed technical assistance.

Mike Lamb, I thank you for your ongoing spiritual advice and friendship along with the rest of the fellas. Jeff, Don and Denise, thanks for your professional input. John, Tim, Bob and Jamie for your first round edits and encouraging comments; thank you. A special sincere thank you to the Father, Son and Holy Spirit; without you, none of this is possible.

Prologue

On July 17, 1945, President Harry S. Truman, Prime Minister Winston Churchill, and Premier Joseph Stalin came together at Schloss Cecilienhof in Potsdam, Germany. It was here at the Potsdam Conference they would agree to disarm and demilitarize the defeated Germany. They would also agree that Nazism needed to be abolished and replaced by a local self-government set up on a democratic basis.

Until the establishment of a permanent new government, the administration of this German nation would be transferred to the military commanders of the United States, the Soviet Union, Great Britain, and France respectively, in their zones of occupation. To resolve issues related to Germany as a whole, a Four-Power Allied Control Council was established.

At this time, there were no specific plans for how they should proceed, and there were differences of opinions on what constituted a democracy. There was never a strategy to divide the country in half. With time, however, political aims and ideological differences became more evident between the Soviet and western powers.

In 1949, Germany was divided. The Federal Republic of Germany was controlled by the western allies, and the Soviets controlled the German Democratic Republic (GDR).

Six years later, on May 14, 1955, as pressures continued to build, the Warsaw Treaty Organization was formed. This alliance was comprised of seven European communist nations. Bulgaria, Czechoslovakia, Hungary, Poland, Romania, East Germany, and the Soviet Union were brought together as one single, united power.

The obvious threat from the Soviet Union prompted the idea among western powers that the Federal Republic should rearm in order to share in the overall responsibility of their defense, particularly in regard to manpower. This ultimately materialized in 1956 with the establishment of the *Bundeswehr* (Federal Armed Forces).

On March 1, 1956, the German Democratic Republic developed its own military by establishing the *Nationalen Volksarmee* (NVA), i.e., "The National People's Army." These forces were basically at full strength from their beginning.

This new "goose-stepping" army was well disciplined and equipped with the most modern military hardware. It was organized on Soviet Communist lines, but with a much greater component of long-established Prussian militarism. The German Democratic Republic, along with the NVA, followed the instructions of their Soviet leaders without question.

West Berlin was a glowing example of western democracy. Huge amounts of money were invested by the United States and eventually by West Germany itself.

Economic and political relations with the Federal Republic became stronger, and West Berlin became increasingly more remote from East Berlin and the surrounding German Democratic Republic.

At this time, there were no travel restrictions between the Eastern and Western Sectors. Observing a better economy and greater freedoms found in West Berlin, the people of East Berlin began to migrate to the West in large masses during the late 1950s. The GDR was in danger of extinction, because most of those who had fled to the West were young and more suitable for employment and were often highly-skilled tradesmen.

Prime Minister Nikita Khrushchev of the Soviet Union came to the aid of the GDR with his Berlin Offensive. It was November 1958 when

Khrushchev notified the three western allies, ending the Four-Power Agreement. His ultimatum stipulated the withdrawal of the western forces no later than May 1959, and the conversion of Berlin into a "free, demilitarized city." Prime Minister Khrushchev also stated he would negotiate a separate alliance of non-aggression with East Germany and would transfer Russian sovereignty over the Berlin air corridors to the Ulbricht government. The United States, Great Britain, and France rejected the Soviet's terms. Indeed, at this point, the proclaimed "Cold War" was beginning to heat up.

The flood of East Germans coming into the West had increased dramatically since June 1961. By July that same year, one in every nine inhabitants of the German Democratic Republic had escaped the country.

On August 13, 1961, United Press International announced that large contingents of the Communist People's Police had sealed off the borders of Berlin between the Eastern and Western Sectors. This was the beginning of a wall that would stand as a physical barrier to freedom for the next twenty-eight years. The political and ideological barriers would prove to be more withstanding.

Chapter One

The German State of Bavaria
Sunday, September 26, 1993

Approximately ten minutes before sunrise, Special Operations Investigator Erich Mueller pulled the midnight-blue Mercedes E300 off Highway 17, the connecting route between Fussen and the Austrian border, onto a nondescript dirt road—two parallel tire tracks mostly overgrown by grass and covered with pine needles. He traveled the length of the path, no more than two hundred fifty meters to a clearing at the edge of a small emerald lake.

Mueller got out of the car and stretched his arms and back. He breathed deeply, filling his lungs with the fresh mountain air, and reflected on how long it had been since he had visited this particular spot. It had been a place to return to nature in his adolescent years, a country retreat. Now he could finally slow down and enjoy a well-deserved holiday.

The past four weeks had been intense. The stress of the trial had mentally drained him, and he could feel the physical drag on his body, as well. A couple of days of trout fishing and total relaxation should recharge the batteries and re-sharpen his edge before reporting back to the National Security Agency listening post in Munich.

Mueller removed a pair of brand new Hodgman chest waders from the trunk of the Mercedes, along with his old Fenwick fly rod and an even older Horrocks-Ibbotson fly reel. Out of sheer habit, Mueller also picked up his personal Beretta 92F and slipped it into the open pouch in the top portion of the waders. The fact was, he felt naked without it.

Sitting on a large piece of granite at the water's edge, Mueller struggled into the chest-high wading boots. Carefully, he stepped into the crystal clear water to keep from spooking the brown and rainbow trout he could now begin to see. Daylight was creeping into the valley.

This end of the lake was rather shallow and was bordered to the north by an open field. Mueller waded slowly, stopping occasionally to take a short cast, until he found what an angler would consider to be "the right spot." He had only taken a single full cast toward the shore when he glanced over his left shoulder and noticed two hunters. One man was tall and slim, and the other was shorter and stocky. As Mueller looked in their direction, the shorter man raised a hand and hollered, "*Guten Morgen, mein Herr!*"

Mueller was no longer fly fishing. He had just been snapped back to the real world. *His world.* Immediately his brain switched into the "on" position like that of a computer microprocessor. It began sorting data in a fraction of a second. Something was wrong.

Mueller's eyes and ears had picked up a multitude of details in one quick glance. The first alert was the audible, "*Guten Morgen, mein Herr!*" said with a distinct American accent.

Why in the hell would anyone out hunting at this time of day yell out "Good morning" to some total stranger fifty meters away? Mueller thought.

For one thing, that would certainly scare off any game within the area. The men were both dressed as typical Bavarian hunters, but what type of game were they hunting? The tall man carried a pump shotgun, large gauge, and the short man held a bolt-action rifle which looked like a Remington model 700, possibly a 30-06 or a .308-caliber with a large, mounted scope. This was September—too early and much too warm for deer. The deer would be much higher in the mountains in early autumn.

Mueller told himself to calm down. *I'm being totally irrational,* he thought. *Two hunters, no big deal! I've been working too damn hard. I really do need to learn to relax, loosen up.*

But his intuition to detect trouble did not give way so easily. His brain continued to report its findings that something was definitely wrong. The alert mechanism had already been triggered, and the corresponding response was very clear and very basic: self-preservation. Protective measures must be taken *now!* Mueller reached for the Beretta and clicked off the safety.

~ * ~

Nearing Sassnitz, East Germany
February 7, 1988

Hauptmann Gerhardt Richter, Nationalen Volksarmee of the German Democratic Republic, stared out of a dirt-smudged window of the northbound train and saw nothing. Richter was totally immersed in his thoughts. Had the world around him actually started to change, he wondered, or was he just starting to wake up to the reality of his situation?

The train was beginning to slow down, still several kilometers from the rail yard and docking facilities of the ferry that would transport them across the eastern edge of the Baltic Sea to Trelleborg, Sweden. If Richter were to have directly answered his own questions, he could have simply responded "Yes" to both queries and would have been totally correct. The young, blond, blue-eyed captain was a victim of his own heritage.

The Richter family was steeped in German military tradition. His father presently held a high political office in the GDR, after having resigned his commission as a general in the NVA due to failing health. Gerhardt's grandfather had served as a colonel in Adolph Hitler's army.

Richter recalled the stories his father often told of his own father's activities at Dachau. Privately, among his family and close friends, he actually laughed and made jokes about how the "mighty" colonel would march the Jews to their death and have their bodies stacked like firewood on a cart to be hauled away to some mass grave. Publicly, Gerhardt's father adamantly denied any connection with the death camp and disassociated himself from anything pertaining to the Nazi party for fear of reprisal. There was never any remorse when he told these stories; they only seemed to become more graphic and more obscene as the years progressed. He often openly admitted he idolized his father and felt that he had been born one generation too late. *These are the men I am expected to emulate? These are the men who had an impact on my military education and actually influenced my instructors?* Gerhardt Richter had had these thoughts before, but lately they seemed to hang on for longer periods of time and were reoccurring much more frequently. In the past, he would force himself to shake these thoughts and clear his mind, but today was different.

All around him things were beginning to change. Young people talked of abstract things like political reform and religion; they uttered words like "justice" and "freedom." Something was about to change; it had to. Richter could feel it in his bones.

Captain Richter welcomed his new assignment as commander of the guard to supervise the safety and well-being of East Germany's finest athletes as they prepared to compete in the European Winter Games. In more realistic terms, it was his responsibility that none of the athletes, coaches, or trainers—or guards, for that matter—should attempt an escape to the free world. After all, that would cause a terrible embarrassment to East Germany.

The GDR had granted permission for its athletes to be showcased in this year's competitions primarily to counteract the increasingly negative political publicity it had been receiving over the last several months, but also because the games would be held in and around Stockholm, and Sweden was considered a neutral country.

Richter was eager to accept any assignment that would remove him from the drudgery of another gray winter in Berlin. He had heard Stockholm was a beautiful city, even in the dead of winter.

Captain Gerhardt Richter got up and stepped over the other five soldiers in the cramped, smelly compartment of the special government train and into the passageway lined with athletes, coaches, trainers, and NVA guards. The captain was beginning to feel claustrophobic. The lack of ventilation made the smell of cigarette smoke, perspiration, and other unpleasant body odors that much more unbearable. An open-air cattle car would have been a huge improvement over this form of travel.

Making his way to the adjoining car, over the small platform above the couplings, he stopped as a gush of frigid air enveloped him. The noise of the train was loud, and the temperature was considerably colder here in a space only protected from the outside air by the flexible accordion-type material, but there was no one else occupying this space. The cold air was refreshing, and he could tolerate the squeaks, the grinding noises, and the clatter of the moving train. Gerhardt Richter lit a thin, wood-tipped cigar and promptly reverted to his previous mode of deep thought. The slightest fibers of an idea were beginning to form. *Possible opportunities?* Halfway through the slim cigar, one could detect only by very close observation, a certain glint in the Captain's eye. The rest of his face remained carved in stone.

~ * ~

After the first three days in Stockholm, Captain Richter could see the pattern in the daily activities that took place prior to the actual competition. Work schedules for the guards had been posted. There was very little free time, as expected, for the officers of the guard detachment.

Housing for the guards and a large group of the athletes was much better than Richter had expected. They were billeted in a large, newly renovated multipurpose building which was part of a private university. The building contained dormitories, a well-equipped gymnasium, and a complete food service facility. The living conditions here were ten times better than what Richter and the other officers had back in East Berlin.

At first, Richter had considered somehow slipping away and making a break for freedom. Considering his position, this would not have been too difficult. But considering how he had grown to despise the communists almost as much as he detested the Nazis of World War II, he wanted to do more than just defect and cause a bit of public embarrassment for the East German Army. Gerhardt Richter wanted to create something positive from this opportunity, something to hit the GDR where it would inflict the most damage.

Captain Gerhardt Richter had decided, while still en route to Stockholm, that he would somehow, someway, reach American officials, probably through the U.S. Embassy, and offer his services as an insider to the GDR. As risky as it may be, he was willing to take the chance. He could not go on living a lie, serving a master he hated with such passion.

Richter knew he possessed the most important tool to accomplish this task. He had their trust. Although he had been accepted into the most prestigious military academies in East Germany on the name of his father and grandfather only, Richter had earned the respect and highest accolades from his instructors on his own merit. He had always been an above-average student, even in the most difficult disciplines of science, mathematics, and foreign language. Gerhardt especially excelled in field tactics and military strategy, and in matters of military intelligence. The Headquarters Corps of the NVA was eager to have this fresh young soldier join its ranks. High-ranking officers were actually recruiting Richter for his services in their various divisions. Gerhardt Richter was somewhat astounded by the attention he had received upon his graduation from the Academy and simultaneous commission as a lieutenant in the East German Army, equal to a second lieutenant in the U.S. military.

In the beginning, he had gone along with the wishes of his family, primarily his father—demands would be more accurate—to follow a military career; it was an obligation. He had no other options.

As a trusted comrade who rubbed elbows with many of the powers within the Communist Party in East Germany, Richter had access to some classified information, but not as much as he wanted right now. With a targeted push in that direction, Richter was certain he could achieve the rank of major and place himself among the movers and shakers of the GDR. Now that he had a goal, he would do everything within his power to achieve it. If his comrades got in the way of his progress, they would pay the price, simple as that. Now he would let his prestigious surname work to his advantage, unlike in the past. If the name Richter opened doors at the top, then so be it. Reaching executive status within a year was certainly not out of the question. *Let the Games begin.*

Timing would be extremely critical, Richter thought as he lay on his bed staring at the ceiling in the only private dormitory room in the building. It would have to be just right, or the whole opportunity would be wasted, or worse—he could be caught and shot by a firing squad as a traitor.

Richter sat up and opened the brown leather satchel next to the bed. After a little digging, he found the dog-eared map of Stockholm. It was old, but prominent buildings and points of interest were numbered. The Academy had always stressed the importance of reconnaissance and familiarization of the terrain. Well, that's exactly what he had in mind.

Without too much trouble, he located the U.S. Embassy on the map. Richter estimated it was only a little over four kilometers away, at Dag Hammarskjolds vag 31. This was encouraging. He committed to memory some of the other main streets near the embassy: Strandvagen, Nobelgatan, and Gardesgatan. He did not dare write anything down.

Now, how the hell do I reach the other side? he thought. He couldn't very well just hop in a taxi in his NVA dress uniform, slip the driver a few crowns, and tell him to take him to the U.S. Embassy.

During one of the preliminary briefings back in East Berlin, the guard officers had been instructed at great length as to their own restrictions. One point was made perfectly clear: none of the guard detachment would be allowed to bring civilian clothes, and there would be a shakedown inspection of all baggage conducted prior to boarding the train.

"This is NOT a holiday!" explained Major Scherer, who had conducted the briefing.

It was evident to most that the NVA was not going to make it easy for anyone who had the notion to sample genuine freedom. Gerhardt Richter resented the fact they always tried to mask the obvious reasons with a childish explanation.

Stay focused, he reminded himself. *Don't rush it.* He had three weeks to accomplish this task and mustn't do anything until the right situation presented itself. Richter folded up the map, placed it back in his briefcase, and headed down the hallway to the gymnasium.

The guards had permission to use the gym and all of its equipment in their off-duty hours, but only if it was not in use by the athletes and their trainers. The gym had all of the most modern equipment: a weight training room complete with treadmills, stationary bicycles, free weights, weight-lifting benches, incline boards, a trainer's table, and a stainless-steel whirlpool bath. Nothing but the best for these East German athletes. This was another thing that irked Gerhardt Richter. While some people in East Germany were nearly starving, these select athletes lived like royalty, only because God had seen fit to grow them larger, stronger, or faster than the others. On second thought, it could just be due to the anabolic steroids most of them took.

At about 1800 hours, Captain Richter had hoped the weight room would be available for a light workout. He felt he needed a little physical activity to release some of the pressure. The husky, white-haired chief trainer of the East German athletes came into the vacant weight room only minutes after Richter.

"Good evening, Comrade Captain. May I help you?" he asked in the polite manner that a servant would ask his master. Richter had placed his uniform jacket and shirt neatly on the seat of the leg press apparatus.

"Good evening to you, sir," Richter replied with the respect he felt was owed the older gentleman, regardless of his own military rank or status. "I would just like to use your weight room, if that's okay."

"Of course, Comrade Captain. You have no workout sweats, sir?"

Richter shook his head.

"Allow me to fix that for you. Follow me, please." The trainer guided the captain back to his glassed-in office, flipping on the lights in the locker room and shower areas as they went. He unlocked the office. Richter realized the older man must have been on his way out of the building when he had spotted the lights on in the weight room.

11

"Ah, let's see. You would be a size extra-large sweatshirt, and probably a large in the sweatpants, correct?" The trainer gathered a set of brand new gray sweats from a large equipment locker. "You'll need a supporter, socks, and what size shoes, please?"

"Eleven and a half," replied Richter, amazed at what was going on. The older man continued to collect the personal gear from other shelves in the equipment locker and stacked them in Richter's arms.

"Comrade Captain, the towels and soap are just inside the showers. Oh, and here is a lock. The combination is on the small tab attached, and you may use any of the full-length lockers that are not in use, over here," he said pointing to a row of mostly vacant metal mesh lockers. "Is there anything else you might need?"

"No. Thank you! You've been most helpful. If you were on your way out, you don't need to stay on my account. I can certainly lock the doors and turn off the lights when I leave," said Richter.

"You wouldn't mind? I've been here since before six this morning, and I'm starting to slow down a little early at my age," said the trainer.

"I don't mind at all. Go on. I'll secure the place when I'm finished working out," Richter said.

"Very well, Comrade Captain." The trainer opened the top desk drawer, fumbled around through miscellaneous hardware, and handed the commander of the guard a single key. "Here is an extra key to the gymnasium. Please feel free to come and go as you wish. I realize your hours are probably somewhat irregular, and I may not be here to let you in during the late hours. Enjoy your workout, Comrade Captain." He put on his heavy coat and fur-lined cap and headed out the door for his lesser quarters in a much older building on campus.

Well now, this is an interesting development! Gerhardt Richter thought as he quickly changed into the gray sweats and new Adidas training shoes. *This might just be the small window of opportunity I'm looking for.*

Richter was skeptical and a little apprehensive about just falling into this possible opportunity. He wondered if he might be rushing things. He had to keep his emotions in check and not be influenced by his strong desire to seek justice against the domineering communist rule. But he couldn't just sit there and wait for someone to ask if he needed a lift to the U.S. Embassy, could he?

He began to search the gymnasium for some additional civilian clothing. Although it wasn't bitterly cold, he knew he would look out of place on the street without a jacket or coat. He must blend into his surroundings like a chameleon and not call attention to himself.

He had seen nothing in the head trainer's office. He tried several lockers and found nothing but a few sweat-soaked t-shirts and jock straps.

Only one door remained that he had not tried: a small broom closet near the back door emergency exit. There, hanging on a metal hook next to a snow shovel and a large bag of rock salt, was a dark royal blue nylon ski jacket. The cuffs were frayed, and the collar was discolored and badly worn, but it fit Richter with some room to spare. As an extra added bonus, the captain found a multicolored ski cap and gloves stuffed in the side pockets. *Perfect!* This would be excellent camouflage for the terrain in which he needed to work.

Richter returned to the locker room, secured his uniform in an empty full-length locker, and brought with him a fairly heavy metal coat hanger and a small roll of discarded athletic tape he had found under the bench in front of his locker. Richter turned off all but one light and locked the gymnasium door behind him, then headed toward the emergency exit door in the rear of the building.

Captain Richter quickly used the metal coat hanger and tape to provide a complete electrical circuit that would remain intact and not set off an alarm once he opened the emergency door. He also taped back the bolt on the lock so he would not be locked out upon his return. Richter knew, because he had personally set up the walking perimeter for guards around the campus "compound," that it was not necessary for the back side of this building to be monitored.

Under the guise of his new instant identity, Richter stepped out into the unfamiliar streets of Stockholm. He could very well imagine how it might be to someday have the freedom to come and go as he wished, to not be constantly preoccupied with threats from senior-ranking officers and political officials. For some reason, the cold night air seemed a little cleaner, a little fresher than before.

Richter wished he had spent more time studying the map. He pictured it in his mind, having committed to memory the names of the main streets that led to the embassy. He would have liked to be better informed on the lesser traveled side streets as an indirect return route, in case he needed to take some evasive measures.

This expedition is strictly reconnaissance, he reminded himself, as he walked quickly to gain as much distance from the training site as fast as he could. Richter discovered his heart was pounding as he stopped at an intersection and waited for traffic to pass. He had considered the underground system for a moment, but quickly rejected the idea of being in an unfamiliar and confined space. Better to learn the lay of the land.

Passing by a storefront window, Captain Richter noticed in the reflection just how shabby he looked—a cross between a street person and a half-hearted athlete out for some exercise. His disguise would have to do for the time being. After several blocks, he finally approached the embassy from the opposite side of the street. "Number 31 Dag Hammarskjolds vag," Richter muttered, making as many mental notes as his memory could hold.

Under the well-lit portico, two U.S. Marines, in dress blue uniforms and with side arms, stood guard on either side of the double white doors. Gerhardt Richter continued to walk at the same pace, which had slowed considerably from when he had started, making certain that his observations were as inconspicuous as humanly possible. He spotted a quiet little café about a half block down from the embassy building. An empty table sat near the window. He entered and sat by the window with a full view of the U.S. Embassy from a distance of about a hundred meters. Richter ordered a small pot of coffee and enjoyed the warmth and comfortable ambiance of this pleasant Stockholm café.

He watched the two guards with a professional eye, for he had the greatest respect and admiration for the U.S. Marine Corps. He had read several books and military journals containing historical information about this particular branch of the U.S. Armed Forces. Richter felt it had to be the personal discipline instilled in these soldiers that made them a superior fighting force. U.S. Marines seemed to be almost all of the same size and build. They all looked like they could be professional athletes. The only distinguishing features that separated the two guards on duty now was that the sergeant, a black man, wore thin, metal-framed eye glasses, and the other Marine was of lower rank—Lance Corporal, Richter believed they called it—thinking it an unusual classification. He also looked to be a few years younger.

Richter sipped his coffee and continued his discreet observation. He noticed some movement. Two more Marines appeared, and the black sergeant exchanged hand salutes with another sergeant. The two original guards smartly stepped away in unison, leaving their post to the new guards who had relieved them. Richter glanced at his watch and made a mental note that the guards were changed promptly at 2000 hours. He continued to watch and tried to formulate some idea about how to make himself and his services known to the other side. Captain Gerhardt Richter was drawing a blank.

At about 2015, from the far side of the embassy, Richter noticed two men round the corner and cross the street directly in front of the embassy building. The first man dashed across the road, seaming to defy oncoming cars. The second pedestrian, a black man with metal-framed glasses, took a more sensible approach and waited for a safer break in the traffic. Without a doubt, these were the Marine guards.

The pair walked directly in front of the window seat at the café. Instantly, Richter got up, left money on the table for his coffee, exited the café, and began trailing the two Marines at a safe distance. He had no idea where this might lead, but it might be a start. The jaunt was not that far: two blocks farther from the café, and then a right turn and one more block to a lively, urban pub.

Richter waited outside for a short time, pretending to be looking over the bill of fare posted next to the entrance. Once inside, it was easy enough to spot the two men. Richter stayed well against the back wall of the pub.

Now things seemed to be happening very quickly. This would be the place to make contact. He might not get another chance like this. Richter realized that what he was about to do was not a normal function of an embassy guard, but he would have to trust the good judgment of these Marines. If everything he had learned of the U.S. Marine Corps were true, this contact would be carried out without incident, if handled properly. That was a pretty big "if." Contact with just one of the men would be preferable, keeping with the concept of a minimal profile.

Richter borrowed a pen from a passing waiter and began to scribble his message on the back of a paper Carlsberg Beer coaster.

U.S. Marine,

I need your help. Matter of national importance. Can provide high-level information on NVA activities from within. Must contact your embassy station chief. Meet with you here tomorrow PM, same time. Acknowledge. Please use utmost discretion.

Captain Gerhardt Richter looked up and paused, realizing this would be the point of no return once his message was delivered. He began to make his way toward the long table where the two Marines had been sitting. The younger man was on his way to the men's W.C., leaving a vacant seat on each side of the Marine sergeant.

Richter pressed between the pub patrons and empty chairs until he was just to the left of Sergeant Edwin Maxwell. As he sat down, the sleeve of his jacket knocked two or three Carlsberg Beer coasters to the floor, and he quickly bent down to pick them up. He placed the coaster with his handwritten note, message side up, just slightly to the left of Sergeant Maxwell, who was already watching the clumsy intruder. As soon as the Marine saw the handwritten note, he made quick eye contact with Richter and began to read the message that had been slipped in front of him.

Maxwell's facial expression did not change; he merely stroked his chin once with his right hand and gave a very slight, almost imperceptible nod to acknowledge this unusual message. With his left hand, he casually flipped over the coaster and slid it into the left pocket of his jacket that hung on the back of his chair.

Lance Corporal Jim Schnietz returned to the table, gulped down his remaining beer, and had raised his hand to order another round when Maxwell gently took hold of Schnietz's arm and brought it back down.

The young Marine looked at his superior with a mildly perplexed expression and asked, "Hey, Max. What's up with that? Didn't you want another beer?"

"No, and neither do you."

"But Max, this was only my first beer! I'll just have…"

"No," the sergeant said more sternly. "You've had plenty to drink, Jim, and you need your beauty sleep. We'll be shoving off now."

With that, Sergeant Maxwell was on his feet, handing Lance Corporal Schnietz his coat. Now Schnietz's expression was very perplexed. Maxwell offered no explanation during their brisk walk back to the embassy compound, and the lance corporal knew better than to ask.

Through the gates, Lance Corporal Schnietz turned left toward the guard billet. Sergeant Maxwell said, "See you at O-six hundred, Jimbo," and kept walking straight forward, up the steps, past the guards, and through the double wide front entrance into the U.S. Embassy.

Much to the surprise of Sergeant Maxwell, the lights were on and the door was open to the office of the deputy chief of mission. Kevin Glenn sat behind the large cherrywood desk, bracketed by two stacks of paperwork. Maxwell centered the doorway and rapped twice sharply against the hardwood doorframe.

"Hey, Maxie, come on in. Have a seat. What brings you here at this hour?"

Maxwell was one of Glenn's favorite "watch standers." Why he was only an E-5 was a mystery to Glenn, but then that was none of his business. The deputy chief of mission expected to see the usual cheerful face come to life and hear some quick retort about himself still in his office burning the midnight oil. Instead, the expressionless Marine came in and sat down in one of the two leather-upholstered chairs in front of Glenn's desk.

"I know that the chain of command calls for me to report to my detachment commander, and I also know that Gunnery Sergeant Feller will not be back 'till much later this evening. I need to pass something very important along to the next higher up on the chain, right away. I suppose I should really speak with Ms. McClintock about it." The sergeant was not feeling at all comfortable with this scenario.

"First of all, yes, I'll try to reach the RSO right away," said Glenn. "Secondly, you're already here in my office, so you might as well tell me what's going on. You seem a little uptight, Sarge. What's up?"

"Well, sir, something very odd just happened about fifteen minutes ago at Falsterbo Pub." Maxwell paused, determining how best to explain his serious encounter. "This guy comes up to me from out of nowhere and gives me this," he said, reaching into his pocket and handing the DCM the pulpboard coaster. "Read the back of it, Mr. Glenn," said the sergeant.

It only took a few seconds to read, and Glenn read it again out loud, as if he might have missed something the first time.

"This *is* interesting," said Glenn in a low voice. "Shut the door, will you Max?" He reached for the phone to call the regional security officer.

Sergeant Maxwell shut the door and returned to the chair.

"Lynn, this is Kevin. I know that it's late, but something has come up you need to be in on. Okay. Thanks. See you in five."

Lynn McClintock, the U.S. Embassy Stockholm RSO, was thirty-one years old and a picture of fitness with dishwater blond hair pulled back in a French braid. She arrived in Kevin Glenn's office in a few seconds shy of five minutes.

McClintock extended her hand and offered a friendly greeting to the sergeant. She, too, appreciated the Marine and the excellent work he did for the embassy.

Upon Glenn's instruction, Maxwell repeated what little he had told Glenn, as Glenn handed the RSO the Carlsberg coaster. McClintock raised her eyebrows in surprise as she read the message and picked up on the questioning.

"Ever see this guy before?" she asked.

"No, Ma'am."

"How'd he know you were a Marine?"

"Don't know, Ma'am."

"What did this guy look like?"

"Didn't get a real good look, but he was dressed kind of funny for being at the pub. Beat-up old coat..."

"Give me as much description as possible," interrupted Glenn, who was busy taking notes on a yellow legal pad.

"Blue beat-up ski coat and a gray sweatshirt underneath. I think he might have had gray sweatpants on, too. Not positive on that. He was dressed kind of like a bum, but he was clean-shaven and had blond hair, cut short. What do you make of it, Ms. McClintock? A possible defector?"

Although the question was directed to the RSO, Kevin Glenn responded.

"I think we've got more than just a defector, Maxie. If he wanted to defect, he would have walked right through the front door. We'll sure as hell find out what we've got, though, and don't make any plans for tomorrow night, either."

~ * ~

Gerhardt Richter headed back toward the university complex. He was extremely conscious of the possibility of a tail and took in several extra blocks in order to observe if someone was indeed following him. The NVA captain would stop occasionally and look in a storefront window, trying to notice if anyone else on the sidewalk was moving and stopping with him. Richter could not detect any synchronized movement on the sparsely traveled street, so he proceeded back to the campus dormitory with great care.

He knew full well it would be tricky getting back in the building. Richter pulled the knit cap down over his ears, not allowing any hair to show, and changed his gait from a brisk step to a much slower pace, that of a much older man.

Once inside the building, he moved quickly to the locker room to retrieve his uniform, return the borrowed coat and cap, and dismantle the makeshift electrical circuit on the emergency exit.

Not a hitch. So far, so good. *So this is what it's like to be a spy,* he thought, chuckling nervously.

Richter bounded up the stairs two at a time to return to his private room. There, standing at the top of the stairwell, was the overly obnoxious Lieutenant Friedrich Ostermann; a large, moderately overweight man who looked much too old to be a first lieutenant. He stood in his undershirt and uniform trousers, unbuttoned at the top to let his gut hang out, holding a bottle of vodka about three quarters full.

Richter had not particularly cared for Ostermann from the time he had been assigned to the guard detachment. To make things even more unsavory, he served as Richter's executive officer. Captain Richter regarded the lieutenant as an overbearing "storm trooper" type, always pushing the limitations of his rank as a junior officer. *Born too late for the Third Reich,* thought Richter. *Too bad. He would have fit in so well in my grandfather's army.*

"Hauptmann Richter! Where have you been? I was looking for you," Lieutenant Ostermann said in a booming voice.

None of your damned business where I was, thought Richter. "And what difference is that to you, Oberleutnant?" he asked curtly.

"I wanted to share my good findings with you, Comrade Captain," Ostermann said, lifting the bottle of vodka.

"And how did you acquire *that*?" asked his superior.

"One of the trainers—the old man. This morning I found it in his equipment bag. I told him he was not permitted to have it. So I took it!" The lieutenant laughed, beaming with pride.

That figures, thought Richter. *An overstuffed bully, pushing his weight around with the old guy.*

"I looked all over, but couldn't find you," continued Lieutenant Ostermann.

Richter had not really considered an alibi beforehand. Probably should have.

"If you must know, Lieutenant, I went to the weight room for a workout…"

"I checked there, and the room was dark, locked up," Ostermann interrupted.

"…and then I went over to the ice rink to watch the figure skaters practice. Next time, Lieutenant, I will be sure to tell you *exactly* where I am going," the captain said, his voice laced with venom.

Lieutenant Friedrich Ostermann did not have the good sense to apologize, although his voice did adopt a much quieter, almost friendly tone.

"What did you think of Christel Angsteller? Very good, eh?" asked the lieutenant.

"A very good skater indeed, and extremely pretty. I'm sure she'll bring our country at least a silver medal, if not the gold. She will make East Germany very proud." A little political bullshit to help mask the lie.

"Yes, I agree. At least a silver," Ostermann said. "Good night, Comrade Captain. Have a peaceful evening."

Richter gave an informal salute to acknowledge his dismissal.

Later he lay in his bunk, eyes wide open in the dark. He had made a commitment, and he would see it through. He was not sure where the road he was on would lead, but he was sure of this: he would do his part to fight the loathsome atrocity called communism.

The duty roster posted in the hallway on the second floor of the guards' billet would be the same as the day before and the day before that. Captain Richter saw no need to change the routine, especially today.

The only thing that seemed to have changed overnight was the demeanor of his executive officer. Lieutenant Ostermann was actually pleasant to his CO; he was not the abrasive buffoon he usually appeared to be. *No harm in that,* thought Richter.

At 1800 hours, Gerhardt Richter watched from his second-story room as the head trainer left the building and walked across the campus toward his temporary quarters. It should now be clear to enter the locker room without being noticed, but it was still much too early. He needed to kill some time and relax, but realistically, relaxing was out of the question.

At about 1930, Richter was finally at his locker, changing into the gray sweats, Adidas shoes, and borrowed dark blue ski coat and knit cap. Once again, he rigged the emergency exit to not sound the automatic alarm system when the door was opened. He again taped back the spring bolt to allow him passage back into the locker room. Richter had allowed plenty of time for the trek and took a slightly different route to the Falsterbo Pub, skirting the U.S. Embassy entirely and taking all possible precautions to avoid being tailed.

At exactly 2030, Richter entered the pub and waited only a moment inside the doorway before spotting the black Marine sergeant, again dressed in civilian attire. The NVA captain walked directly over, pulled back a chair, and sat down beside him, near the same spot as the previous evening.

Across the street and down about sixty or seventy meters from the entrance was a white VW minivan. Inside the van were two very skilled NSA technicians, equipped with the latest audio and video surveillance equipment, as well as 35 mm cameras with 100X infrared lenses for detailed close-ups of the man claiming to be able to provide high-level information on NVA activity. Sensitive listening devices were also in play tonight for this rendezvous. Sergeant Maxwell had been wired for sound. Deputy Chief of Mission Glenn had insisted that he also be inserted into the pub, and because of the apparent shortage of available intelligence officers, he was permitted to take an active role in tonight's clandestine meeting.

Kevin Glenn was equipped with a tiny radio transmitter and earphone no larger than the smallest modern hearing aid. He could communicate with the techs in the van to give a play-by-play of what he was observing from within the pub; for this, Glenn asked the assistance of the regional security officer, Lynn McClintock. What Kevin Glenn completely understood from the get-go was that McClintock was going to be there whether the DCM had requested it or not. She called the shots when it came to security issues, and no one was going to keep her away from this main event. Glenn had requested to work with a member of the opposite sex for the simple reason of not appearing to be talking to himself or to be whispering into the ear of another male. Unofficially, he enjoyed Lynn's company more than he let on. She was fascinating to work with.

Everyone was in place; the stage was set. The NSA tech personnel and the embassy staff were taking all of the precautions not to let an outsider in who could possibly turn into a double agent. The photos would be processed and directed to Fort Mead, Maryland, at once and then run through the computer to insure his proper identity. Even if this man with no name could produce valuable inside information to them immediately, they would watch his every activity very closely, because absolutely no one was trusted until they had turned his very soul inside-out, looking for anything that might even hint of loyalty toward East Germany or the USSR. "Take what you can get, qualify it, but never give anything in return," was their unwritten credo.

"Is this seat occupied?" Gerhardt Richter politely asked the Marine sergeant.

"No, please sit down."

The meeting was more than a little tense at first. Both men seemed to wait for the other to take the lead. Sergeant Maxwell had been thoroughly briefed by McClintock and Glenn on how to handle the NVA officer: "Let him talk. Do whatever you can to make him feel comfortable. Most important, make sure he receives and understands the instructions as to where to meet his contact."

The East German produced a pack of cigarettes from his jacket pocket, lit one, and extended the pack to his new colleague.

"Care for a smoke?" Only two cigarettes remained.

"Yes, of course. Thank you," replied Maxwell.

"Keep the pack."

Upon taking out a cigarette, Maxwell noticed a paper neatly folded in the HB box-like pack.

"Thanks," murmured Maxwell, remaining cool as a cucumber, as if he did this espionage thing every day. He left the pack on the tabletop for a while before putting it in his pocket.

Richter remained silent. He had written a brief resume, explaining his reason for wanting to ally himself with the free world and that he was willing to risk his life for the cause of freedom. He went so far as to include his military service number and half a photograph picturing only himself. Richter had kept the better half. She was much too pretty to pass along, but more importantly, he did not want to involve anyone else in his personal mission. Captain Richter was just trying to make the NSA's job a little easier when they checked him out. He didn't know they were already several steps ahead of him in that department.

The NVA officer said in a very low tone, just barely audible over the noise of the pub, "Is there someone else here I should meet?"

"You are to go to the nearest underground station. Do you know where that is?" asked Sergeant Maxwell.

"Yes, about three blocks east of here, correct?"

Maxwell nodded. Obviously Richter had studied his city map very well.

"A diagram of the metro system is on the wall there. Stand in front of it as if you are studying the map. A woman in a long, green coat, carrying a single shopping bag, will approach you and ask if you need any help. She is your contact. Do exactly as she tells you. You will meet her there at 2100 hours sharp. This is all I can tell you."

Richter said nothing, but gave the Marine sergeant the slightest smile that conveyed his sincere appreciation for helping him through this first step toward a new life. Then he got up and walked out, turned right, and headed for the metro station.

Maxwell waited and finished his beer, looking across the room to where Glenn and McClintock were seated. Glenn gave the predetermined signal, a green light for the Marine sergeant to leave. Glenn and McClintock waited an additional three or four minutes before making their exit. The white minivan had pulled away, following Richter at a safe distance.

Maxwell walked back to the embassy while the DCM and "his date" hailed a taxi and took a roundabout way back to his office where they would all soon meet for the debriefing. Glenn was happy the ambassador was out of the country on a two-week vacation in Ocho Rios. Things always went a lot smoother when the boss wasn't there to get in the way.

~ * ~

At 2059, Richter stood looking at the diagram of the Stockholm Metro System as instructed. Just ninety seconds later, an attractive woman in her late twenties or early thirties, sporting a full-length green coat and shoulder-length, stylishly-cut dark brown hair, stood by his side. Richter tried to be as inconspicuous as possible. He noticed the woman's beautiful brown eyes and an almost friendly smile. He wondered if she might be Italian. With a second glance, he noted she did in fact carry a single shopping bag.

Another minute passed as they both looked at the color-coded diagram. Finally, she spoke.

"Can I possibly be of any help?"

Her German was perfect, which surprised the NVA officer. No one was in the near vicinity of the two. A few people waited on a bench farther down the wall of this grotto-like metro station. Richter felt as if he was in an art museum rather than an underground rail station, for this was far from the typical U-Bahn station he was accustomed to in Berlin. One neatly dressed man stood near the north end of the subway tunnel, and a middle-aged man and woman stood at the south opening of the dark tube.

"Yes, I hope so," replied Richter.

"I think you should take the north-bound red line, the T13, toward Ropsten. I'm going that way myself, if you wish to accompany me. The train should be here in about…" She glanced at her watch. "…one minute. The Stockholm Metro is always on time."

She gave Gerhardt a slight smile, maybe just for a little well-needed reassurance.

They walked to the edge of the polished, green-tiled platform, only waiting seconds before a gush of air pushed through the south opening of the tube, followed by the bright blue metro train.

Richter reasoned that the lone man at the north end and the couple at the south were party to this rendezvous. They were inconspicuous, but both locations kept in visual contact with Richter and the woman in the full-length green coat. *How many others here are watching me?* he wondered.

Words were not spoken until they were seated on the train at the rear of one of the middle cars, with no other occupied seats for five or six rows.

"You may call me Jennifer," she began. "No need to be nervous. Why do you want to offer East German information to us?" she said, getting straight to the point.

Richter stated in brief exactly those points he had included in his resume. His reasons were justifiable, and he hoped his words, spoken in person, conveyed a feeling of credibility that written words could not fully express.

~ * ~

The young NSA Intelligence officer, Jennifer Ann Frost, would be 99 percent sure if this guy was for real within the first couple of minutes of her interview. She had positive feelings about the East German Army captain right from the start. Ms. Frost decided to give him a chance to prove himself. She asked him technical questions about the information he had claimed he had access to back in Berlin. He would not know that she, the NSA, already possessed these answers in detail. Nothing more than a simple test.

"How do I get this information to you?" Richter asked.

"You are working out of the NVA Headquarters building in East Berlin, correct?"

"Yes, that's correct."

"Well, then, I have a little something for you," she said as she reached inside the shopping bag, producing a small gift-wrapped package. "We have an asset in place, near your sector of East Berlin right now. When you retrieve the data I've asked for, you will use this." She handed him the package, slightly larger than a pack of cigarettes. "This is a microfilm camera and several rolls of microfilm; instructions are inside. Very simple.

You take photos of *all* written information. If it's verbal information, then you write it down and take photos of it, and make sure you completely destroy any of these written notes. You will then take the exposed microfilm, along with a roll of regular 35 mm film, exposed…you do have a 35 mm camera?"

Richter nodded.

"…to the pharmacy at the corner of Graustein and Hirschgarten Strasse. Are you familiar with this location?"

Again he nodded.

"You will label the film envelope: 'Alfons P. Zenker, #66 Beulow Strasse, Apartment C, East Berlin.' There is no Alfons P. Zenker, and there is no such address. You drop the microfilm, along with the 35 mm film, into the envelope. No big deal. Some person along the line will always be on the lookout for envelopes from Alfons P. Zenker. It could be somebody at the pharmacy, could be the driver making the pickup, could be any of a number of people at the photo processing lab; you will never know, because you don't need to know. Just give us good information. The rest is our job," she said curtly. "We will use different methods of communicating, if you prove to be trustworthy and if your information is accurate, but this method will do until further notice. Good luck, and do try not to get caught. Okay?"

The subway slowed to a stop. Jennifer was on her feet and out the sliding doors. Her other companions stayed in place, not indicating any interest, just standing their post as ordered, Richter figured.

Richter got off at the next station and went to the street level to reorient before starting his long walk back to the university compound. Things had gone well. Everything seemed to be moving pretty fast. *Too fast?* Richter was somewhat surprised the Americans did not receive him with outstretched arms, smothering him with hugs and kisses of gratitude, but in retrospect, he could certainly understand, from their point of view, how carefully a situation like this needed to be handled. He could have just as easily approached them as a double agent with the intention of getting into their rank and file to find out who the inside people were and to discover where the leaks appeared from the East German side. He would definitely have to prove himself. It would be a "one man force" from his perspective. The commitment was made, and he would see it through to the bitter end, whatever and whenever that might be.

~ * ~

The antique clock on the bookcase in Kevin Glenn's office struck one time, announcing the half hour, as Jennifer Frost joined the assembled group.

"What do we have, Ms. Frost? Is he for real?" Glenn asked.

"We approach it with caution, as always, Mr. Glenn, but my gut reaction is he might be a real winner. Did you get pictures and voice prints?"

Lynn McClintock responded, "That, plus a few extras. We've got fingerprints from a cigarette package and a nice little stat sheet, plus a personal profile complete with photo and military I.D. numbers, just to help us check up on him. We'll have confirmation on these things in the morning, first thing. Sergeant Maxwell here handled this like a pro."

"You understand, Sergeant Maxwell," the young NSA Intelligence officer said, "this is all highly confidential, and your activities with this man in the pub and the people gathered here are strictly classified, to be discussed with no one outside of this office. In fact," she said, pausing for emphasis, "you can completely forget your contact with this man ever took place. Do I make myself clear?"

"Yes, Ma'am," answered the Marine sergeant.

~ * ~

Captain Richter opened the weight training room door. It was unlocked, to his surprise, but he found an even bigger surprise inside. Lieutenant Friedrich Ostermann sat on the edge of a weight lifting bench. His uniform shirt was off, and signs of perspiration showed through his undershirt.

"Well, Comrade Captain, I see that some of us have special privileges."

Richter could instantly taste the acid from his stomach and hoped his face had not turned totally white. He felt like a student caught by the teacher while cheating on an exam.

"How did you get in the gymnasium, Lieutenant? This area is to be locked after 1800 hours!"

Reaching into his pocket, Ostermann pulled out a large ring of keys and dangled them in front of his commanding officer.

"I took them from the old man, of course," the lieutenant said matter-of-factly. "You have civilian clothes, and obviously you have been out enjoying the city, eh?"

How much does he know? wondered Richter.

"Obviously, *Lieutenant* Ostermann, you have trouble determining the chain of command." Richter struggled to remain calm. "Let me help you with that for the last time," he continued. "I am a *captain*, your commanding officer. You are a *lieutenant*. *Captain* outranks *lieutenant*," he said, his voice rising. "Check the book! I will *not* tolerate your insubordination any longer!" The anger was clearly visible in Richter's face. "Tomorrow morning, I will…"

"Tomorrow morning, you will do nothing," Ostermann calmly interrupted. "You see, I now have the upper hand. I now control *you*," he said, jabbing a finger in Richter's chest, "even if you do wear the rank of captain. You see, last night when you came back to the dormitory, I asked you about our premier figure skater, Fraulein Angsteller. A trap that I set for you, and you fell right in." Ostermann beamed and thrust his chest out like a rooster, proud of this psychological victory.

This has to be the first time he has ever, seemingly, outwitted anyone in his life, thought Richter.

"Had you actually been at the ice arena last night, you would have known that Christel Angsteller had tripped and fallen in her practice routine and suffered a terrible injury to her right knee. She will be out of the competition. You were totally unaware, or you certainly would have commented on this unfortunate situation. I sensed that you must have been doing something against our orders," Ostermann said.

What a quick wit this one is, thought Richter, remaining silent, realizing this sorry excuse for an officer would tell him all he knew and then probably would guess at what he did not. "And I knew you were out *again* this evening. I looked all over and could not find you. Oh, nice job on the emergency door, by the way." Ostermann paused. "You have a girlfriend, eh? You know Major Scherer would not take kindly to hearing that his commander of the guard likes to slip away at night for a little 'action,' would he?" Ostermann gave a loud belly laugh.

Captain Richter knew that Major Scherer would suspect something more in depth—more serious—than simply sneaking out for a romantic interlude. Anyone other than Ostermann would see right through this potential opportunity to link up with the western world.

"Don't despair, Comrade Captain. I'm sure we can work something out between us. It's really very simple. You give me the duty I ask for, time off, extra leave, and, of course, a high recommendation for promotion to captain. That's not such a big price to pay for me to keep my mouth shut, is it?"

"That's blackmail!" replied the NVA captain, relieved to a large degree that he was dealing with a complete idiot.

"That's exactly what it is. I can be on the phone to Major Scherer in one minute, if you choose not to pay the piper. What will it be, Captain? I would probably receive a nice commendation, or possibly even that promotion, if I turn you in. I don't really care which way you choose, but believe this: I *will* tell everything I know."

Richter had no doubt he would do just that and then some to embellish the tale with a little added spice. But equally as important, if he did go along with Ostermann's scheme, he could never trust the man to remain silent and keep his word. The man had absolutely no moral fiber. He would not stop at asking mere favors. He would hold it over his head indefinitely, eventually spilling his guts when he grew tired of playing the game or had had a little too much to drink, which could be any given day. Ostermann presented a real threat. Richter could not ignore him, and he refused to trust him or to play his ridiculous game.

Richter appeared to contemplate his options in silence for some time, while Ostermann sat back down on the weight bench with a smirk, already proclaiming victory.

"You're right," Richter said, breaking the silence. "You've caught me. Yes, I was out with a woman. I have to admit, you are very clever to have detected my activities. I give you credit for that."

This is precisely what Lieutenant Ostermann wanted to hear.

"I'll go along with your wishes. I have no other choices, do I?" said Captain Richter.

"I knew you'd see it my way," said Ostermann. "You're a smart man. We'll work as a team, eh?"

"Yes, a team," replied Richter, feeding the ego of the shallow man. "We'll work well as a team." He took off the old, blue ski jacket and hung it on a nearby hook. "Mind if I join you in a workout?"

"Of course not, Comrade Ca—I mean, Gerhardt," replied Ostermann, smirking. "If you still have any strength left after your night out on the town."

"That's quite a bit of weight on the bar," said Richter, indicating the weight bar supported on forks over the weight lifting bench.

"Yes, it's nearly my body weight. I can bench press at least a hundred kilos," Ostermann boasted.

Yeah, sure you can, you fat ass! thought Richter. "How about if I spot for you, just in case?"

"Go ahead, if you wish, but I can lift it, no problem," Ostermann said as he slid under the bar, taking a grip about a shoulders width.

Richter positioned himself behind the bench, hovering over the lieutenant's head. He could hardly believe his executive officer was so naive or so terribly stupid to not be aware of the imminent danger. *Seize the moment?* pondered Captain Richter for about two seconds.

As Ostermann had laid a trap for his commanding officer, Richter now had an opportunity to return the favor. Ostermann lifted ninety-five kilos off the fork with little enough effort, then brought it down to his chest and began to breathe out and push the weight back up. Richter helped lift for the first two forced reps, as any training partner would do. The third repetition would be different. Instead of continuing to assist, Ostermann soon realized that Richter was now applying downward pressure. The bar was touching Ostermann's throat, and the lieutenant thought Richter was testing his strength by applying more pressure. He began to struggle, trying to muster all his strength, but it was no contest. By the time Ostermann actually realized what was happening, he had no air left in his lungs to scream for help. The added weight of Richter's hands and arms and just a little extra push on top of the existing 95-kilo bar was too much. Now the entire weight of the bar was just below the larynx. Lieutenant Ostermann's eyes began to bulge, and all of the veins in his neck and head looked like they'd explode from pressure any moment. Richter was surprised at the extra effort a body would expend to hang onto life. Seeing that the struggle had finally left the surly lieutenant, Richter allowed the bar to rest on his throat, cutting off the oxygen supply to the brain at the windpipe. Cause of death: suffocation.

"The poor bastard should have known better than to do bench presses without someone to spot for him," Hauptmann Richter explained to his immediate commander, Major Helmut Scherer, on the telephone.

There was no need for an investigation. This was obviously just a stupid, careless mistake made by a predictably incompetent junior officer.

Gerhardt Richter was surprised at the lack of his own emotions. He had just killed a man in cold blood, and he had not felt the least bit shaky or weak in the knees. In fact, he felt untouched by the whole encounter. This he found to be a positive sign, considering his new field of work.

Chapter Two

Eastern Europe
1987–1989

On June 12, 1987, President Ronald Reagan made his speech in Berlin at the Brandenburg Gate. Approximately 45,000 West Berliners awaited the address. President Reagan told the assembled:

"We welcome change and openness, for we believe that freedom and security go together, that the advance of human liberty can only strengthen the cause of world peace. There is one sign the Soviets can make that would be unmistakable, that would advance dramatically the cause of freedom and peace. General Secretary Gorbachev, if you seek peace, if you seek prosperity for the Soviet Union and Eastern Europe, if you seek liberalization, come here to this gate. Mr. Gorbachev, open this gate. Mr. Gorbachev, tear down this wall!"

Further into his speech, Reagan also said, "As I looked out a moment ago from the Reichstag, that embodiment of German unity, I noticed words crudely spray-painted upon the wall, perhaps by a young Berliner: 'This wall will fall. Belief's become reality.' Yes, across Europe, this wall will fall. For it cannot withstand faith; it cannot withstand truth. The wall cannot withstand freedom."

In the same address, President Regan called an end to the arms race, referring to the Soviets' SS-20 nuclear weapons and of our having "within reach the possibility, not merely of limiting the growth of arms, but of eliminating, for the first time, an entire class of nuclear weapons from the face of the Earth."

~ * ~

The legendary day of November 9, 1989, began with an extraordinarily dull press conference in East Berlin. Following the mass migration from Hungary and the weekly protest rallies throughout East Germany, citizens were still waiting for a change of heart within the Central Committee.

At exactly 6:57 p.m., at the conclusion of the press conference, one of the members of the press posed a question. The Politburo spokesman for information and the media, Gunter Schabowski, retrieved a letter from his pocket that had earlier been passed to him by Egon Krenz. Schabowski appeared uncertain as he read the contents of the transcript. It was obvious to everyone present he was genuinely surprised at what it contained. Schabowski understood that something was not right with this message, but he was too inexperienced to mask his own astonishment.

Schabowski read: "The Council of Ministers of the German Democratic Republic has decided that until a permanent regulation approved by the People's Chamber is brought into force, the temporary regulation governing exit rights, i.e., the right to leave the country, shall be lifted."

The statement was totally incomprehensible. He was asked whether the new rules applied to Berlin, as well. Schabowski referred to the letter for a second time and confirmed that they did in fact also apply to Berlin. Schabowski's statement simply meant that the border was open. Within an hour after the press conference, a mass march to the Wall was underway.

There was never any intention on the part of the East Berliners to wait to apply for visas the next day. The border guards still stood impassively at their posts. At this point, hesitantly at first because the situation seemed unreal, a multitude of people approached the Wall by car and on foot. The fear and the memories of living behind the Wall for so many years still outweighed the desire to cross the border, but gradually the growing crowd of East Berliners surged into the Western Sector. In spite of the suppressed fears that the guards might suddenly open fire on them, keeping them from freedom, nothing happened.

Then there was euphoria. People were celebrating in the streets. The Wall was finally broken.

Almost simultaneously, other uprisings took place. Communist leaders were overthrown and replaced by new freedom fighters in countries throughout Eastern Europe—Czechoslovakia, Hungary, Bulgaria, and Romania.

It appeared to be the beginning of the end of communistic rule in Eastern Europe. Russia, on the other hand, was a completely different story.

~ * ~

In the Eastern Sector of Berlin
31 December 1989
1800 Hours

Major Gerhardt Richter sat alone at his favorite corner table at the Café Opern, enjoying a tureen of lentil soup and contemplating what delectable pastry he would choose for dessert. He had always enjoyed the quiet, warm ambiance of this well-known café along the Avenue Unter den Linden, but this evening it reflected a totally new atmosphere, as did all gathering places within the newly unified city. The café was alive with friendly chatter, singing, and laughter as it had never been before, at least not for the past twenty-eight years. Richter dared not show the least bit emotion or excitement, for that would not be fitting of a true NVA officer. At this particular moment, however, he felt a real surge of pride and genuine happiness for all those who surrounded him in the café and out on the street.

As with any New Year's Eve, Richter reflected on the events of the past year or, more accurately, the previously twenty-three months. He had accomplished all he had set out to do during this time, and then some. Most important of all to Richter, he had won the trust of the National Security Agency and had proven himself to be a very valuable asset. He had also proven himself to be a highly revered and very qualified officer in the NVA, earning him a promotion to the rank of major at a very early age.

Of course, Richter had paid extremely close attention to all of the political changes and events as they had taken place. He would not be caught flat-footed. He constantly adjusted his sites to align himself with those people who were in authority and wielded the most power.

It had come as a shock to most, although not to Gerhardt Richter, when the Soviets offered no support whatsoever as the regime in the GDR began to falter in late '88 and throughout '89. Richter could also foresee that the Federal Republic of Germany was clearly the much stronger of the two economically and would just swallow up the German Democratic Republic. This would also hold true for the military. In fact, rumors were already beginning to spread within the ranks of the National Volksarmee about how the Bundeswehr would simply take over the NVA. Word had it that all senior NVA officers, majors and above, were to be pensioned off, no exceptions. Some select junior officers and senior noncommissioned officers from the Bundesheer (Federal Army) would be sent into the territory of the GDR to reorganize and retrain the presently existing NVA.

Many westerners naively believed that now that the Wall was down, their troubles were over and communism was on its way out for good. Gerhardt Richter knew it was not over by a long shot. The Iron Curtain was not about to go away that easily. Too many Communist Party leaders and high ranking military personnel had fought tooth and nail and had even killed to reach the level of power they now held.

Richter had to sniff out exactly who would emerge as the leaders of a new Communist Party. This was his primary task; reporting the development would follow. The thought of being "pensioned off" was out of the question for Richter.

Hell, he thought, *I'm just getting warmed up!* The young major had some ideas about how to confront this problem.

Richter finished the last bite of his cheesecake tart and washed it down with a final sip of black coffee. He would be visiting with people in high places tonight. He figured he had better make his way back to his apartment to prepare for the private gathering of Red Army officers and several SED officials scheduled to attend this evening. It was Richter's father who had extended the invitation to him, even though he would not be able to attend, due to his poor health. No other NVA officers were invited. Richter accepted this preferential treatment with great pleasure and satisfaction.

This would not be a New Year's Eve celebration—for there was nothing this group of communists had to celebrate at this time—but more of a "rally" to add cohesion to their once powerful political following. The existing Communist Party needed unity within their ranks, now more than ever. Richter considered it to be a time for them to re-group and lick their wounds.

~ * ~

Soviet Military Headquarters, East Berlin
31 December 1989
2000 Hours

Peering into the ornate, gold, scalloped mirror, Major General Stephan Krause inspected the alignment of the various campaign ribbons and personal achievement medals on his chest. He fastened the subdued metal buttons of his olive drab parade uniform and spent a rare frivolous moment comparing the similarities and differences of the NVA uniform he had worn for the majority of his military career to that of the Soviet Rocket Forces, which he had worn not long ago, to the present uniform he now wore. It was somewhat odd, thought Krause, that the most elite military force in the USSR did not display any special insignia that would distinguish them as members of this select group of warriors.

Spetsnaz soldiers wore the same uniform as the Soviet Airborne Forces and Air Assault Troops, except for the Guard Unit insignia. Krause realized the need for the anonymity and also realized that there was actually a certain recognition achieved by the absence of a unit badge.

Krause prided himself for always being a step-and-a-half ahead of everyone else. He attributed this, in part, to his skill as a meticulous planner and some gut reaction, but mostly to his superior intellect. Stephan Krause had always used whatever means available to him to increase his military status. To Major General Stephan Krause, power was *everything*.

In 1962, Krause had begun his military career as a young lieutenant in the National Volksarmee. Even though he was very well-accepted by his Soviet counterparts and higher ranking officers, Krause had always resented the limitations and restrictions placed on the NVA officers. They were basically treated as second class soldiers by the Red Army. All operational orders, military policy, and procedures were set by the Soviets. The Red Army gave the commands and the NVA carried them out; it was as simple as that.

The resentment of this denied power had persisted, and Krause eventually came to the conclusion he did not care to spend the rest of his military career taking orders from another man's army. This would need to change, and he was determined to change it for himself. No one else.

Stephan Krause's father, Günter, was a physicist born and raised in Garmisch-Partenkirchen, who later relocated to Berlin. His mother, Nadiya Alenichev, was an accomplished classical musician from Leningrad. As a result of this international union, young Stephan grew up bilingual, speaking perfect Russian as well as German. Considering the Soviet dominance over the NVA, this proved to be a terrific advantage to be able to communicate directly with his peers in the Red Army, *almost* placing him as an equal.

Much of Krause's time in grade had been spent as an executive officer assigned to one of the many SS-20 and SS-A-20 missile outposts along the western borders of East Germany. These missiles were targeted at various U.S. Army and Air Force installations as well as Bundesheer bases throughout West Germany.

It was in the spring of 1985 that Oberst (Colonel) Krause volunteered his professional services to fight in Afghanistan in exchange for the privilege of having his commission transferred from the NVA to the Red Army. His military record was proof enough that he was a very qualified NVA officer. He now needed to prove he was capable of being a *Soviet* officer.

One particular issue with the Soviets was a long existing attitude—an obsessional fear—that the Russians had felt toward the East Germans since the late '60s. The Russians questioned just how far the East Germans could be relied upon to fight the West Germans. Krause was aware of this concern, but he felt it was nothing that his experience, perfect record, and superior qualifications could not overcome. After all, it basically boiled down to a matter of trust.

Soviet scientists had been experimenting with a new anti-personnel, high- explosive fragmentation device that was somewhat a cross between a grossly oversized mortar and a small, tubular-launched missile. Because this new experimental missile was propelled by liquid rocket fuel and guided by a laser beam, it fell within the technical parameters of the Strategic Rocket Forces, as opposed to the Red Army infantry.

Partially because of the Russian blood line on his mother's side, but more because of his superior military record, his offer was accepted by the Soviet Rocket Forces. In reality, what the Soviet Rocket Forces really needed was a well-trained, intelligent guinea pig for their experimental weapon. That, coupled with the fact that there was also a severe shortage of qualified officers at this level in Afghanistan, carried an appreciable amount of weight in their decision.

Now that Stephan Krause had broken into the ranks of the Soviet Armed Forces, he would prove his worthiness to his superiors and would proceed to strive for more power. As time went on, he would also refuse to stop until he reached the highest rank of general of the army, commanding the most powerful and prestigious forces within the USSR.

During his two-year tour of duty in the rugged mountains of Afghanistan, Krause received three personal commendations: one of which was the highly-honored Order of Suvorov, First Class. Colonel Krause was probably responsible for more carnage in that two-year span than any other senior officer since the Great Patriotic War. For this he was promoted to the rank of major general (comparable to a brigadier general in the U.S. Armed Forces).

Upon completion of his bloody tour in Afghanistan in the spring of '87, General Krause was offered the command of the Third Rocket Regiment, positioned in the Ukraine near the borders of Czechoslovakia and Hungary. His command responsibility included the supervision of the SS-20s, SS-A-20s and SS-25s, totaling three-hundred-plus rockets and complete ground control of the two Cosmos satellites that were originally put into orbit from his command/launch site in the western Ukraine.

No more than three or four weeks after the new boss of the Third Rocket Regiment was in place and had inspected each of the missile sites under his command, there began a rekindled interest in the Strategic Arms Reduction Talks (START) in Geneva. There was a new, stronger push from the United Nations, more specifically from the western European countries, to strictly enforce the number of intermediate range nuclear weapons in the Soviet Union's arsenal. This would certainly affect Krause's SS-20s and A-20s, *if* it was to be enforced.

SALT II had never actually been ratified, due to the Soviet invasion of Afghanistan, but oddly enough, the U.S. and USSR now voluntarily observed those arms limits that had been previously agreed upon. This was highly unusual and not good news for General Krause. Not good at all. This would impact roughly two-thirds of the weaponry he presently had on the line.

The SS-20 was an intermediate range, solid-fuel ballistic missile, with a range of fifteen hundred to three thousand miles, mounted on a huge mobile launcher. It was the perfect threat to any European target.

The SS-A-20 had a great deal of the same characteristics as the SS-20, but was powered by a liquid-fuel propulsion system, was considerably smaller in size, and had only about half the range. The advantages of the A-

20 were that it was newer, more accurate, more dependable, and considerably more mobile than the old 1960s vintage SS-20.

At least his SS-25 ICBMs were not scheduled for the scrap heap yet.

~ * ~

By the fall of 1987, NATO was *demanding* the removal and destruction of all of Krause's SS-20s and SS-A-20s.

"Pizdet!" cursed Krause, learning of the new decree. "If they think I am going to remove and destroy these perfectly good weapons, they will be sadly mistaken."

Stephan Krause was not one to simply obey commands from a virtually powerless NATO force. He would, however, need to comply with orders from the commandant of the Strategic Rocket Forces or the Red Army Command if it came down to that.

What's going on? he thought. *The strongest nation on earth is being dictated to by a powerless group of bureaucrats!* He shook his head in disgust. *Things are just not the same anymore.*

After ten or fifteen minutes of serious deliberation, Major General Stephan Krause began to reevaluate the situation. After another fifteen minutes or so, he smiled inwardly and concluded that this new edict might not be so bad after all. This would call for some very serious planning indeed.

Chapter Three

DFW International Airport
April 24, 1987

Colonel Alvin Pallosic looked up at the departures monitor to check the status of American Airlines flight #886, nonstop to Detroit, and determined that he had enough time for one or two drinks before his 10:42 a.m. flight. The U.S. Army colonel, in civilian attire, searched the overhead signs for a cocktail lounge. It was early, but Pallosic knew it wasn't too early for an airport bar. He had been down this path before.

Halfway down the busy terminal, Pallosic found a semi-deserted lounge and ordered a double scotch.

Although the veteran 1st Cav officer usually had the personality of a rattlesnake, this morning his demeanor was almost mellow. Sitting back in the black, padded-vinyl chair, he lit a cigarette and took a long pull from his scotch.

The Pentagon was making progress toward approving the design plans of Colonel Pallosic's "baby," the new M-5. The upcoming meeting with General Motors Design Group should help speed up the process by confirming several of the cost issues originally brought up by the Defense Department. Pallosic would remain only cautiously optimistic, however, until he had all of the answers and could convince the Pentagon that his M-

5 was truly a bargain. Past experience had taught him that the Army had the capability of screwing up just about anything.

Pallosic reached for a discarded copy of *The Dallas Morning News* on the neighboring cocktail table and perused the front page. Nothing of major interest there, but an article on page two certainly grabbed his attention.

"Are these people completely *nuts?*" Pallosic said aloud, slamming his glass down on the table. "Get rid of our Pershing-2 rockets? They gotta be kidding!" One thing was for sure, you could bet your sweet ass the Reds weren't going to dump all their SS-20s into the Black Sea just because NATO told them to.

It had only been about four years since the medium range Pershing-2 ballistic missile had been developed to counter the much older Soviet SS-20 series missile. Colonel Pallosic at first found it hard to believe that his government would actually turn around and scrap a multi-million-dollar— possibly billion-dollar—project like the Pershing-2. But on second thought, it was very believable. The U.S. government made a habit of making illogical, wasteful, or just plain stupid moves.

Alvin Pallosic knew he was cynical, but with good reason. His bitterness stemmed from a recent Pentagon screw-up which had resulted in his being passed over for promotion to brigadier general. Apparently some critical paperwork had been misplaced or overlooked. A very weak attempt to explain the mistake, followed by an even weaker promise to correct it, was his only consolation from the Pentagon. The veteran colonel was told the matter would be investigated very soon. "Very soon" was just a little too damned ambiguous to accept. He wanted it corrected *now*!

Pallosic had spent a total of eighteen months in Vietnam as the CO of an armor company. His second tour was cut short by six months due to a VC sniper round that shattered his left wrist and left his hand dangling by some splintered bone, a few strands of ligament, and muscle tissue. After immediate "meatball surgery," performed by a Mobile Army Surgical Hospital team, followed by two more state-side operations, Pallosic's left hand and wrist were almost completely functional. Through long and intense rehabilitation sessions, he was able to squeak past the mandatory physical required to stay in the U.S. Army.

Pallosic had no intentions of accepting a medical discharge. Residual nerve damage still caused him a great deal of pain more often than he cared to admit, but mechanically he was okay. He had learned to live with it. He had also learned to become more and more dependent on support from his closest friend, Johnnie Walker, who was always there to ease the pain. Apparently, the Pentagon pencil pushers didn't give a rat's ass how he'd sacrificed for his country.

~ * ~

In May 1988, the governments of the United States and the USSR ratified the Intermediate-Range Nuclear Forces Treaty. The INF Treaty allowed each signatory to carry out onsite inspections of the other party's territory.

As a result of the enforcement on the limitations contained in the treaty, General Stephan Krause was ordered by his superiors to dispose of his entire stock of SS-20 and SS-A-20 intermediate range missiles. His SS-25 ICBMs would stay in place for the time being, although future production of the SS-25s at the Votkinsk Machine Building Plant, some six hundred miles east of Moscow in the Udmurt region, would soon shut down.

General Krause's letter of resignation did not come as much of a surprise to the commandant of the Strategic Rocket Forces, due to the impact and enforcement of all of the various treaties restricting nuclear weapons ranging from intercontinental to intermediate and medium-range ballistic missiles. It was the letter to Valentin Zhandov, director of the GRU (Glavnoje Razvedyvatel'noje Upravlenije), the foreign military intelligence directorate of the Red Army general staff, requesting a private meeting that did come as a complete surprise to the upper echelon of the Soviet military commanders.

The GRU was known for its fierce independence from its rival government power blocs, including the Communist Party of the Soviet

Union and especially the KGB. Along with being the USSR's largest intelligence agency, the GRU was also the governing force of the Soviet Army's Special Forces, the elite Spetsnaz troops.

Krause's pitch to General of the Army Zhandov was simple and straightforward. He wanted to be a member of Spetsnaz, and he wanted to retain the rank he had legitimately earned. Krause explained quite logically why he should be allowed into the military's prestigious fold, stressing his broad experience, outstanding military record, and the necessity for someone of his intellect to join their ranks and help stop the terrible skid toward capitalism that was becoming all too obvious to the governing body in Red Square.

As a final point to support his argument, he reminded Zhandov that his mother was one hundred percent Russian, in case the director might be the least bit skeptical of Krause's German surname.

Once again, the charismatic Krause had presented such a watertight case that even the members of the GRU could find no good reason to not accept the generous offer of service. In fact, they were quite thrilled to have this warrior who had earned the honor of a hero in Afghanistan only less than three years before. The transition took place immediately.

~ * ~

31 December 1989
2100 Hours

General Stephan Krause walked down two flights of stairs from the VIP guest quarters of the Soviet military headquarters building to the second floor assembly hall. Krause did not particularly want to attend this gathering of grumbling, gossiping old men. If the truth be known, the only reason for the general's return to Berlin was for one last opportunity to listen to his beloved East Berlin Symphony Orchestra before the West took complete control of the city. He had arrived two days earlier and had taken in the symphony the night before, but he hoped to catch at least one more performance before he returned to Moscow.

Thinking his time could have been better spent at one of Moscow's New Year's Eve gatherings among more prominent, influential people, Krause decided to make the most of things and at least enjoy the caviar.

~ * ~

Two Red Army corporals stood at attention as the snow continued to fall. A couple of inches had accumulated on their gray, wool winter caps, earflaps in the upright position, as the corporals waited to open the brass-plated doors for arriving government dignitaries and guests.

Major Gerhardt Richter stepped out of the taxi several yards from the main entrance, not wanting to cause any interference with the arrival of the higher-ranking officers as they made their grand entrances into the building. As Richter approached the magnificent brass doors, he returned the salute from the two corporals and gently kicked off the thin layer of snow that covered his freshly polished boots, careful not to scuff the mirror-like surface. The entrance foyer and wide marble stairway leading to the next level only seemed slightly warmer than the temperature outside. *Welcome to Moscow in East Germany,* he thought.

The second floor assembly hall of the USSR government building in Berlin was a sorry excuse for even the Communist Party leaders and the high-ranking Soviet military to meet for a social function. The room was cold and bare, with the exception of three long serving tables along the north wall and fifty straight-backed chairs that lined the south wall. The room was void of any decorations unless you counted the two huge pictures of Karl Marx and Vladimir Lenin on the east wall above the doorway. This was not your typical New Year's Eve bash, but it was perfect for the political hobnobbing that Gerhardt Richter was counting on.

Across the room, Richter spotted a figure who looked somewhat familiar. From behind, the tall, slender man with perfect posture reminded him of the NVA colonel who had been in command of the airborne training center at Neurippen, where Richter had earned his silver "jump wings" immediately following graduation from the academy. But this man wore the uniform of a Soviet Airborne Forces officer. Thinking it nothing more than a coincidence, Richter walked over to a porter carrying a silver tray with a dozen, fluted champagne glasses, then toward the serving table that held the dark gray, almost black caviar and thinly sliced pieces of dried toast on silver trays. *Beluga caviar?* wondered Richter. He tasted it. If it wasn't Beluga, it was the next best thing. *One of the very few things the Russians did well,* he thought. Enjoying the expensive delicacy of sturgeon eggs on toast and washing it down with a very mediocre, straw-colored champagne, Gerhardt Richter felt a firm tap on his shoulder.

"Major Richter!"

Richter turned toward the familiar voice to find the man in an Airborne Forces uniform—a Spetsnaz uniform on closer glance—looking directly into his eyes.

"Colonel—er, General Krause, it's a pleasure to see you again, sir!" Richter switched from German to Russian as smoothly as moving from fourth to fifth gear in a Maserati. "Excuse me, sir, but you've taken me by surprise. I didn't expect to see you in anything other than an NVA uniform."

"Times change, Major Richter," Krause said, sounding like the voice of reason.

"I'm rather surprised and quite flattered you would remember me, Comrade General."

"Not at all, Comrade Major. You graduated with honors from the academy, you were first in your class at Neurippen, and your name is often spoken by your commander and his staff. I hear very good things about you, Major Richter."

Gerhardt Richter's pulse quickened. This could be his big break; it had to be. *Play it cool, don't press, don't rush it,* he told himself.

"Well, thank you, Comrade General. Those are very kind words. And you, sir, how did you come about Spetsnaz?"

Krause explained exactly what had prompted both of his changeovers, then went on to explain his service in Afghanistan and finally his latest assignment.

Now is the time, Gerhardt thought. *Turn on the charm.* "Comrade General, may I speak with you confidentially?" he said almost in a whisper.

Krause nodded and casually walked away from the serving tables and toward the opposite wall, indicating Richter should follow.

When well out of ear shot of the other guests, Richter began to speak, still very quietly. "Sir, to be very straightforward with you, I am concerned about my future."

Krause nodded, showing that he understood the concern.

"I have heard, and I believe it to be true, that *all* NVA officers will soon be pensioned off, and the People's Army will be under the complete control of the Bundeswehr. Comrade General, I am much too young and have too much to offer, in terms of military skills, to be cast aside like an old boot. I don't mean to sound my own horn, but it would be a profound waste of many years of excellent training to put me out to pasture when I can still offer my experience and the best years of my life to another army. We've worked toward the same goals, General." Richter paused briefly. "I look up to you as someone with extraordinary vision to have made a very intelligent decision to change, well in advance of this time of crisis and chaos." He spoke as if a true patriot.

"Comrade General," Richter paused again, taking a breath. "I am asking you to find it within your power to take me into your ranks as a Soviet soldier. I would be extremely proud to wear the Hammer and Sickle and to serve the USSR in any capacity you would consider appropriate. I am at your service, Comrade General."

Krause was silent. He eyed the young major as one would inspect a thoroughbred race horse before buying it. As with anything else, Stephan Krause was already a full step and a half ahead of the NVA major.

~ * ~

The seed of his plan had actually been planted as far back as the spring of '87 when the Strategic Arms Reduction Talks had begun to sound like a legitimate threat. The next fall, the threat of disarmament would become an outright demand. It was then that General Stephan Krause had made the decision to systematically begin building his own army.

There were obvious signs that the massive structure of the Communist Party was now beginning to weaken under stress, eroding and decaying at the foundation. This was Krause's opportunity to grab the power and take control. With the right cadre and proper equipment, he was confident he could form *his own* new communist party. It would be a rebuilding process that would take time, and he was prepared for that.

The first step would be to choose a team of select players as his nucleolus: specialists in technical fields like computer programming, communications, linguistics, radar systems, and countless other disciplines as needs arose. The only qualification more important than technical skills was unquestionable loyalty to him and to the principles of communism. He would seek only the very best, from the lowly NCO in charge of a single squad of soldiers, to single-star generals at the brigade level.

~ * ~

Krause's position as the commander of the 3rd Rocket Division had offered ideal access to a multitude of weapons and equipment that he would need to carry out his mission. At the very top of Krause's list of "Essential Weaponry and Equipment," he had highlighted two items in bright yellow: 20 ea. (minimum) SS-A-20 missiles, and 1 ea. Cosmos 1800-series satellite.

All military hardware in any army is inventoried and, somewhere down the line, someone is accountable for everything, from the common entrenching tool to a nuclear armed missile. According to the general's plan, appropriating twenty missiles and a satellite would pose no real problem. In fact, they would be easier to steal than a rifle or a case of ammunition. Krause's plan was simple but well-thought-out. He would skillfully backtrack into the A-20's performance and maintenance reports that were filed at regular intervals and following all field training exercises.

Krause began the process of entering post-dated reports stating that the weapon had either been expended in test firing exercises (minus the nuclear warhead, of course) or showing a variety of pieces of technical proof as to why the missile had been redlined: dangerously defective ignition systems, faulty wiring, and so forth. The maintenance reports for these defective missiles clearly indicated that they had been shipped off to other larger sites for further inspection and repairs, thus enabling Krause to strike these weapons from his inventory.

As General Krause rendered each of these weapons "inoperable," he personally accompanied the transport crew to a small abandoned Soviet airbase, fifteen kilometers southeast of the Ukrainian city of Mukachevo, for their disposal. The vacant aircraft hangers, once occupied by MIG-21s, provided excellent cover and concealment for these intermediate-range, nuclear tipped missiles.

Each and every one of his rockets had official documentation to confirm its readiness status and location. If anyone wanted to try to physically track them down, he had forged documents to prove that the other site had received them in good order. They were no longer his responsibility, nor could he be held accountable for them. The entire process was no more than a paper shuffle.

By May of '88, Krause had successfully transferred nineteen fully-operational SS-A-20 IRBMs to his side of the ledger. He had hauled away twenty of these slender rockets, but one actually did prove to be defective.

The second item on the "Essential" list was a Cosmos 1813C satellite that orbited the globe exactly midway between Gdansk, Poland, and Vienna, Austria: parameters that were perfect for what General Krause had in mind. This project, too, would take some time, and it was considerably more complex. It would definitely not be as easy as stealing the A-20s. It required a fairly lengthy procedure of secretly feeding the Cosmos 1813C misinformation from a second command disk: a "garbage in–garbage out" type of thing. After seven months of spoon-fed, "inaccurate" data, the satellite would appear to be malfunctioning whenever the bogus 3.5 floppy disc was inserted. The differences between the two disks were very subtle. One could not easily detect the good output from the original command disc from that of the altered one. The general began, from early on, to let some of the technicians find some of these glitches from time to time, minor errors in calculations that were of no consequence. When informed of these reoccurring problems, he would go into a mild tirade, always blaming the techs and the programmers that had built the damn thing.

Krause needed only to wait for the appropriate time to call upon the satellite for some critical bit of information so he could actually prove the data received from the satellite was incorrect—something important enough to jeopardize the security of the USSR. Then he would be forced to deactivate it and pronounce it dead or "decayed," as the Soviets liked to label malfunctioning equipment, and the satellite would become just another piece of space junk.

The Cosmos 1813C satellite was essential to Krause for several reasons: It gave him a secure ban to be able to communicate simultaneously with multiple locations that could link-up anywhere in the world, and it provided the capabilities to control and direct certain television and radio waves that could also be used to jam other existing television or radio waves. Primarily, however, he needed the satellite for its capacity to serve as a fire control center for the SS-A-20s. Ground coordinates could be entered for as many missiles as one possessed and, with a short series of key strokes, could launch those missiles to strike anywhere throughout Europe. Stephan Krause took a great deal of personal satisfaction in having this kind of power at his fingertips.

For seven and a half months, Krause also carefully gathered small arms, ammunition, computers, and various electronic gear and other bits of equipment that might prove useful, like a squirrel gathering nuts to sustain himself for a long winter.

~ * ~

Krause's "extraordinary vision," the term Richter had used to stroke the man's already inflated ego, had been grossly understated.

The collapse of the Berlin Wall was a shock to most. Some political analysts and historians may have been able to predict the eventual fall of communism, but no one else had the foresight and conviction to begin rebuilding the structure before it was actually completely knocked down. No one else had taken the risks involved in planning for the future as

Krause had. Stephan Krause actually did envision a powerful return of the communist régime, with himself at the forefront of the campaign. A highly intelligent man, Krause understood the severe strain the people would feel when the wheels of democracy did not turn fast enough to suit most. He knew that the same people who were now celebrating in the streets, celebrating their so-called freedom, would be among those who would wonder why there was not enough fuel in the winter to keep their apartments warm, or why there was not enough bread to feed their families. He laughed, thinking that every one of these fools expected to be wearing Levi jeans and eating Big Macs and fries within weeks of lowering the red Soviet flag.

They would come crawling back to communism, begging to be taken care of again. When the time was right, he would be there to take charge.

Krause had made significant strides in preparation for his ultimate goal. He had assembled much of the needed equipment and weaponry, and he had recruited some of the key personnel, but the general was still very much in the market for the right men to form his officer corps. Gerhardt Richter could be an asset. By saving him from the imminent sentence of being pensioned off by the NVA, he could acquire a highly qualified indentured servant. *Yes, this could be a very good acquisition indeed!*

After a full minute of silence, Krause spoke. "Major Richter, because I am a compassionate person, I will accept your offer. I have no immediate slots open in my command at this time, but I will notify Colonel Romokovitch at the Airborne Division headquarters at Maykop that you will be reporting to him on Monday of next week. I know he can use an officer of your caliber in his brigade. I will also have my staff pull your file and transfer it over to "our side," he said with a grin.

The young major offered Krause the expected gracious thanks and a solemn reassurance that the general would not be disappointed in his performance.

Even though Krause *did* have an open slot in his command, he would not let Richter just step right in. He would have to observe the NVA major—or rather Colonel Romokovitch would observe Richter and report his findings directly to Krause. Too many covert things were taking place in his headquarters now for this newcomer to be privy to right from the start. Later, possibly, but not now.

~ * ~

March 18, 1990

West Germany had announced its commitment to reunification shortly after the collapse of the Berlin Wall. Three months later, the results of the East German election signaled the official demise of the communist régime. By March 1990, the total number of East Germans who had relocated to West Germany reached a half million.

This news only reconfirmed what Krause had already predicted. The sudden influx of East Germans into the western side would create pandemonium. The financial burdens of reunification were a major concern to the West Germans, not to mention the cost of economic development in the former East Germany.

General Stephan Krause took full advantage of his position of power during this period when most military and political figures were keeping a very low profile. He continued to quietly build his war chest and to spend more time poring over personnel files, recruiting a faithful following within the ranks of the military, much as a politician would do on the campaign trail, all under the guise of being a super patriot.

Chapter Four

Fort Hood, Texas
19 September 1990

The convoy of M2 and M3 Bradley Fighting Vehicles and M1A1 Abrams Tanks created a cloud of dust so thick the troops and vehicles were nothing more than a blur. The tan and brown shades of the desert camouflage blended in perfectly with the parched surroundings of central Texas.

Advanced units of the U.S. Army's 1st Cavalry Division and 3rd Armored Cavalry Regiment were *en route* to their primary staging area for deployment to the Middle East. This defensive action was precipitated by the Iraqi invasion of Kuwait on 02 AUG 90. Approximately seventeen thousand, four hundred soldiers and seven thousand fifty pieces of heavy equipment were in the "move out" phase, bound for Saudi Arabia. The 1st Cav and the 3rd ACR both had proud combat histories dating as far back as the Indian Wars of the last century, when the cavalry was a quick-strike force of mounted riflemen. Oddly enough, the most basic tactics of the cavalry had not changed all that much over the years. Now they were mounting up for Operation Desert Shield.

The only thing hotter than the September sun in Fort Hood, Texas, was the temper of Brigade Commander Colonel Alvin Pallosic. Colonel Pallosic stood alone, watching the troop movement in the baking heat. The dust combined with sweat instantly formed a thin film of mud on his exposed face, neck, and arms. He had not seen this much activity at Hood since the fall of 1967 during the build-up for the Tet Offensive, when the soldiers of the 1st Cav wore OD green fatigues with Woodland green camo covering their steel pots and slung the old reliable M-14s over their shoulders as they similarly moved out for Southeast Asia. A lot had changed since then. Pallosic had been part of that action. He was a leader on that team when they took the field in '67, and now he had just received word that his orders had been yanked and he would be sidelined instead of making the trip to Saudi. Pallosic read the revised orders for a third time; he couldn't believe the Army had just shafted him once again.

The importance of being part of Desert Shield went way beyond Pallosic's desire to be involved in an actual combat situation once more, to feel the stimulation one can only experience when you match wits with the enemy in a contest where second best just won't cut it. Operation Desert Shield meant that Pallosic would almost certainly return stateside with the single star of a Brigadier on his collar. Nothing accelerated promotion like a little one-on-one with an enemy overseas.

To add insult to injury, Colonel Pallosic's revised orders called for his transfer to some kind of administrative position at Fort Knox, Kentucky, and to report in on 01 October. Pallosic could not understand this lunacy and promised himself and others he would "cut through all this bullshit and get to the bottom of it."

"I am OUTRAGED!" he shouted directly at the base commander, Major General Jeffrey R. Robertson, after a very brief explanation as to the nature of his unscheduled visit.

General Robertson was an even six feet, one hundred eighty-five pounds of pure Army Ranger, several years younger than Pallosic, with only about half the fruit salad on his left chest.

Robertson slammed the high-backed chair into the credenza behind the large mahogany desk as he came to his feet, fists clenched with knuckles pressed against the surface of the desk, leaning forward to the point that

Pallosic could feel his breath. "Colonel Pallosic, let me point out to you that I don't give a *damn* as to who's happy and who is *outraged* around here! I run a U.S. Army post, not a day care center."

Struggling to gain at least a little bit of composure, Pallosic tried again. "Sir, can you tell me *why* this decision was made and *who* is responsible?"

The general sat back down behind the desk, leaving Pallosic standing in place. "Negative, Colonel. That is classified, and I suggest you start packing your duffel bag, or will I need to instruct the MPs to do it for you." Robertson paused, locking eyes with Pallosic for a long moment. "You are dismissed, Colonel."

Pallosic could see nothing but red. He did a sharp about-face and left the base commander's office, slamming the door behind him.

Jeff Robertson did not even look up from his paperwork; he just shook his head in disgust and disbelief. *Conduct unbecoming of an officer,* he thought. *It's hard to help this guy when he pulls crap like that.*

"That son of a bitch!" Pallosic muttered under his breath. "He's the one who shot me down. I know he is." He stepped out of the Fort Hood HQ building, back into the heat of the afternoon.

Part of Pallosic's more obvious problem was that he was just too outspoken. It would be a gross understatement to anyone who knew him. Pallosic considered the base commander to be an inexperienced jackass, and he made no attempt to conceal his opinion. This did not make for good politics within the military hierarchy. Colonel Pallosic's question, "Why?" had remained unanswered. The "who" part seemed pretty obvious to him.

Alvin Pallosic was a fighter, not a quitter, and he would not take this lying down. Something had to be done. He knew he had at least one ally who held an influential position; his former battalion commander during his second tour in Vietnam, now a "three star" at the Pentagon. Pallosic could lean on him to find the answer to his question. He would also do his damndest to have him intervene and kill the orders for Fort Knox and ship him to the desert where he rightfully belonged instead of behind some damned large metal desk.

~ * ~

The last of the Air Force C-5A Galaxy transports shuttling the 1st Cav and 3rd ACR from Fort Hood to Saudi Arabia was scheduled for takeoff at 1300 hours on the twenty-first. Pallosic considered getting his old boss, Jim Donovan (no direct relation to the famed Colonel Bill Donovan who headed the OSS during WWII), on the horn right away in hopes of getting a quick approval of his petition, but then he realized nothing could possibly work that fast, not even if the lieutenant general was behind it a hundred percent. *Get real*, Pallosic thought. The colonel walked at a quick pace back to his office and immediately reached for the phone. He had his strategy together now and would attack the situation employing better logic:

Plan A: Request his orders be reversed and that he be sent to Saudi on the next available transport. The Air Force was hauling troops and equipment every day from a dozen bases all around the country.

Plan B: The alternate plan if the Saudi deal didn't fly: Make damn sure his orders called for him to remain at Hood at least until the M-5 was put to bed. Quite simply, his continued involvement was essential to the success of the project. It was so close to completion. The only logical choice was to let him see it through. Wouldn't that be obvious to them?

Pallosic had devoted three and a half years as the chief military advisor on the M-5, in addition to his regular appointed duties as brigade commander. It would kill Pallosic to see this project taken over by some half-whit who didn't know shit from Shinola about his M-5. Certainly the recognition he would receive from his technical involvement on the M-5 project would be overwhelming. It would create an almost celebrity-type status within military circles. *This alone*, considered Pallosic, *has enough merit to earn me the right to be addressed as Brigadier General.*

Colonel Pallosic resisted the urge to call Donovan at the Pentagon during business hours and waited impatiently until he could reach the general at his Arlington, Virginia home. It made for a very long afternoon, but at 1800 hours, Pallosic placed the call. *Time to bring in a little extra fire power.*

The conversation was friendly with very minimal small talk. Pallosic said he was coming to DC the day after next and wondered if he could pay him a visit, strictly unofficial, of course. The two senior combat veterans agreed upon a dinner meeting at Hogate's, a well-known seafood establishment, located directly on the banks of the Potomac River.

~ * ~

Lieutenant General Jim Donovan did not look at all out of place in his single-breasted, dark gray pinstriped Hart Schaffner and Marx suit, perfectly tailored and accented with a red and gray striped neck tie. Along with a full head of silver-white hair, he looked more the part of a Wall Street executive than a seasoned military man. Alvin Pallosic, on the other hand, never did look natural nor feel comfortable in civilian business attire. Lucky for him, navy blue blazers never really change much in style; however, his red and blue diamond design tie could have been a little less wide.

It had been an excellent dinner: fresh, steamed little-neck clams, shrimp bisque, Caesar salad, Hogate's famous Rum Buns, and a two-pound live Maine lobster served with drawn butter, not to mention several rounds of Johnnie Walker Black. The two sat at a corner table near the back of the restaurant and talked of old times, some good, some tragic. They shared experiences that had created a genuine mutual respect.

Soon the conversation began to taper off. The reunion had been nice, but now it was time to get down to business. Donovan let Pallosic bring up the main subject, anticipating precisely the real reason for this meeting.

Pallosic first wanted to confirm the "who" part of his question, followed directly by the "why." Donovan was prepared for the battery of questions. He explained that General Jeff Robertson had absolutely nothing to do with the decision to pull his orders for Operation Desert Shield. The decision was actually made at the Pentagon level, based on the results of the compiled scores from a team of so-called "experts" that had presided over the last set of proficiency tests Pallosic had taken about five months before. The input from the scorers was digested by a department of the Army computer and then subsequently spit out in the form of a lengthy report printed on green bar paper.

"The scorers gave you some pretty low marks, Al. In fact, so low they rated you no longer combat ready. Your proficiency test scores dropped right off the table. I know you don't like to hear it, but it was not Robertson's fault. If you're looking to blame somebody, you've only got one person to blame, and that is yourself. And regarding your anticipated promotion, it's all tied together. Even though the rank of "brigadier" is essentially a presidential appointment, you still need to have your name submitted and then screened by an in-service promotion board just to get it in front of the president. Look, Al, if the brass isn't on your side, it just isn't going to happen. Simple as that."

Donovan had been painfully honest. He was not one to stand by and watch another become the scapegoat for something for which he was not responsible, especially if that person was not present to defend himself.

Alvin Pallosic was predictably angry. He was not angry at Jim Donovan; he anticipated his straightforward, no bullshit answer. He trusted the three-star general as he always had. Pallosic was no longer angry at Robertson. He was angry at the system; he was angry at the U.S. Army. They were putting snotty-nosed young officers in positions of evaluating professional soldiers like himself, when they didn't even know an M-1 tank from an M-1 rifle. *They were playing God,* thought Pallosic. This group of nameless, faceless computer jockeys possessed all of the power needed to condemn him. *Thumbs down on the aging gladiator.*

Once again, Colonel Pallosic had to suppress his outrage. He was able to accomplish this by setting it aside intact, like putting a box up on the shelf, assuring himself he would deal with it another time. It was the prudent thing to do.

Al Pallosic realized that his Plan A was dead in the water, and he had better concentrate on Plan B.

"Jim, you've gotta help me. Haven't I done my part? Haven't I contributed more than my fair share? I don't deserve this kind of crap, do I?" This was a last ditch effort that came from the heart.

Donovan knew exactly where Pallosic was coming from. The picture in his mind was as clear as if it were yesterday. It went back to a sweltering afternoon in early June 1968, in the northern Quang Tri Province of Vietnam near the Demilitarized Zone.

Word from Marine Recon Group Delta was that a well-armed, uniformed unit of North Vietnamese (regular) Army was moving south across the DMZ into Quang Tri Province. Recon Group Delta came under unexpected heavy small-arms fire. Quickly realizing they were far outnumbered and outgunned, it became obvious to Delta that they would soon be pinned down on three sides, making it increasingly difficult to maneuver out of their position. The Marine platoon leader, Second Lieutenant Patrick Stephenson, radioed for reinforcements ASAP!

Captain Alvin Pallosic, on temporary duty assignment with A Troop, 2nd Battalion, 34th Armor, could hear the chatter of light-weapons fire from off in the distance and picked up on the Marine Recon's radio for help. Pallosic turned his company of M48 Patton tanks off their course on Route 9 and headed toward Hill 207 at top speed.

Another two platoons of Marine infantrymen with a couple of M60 machine guns, trailed by an M67A1 flamethrower tank, arrived from the west as Pallosic's team converged on the NVA from the east. The combination Army and Marine reinforcements made quick work of the North Vietnamese regulars, delivering a one-two knockout punch before the Marine "Zippo" flamethrower tank ever reached the fight.

As the smoke cleared and there was no more return fire from Hill 207, the Marine Recon platoon leader radioed his thanks to Pallosic for the Army coming in and "saving his bacon." Alvin Pallosic smiled inwardly, as he could sense the bruised pride of the Marine Corps officer over the air waves.

Sitting in the open hatch of his M48 command tank, Captain Pallosic was adjusting the microphone and earpiece on his communications helmet when a single AK-47 shot rang out, striking the company commander in the wrist, only two or three inches from his face. After hearing the scream of pain over the noise of the V12 diesel engines, the gunner turned around to see his captain's face splattered with blood. He was clutching his left wrist, which was bleeding profusely. The gunner immediately got on the battalion network and franticly explained that his CO was hit and seriously wounded.

Lieutenant Colonel Jim Donovan, battalion commander, 2nd Bn, 34th Armor, had been monitoring the net and heard the news directly. Luckily, he had been *en route* to the skirmish and was only five minutes away. Donovan vividly recalled picking up the field phone himself and demanding, not requesting, the immediate evac of his best company commander. He could still envision the medics loading Pallosic into the UH-1 chopper amidst the yellow smoke marking their position. He also remembered the Marine second lieutenant giving the order and directing a steady stream of flame from the M67A1 Zippo, covering the lower half of Hill 207 in a sea of orange. The VC sniper was in there somewhere among the thick, green foliage. This was like going after a gnat with a shotgun, but Second Lieutenant Stephenson wanted to make damn sure that he was able to repay his debt of gratitude.

As the battalion commander looked on at the inferno before him, he had the slightest feeling of satisfaction, or maybe it was simply a feeling of justice being served; he really didn't know. He did know that he did not believe in "an eye for an eye," because the Bible clearly taught against that. However, he could never lose sight of the fact that he was a soldier, and this was war, and somehow the Marines had managed to even the score for that day.

No, Donovan thought now, *Pallosic does not deserve this kind of treatment.* The Pentagon did not have a reputation for being too sensitive about these kinds of incidents, either. Donovan understood the situation completely.

"I've been working on the M-5 project since day one," Pallosic said. "I only wish we had this baby available for this desert action in Saudi Arabia. It'll be up and running for whenever the next skirmish takes place, I guarantee. It's gonna be the single most valuable piece of equipment in the entire U.S. arsenal. It's *that* important, Jim. I'm not just blowing smoke, either. It's the quick strike machine we've always needed. The first prototype will be delivered to Hood early next month. I should be the one to put her through its paces. I've brought it this far, and I don't think anyone else is really qualified to give it the proper testing."

Donovan said nothing, but nodded in agreement.

"And Jim," Pallosic continued, "I know for damn sure I don't want to go to Fort Knox. You know I can't stand the spit and polish there, and besides, I never did look very good in Class As," he said, trying to interject a little levity.

Neither man spoke for a while, lost in thought amid typical restaurant sounds. Pallosic broke the silence. "Ya know, Jim, I'd really like to stay at Hood for the duration if at all possible. Retirement isn't that far off, and Fort Hood is about as close to a home and family as I'll ever find."

Donovan could see that it was a matter of pride. Pallosic should be entitled to some degree of respect and dignity. "I'll do everything within my power, Al, you can be assured of at least that much. I'll work at getting you an answer as soon as possible." He was sincere, but careful not to create any false hopes for his old comrade in arms.

~ * ~

Rambo 5

The old 8-inch diameter, 215-pound XM-753 rocket-assisted projectile was classified as an "enhanced radiation" weapon. It contained a single stage W-79, low-yield warhead, rated somewhere between one to two kilotons. Range 18.64 miles.

The XM-753 was developed by the Army in 1976 at the direction of the U.S. Congress. The congressional directive specifically called for "a technologically updated artillery projectile that could deliver maximized personnel casualties while minimizing collateral damage to the surrounding environment."

This nuclear artillery gave the U.S. Army a tactical punch that was more accurate and less susceptible to bad weather than the low-yield atomic weapons delivered by aircraft. Politically, the AFAP (artillery-fired atomic projectile) gave the Army a new, important role on the nuclear battlefield that had always been dominated by the Air Force.

The XM-753, as well as the original conventional high explosive 203 mm round, were transported and fired by the U.S. Army's M110A2, a tracked vehicle that resembled a tank with a 203 mm cannon mounted atop. The M110A2, most recently in service in Viet Nam, had a total crew of thirteen. Seating only five crew members, the remaining eight were transported by an M548 tracked carrier. Although this eight-inch gun was self-mobilized, it was slow and less than efficient with such a large crew and required a support vehicle of comparable speed.

By late 1986, another congressional committee had concluded, after a lengthy re-evaluation of the XM-753/M110A2 combination, that there was a definite need to improve this concept of a mobile tactical warhead and bring it up to the standards of modern warfare. The fact that there were slightly over one thousand of these M110A2s in service and some outlandish number of XM-753 projectiles salted away somewhere as a result of President Gerald Ford's 1977 Stockpile Memorandum had very little bearing, if any, on the decision to develop the M-5 Rapid Mobile Launch Vehicle.

The M-5, nicknamed RAMBO 5, would revolutionize the traditional role of an Armored Cavalry Regiment.

Colonel Alvin Pallosic was recognized as the man to turn to for his vast experience with armored vehicles. Most just assumed that Pallosic had cut his teeth on the tread of an old M48 Patton tank, but he had actually spent his first two years of service as an MP, patrolling the confines of Fort Riley, Kansas. Military police work was incredibly boring to the young second lieutenant. A change of MOS was imperative and not that difficult to do. It would mean more training, but that was an acceptable tradeoff, if the new field offered him a challenge.

Everything about Armor and Armored Cav agreed with Pallosic. Hot and dirty was just a way of life. The smell of grease and diesel fuel early in the morning at the tank park was an aroma as satisfying to Pallosic as freshly-brewed coffee was to the common man. Pallosic had found his niche. His ability to command and maneuver these powerful machines made of steel was second nature to him, and eighteen months of combat in Vietnam in the turret of an M48-A3 gave credibility to claims of fame he received, along with a Bronze Star and a Purple Heart.

Alvin Pallosic was the obvious choice to be the primary advisor on this project. The Colonel also had a special aptitude that allowed him to quickly grasp some rather complex mechanical and electrical engineering concepts, making him that much more valuable to the overall development of the M-5.

The RAMBO 5 combined with the XG-777 guided missile was the ultimate quick deployment weapon. The M-5 Rapid Mobile Launch Vehicle was unique. It was a light armored vehicle, Kevlar-plated, and not much larger than a GMC Suburban.

Pallosic's influence was apparent in the M-5's mobile capabilities. He realized that all wars would not be fought in the jungles or in the desert, and that super highways link all major cities throughout the civilized world. With this in mind, he developed a vehicle to travel at a cruising speed of up to eighty plus miles per hour on the open highway, with a range of three hundred miles on one tank of regular gasoline. Special tires were developed to accommodate for conditions found in the desert, muddy rain forests, and rocky, mountainous terrain, as well as for asphalt or concrete surfaces. A state-of-the-art four-wheel-drive transmission was also developed by General Motors engineers, making it the fastest, most sure-footed ground weapon in the U.S. arsenal to date.

Not only was the M-5 quick and agile, it was also smart. It had been referred to as "a computer on wheels." The electronic wizardry of its onboard, high-tech computer could locate targets and guide the XG-777 with surgical precision. A portable, 24-inch satellite dish mounted on a collapsible ten-foot, telescopic pole and tripod was tethered to the M-5 with a fifty-foot coaxial cable. This basic satellite link was designed for quick assembly by one man. The interior of the M-5 looked more like the cockpit of an F-15 Eagle than the dashboard of any other military ground vehicle, complete with digital displays, keyboard, and color imagery on a thirteen-inch screen.

One of the other key selling features of the RAMBO 5 was that it only required a crew of two: the driver (operator) and a computer technician referred to as the "fire control officer."

The firepower on board the M-5 was also a gigantic improvement over the old XM-735 rocket-assisted projectile. Three XG-777 missiles were mounted side-by-side in the electrically controlled launching rack atop of the M-5 chassis. Two hundred twenty volts of electric current moved the entire rack vertically and horizontally as quickly as the FCO could punch in the coordinates on the keyboard situated on the center console.

The sleek "7s" were nine and a half feet long and twelve and three-quarters inches in diameter, extending the sharply-pointed nose over the cab portion of the vehicle. Each rocket had the capability of delivering a conventional high explosive ordinance or a 10K "tactical" nuclear warhead with a maximum range of thirty-five miles. The choice of these two weapons was generally in the hands of the battalion commander. The combination of the mobility of the M-5 along with the range and striking power of the XG-777 made for a very versatile and extremely lethal package.

~ * ~

29 September 1990

Alvin Pallosic had taken a few hours off to pack his personal belongings before going to his office at brigade headquarters. There really wasn't very much to pack. Still no word from Jim Donovan. Only two days remained before Pallosic was to report to Fort Knox, Kentucky, for his reassignment. Transportation arrangements had been made the day before when Pallosic became resigned to the fact that if it had taken this long to get a reply from the Pentagon, the news would not be good.

Pallosic had grown even more bitter over the past week waiting to hear from his so-called friend who had obviously forgotten about him, or worse yet, had lied to him.

There in his office, lying in the center of his bare desk, was a Federal Express envelope marked for Priority AM Delivery. It was from Lieutenant General James Donovan, Department of the Army, Pentagon.

Pallosic opened the cardboard envelope without a trace of enthusiasm. *At least Donovan proved to be a man of his word*, considered the colonel as he extracted the official government forms with a note paper-clipped to the documents. The note was written in Donovan's own hand. It first expressed the general's personal regard for his colleague's requests, followed by his regrets he could not influence the ultimate decision maker (name withheld) to totally comply with his wishes, but all was not lost.

The good news was that Colonel Pallosic's revised orders stated he would be retained at Fort Hood; he would not be required to report to Fort Knox on 01 October. The bad news was that Pallosic would no longer even be associated with Armor or the Armored Cavalry. This essentially proclaimed the end of his involvement with his beloved M-5.

The new orders called for Pallosic to take command of the 89th Military Police Brigade, HQ, Fort Hood, Texas. On October first, Colonel Alvin Pallosic would carry the official title of Fort Hood Provost Marshal. It took a couple of minutes for this news to sink in, but finally Pallosic followed the reasoning behind this latest stroke of genius from the Pentagon. He understood it, but nevertheless, he didn't like it one bit.

As best as Pallosic could figure, the 89th MP Brigade provided combat military police support to III Corps in Saudi Arabia. About two-thirds of this brigade had already shipped out to take part in Operation Desert Shield, along with its present colonel, still retaining his command of those troops.

Technically, Pallosic had met the minimum requirements for this position. He presently held the rank of colonel; he had completed the ten-week Military Police Basic Officer Leadership Course from the U.S. Army MP School at Fort Leonard Wood, Missouri; and he had served as a military police officer at Fort Riley, Kansas, for twenty-five months. Not exactly what one would call impressive credentials for a job that carried the responsibilities of provost marshal for one of the largest military installations in the country, but it was good enough. Even if Pallosic had not met these minimums, it would not have impeded the Pentagon in this particular change of MOS. Nothing that a simple waiver couldn't fix.

This is bullshit! thought Pallosic. *Hell, I'm nothing more than a caretaker here. Everybody has been shipped over to the desert. The base is over half empty; this place is a ghost town! Who or what am I supposed to be protecting? I'll bet I don't have more than one or two companies of men left under this command, with nothing more than 45s, a few M16s, and a dozen four-door sedan squad cars!*

Once again, Alvin Pallosic was seething. He seemed to be doing a lot of that lately. *I guess they needed a new crossing guard at the elementary school or someone to write parking tickets in front of the main PX. Thanks a lot, Donovan.*

Pallosic considered his new orders to be a huge slap in the face. The colonel did not look at this as a position of great responsibility, as Donovan had genuinely intended, but seemed to measure his self-worth in terms of the number of men and the amount of military hardware that were under his command.

Colonel Pallosic had achieved his success by being an aggressive soldier. He thrived on the military power that he had possessed for so many years. Now it was over. If it wasn't for his maximum retirement benefits, he would drive off the post right now. The more he thought about it, the more disgusted he became. He now hated his surroundings and the military way of life that he had cherished for all of his adult years. Pallosic had reached a point of no return. Nothing could right the wrongs that had been inflicted upon him now. It was just a culmination of all of the past injustices that he had had to endure. Well, not any more.

Who was it who had said, "Pay backs are hell"? Pallosic thought. *Well, by God,* somebody WILL *pay for this!*

It did not take long for word to get out that the new provost marshal was one mean son of a bitch. MPs are known for having a rough exterior, but this guy was way beyond logical explanation. Absolutely *everyone* steered clear of the "full bird" with an attitude.

Chapter Five

Eastern Europe
1990–1993

The year 1990 continued to bring about radical changes in Eastern Europe:

Democratic elections were successfully carried out in Hungary, Czechoslovakia, Poland, and Bulgaria.

Czechoslovakia held its first free democratic election since 1946. Pressure from Slovak nationalists forced Czechoslovakia to change its name to the Czech and Slovak Federal Republic.

Solidarity swept local elections throughout Poland. Lech Walesa was elected president.

On October 3, 1990, slightly less than eleven months after the Berlin Wall had fallen, Germany could at long last officially proclaim "Reunification." All of the political events that had taken place in eastern Europe during 1989 and 1990 were a build-up of what was to take place at a conclave in Paris on November 19, 1990. It was here that Mikhail Gorbachev, leader of the Soviet Union during the final stages of the Cold War, accepted the conditions of the victors and recognized Germany as a unified state. This marked the end of the Cold War and was functionally equivalent to the act of capitulation in the railroad car in Compiegne in

1918 that officially ended World War I, or the signing of the unconditional surrender of the Japanese to the Allies on the deck of the USS Missouri in Tokyo Bay on September 2, 1945, which officially ended World War II.

~ * ~

16 June 1991

Lieutenant General Stephan Krause was definitely feeling the pressure. Unlike most, Krause found stress to be exhilarating; a special kind of motivation.

The Warsaw Pact would be formally dissolved on July first. Most Soviet troops had already pulled out of Hungary, knowing well in advance that orders to evacuate the country would be strictly enforced as of that day.

Krause viewed this as just one more opportunity. He was beginning to be recognized as one general who was not just part of the establishment. For the most part, with the exception of General Aleksey Chesnokov and several of his faithful, the others had been defeated; they were like sheep being led to slaughter. Not Stephan Krause. He chose to play the role of a rebel and, oddly enough, no one was getting in his way.

Krause had staged a full-scale field training exercise, basically "war games," in northwest Hungary near the Ukrainian border. The exercise would be carried out for two full weeks, running all the way up to the thirtieth of June. A defiant move, obvious to all, but that was exactly the message Krause wanted to deliver.

"Saber rattling" was meant to demonstrate the might of Mother Russia, but in reality, Krause was using the field exercise to provide an excellent smoke screen to appropriate whatever weapons and equipment he still needed to complete his arsenal. Everything from small arms, anti-personnel mines, and machine guns to shoulder-fired ground-to-air missiles and anti-tank weapons, along with vehicles of every size and purpose, were at his disposal. There was still some accountability for this equipment beyond the normal amount destroyed or expended during training exercises, but nothing like the tight security that had once been imposed on division commanders.

Part of the beauty of this scheme was that Krause was rarely questioned by higher authority. For one reason, there were not all that many who actually outranked him. Second of all, he was highly respected by most of his peers and feared by a few who would never admit to it. As a rule, Krause did not interfere in the routines of the other senior officers, as long as they did not stand in his way or present an obstacle to something he might need.

~ * ~

30 June 1991

The General got out of his staff car and climbed a small rise that overlooked the Hungary/Ukraine border from the Ukrainian side.

The sun was setting as the last vehicles crossed the dividing line that separated the two countries. It was a beautiful sight to behold for Krause. The efforts of so many months of well-orchestrated planning were becoming more visible every day. There would always be more work, more planning, more political maneuvering to do, but for this moment, Stephan Krause reveled in the success of his progress thus far.

Krause's cache had outgrown the abandoned MIG hangers outside of Mukachevo, and the general was now dispersing his newly-acquired arms and equipment in several small safe-havens throughout western Russia.

~ * ~

General Krause had been very much aware of the planning and the formation of what was to become the new, loosely-bound confederation known as the Commonwealth of Independent States. No longer would there be a Union of Soviet Socialist Republics, but a mere Commonwealth. Even the feeble sound of Commonwealth of Independent States made Krause cringe. It lacked any resemblance of having a backbone or even the slightest amount of strength. Although Krause had openly opposed the formation of the CIS, he knew there was nothing he could do to stop it right now. He would simply have to accept it at the present time and not lose sight of his ultimate goal.

The best estimation as to when the U.S.S.R. would officially become the Commonwealth of Independent States was somewhere around the middle of December. This came firsthand from a reliable source within the Kremlin. Probably just before Christmas to give these "freedom fanatics" another thing to sing and cheer about, Krause suspected.

In a sense, it was like moving all of your belongings to higher ground just before a flood. All of Krause's military hardware was now safely stored in various sites throughout western Russia, with the exception of his nineteen SS-A-20s, still in the Ukraine.

After several months of on-and-off-again searching, as time would permit, Krause found the ideal location to store the A-20s.

~ * ~

08 December 1991

A convoy of ten flatbed trucks, each with black, weather-proof tarpaulins securely tied down, covering their cargo, had traveled the Ukraine from its eastern border near Sumy to their destination near Kursk in western Russia, a boneyard for obsolete and nonfunctioning equipment.

The sole purpose of having this almost nonmilitary-type military base was to provide a quick source for spare parts for inoperable weapons and equipment. In theory, it was an excellent cost-saving and time-saving facility. In actuality, this small, understaffed base was as nonfunctional as the rusted tanks, artillery pieces, and antique helicopters that occupied this burial ground of Soviet weapons. The main problem with the Kursk Salvage Depot was that hardly anyone used it. Whether it was a case of not knowing of its existence or not having faith in secondhand parts, or possibly the inability to access an accurate inventory record of what was on hand, most Red Army maintenance officers did not take advantage of this facility. It was a place distant in the minds of those in the Soviet military, because the only obvious proof of its existence was the payroll record and the fact that the facility drew provisions from central supply. Aside from that, it was virtually invisible.

That is precisely what made it such an attractive location for Krause's stash of SS-A-20s.

~ * ~

It was going to be an exceptionally long day for the Red Army corporal who normally operated a variety of heavy equipment throughout the yards and in the bowels of the underground storage bunkers of the Russian Army Salvage Depot at Kursk. Mladshiy Serzhant (junior sergeant or corporal) Grisha Baturin had watched the convoy of ten flatbeds roll through the high gates of the depot as he strolled, half asleep, to the mess hall, about forty-five minutes before the sun would rise over the hills on the eastern horizon.

Corporal Grisha Baturin worked his hardest at avoiding work. The ten long trailers with their mystery cargo covered with black tarps could only mean one thing to the corporal; someone would have to unload these vehicles, and that certainly looked like more work than he cared to do for a week. Being a heavy equipment operator usually worked to Baturin's advantage. He believed that sitting and riding were always preferred over standing and walking. Rarely did Corporal Grisha Baturin ever break a sweat while on the job.

"Baturin!" bellowed the Starshiy Serzhant (senior sergeant) from behind, jolting the corporal a few inches from the surface of the wooden bench.

Grisha Baturin had been perfectly content to nurse his oversized mug of tea in the warmth of the small mess hall.

"It's your lucky day, Grisha! I'll give *you* the choice of job assignments this morning. Do you want the crane or the forklift?"

"What are we unloading, Comrade Sergeant?" asked Baturin.

"I'm not telling you," the sergeant said with a grin, making the monotony of daily duty assignments into somewhat of a little game. He repeated his question: "The crane or the fork?"

"The big crane or the small one?" asked Baturin.

The sergeant thought for a moment or two and then responded, "The small one."

That was a good enough clue for Grisha Baturin to make a decision. "Okay, Comrade Sergeant, I'll take the crane."

The sergeant laughed loudly, having anticipated this response. "Of course, of course. Small crane, small work, correct? Not so, my lazy comrade, not so. Come with me, Grisha, I'll show you what needs to be done." The sergeant pulled on his thick, oversized mittens and donned his heavy, gray woolen cap with the fur-like pile ear flaps.

The lead truck in the convoy had been directed to pull up in front of bunker number one; the remaining nine vehicles formed a neat line leading to the entrance of bunker two about a quarter of a mile farther down the road. The driver of the lead truck was already in the process of turning back the tarps that masked the cargo on his flatbed truck.

"Look, Grisha," said the Red Army sergeant, as his breath crystallized in the freezing morning air, "had you chosen to operate the forklift today, you would have only had to unload those nineteen wooden cases and nineteen pallets holding those tail fins. That large cylinder on the other side of the flatbed is a SS-A-20 missile. You will become very well-acquainted with these A-20s," he said, pointing to the long line of tractors and trailers, "because you will be unloading those eighteen missiles plus the one here in front of bunker one. Oh, and Grisha, you *will* have this job completed by the end of the day." The sergeant chuckled sadistically.

The nose cones that contained the disarmed nuclear warheads had been packed in large wooden crates, and the tail fin assemblies had been removed and stacked onto wooden pallets for the best possible economy of hauling this valuable freight.

Once the crates and pallets had been unloaded by the forklift and safely stored in bunker one, the flatbed truck, now hauling only the single SS-A-20, joined the end of the line to be unloaded in bunker two.

Underground storage bunker two was a huge cavern of reinforced concrete about three times as large as bunker one, originally built to safely store Russian ordinances from possible attack by the Germans during WWII. Three and a half feet of concrete reinforced by steel rods provided a protective shell well below the thick layer of earth that provided total concealment from the air.

Bunker two had been equipped with an underground railroad siding that had been functional up until the early 1970s. Due to the lack of use and no maintenance whatsoever, the walls and the ceiling of the lead-in tunnel had deteriorated so badly the track was taken up and the entrance was securely sealed by a double thickness of red brick. Now the only entrance to bunker two was the descending ramp that was just wide enough and high enough to accommodate most modern tractor/trailer rigs.

It had taken Corporal Baturin the entire day to unload the eighteen missiles. Two missiles per flatbed trailer were cradled in concave, grooved wooden planks, forming a protective rack to prevent them from shifting during transport. Technicians had been instructed to drain the liquid rocket propellant from each of the SS-A-20s before leaving the hanger in Mukachevo to insure a lighter and safer load for the journey to the Kursk depot.

By 1800 hours, Corporal Grisha Baturin was cold, tired, and very hungry. He knew the mess hall would be locked up tighter than a drum by 1900 hours, but he was sure that he could unload that last missile, turn in his equipment to the motor pool, and still make it back in time for a hot meal. In his mind, he could smell the almost home-like aroma of potatoes, cabbage, and sausage simmering in a pot on the large cast-iron stove in the mess hall.

The harness had been strapped in place, and Baturin began to raise the boom of the crane to lift the final rocket from its wooden cradle. The cable was taut, and Baturin could feel that this one was considerably heavier than the other eighteen. Some inept rocket techy had failed to drain the fuel from this missile!

The winch strained as it began to lift the long, gray cylinder. Baturin considered setting it back down in the cradle on the flatbed truck. He knew in the back of his mind that he should get extra help or, better yet, use the larger crane, neither of which he chose to do. He knew that none of his other comrades would be around in this area or in bunker one, with the possible exception of his sergeant, and he knew better than to bother him with a problem like this at this hour of the day. Besides, he was probably well into his vodka by now. The trip all of the way down to the motor pool would take at least another ten minutes or so, plus he'd have the additional hassle of filling out the paperwork for the larger piece of equipment. Basically it all boiled down to taking too much time and, as a result, would cause him to forfeit his evening meal.

"Screw it," he growled. "This will have to do."

The cables and gears creaked under the strain of the additional eighteen hundred pounds of the highly-volatile liquid rocket fuel. Baturin had lifted the missile fuselage about two and a half feet above the cradle when the weight shifted slightly, causing the lower portion to begin to slip from the harness. Seeing this happen, Baturin slammed the control lever to the "Stop" position, not considering the repercussions of an over-reaction. The payload jerked violently, adding pressure to the already overloaded cable. The cable snapped like a broken rubber band, just above the fastening device, and the loose rocket careened off the metal edge of the flatbed with force, about three-fourths of the way down the length of the missile.

The thin, gray skin of the rocket could not protect the internal fuel cells from this impact. Immediately, the ruptured fuel cells began spewing the clear liquid dynamite onto the concrete floor. The boom operator froze in his seat as he soon realized he had just committed an error that would cost him his life. The sick feeling from the pit of his stomach lasted only a second or two. The truck driver, napping comfortably in the enclosed cab never had the slightest inkling of what had just taken place.

When the forward portion of the rocket struck the floor, it created a spark that ignited the highly-volatile fuel mixture already puddling on the ground. Or possibly just the fumes were first ignited; it really made no difference. Storage bunker two was immediately engulfed in a huge ball of white flame. With only the relatively small opening up the ramp leading outside, the inferno was trapped beneath the earth's surface. The explosion forced the entire dome of reinforced concrete and tons of packed dirt to be hurled into the air simultaneously with a great plume of flame that resembled a massive volcanic eruption.

One rocket loaded with fuel would certainly have been enough to cause the total destruction of the bunker and its contents, but the small amounts of fuel residue in each of the other eighteen rockets had created enough vapor within the fuel cells and fuel lines to cause them to also explode from within when hit with the blast of intensive heat. The large diesel fuel tanks of the truck pulling the flatbed trailer, along with the propane gas canisters fueling the crane, contributed to the massive explosion. Because of the highly-volatile fuel in this confined area, the explosion produced what would appear to be one enormous flash and deafening boom instead of several separate explosions, but the end result was the same: one gigantic crater. Miraculously, only two lives were lost.

The mysterious explosion at the Kursk Salvage Depot proved to be a turning point for General Stephan Krause. Although the paper trail concerning the SS-A-20s offered no conclusive evidence as to who was responsible for nineteen medium-range ICBMs showing up at Kursk, most rumblings throughout the Kremlin and in high military circles seemed to implicate the rogue Spetsnaz general in one way or another.

Krause was understandably upset at the loss of his cache of missiles. He was *temporarily* down, but a long way from being out. If anything, the setback seemed to spur Krause on. Now, more determined than ever, he resumed his crusade to recruit a greater following for his new communist party. As far as losing the nineteen missiles that represented the offensive might of his authority, well, that was just hardware. There was time, and there were still thousands of nuclear missiles scattered around the globe; he would just have to start from square one on that count and begin at once to rebuild.

~ * ~

NSA Station M in Munich, Germany, was under the direct command of Senior Operations Officer and Station Chief Henry Talbot, with Erich Mueller serving as the lead special operations investigator.

Talbot, a man in his early fifties, had devoted his entire adult life to his job. People close to Talbot agreed that his confirmed bachelorhood was a result of his "marriage" to the NSA. Hank Talbot's bond was with the NSA, and he could not serve anyone or anything else without detracting from the one hundred percent he gave his career.

Talbot had always worked at keeping his six-feet-two-inch body in reasonably good condition, but lately, the work load prohibited him from his regularly scheduled exercise. Having had the privilege of playing football for Woody Hayes at Ohio State University, Talbot knew the importance of staying physically fit. Now it had become a struggle to work out as he was used to. Talbot didn't know if it was an age thing or if he was just that much busier than he had been in the past. It seemed strange, but it appeared to Talbot that the spy business had actually picked up since the end of the Cold War. At least that's how it was at Station M.

Hank Talbot had been Gerhardt Richter's contact since he had become an established source back in early 1989, working out of Berlin. Talbot continued to receive Richter's feed of information when he made the big switch to the Russian side, joining the North-Caucasian Military District and moving to a remote training site in the Caucasus Mountains back in January 1990.

Richter's information was always accurate and reliable, so there was no reason to doubt his account of the explosion at the Kursk Salvage Depot. Richter had pegged Stephan Krause from early on as the one to watch in this horse race. A lot of very legitimate concern was being paid to General Armii (equivalent to a four-star in the U.S. Army) Aleksey Chesnokov. General Chesnokov had a large following of Russian military brass in his camp; he was a figure who needed a close eye and could not be overlooked.

In Major Richter's estimation, Krause was the guy who was most likely to upset Yeltsin's applecart. General Stephan Krause, along with three or four political movers and shakers, could not be trusted, according to Richter's reports. It was terribly frustrating to Gerhardt Richter not to be within the inner circle of General Krause's command. There was always so much more going down in Moscow that never reached him in this most God-forsaken part of southern Russia.

~ * ~

December 21, 1991, marked the official formation of the Commonwealth of Independent States. The monolith known as the Soviet Union had been shattered.

Political soothsayers, along with the news media, did not give this loose confederation of former Soviet republics anything more than a slim chance of survival.

~ * ~

16 June 1992

Although Alvin Pallosic no longer had any involvement with the M-5, he was still highly critical of the decision to scrap the entire project. Ever since the end of the Cold War, Pallosic had been afraid that his government was being lulled into a false sense of security. The U.S. Congress had killed the bill to proceed with the production of the M-5. *Was their thinking so shallow as to believe there would never be another need for the M-5?* Pallosic wondered.

The majority of members of Congress could not go back to their tax-paying constituents and ask for additional money for defense. To the contrary, defense programs were being slashed right and left to cut the budget, and the M-5 was no exception. The colonel shook his head in disbelief. There sat sixteen perfectly engineered, perfectly-functional M-5 prototypes used for field testing that would do nothing more than take up space in the confines of the tightly secured, fenced-in section of the North Fort tank park. *What a waste,* thought Pallosic. It was really no big surprise to the colonel. It stoked a fire in the pit of his stomach, fueled by a persisting anger that he could not suppress.

January 1, 1993 - Czech and Slovak leaders split the seventy-four-year-old Czechoslovakian federation. The Czech Republic and Slovakia became fully sovereign and separate countries. Vaclav Havel was elected president of the new Czech Republic by the parliament.

January 3, 1993 – U.S. President George Bush and Boris Yeltsin signed START II in Moscow, further reducing the strategic nuclear arsenals by seventy-five percent.

March 21, 1993 – Russian legislators voted to strip Boris Yeltsin of his power, asserting that the parliament, not the president, is constitutionally charged with running the country. Public sentiment was mixed. Many Muscovites disliked Yeltsin, but realized that reform was needed.

On March 29, 1993, the newly formed Czech Republic was struggling with an enormous bureaucratic overload. That was to be expected. Newly appointed government officials were either overstepping their prescribed duties or, more often than not, were not aware of all the duties for which they were responsible. Radical changes were being made every day. Some changes were very necessary and well thought out, while others seemed to be changes just for the sake of change.

Stephan Krause sat back like a hawk perched high in a tree, waiting to swoop down upon his prey. Amid this chaos, Krause could see yet another opportunity. Of primary importance, the Czech Republic was starving for capital. Secondly, the newly formed government was in the process of de-emphasizing the role of their military by disbanding the People's Militia, a part-time force of one hundred twenty thousand troops. Word had it that they would also be shutting down their antiquated but still functional radar system along the entire western and southern borders, stretching from Cheb to Mikulov, while continuing to maintain a nominal force of thirteen thousand border troops.

The logic behind this cost-saving measure was sound. Why maintain a radar system if you could no longer defend against an air assault? Plus, it was a popular notion that all of eastern Europe could now pretty well put aside the fear of being attacked by an outside force. The big black bear of communism had been severely beaten and chased back into its cave to die a peaceful death.

The closure of the radar outposts was a welcomed budget cut by most of the Czech government and especially by Havel's finance ministry. As if the gods were really smiling upon this new Czech Republic, there was an offer from a German businessman, representing a Frankfurt electronics firm, to purchase these radar outposts for salvageable parts and equipment. The German businessman explained that his company could refurbish and resell a good deal of the Czech air defense system for commercial use.

Stephan Krause thoroughly enjoyed playing this role. He also considered himself to be quite dapper, dressed in a navy blue Armani suite, Italian silk shirt, a burgundy "power tie," and a pair of Gucci loafers. *Were these Czechs that easily duped, or was I putting on that good of a performance?* Krause wondered. Of course Krause chose to believe the latter.

The new Republic desperately needed this cash infusion. They jumped at the chance to unload the surplus electronic gear, not realizing that they would only see a relatively small down payment and none of the money from the 120-day terms they had agreed upon.

Once the Czech Army troops moved out, teams of civilian clad Red Army radar technicians soon began occupying these remote radar sites along the western and southern borders. No one would be allowed close enough to see that instead of dismantling the present equipment, they were actually repairing and improving the Czech radar system that was already in place.

This string of border radar outposts was the beginning of what Stephan Krause envisioned as the next "iron curtain" for his new communist stronghold.

The 120-day agreed-upon terms virtually guaranteed that he and his troops could work unmolested for at least the next four months. If the general had not made his move by then, putting the coup into motion, he would at least be in a very strong defensive posture along the Czech border.

Krause now had amassed the manpower and most of the military hardware he needed, with the exception of an offensive strike system as he had with his SS-A-20s. But now he also realized he would need recognition when the time came—recognition of his new order of communism as a world power. He needed to be recognized by the United Nations and particularly by the United States and every European country as a force to be reckoned with.

He could not afford to be taken lightly or to appear weak. He needed an offensive strike system that could be a visible threat if the West should decide to ignore him. Whatever it took, he would have no problem issuing an ultimatum and then following through with the necessary force.

The world will soon learn that you do not question the authority of Stephan Krause!

The two key elements that he lacked were an offensive strike system capable of delivering a crippling if not fatal blow to Central Europe and enough funding to buy a few more officials in the Kremlin who could make his task a great deal easier.

Patience was a virtue that even Stephan Krause occasionally realized needed to be honed.

Chapter Six

South America
1945

Toward the end of World War II, when most Germans came to the realization that the Axis forces had indeed been defeated and there was no longer a shred of hope to revive the Third Reich in Europe, many high-ranking Nazi officers fled to South America. Some of these officers were faithful to Adolph Hitler's notion of a superior Arian nation and chose to keep the Fuhrer's ideals alive by transplanting themselves on new soil. For the majority of these refugees, however, it was a simple matter of escaping to avoid certain conviction and punishment for war crimes and atrocities committed at the various concentration camps in Germany and Poland. Specifically, they would be tried for the murder of about six million Jews, two million gentile Poles, and two thousand Polish Roman Catholic priests and bishops.

They settled in several different areas of the continent; locales in Argentina and Brazil were among the two largest concentrated areas for these exiled Nazis. One very small community of these native Germans settled on the secluded mountain slopes of northern Venezuela, halfway between the capital city of Caracas and the Caribbean Sea. Mountain slopes were not at all uncommon to these new inhabitants. In some cases, with a bit of imagination, the mountains resembled the steep foothills of the refugees' homeland in the Bavarian Alps.

Of course the climate and most of the vegetation was entirely different, but the principles of farming on steep grades was still essentially the same. This handful of Bavarians that banded together, hell-bent on maintaining their German heritage, could survive here very well, it seemed. Secluded from the rest of society, their chances of ever being detected were very slim.

Among the new residents of this remote mountain dwelling was the former Gestapo Captain Wilhelm Krause from Garmisch-Partenkirchen. As a Gestapo officer, Wilhelm Krause was a man with a heart as cold and hard as a piece of steel. But he exhibited a completely different personality when it came to matters involving his own family.

It was not an easy transition to Venezuela. He often wondered whether it was so much a matter of missing his parents and his only brother, or if it was the issue of knowing that he could never return to his family and his Fatherland.

The family ties were much too strong to be broken. About eleven months after his hasty departure, when it was relatively safe, Wilhelm wrote home to his brother Günter, informing him that he was well, and gave him a post office box number in Caracas that he and his family could respond to.

Günter Krause was a physicist, an intellectual type who had been declared exempt from military service in order to continue his scientific research with his associate and fellow scientist, Wernher von Braun.

Although Günter Krause gained a great deal of credit for his scientific contribution toward the development of the V-2 rocket, he had always considered his younger brother, a captain in the Fuhrer's elite police force, the true hero. The admiration of the younger of the Krause brothers was obviously instilled in Günter's first born son, Stephan. From early childhood on, young Stephan envisioned his uncle as someone larger than life: a war hero forgotten by Germany, but never to be forgotten by his family.

Stephan Krause could remember the excitement whenever his father or his grandparents would receive a letter from Caracas, Venezuela, from the mysterious sender "Guillermo Lossada." His father would chuckle at the amateurish code name Wilhelm had adopted in order to throw off anyone who might be trying to stalk the former Gestapo captain, but he understood that this was essential in establishing Wilhelm's new identity.

Within the first eleven months of Wilhelm's exile, he had found a bride, Eldora Carache, from the village on the neighboring hillside. A few short months later, she gave birth to Guillermo Lossada II.

Correspondence by mail was a regular occurrence now. Photographs of the families were frequently exchanged, especially pictures of the children. The photos, combined with the letters, became links of a chain that could not be broken, connecting the family over sixty-five hundred miles. The separation was most difficult for the grandparents, who knew they would probably never get to hold their second grandson.

Telephone calls were limited to one annual call on Christmas Day, so when the elder Guillermo received a call from his brother Günter on a steaming hot summer morning in August 1951, he knew it could not be welcome news. The death of his father was terribly difficult to deal with from such a distance. Guillermo wanted to fly back to Germany to comfort his mother and to be at his brother's side, but he realized the cost plus the time and confusion of arranging the transatlantic flight from South America to Europe on the spur of the moment were prohibitive, not to mention risky: he could be identified as a war criminal if he were to return to Germany.

Wilhelm Krause, former Gestapo captain, with almost god-like power over life and death and with all of the prestige that accompanied that position, was now Guillermo Lossada, a dirt farmer on a mountain slope in Venezuela, with no power and certainly no prestige. Guillermo Lossada could barely provide adequate food and shelter for himself and his small family. This was a terrifically humiliating experience for Lossada.

It seemed that Lossada had lost sight of the situation that brought him to South America in the first place. He had been running for his very life and had paid nearly all of his worldly possessions to a freighter captain who guaranteed his safe passage to South America. At that time, he had been quite satisfied with any proposition that would protect him and offer him a new identity and a new life, even if it meant being a poor dirt farmer.

In the spring of 1954, Günter Krause made plans for his family and him to visit his brother and his family in Venezuela. For three weeks in June, the Krause brothers were reunited. They seemed to spend every waking minute catching up on the previous nine years. The sisters-in-law, Nadiya and Eldora, co-existed as well as any two people could with a complete language barrier. Nadiya spoke no Spanish other than "please," "thank you," "hello," and "good-bye." Eldora spoke not a word of Russian or German.

Stephan, age nine, and Guillermo, Jr., age eight, became instant best friends. Growing up on two separate continents had no impact on the likes, dislikes, and interests of the two young boys.

There was never a question as to which parent young Guillermo resembled. His black hair, brown eyes, and dark skin gave no indication of his half-European heritage. It was only when the youth began to speak in his father's native language, in a dialect common to southern Germany, that one could tell he was anything other than a hundred percent Venezuelan.

Günter was surprised and very saddened at seeing his brother living in near poverty conditions. He vowed never to tell his aging mother the truth about his brother's financial condition, because it would break her heart to know her son and grandson had less than other families in Garmish.

It was a wonderful visit for Guillermo, at least until the morning Günter and his family were to leave. Touched by the Spartan dwellings and total lack of creature comforts, Günter took his younger brother aside and handed him a role of several thousand bolivars. It was no king's ransom by any means, but it was enough for them to buy some new clothing, a little furniture, and groceries to sustain them for three or four months.

Rather than gratefully accept his brother's generous offering, given with sincere, good intentions, Guillermo rejected the gift and took the offer as a personal insult. He refused to take any handouts from his brother or from anyone else, for that matter. It was no one else's business how he was able to provide for his family.

Günter apologized, assuring his brother he had no intentions of interfering with his life. The apology received superficial acceptance. Once Günter and his family waved goodbye at the airport, the younger brother seemed to settle into a state of depression for several weeks to follow.

The two cousins, however, had enjoyed the time of their young lives together. Nothing could have been more fun than exploring the hillsides and jungle-like valleys and playing in the rushing streams with a new best friend. Once back home, the boys began exchanging their own letters; they had their own interests to discuss.

Sadly, correspondence between their fathers diminished. It never came to a complete stop, but it did become less balanced: more letters from Germany, fewer from South America.

~ * ~

Along with the techniques of contour farming, the small community of Bavarians had adapted to the mountain slopes of Venezuela. One family had brought with them the trade craft of blown glass. The art of blowing glass is normally associated with craftsmen from Venice. In the case of the Koehler family, there had been a direct link to an accomplished Venetian glass blower only one generation removed.

At first the exiled Germans were only interested in growing crops to feed their families, but as time passed, they were harvesting the maximum yield their small parcels of land could produce. They had to turn toward some other sort of light industry, something without having to invest large sums of money that they did not have, so they turned to the experience and talents of the Koehler family.

A small glass factory was assembled near the top of the neighboring mountain, due north of the Guillermo Lossada dwelling, the same mountain from which Eldora (Carache) Lossada had come.

The factory produced small quantities of a variety of ornamental objects that were sold in shops in Caracas, appealing mostly to the tourist trade. In time, orders for the glass trinkets began to grow and the factory gradually began to expand.

One spring in the early 1960s, after severe rains had completely washed away the freshly seeded acreage of the Carache family farm, Eldora's three brothers sought employment at the glass factory. The glass business remained steady, and the brothers were content to stay on at the factory, abandoning their lives as common farmers. They now considered themselves businessmen.

~ * ~

Correspondence between Günter and Guillermo now consisted of only one letter per year at Christmas time, replacing the annual telephone call. The young cousins still wrote to each other occasionally, but as typical of those in their late teens, they, too, did not find the time to write as often as they had a few years before.

In the mid-1970s, young NVA Major Krause received an unexpected letter from his cousin in South America. Oddly enough, there was a strong suggestion of better economic times for the Lossada family. Guillermo, Jr. mentioned that his family had bought a television set—their very first one—and an electric washing machine for his mother.

Two months later, another letter proudly boasted of buying a car and mentioned plans of building a larger home. Obviously things were looking *much* brighter for the Lossada family.

Letters received over the next months revealed in a subtle way that Guillermo, Jr. and his father had become involved in the nearby glass factory business. He would occasionally speak of their lucrative "export business." Stephan naturally assumed that his cousin was referring to his family's involvement in the blown-glass industry.

It was in the fall of 1973 that the Carache family began construction of their crude cocaine refinery on the opposite side of the mountain from the glass factory. It was an ideal location. The winding mountain road lead directly to the front of the glass factory and then dead-ended, leaving a distance of only about two hundred yards to the cocaine processing plants concealed by thick vegetation. This created the perfect "front" for truck shipments departing the glass factory with their payload of white powder.

The Koehler family who had originally established the glass factory had been bought out by several of the local families, and a convenient partnership was created between the glass factory and the cocaine processing plant.

The cocaine was actually transported by handcart over a narrow dirt path that wound through the heavy, green foliage and into the backdoor of the glass factory. Once inside the factory, the cocaine, measured and neatly packaged, was then packed in with the blown glass products in many ingenious ways. Serious precautions to conceal the cocaine were taken, but the real protection came from the local police and customs officials paid off by the Carache family.

Chapter Seven

Munich, Germany
April 26, 1993

"Mike, I'm telling ya, I need more help down here!" Henry Talbot pleaded with his long-time colleague and present boss, NSA Deputy Director of Operations Mike Agnussi. "I'm starting to get more vibes from our buddy Major Richter down in the Caucasus Mountains. He's talking more about the Spetsnaz general Krause gaining not only military but political clout among some of the Red Army brass and Ministry of Defense people. It could be very good stuff, but I'm spread so damn thin right now, I can't be as thorough as I need to be."

"How about handing over some of your workload to Erich Mueller? He's capable," suggested Agnussi.

"You're right; he is capable, and I've already considered that, but he's already up to his ass in alligators, too. I can't risk giving him any more than what's on his plate right now. You've said it yourself, Mike, you get too much dumped in your lap and you start getting sloppy, and then that gets dangerous. We sure can't afford to lose good people, right?"

"You're absolutely right, but I don't have any warm bodies to send you. Believe me, I'd help you if I could, Henry, but we are completely tapped out. If things weren't tight enough, we're now working closely with MI6 on that bombing in London two days ago. We've got more activity in Baghdad, again, to keep a close eye on. The present political climate in Moscow is also—"

"I know, I know," Talbot interrupted. "I get the message."

"And I'm afraid it will probably get worse before it gets any better; at least that's how it looks from where I'm sitting, Hank."

Talbot knew that his boss was telling him the straight story, and no one knew the facts better than Mike Agnussi. Although newly appointed to this position as the senior civilian of the National Security Agency, Agnussi was no newcomer to the intelligence community. Retiring from the U.S. Navy after twenty years with the rank of rear admiral, Agnussi had spent the last nine years in Naval intelligence and as Visiting Professor, Department of Computer Science and Communications at the U.S. Naval Academy in Annapolis.

Hank Talbot was frustrated, but experience had taught him how to cope with it. Talbot wondered how the younger ops investigators would learn to cope. Erich Mueller was frustrated, as well; he'd been working very hard and seeing very few results in return.

Gerhardt Richter was stuck in the southernmost tip of Russia, picking up bits and pieces of good intel, but finding frustration in not being closer to the powers in Moscow and not getting the full picture. Hopefully he would also learn to cope quickly before making any fatal mistakes prompted by clouded judgment.

~ * ~

Kotelnikovo Military Airfield, Russia
27 April 1993
2100 Hours

In the privacy of his senior officer's cabin, Lieutenant General Stephan Krause sat at the foot of his simple but comfortable government-issued bed and unlaced his mud-caked boots. The two weeks of division level, intensive field training or "war games," as most others called them, were finally concluded. Krause believed these two weeks in snow and freezing rain in the Khokh Mountain Range, north of the Greater Caucasus Range near Mount Kazbek, added an extra layer of toughness and character to his already gristly troops. In spite of being tired and wet from the foul weather that could always be expected in the Caucasus Mountains during the month of April, Krause was in splendid spirits as he contemplated the events of the last fourteen days.

His Spetsnaz troops had been pitted against an entire division of Red Army regulars and several airborne companies and a few other additional specialized units thrown in for good measure. Krause's elite group of specially trained and dedicated Spetsnaz soldiers had basically rolled over its opposition. The only instance where Krause's men incurred any serious casualties was when they encountered the airborne troops under the direct command of Major Gerhardt Richter. *Impressive,* thought General Krause. *Very impressive, indeed!*

After a lukewarm shower and a change into a clean set of utilities, Krause poured an ounce or two of Courvoisier into a glass snifter and sat down at a small wooded table to sort through a stack of personal mail.

"Ah, Caracas, Venezuela!" he said, reading the return address as he slit open the red, white, and blue-trimmed airmail envelope. *I wonder if Cousin Guillermo is making plans to purchase the Taj Mahal this week?*

After reading the first two lines, the expression on the general's face went from a curious smile to one closely resembling shock or total disbelief.

The words that described the morbid slaying of Guillermo Lossada, Sr. contained more anger than sadness. Details were that a single .45-caliber bullet was fired through the back of his uncle's head, at point-blank range, with his uncle bound to an old, wooden chair and his hands tied behind his back.

Guillermo Lossada, Jr. swore that he would avenge his father's death. He did not know how or when, but he did know who, and he would somehow find a way to pay back the party responsible for this intolerable act of violence committed against his family.

Maybe in his younger years, Stephan Krause would have been touched by the words his cousin had written about his uncle's murder, but too many things had changed over the years that had forged the Spetsnaz general's cold steel character, and besides, mysterious changes had taken place in his cousin's life over the past several years. In closing, as usual, Guillermo extended an invitation to come to Venezuela for a visit, but this time there seemed to be some sort of underlying or subliminal message in his words that could be interpreted more as a request or possibly an offer, rather than simply an invitation for a holiday as they had been for so many years prior.

Stephan Krause decided this might be a good time to make a return visit to Venezuela, not to be misconstrued as a visit of mercy or to mourn the tragic death of a family member, but purely a matter of intrigue and possible opportunity.

The general made arrangements to be flown back to Moscow immediately. He also phoned his cousin Guillermo, expressed his sympathy, and informed him that he would be making the trip to South America within the next few days. Once travel plans were completed, Krause's staff would relay the date, flight number, and arrival time in Caracas.

Krause had carefully read between the lines and managed to put the pieces of the puzzle together as it best seemed to make sense. The drama had not begun with this letter, but with a collection of letters over the past decade. Each letter spoke of newly purchased cars or motorcycles, electronic equipment for his cousin's home, or vacations to the U.S. or Mexico with different lady friends. The letter informing Krause of his uncle's execution-style murder only helped to confirm to Krause that his family in Venezuela was very much a part of the illegal drug industry that flourished in northern South America.

The rapid rise from poverty to wealth in the Lossada family, the "gangland" style execution of his uncle, and Guillermo's knowledge of who was responsible all added up to be typical actions and reactions of rival South American drug lords.

Normally, General Krause would have been eager to learn the results of the field training exercise, but he already knew how good his men were, and he really didn't need any evaluation or critique to bolster his ego. At least not right now. There were more pressing issues to take care of.

~ * ~

April 29, 1993

Air France flight number 222 departed Charles de Gaulle Airport promptly at 10:35 a.m. en route to Caracas, Venezuela. Krause's aide-de-camp had made the hasty travel arrangements and had notified the minister of defense that the general would be taking a brief leave due to a family emergency. No further information was given. "Why offer more information than what they need to know?" Krause would constantly remind his personal staff members.

Traveling in the first-class section, wearing a mock-turtleneck, light weight leather jacket, chino slacks, and soft Italian leather loafers, the general fit the description of a well-to-do European bound for a South American holiday. Krause insisted on traveling in maximum comfort for the ten-hour long trip that cut a sharp diagonal course across the Atlantic.

The meeting of the two cousins at the airport, just outside of customs, was not entirely jubilant. Guillermo, Jr., having inherited the genes not only for his Latin physical characteristics but also for his passions, hugged and kissed his cousin on the cheek, displaying his emotions publicly. Krause, on the other hand, remained stoic, the typical military man, showing no outward signs of emotion at all.

Stephan Krause observed the tin and cardboard shacks and all of the other obvious signs of poverty as they drove up through the mountains that jutted up directly from the coast. Most of the cars and trucks, Krause observed, were older-model Chevrolets and Fords. The vehicle that Guillermo Lossada, Jr. was chauffeuring him in was a brand new black Mazda Miata convertible, another point helping to confirm Krause's original conviction.

Turning off of the main highway leading to Caracas, Lossada made a left turn onto a freshly asphalted road leading to the iron gates of a heavily protected, palatial villa with a manicured lawn surrounding elaborate gardens with fountains and cascading streams meandering throughout the estate.

Upon entering the villa, again achieving the "homefield advantage," Guillermo became very business-like, eliminating all small talk. He spoke of his father's death with little emotion at all, so different from only a few minutes before. He was now displaying the characteristics more common to his Russian/German ancestry. In his newly transformed business persona, Guillermo *now* seemed quite interested in learning more about his guest's position in the Russian military. He asked many direct questions pertaining to Krause's responsibilities. Guillermo Lossada II seemed especially interested in the size and overall strength of his cousin's command, and nearly lost his businesslike composure upon learning that these troops were specially trained, specially equipped commandos.

"Like the Green Berets of the United States military?" asked Guillermo.

"*Much* better than the Green Berets," sneered the general. "My men would make the U.S. Special Forces look like a bunch of Boy Scouts!"

His Latin cousin unconsciously released the slightest hint of a smile from his dark eyes. Only someone looking for such a reaction would have picked up on this minor change of facial expression.

The situation was developing as Krause had hoped it would. He could sense where his cousin was leading, but he would not offer any assistance by claiming that he understood what Guillermo might be looking for. Krause would force Lossada to ask for his help in an outright manner. This would give the general the control, the bargaining power that he wanted. Even though he needed the financial aid that Lossada was capable of producing, Krause now could appear to be his cousin's comrade-in-arms, rushing to the rescue of his family, and this would come with a very high price tag attached. Again, Krause had to remind himself to be patient and not to jump to the rescue until the most opportune time; he didn't want to leave money sitting on the table. Timing was always a very critical factor to Stephan Krause.

Guillermo Lossada, Jr. was the perfect host, serving his guest a light meal of locally grown fresh fruit and imported cheeses from the Netherlands, followed by a very nice Malbec from Argentina. He understood that the body does not respond well to overeating and drinking after such a long journey. He told Krause to get some rest, that tomorrow they would have a very full day.

The guest quarters at the Lossada Villa were equivalent to a presidential suite at most major luxury resorts. Freshly cut flowers and tropical plants adorned the second level sitting room of the suite that took in a panoramic view of the surrounding mountains and the lush gardens below Krause's balcony.

~ * ~

April 30, 1993

Krause had a surprisingly restful night's sleep, as he was not affected by any of the common abnormalities brought about by jet lag. At 8:00 a.m., there was a gentle tap on the door, and a chamber maid whisked in silently, depositing a silver tray with matching silver coffee service and a fine china cup and saucer. On a second silver tray was a tall glass of chilled fruit juice, from fruit that must have been locally grown based on the remarkable freshness, and a copy of the *International Herald Tribune*. A neatly printed notecard on the tray announced that breakfast would be served at nine o'clock on the veranda.

Breakfast was far from the traditional hard rolls, mild cheese, and thinly sliced ham that Krause was accustomed to. A side table with silver-covered chafing dishes offered local breakfast specialties such as shredded beef in a slightly tangy tomato base, cooked black beans, fried bread, and a wide assortment of fresh tropical fruits and melons. English style bacon, scrambled eggs, and pastries were also served for the benefit of the guest.

"Eat well," Lossada told his cousin, "we have a busy day ahead of us. There is much to do and a lot to talk about."

After several cups of a delicious blend of domestically grown coffees and one last French pastry, the men retired from the breakfast table. Each picking up a pair of Ray Ban sunglasses from the glass table in the entrance foyer, they climbed into the black convertible parked under the portico with keys already in the ignition.

A short drive to a neighboring hillside brought them to a small Catholic church. Through an iron gate behind the church was a small parish cemetery. Neither man spoke. Guillermo Lossada led the way to the gravesite that was covered with loose dirt and the remains of several sprays of flowers. A strong, sweet smell from the decaying flora filled the air. Lossada made a reverent sign of the cross and stood erect with his hands balled into fists at his sides. His jaws clenched tightly, and he stared at the grave as if he could see right through the crumbled earth. Two or three minutes of perfect silence passed, except for the chattering and chirping of a few small birds.

Lossada turned and walked away. Krause followed him to the car. Still nothing was said for about a half a mile back down the hillside.

"It's time that I tell you exactly what's going on here," Lossada said, breaking the silence. "You are an intelligent man, an experienced soldier, so I'm sure you have put some of this together by now. My family, well, I should say *our* family, is on the brink of war with another: the powerful Vargas family. Let me start from the beginning so that you will understand the situation completely.

"When my father married into the Carache family, he was accepted as almost one of the three brothers. Their family was very poor, as my father was at that time, too. You already know that from your visit when we were children.

"As I understand," Lossada continued, "many years ago, the second brother, Emilio, had gone to Colombia, Medellin probably, and became somewhat involved with one of the local drug lords. The brother was nothing more than a worker in one of the many processing plants.

Obviously he had a keen eye and some good business sense. When he saw how outrageously prosperous this family business was, he left, unannounced of course, and came back here. He was able to adopt similar growing techniques and, with the help from a chemist in Caracas, developed his own cocaine processing plant.

"My father watched the business grow. Wanting a better life for himself and his family, he became as involved in the business as the three Carache brothers. The oldest of the brothers died of heart failure a few years ago. The youngest brother is basically nonfunctional; his brain has been ruined by overindulging in his very own product, I'm sorry to say. It's really very sad. We warned him about the danger, but he wouldn't listen. This left the entire business to Emilio, my father, and me. Because Emilio Carache was extremely generous, and because he acknowledged the fact that my father and I played a large part in bringing the business up to where it is today, along with the realization that he could not handle the management side of the business alone, he divided it fifty-one percent for Emilio and forty-nine percent for my father and me. At least it *was* fifty-one/forty-nine up until the death of my father. With that, Emilio became extremely frightened, withdrew every dollar from every one of his many bank accounts, and simply disappeared. Emilio realized that he would be the next victim of the Vargas family. I will explain in more detail."

Krause sat impassively listening, taking in the information he had pretty well expected. "Where is the processing plant?" he asked, to simulate interest.

"We are heading there right now," Guillermo replied. "It's on that mountain over there, near the top, on the opposite side of the glass factory. Our operation," Guillermo continued, "is very small compared to the other factories that operate out of Colombia. Our production capacity is limited, and we don't have a real marketing system. No single big user, and no organized distribution set up. We sell to the locals in Caracas and do pretty well in the Dominican Republic and some of the tourist islands in the Caribbean.

"On a business trip to New York about a year ago, Emilio became friendly with another family in New Jersey: the DeGraci family. They had the seed money that our family lacked. To make a long story short, we developed a partnership. This was great, but we didn't realize at the time that we were taking some very serious business away from the Vargas family in Colombia. That didn't really matter much, because we would have gone after it anyway. Well, the business has been developing nicely, and it obviously antagonized the Vargas people greatly.

"The murder of my father was either a very strong warning sign to drop the DeGraci connection or the opening salvo to an all-out war. The problem is they are a very large and powerful family with weapons and other resources that we could not even begin to match."

"How can you even consider going to war with a force that has you outnumbered and that possesses superior firepower?" asked the general flatly, as if he were speaking with a ten-year-old.

"This might sound absurd to you, but I have a plan that would involve you, and it would bring you a terrific amount of personal wealth. I do hope that you can help me," Guillermo said solemnly.

"What in the world are you talking about?" Krause asked, playing dumb so as not to tip his hand.

"You command a battalion of men. Am I correct?"

"No, I do not. I command a *division*. My division is comprised of *several* battalions."

"You have mentioned that you have some elite 'strike force' troops," stated Lossada in a challenging tone.

Krause nodded his head, affirming the statement. "Actually they are all elite soldiers; it's just that there are some who happen to be the 'crème de la crème.' The elite of the elite, as it were," he said with a smirk.

After a few seconds, Lossada spoke. "I need to ask if I can use some of your men and weapons to help us wipe out the Vargas family."

Stephan Krause laughed out loud and shook his head in disbelief. "Cousin, I would like very much to be able to help you, but you must understand that the Russian Army does not loan out mercenaries. We are not soldiers for hire. We have our own wars to fight."

Krause continued his game while he internally basked in the delight of having read his cousin's mind with such accuracy.

Lossada persevered. "With your position, could you not find some way to lend us a few men and weapons? I'm not even asking for your best. Even send me your least skilled soldiers and your old equipment; I don't care! I just need something to put us on an equal level with the Vargas family; that's all I ask. You would be paid *extremely* well, I might add. I can promise you that. I discussed this with Carmen DeGraci last night on the phone, and he agreed to help finance this in order to protect his investment.

"Your pay for this 'mercenary' job, as you put it, would only be the first phase of your payment. We would actually include you in our partnership. You would continue to earn a percentage of our revenue. Let me explain, Stephan. You see, with the Vargas family out of the picture, we could take over all of their business, as well. The possibilities are virtually limitless!"

Guillermo's expression and tone of voice reverted quickly back to a more somber character. "I'm afraid to say that without your help, we will be crushed." Lossada paused for a moment, waiting for his line to sink in. "I have heard military men speak of 'the element of surprise' and what a terrific advantage it is over the opposing forces. This is true, is it not?"

Krause confirmed with a single nod of the head.

"Vargas would never in one hundred years expect any type of formidable opposing force from our side." After another lengthy period of silence, Guillermo said, "I ask you to think of two things, Stephan. First, your uncle's ruthless murder. This is *your* family, too, you know. And secondly, if nothing else, think about the money I am prepared to offer you."

This is supposed to shame me? thought Krause, showing no emotion whatsoever.

"Stephan, you could live like this!" Guillermo swept the air with his free arm, "instead of serving your masters in Moscow. You could be your *own* boss!"

Krause was light years ahead of his cousin on that idea.

"Consider my offer. Please. If not for your uncle, your family, then do it for yourself." Lossada took a deep breath, mainly for dramatic effect. "You know, Stephan, it has taken a great deal of courage on my part to have this conversation."

What conversation? the general thought. *You've done all of the talking!*

Lossada continued soberly. "I have laid it all on the line for you. If I didn't trust you, I never would have mentioned any of this to you. If I didn't think you could help us, I would never have even brought it up."

The two rode in silence as the black Mazda Miata convertible wound around the narrow mountain road, through the thick vegetation, toward the building inscribed "Carache Blown Glass." The sign was neatly printed in red full-block letters on white clapboard, but it had obviously not been done by a professional sign painter.

They parked on the side of the factory and walked through the large, open barn-like doors, past the workers and craftsmen, and out again through the smaller set of back doors and onto a dirt path that bent to the left. Through some one hundred fifty meters of thick, jungle-like terrain they walked until they came to the first-phase processing shack. It could easily have been mistaken for a fairly large peasant dwelling. Scattered farther along the trail were three other similar shacks. Guillermo gave a tour of each of these four processing stations in order.

After leaving the fourth shack, where the white powder was weighed and packaged tightly in clear plastic bundles, Stephan Krause suddenly came to a very startling revelation. If he had not actually been seeking his cousin's financial aid for his own benefit and chose to withhold the military assistance Lossada truly needed and that he was capable of delivering, he would never leave this mountain alive! He now knew all there was to know about the Carache/Lossada cocaine business. These things you just don't walk away from, blood relative or not. Krause understood that if he gave his cousin a flat rejection or balked at the immorality of manufacturing hard drugs, he would end up with a bullet in the back of *his* head and be tossed into a shallow grave just down the steep incline on the leeward side of the mountain. He could pretty well visualize his final resting place from where he stood. All of a sudden, there was another player in this game.

Something extremely rare had just occurred. Stephan Krause admitted to himself that he had not considered a cold, hard subsurface character in Guillermo Lossada, Jr. until now, thereby underestimating the capabilities of his younger cousin—a judgment flaw that could prove fatal. Krause's ego, being what it was, did not accept this mistake very well, so he quickly altered his mindset to a much lighter, less fatalistic point of view.

Ah, there is a definite likeness between my cousin and me that does not meet the eye at first glance, he thought. He did not permit himself any further self-criticism, but made a mental note that his cousin and possible future business partner was now to be viewed in a much more serious light. Guillermo Lossada had actually gained respect in the eyes of the general.

Krause decided to remain *cautiously* uncommitted to Lossada's plea for help as long as he could. The longer he kept his cousin on a string, the sweeter the deal he could walk away with. To avoid the shallow grave at the present time, Krause simply said without a trace of enthusiasm, "I'll consider your offer, Guillermo, but I cannot make such a decision at this time. Understood?"

"Sure, Cousin Steve, I understand."

Krause abhorred the Americanization of his name, but decided to let it slide. This time.

"Okay," said Guillermo, slapping the general on the back. "Enough business for now. Let's go into the city and have a good time. You know, relax, let your hair down a little. When we get to the city, I'll show you one of my other very profitable businesses. I think you'll like it."

The two men entered Red Beards in the heart of Caracas. The entire restaurant staff fell all over themselves to serve Senior Lossada and his guest.

"So, this is your other business. Very busy! All of the tables are filled with customers. I can see where this could be a very profitable business for you," Krause commented as he surveyed the bustling casual dining establishment.

"No, this is not mine," Lossada laughed out loud. "You'll see in a little while. I'll take you there after we've had something to eat and drink. Trust me."

The sun had dropped below the horizon by the time they drove through the back streets of Caracas to a section of the city that was lit up like jewels in the night. Neon lights with dark windows and the glow of black lights and revolving mirrored balls scattered multiple beams of light in all directions.

It was early, so most of the "girls" were still in the main greeting room—or parlor, so to speak—and some were sitting beside the long bar, sipping nothing more than iced tea or fancy colored fruit juices. The high bar stools were excellent stage props for the women of Victor's Place to display their long shapely legs and other selling features, which were virtually unimpaired by tight-fitting evening gowns split up the side or micro-mini skirts with black fishnet stockings that left very little to the imagination.

"These are my finest!" proudly proclaimed Lossada with a broad smile, gesturing with a slow wave of his hand to indicate the girls who inhabited the large room lit in a soft red glow from indirect light. Indeed these were all beautiful women. A wide variety to choose from, all different shapes and sizes, all dressed in unique attire. Some were dressed in erotic fashions, and others looked as if they had just stepped from the doors of a Fortune 500 New York ad agency.

"I have two other establishments just down the street, but they cater more to the working class. I save my best, here, for the high rollers: the traveling executives, high society people, and of course the local police and the politicians. A lot of the government officials, police, and customs officials receive extra special service for no charge at all. This, my friend, is *essential* to my other business. Without this, you understand, the other business would not exist. Oh, and yes, this too is very profitable. Enough shop talk. I promised you that we were just going to relax and have a good time tonight. You choose any one of these beautiful girls you desire. They are all professionals at providing the ultimate in pleasure. Choose two or three, if you wish. Compliments of the management!"

Krause had to admit to himself that the offer was certainly tempting, but he had to show that he was made of sterner stuff than those who made their decisions from below their belts. He would not appear to be sucked in by the weaknesses of the flesh. Krause still had to play out his part and negotiate from a position of strength. He would accept no handouts, attractive as they might be. *Another very slick move on the part of my cousin*, considered Krause.

"I appreciate your generous offer, Guillermo, but I must decline. I need to make a decision on your proposal, our "partnership" as you call it, and I need a clear mind. These are very lovely women, but they would be a great distraction to me right now. I need to concentrate on your offer and decide if there is some possible way for me to help you. I hope that you understand."

"Of course. You are completely correct, and I appreciate your professionalism. Please don't think of my offer here as a bribe. It was only a gesture of hospitality to a weary traveler many miles from home."

"Not at all." replied Krause. The two turned toward the door and made their exit.

~ * ~

At breakfast the next morning, Krause asked his host a litany of questions: "What type of force are we up against? How many? Are they well-trained? What equipment and what weapons do they have? When would you anticipate them launching a strike against you? Do they expect you to build up any type of defense, or possibly even launch a counter or preemptive strike of some sort? These are questions which need to be answered in order for me to even consider if it would be feasible for me to bring any of my men over here. I cannot risk the lives of Russian soldiers for a personal vendetta. You understand that, don't you?"

"Yes, I do, and I can answer your questions without hesitation," Lossada responded. "Then I think you will feel more comfortable with my offer."

"First of all, at the most, they would probably have no more than thirty-five or forty men. Are they well-trained? No, not at all. You would be lucky to find ten men who could shoot straight. They have no military training and no discipline, although they will respond to their leader, Cesar Vargas, mainly out of fear.

"They would be armed with light weapons: automatic rifles, shotguns, semi-automatic pistols for sure. Possibly some hand grenades and small explosives. Nothing that your men could not handle, I'm sure.

"When? Soon, I would expect. I think they would like to hit us all at one time, eliminating the possibility the rest would go to ground after another individual hit. This 'when' part concerns me very much. Even if you *can* help us, will we have time? They could strike today, tomorrow, or next week. We have to act fast, Stephan. I don't suspect that they would even anticipate any kind of warfare from us. They will probably be planning their assault for some time when all or most of our organization's members would be together in one location, so they can gun us down in cold blood like shooting fish in a barrel. That would be their style, but it doesn't eliminate the risk they wouldn't settle for picking off myself or any of my officers individually. Realistically, that could take place at any time and almost any place."

"How often does your entire organization come together?" asked Krause, looking for as much insight into the situation as possible.

"We have two business meetings per year, here at the Villa, when we all come together to discuss our sales strategy, distribution problems, or any other business that needs attention."

"And the last meeting was…?"

"The week before my father was murdered. My father had spoken out strongly against the Vargas family, which supports my suspicions that there must be a traitor within our ranks."

"A traitor! Why didn't you mention this to me before, Guillermo?"

"I didn't know that it made a difference. Does it?"

"It could make a big difference. First of all, you are in a great deal more danger than I had originally suspected. Not having wiped out your entire organization at the semiannual meeting, I would think the Vargas family would be planning to eliminate you and your officers individually. You are quite vulnerable here to anyone who would like to take you out. Your large gate, iron fence, and electronic sensors around the perimeter would not protect you from a sharpshooter over there or anywhere on that hillside," the general said, pointing in the distance.

"I would take all possible precautions starting right now." Krause stood up, pushed himself back from the glass breakfast table, and started toward the house with Lossada following. "As lovely as it is here on the veranda, you are a perfect target from these two directions," he said, pointing to the adjacent green hillsides. "Keep yourself isolated as much as possible. Your very right-hand man could be your worst enemy. Keep your distance from everyone. I mean it. You can't afford to make any mistakes at this point."

Walking into the kitchen and pouring a fresh cup of coffee for the general and himself, Guillermo invited his cousin to sit with him at the small table usually used by the kitchen staff.

After a while, Stephan Krause tilted his head to the side and rocked back in his chair, obviously on the verge of some new plan or idea. "Come to think of it, if you do in fact have a traitor amongst you, it could possibly make this task somewhat easier." Still thinking out loud, Krause said, "If you have a mole within your organization, I would bait a trap."

"Plan an emergency meeting within the next week or so, somewhere other than here at the Villa. You need to give him enough time to get the word back to Colombia and for them to plan their attack, and then—"

"Stephan," Guillermo interrupted, "does this mean that you will help us?"

"Yes, I thought about it last night as I lay in bed. I could not stand by to see my cousin murdered as my uncle was. We do need to retaliate and seek revenge." It was a bold-faced lie, of course, but Krause knew that it was exactly what Lossada wanted to hear.

"You'll need to tell me as much as you can about Vargas and his men so I can plan and prepare for our attack. The lives of *my* men will be at stake. I do *not* want any surprises, so your accurate information is absolutely critical to the success of this mission. Understood?"

"Yes, sir. I understand completely," Lossada said, uncharacteristically humbling himself.

General Stephan Krause requested that his "laptop," a new IBM ThinkPad 700C, the latest in portable electronic personal computers, be brought down from his room so he could begin taking notes. Lossada gave every possible detail about his foe that he could remember, building a psychological profile with the aid of the general's insightful questions.

It was established that Cesar Vargas was extremely bold and self-centered, which came as no surprise to Krause. *Was his self-absorption strong enough to be his Achilles' Heel?* He would not suspect that anyone else could be making plans of attack other than himself, for he considered himself to be more powerful than anyone else in South America. For Colombian drug lords, as a whole, this was not an exaggeration.

The concept of an inside informer became more evident through further questioning. Only someone from the inside could have known where and when Senior Lossada would be alone and unprotected on the night he was killed. It would be through this mole, whoever he or she was, that Krause and Guillermo planned to feed the information that would end up back in Colombia.

Krause instructed his cousin, "Tell your people you are going to have an emergency meeting. *All* of your officers and soldiers will be there. Tell them it's about improving your security since the death of your father, etc., etc. That's believable enough without going into greater detail."

"Think of an appropriate location to hold this conference. It should be somewhere we can draw them into an ambush. It sounds very basic, but that's exactly what we want. You start getting too crafty, and you increase the amount of things that can go wrong."

Krause checked his watch and said, "I can leave this afternoon on the four-ten flight for Paris. I will be in touch with you as to how much time I will need to prepare my troops and gather the appropriate equipment. Oh, and I need to stress that when you select the site for your meeting, make sure it's as secluded as possible. We can't have any outsiders getting in the way of pulling off a successful ambush. This is your primary concern."

"Now listen to me very carefully, Guillermo." Krause did not care if he sounded condescending. "*Do not*—I repeat, *do not*—breathe a word of this conversation to *anyone*! Not even your closest captain. You only speak of the conference, and nothing else. I am sure it will leak out to the right person, if what you tell me is true. And understand one thing very clearly, dear cousin, this service will not come cheaply. Your ideas of partnership and long range plans are all well and good, but I will need money to pay these troops, hire an aircraft, and purchase other miscellaneous equipment. This will be a "volunteer only" mission, and money will be the only carrot that I can dangle in front of these soldiers. This is not for Mother Russia."

"Money is no problem; I told you that earlier, Steve."

The price just went up, you fool, Krause thought.

"I need five million in U.S. dollars now, and five million when the mission is completed, plus the partnership you offered earlier, say ten percent of your profit. Fair enough?"

The general had him exactly where he wanted him. After Lossada's long dissertation on how desperately he needed his muscle, he could hardly bargain for a cheaper price, much less reconsider.

"Ten million U.S. dollars! You are killing me! You are my own cousin, my family!" Lossada shrieked in disbelief.

"That is true, but *this* is business, don't forget. You *are* in it for the money, aren't you? You *need* me, Guillermo. First, to keep you alive, and second, to keep your business alive. No, more than that. Your business will increase…what? Tenfold, twentyfold, with Vargas out of the picture? Now think about it; is my price too much to ask? I think it's actually quite a bargain," Krause said, exuding confidence with every word.

By 3:20 p.m., Stephan Krause was walking toward the Air France gate at the Caracas International Airport with two large, black nylon, square-shaped Nike athletic bags. Each of the bags was neatly stuffed with 1.25 million U.S. dollars, all very large bills. Realizing that five million in cash was impossible to produce on such short notice, Krause had agreed to have the remaining 2.5 million placed in a special account under his name in the Banco Central de Venezuela. U.S. dollars were much easier to work with and easier to spend. Rubles or bolivars were both unstable currencies, and they would have literally required several footlockers to transport it all.

Guillermo Lossada had led his cousin to one of the customs officials who was always willing to take a bribe, thereby eliminating the risk of having the Nike bags inspected. French customs at Charles de Gaulle Airport had never been a problem. Krause would merely flash his military ID along with his Russian passport, and they would wave him through as if he had some kind of diplomatic security clearance. Basically the French customs officials were frightened out of their shorts of any Soviet males, much less a general officer of the Red Army. At this stage of the game, no one wanted to upset the so called "peace" between Russia and the western world.

The general's last words of instruction to Lossada as they waited at the gate for the boarding call for flight 211 stressed the importance of finding a suitable location to ambush Vargas and his men. He explained again the ideal ambush scenario, describing the desired physical characteristics of the land that would be best for tripping the snare on their opponents.

Lossada was quick to understand the game plan; there was nothing terribly complex about it. He could easily picture the setting in his mind.

Krause spent the next nine hours traversing the Atlantic, working out the detailed preparations on his laptop computer. Upon arrival at CDG Airport, there would be a one-hour and forty minute layover before boarding the 07:55 Aeroflot flight to Moscow. Another four and a half hours in the air seemed almost unbearable with so much work to be done. The wheels would be set into motion as soon as he set foot on Russian soil.

He planned to utilize a select team from his 1st Battalion. They had all just been put through their paces no less than a week ago, but this would be his handpicked team of Spetsnaz specialists. With a few days' rest, they would be sharper than ever. The general was confident that these men could adapt themselves to the jungle-like terrain of South America without any trouble.

Chapter Eight

Moscow
02 May 1993
1545 Hours

With only two hours of sleep on the plane and the help of a large cup of strong tea, General Krause charged through his office door, giving orders to locate Major Petya Starikovitch. Until Lossada called with a time and details of the ambush site, he could only brief the major in general terms about the basic nature of their mission. Details given prematurely would only cause confusion and could possibly lead to a flaw in the execution of the assignment. Krause would simply have to wait for his call.

Although Major Starikovitch was technically not his second in command, this was the man he had chosen to prepare and organize his First Team for this highly covert mission to South America. Five minutes later, behind closed doors, General Krause explained to the veteran Spetsnaz major that this new mission would be classified as "Specialized Jungle Warfare Training." With the growing political unrest throughout most of Central and South America, it would be wise to have a strike force trained and available for quick deployment if it would ever become necessary to protect any Russian interests or assets that could be endangered.

Before Krause was able to conclude his first mini-briefing, he was interrupted by a two-beep sequence on his private line.

"Yes, put him through immediately," he instructed the switchboard operator. Krause dismissed the major and told him not to wander off too far. He would have more information forthcoming.

"Cousin Stephan," came the clear voice from the handheld receiver. "I think I've found the perfect spot. It's just as you told me it should be." Guillermo went on to describe in detail the terrain and all of the physical characteristics of the land. Other details were given pertaining to how the trap was to be baited. Guillermo even had plans for where a large aircraft could land in relative seclusion and also be refueled for the return flight.

It all seemed quite logical and well thought-out, even though it had only been a matter of about eighteen hours since the cousins had discussed their basic plans at the Air France gate at the Caracas airport. Krause was pleased with his cousin's plans and somewhat astonished at his efficiency and tactical aptitude.

"Excellent work! Guillermo, I must admit I am very impressed! Have you determined a date for this to take place?" asked Krause.

"I have set the tentative date for the sixth of May, but I was waiting to see if you needed more time before I finalized any plans."

Looking at his desk calendar, Krause agreed that he was certain he and a select team of his best men could be fully operational for combat within thirty-six hours. The general thanked his cousin and closed the call. Many details still remained, with very little time.

Transportation for this mission on such short notice could be a problem, but he would just have to verbally kick someone's ass to speed up the system if necessary. Actually, it would be no problem at all.

Krause's first call was to Polkovnik (Colonel) Yuri Berezhnaya of the Voyenno- Transportnaya Aviatsiya, the Military Transport Aviation Command. The VTA was responsible for all airlifts of Russian airborne forces. It was comprised of seventeen hundred various cargo/ personnel-type aircraft and was operationally subordinate to the Soviet general staff.

Colonel Berezhnaya and the general's association went back to the days when Krause served in the East German sector at Neurippen. Krause had always regarded the colonel as a trustworthy and competent officer, a professional soldier in the strictest sense of the word.

Brief pleasantries were exchanged, and Krause went straight to the point. "Comrade Colonel, I need your assistance for a special training mission. The nature of the mission is *strictly* confidential. The fewer people in the loop the better." Krause paused a moment for effect.

"Yuri, I need to rely on you, and only you, for your expert advice."

Flattery always seemed to work pretty well.

"Of course, Comrade General, you can put your trust in me. Just tell me what you have in mind and I will do my best to accommodate your needs," said Yuri Berezhnaya.

"I knew I could rely on your full cooperation, Colonel." Krause booted up his laptop computer and retrieved the notes he had written on the return flight. "I will need transportation for a total of nineteen men with light equipment, one KamAZ-4310 (2½-ton truck), and one UAZ-469 (3/4-ton truck). A flight plan should be drawn up for a departure from the airfield at Kotelnikovo to the northern coast of Venezuela near Caracas. I cannot be too specific at this time."

"Will you be deploying paratroopers, General Krause?"

"No, I will not, but I should add that our landing and takeoff area in Venezuela might be in limited space, and it will probably be an unpaved surface."

"Very well, Comrade General. From the details you've given me, primarily the takeoff and landing conditions, it rules out jet transportation. We'll need to go with a large turbo-prop," Berezhnaya said, jotting some figures on a note pad. "So the best aircraft for your mission would have to be an Antonov An-12. Specifically the An-12BK would work best in this situation. By my quick calculation, your destination is roughly seventy-five hundred miles from point A to point B. Considering the load," he said, pausing briefly to scribble more numbers on his work sheet, "you will need refueling twice. I can arrange for inflight refuel—"

"No, Colonel, that would involve more aircraft and more personnel. As I said before, we must keep the number of people with any knowledge of this activity to the bare minimum. Make arrangements for refueling on the ground."

"Yes, Comrade General, this should not be a problem. I would think that your first refueling stop should be somewhere in Libya or Tunisia." Berezhnaya checked his options of landing sites. "Ah! Yes. Here." He stabbed the wall map behind his desk with his index finger. "We can set you down in Daraj, Libya, and then proceed to the miniscule island of Fogo in the Cape Verde Islands off the coast of Senegal, West Africa for your second stop. Both of these refueling stops and the same stops on your return can be arranged with two phone calls. I cannot foresee any problems with your refueling. If parts or repairs are needed, that is a very different matter. We will just have to make certain all systems on this aircraft are finely tuned and thoroughly inspected before your departure."

"An excellent idea, Colonel Berezhnaya!" replied Krause, with a distinctive note of mild sarcasm. "And what would be the estimated flying time?"

Berezhnaya paused to calculate the miles, payload, plus air speed and estimated prevailing headwinds. "Including the two refueling stops, it will take approximately twenty-three hours going over, and about an hour less on your return, General. Tailwinds on your return, sir. And you should also figure that each refueling stop will take approximately one hour, maybe a little less."

"How soon could you have this An-12BK to me at Kotelnikovo, completely checked and ready for the mission?" asked Krause.

"Twenty-four hours, Comrade General," Berezhnaya responded with pride.

"Excellent, Yuri. Then arrange for the An-12 to touch down at Kotelnikovo at 0500 hours on the fourth and—"

"Excuse me, Comrade General, but I need to remind you while I'm thinking of it that even though you are going into a tropical climate, you will need to instruct your men to bring their cold-weather gear and plenty of blankets for the flight, because the cargo area in this aircraft is not pressurized and it gets pretty cold at cruising altitude."

"Colonel Berezhnaya," Krause said in a somewhat exasperated voice, "this is not exactly my first ride in the An-12. Once your lips turn blue and your finger tips and toes become numb at eight thousand meters, you don't ever forget, but thank you for bringing it to my attention just the same."

"Now, listen very closely to what I am about to tell you," Krause said, pausing to let the importance of his message sink in. "When you draw up these flight plans, you will *not* file them as you normally do. The flight crew will receive a copy for navigation purposes and will not be aware of anything out of the ordinary. You will send the remaining file copies to me. Is that clear, Comrade Colonel?"

"Perfectly clear, Comrade General," responded Berezhnaya.

Major Petya Starikovitch was recalled to Krause's office for the continuation of the emergency briefing. Krause could now fill Starikovitch in on the entire scope of the mission. He trusted the major implicitly; he had to. Everyone else involved would be on a "need to know" basis.

The general scrolled down the list of needed weapons and equipment he had entered into his laptop on his return flight from Venezuela. Major Starikovitch took accurate notes:

1 KamAZ-4310: all identification markings painted over

1 UAZ-469: all identification markings painted over, with NSV-12.7 machine gun mounted

20 MON-50 directional, antipersonnel mines

10 RPG-7 antitank, rocket-propelled grenade launchers

In addition, they would need several various light weapons, ammunition, and equipment, as well as the regular combat load of the Spetsnaz soldier. Krause conferred with his major to select their best seventeen men.

Jungle camo utilities would need to be issued. It was standard operating procedure for these soldiers to have no form of identification or rank when on any type of mission. Starikovitch's men and equipment could easily be in place at the air strip in Kotelnikovo within twenty-four hours.

~ * ~

Caracas, Venezuela
May 2, 1993
9:20 a.m.

Guillermo Lossada, Jr. announced a special business meeting and celebration to be held on May sixth at the Blue Caribbean Beach Resort. The Blue Caribbean was not the largest or the most luxurious resort on the coast, but it was definitely the most secluded. In order to insure the privacy needed and eliminate any traffic on the private road leading to the beach resort, Lossada had to purchase all of the existing reservations for the fifth and sixth of May, plus the upcharge to have those guests relocated to one of the five-star beach resort properties owned by the same company that managed the Blue Caribbean.

The business meeting would begin at 9:00 a.m. sharp in the Twin Palms Cabana adjacent to the large, free-form swimming pool and tropical waterfall grotto. Business topics to be discussed were:

New security procedures.

Redistribution of top level assignments (due to the sudden absence of Emilio Carache).

The celebration was in honor of their newly formed partnership with the DeGraci family, which promised a terrifically prosperous future for the entire Lossada organization. This was designed as a direct "in-your-face" type of an insult to the Vargas clan. If that didn't fire them up to take the bait, nothing would.

There would be a gala poolside banquet scheduled for noon, with "entertainment" to follow. Attendance for this meeting/celebration was mandatory; no exceptions.

Guillermo Lossada had sent out the word. He wondered which one of his sixteen trusted officers and soldiers would be the turncoat and deliver the message to Cesar Vargas.

~ * ~

04 May 1993

The morning sky was still dark and perfectly clear. In the distance, you could hear the low drone of the turboprop engines. Krause checked his watch. It was 0457, exactly as Colonel Berezhnaya had promised.

The bulky-looking An-12BK "Cub" touched down with the grace of a swan on the secluded, unmaintained runway at Kotelnikovo. The single east/west runway had been built fifteen years ago to support the Red Army during the Soviet-Afghan War. Now only a skeleton ground crew was available to maintain the infrequent incoming flights.

A young VTA Lieutenant stood at the general's side, waiting for the massive, dark gray cargo plane to come to a complete stop. A small squad of three men—two mechanics and a fuel truck driver—dashed out to the An-12 before the propellers had stopped turning.

The mechanics each pushed oversized rolling ladders and carried large, high-beam flashlights to inspect the four turboprop engines and the hydraulic lines which were easily accessible. Landing gear and tires were also quickly inspected as the fuel tanks were being topped off for the first of a three-leg journey crossing Turkey and the Mediterranean Sea, the top of North Africa, a long stretch over the Atlantic, and a corner of the Caribbean Ocean.

"Do you have a de-icing vehicle?" the general asked the VTA lieutenant.

The lieutenant wondered if this Spetsnaz general had possibly lost his mind. It was the fourth of May, without a cloud in the night sky. "Yes, sir, we do."

"Do you have any gray or dark-colored paint?" Krause asked.

"I'm not sure, sir, but I can probably find some in the maintenance shed somewhere."

"Good. I want these large numbers and the red star on the tail painted over, and the serial numbers toward the forward section of the fuselage, as well. Get in the snorkel of the de-icer and throw some paint on that tail and the other identification numbers before the fueler is finished filling the tanks. Nothing fancy, just fast. Understood?"

"Yes, sir!" responded the lieutenant, saluting and turning to sprint for the maintenance shed.

Five minutes later, the lieutenant came running back, carrying a large cardboard carton. Out of breath, he explained to the general, "Sir, I'm very sorry, but the only paint we have is dark olive green. We also had some red, but I didn't think you would want that."

"The green will have to do. Now get on it, Lieutenant!"

Krause ordered two of his corporals to accompany the lieutenant on the painting detail, and two others to remove the twin machine guns mounted in the tail gun turret. The two vehicles waiting to be loaded onto the aircraft had already undergone the de-identification process by order of Major Starikovitch.

The 2½-ton KAZ-4310, the smaller ¾-ton UAZ-469, and the specialized weapons were loaded into the belly of the An-12BK cargo ship, followed by Krause's select team of soldiers carrying their own personal gear and weapons.

Everything had gone according to plan, with the exception of Captain Asimov, the company commander. He had become ill with a case of the flu, along with severe diarrhea the day before. The captain insisted upon making the trip and leading his men on this training mission. Gallant, yes, but not practical. General Krause vetoed his request to continue on, knowing that anyone who was not a hundred percent physically able should not be involved in a live-fire situation. The captain's physical condition could alter his agility and reflexes and possibly even put his men at greater risk. The order to sideline Captain Asimov was made without a second thought. Krause was confident each man knew his job inside and out, and that Major Starikovitch had been in on all of the training exercises and could fill in for the captain without missing a beat. This was one of the advantages of working with the very best.

The mechanics had completed their checklist, the fuel truck was coiling up the fuel hose, and the lieutenant covered with dark olive green paint was just being lowered in the bucket of the de-icing snorkel after spray-painting the second side of the tail of the large transport.

A member of the flight crew walked back from the flight deck to ensure that the two vehicles were properly lashed down to the metal decking of the aircraft and that the troops sitting along the port and starboard bulkheads were strapped in on their bench-like seats. The crew chief used the intercom at the rear of the An-12 Cub to inform the pilot that the cargo was properly secured for takeoff.

Once airborne, the troops appeared to be a little on the cagey side, not as relaxed as they normally were. There was a gut feeling among these Spetsnaz soldiers that this was not just another training exercise. There were too many subtle hints that appeared just before takeoff at Kotelnikovo. The last-minute order to camouflage all of the identification on the aircraft was one rather obvious clue, as well as the fact that the larger of the two trucks was loaded with nothing but live ordnances: several metal boxes of live ammunition for their AK-47s and the NSV-12.7 machine gun, wooden crates of hand grenades and RPG-7s, and several cases of MON-50 antipersonnel mines. There was not a trace of any blank ammunition or anything that would indicate any sort of simulation. It was all the *real* stuff.

The sixteen warriors were waiting in anticipation like school kids on a field trip to the zoo. Major Starikovitch and General Krause could read this in their faces and decided to brief the men on their mission now, as opposed to briefing them on the last leg of their journey, before they reached cruising altitude and the cargo hold became too damned cold and uncomfortable. More importantly, their minds were still fresh now, and they could possibly relax and get some sleep once they were aware of the nature of their mission.

Major Starikovitch called the men to huddle around the general and himself toward the aft section of the cargo bay.

"Comrades," the general announced in a loud voice over the noise of the four Ivchenko AI-20M turboprop engines, "you are to be congratulated! You have been selected by Major Starikovitch and me for a special mission. We are en route to Venezuela, South America, but do not get the wrong impression," he quickly added. "We are *not* on holiday, comrades, not by any stretch of the imagination. I think that all, or at least most, of you have observed by now that we have a substantial amount of live ammunition and various weapons on board. There is a good reason for that. This is *not* a training exercise. You will be engaging armed soldiers who will be returning fire."

Krause stopped short of telling his soldiers that it would be more like shooting fish in a barrel. It was not worth the risk of having them go in overly confident or becoming the least bit lax.

"I have planned a very basic ambush. I do not expect any of the enemy to escape, nor will we be taking any prisoners. Major Starikovitch and I will need to recon the area upon our arrival, so I cannot give you details of the terrain and other specifics at this time, but I *can* tell you about our opposition. These are civilian soldiers we will be fighting, basically untrained and undisciplined. They *will* be well-armed, however, and we need to be extremely cautious, even though they are not quite the threat that well-trained soldiers might be. We will be outnumbered by roughly two or two and a half to one, but we will have the element of surprise, and you are Spetsnaz, so I see no real problem."

The team of handpicked soldiers now looked like a pack of hungry wolves, licking their chops, waiting for their prey. It actually showed in their eyes.

Krause gave his men the other minor details regarding the refueling stops and their ETA in South America. The men were instructed they would not be permitted to leave the aircraft during these stops. He would not have any of his troops spotted touching foot on foreign soil. For all anyone else needed to know, it was an empty aircraft with no military markings; there were, after all, hundreds of these An-12s in commercial use all over the globe. Krause told them to get some rest. The general had learned years ago to take advantage of any opportunity to sleep before a battle. Any edge you could create on your enemy could mean the difference of victory over defeat. Even though their foe was nothing more than a bunch of pistol-toting bandits, Krause and his men would not be caught off guard.

~ * ~

The flying time plus refueling stops had been calculated for Krause and his specialized troops to touch down at the secluded airstrip, twenty-three miles southeast of Caracas, under the cover of darkness. The pilot notified General Krause as they approached the coast line of Venezuela, as he had been instructed to do. Ahead and to the right, the city of Caracas glittered like a starburst of light as they crossed over the mountains that ran along the coast.

The pilot's instructions were to turn on the landing lights five minutes after crossing the coast. The airstrip, which had once been used exclusively by the Fama de America Coffee Company for its executive aircraft, would in turn activate its green and white beacon once the cargo plane was in sight, or at precisely 2100 hours, whichever occurred first. At that time, the white ground lights which outlined the north/south single runway would be illuminated. There would be no radio communication at all. Guillermo Lossada had made a very lucrative offer to the manager of the airstrip for the use of his field and to keep his mouth perfectly sealed.

As the An-12BK Cub began a moderate decent, the copilot was the first to notice the green and white sweeping motion of the beacon only seconds after the plane's powerful landing beams had been switched on.

Krause was on the flight deck, strapped into a jump seat for the landing.

"Landing on an unfamiliar, unpaved airstrip is always cause for a little concern," admitted the pilot to the general, after performing the maneuver with the skill of a surgeon. "If the surface is too soft, you might just snap off the landing gear and bury this big bird up to its nose in the mud!" he chuckled, prompting the copilot and navigator to laugh out of respect to the higher-ranking officer's attempt at humor.

The time was 2046. Fourteen minutes ahead of schedule.

The runway lights had been killed before the hinged aft doors folded up and in and the large metal ramp touched the ground. Krause and

Starikovitch were first to exit, followed by the two trucks filled with their payload of soldiers and equipment. The only visible lights were the red interior lights in the cargo hold of the plane, the tiny red "cat eyes" on the two vehicles, and a million stars that filled the clear night sky.

Lossada, in the small, two-story corrugated metal hut that served as a makeshift control tower, noting the "cat eyes" through his binoculars, took the hint to maintain light discipline and drove out to meet his mercenaries using only the amber parking lights of his Jeep Grand Cherokee.

Krause continued to be impressed with how well his cousin had organized his end of the battle plan.

After brief introductions between Guillermo Lossada and Major Starikovitch, Lossada led the short convoy to a bivouac site he had selected about a half mile away from the airstrip, in a small clearing on the edge of the Fama de America Coffee Plantation.

The Russian soldiers truly enjoyed the warmth and the clean, fresh night air, as well as the opportunity to stretch their limbs after the twenty-three hours spent confined to the frigid, smoke-filled belly of their An-12 transport.

Lossada popped open the back hatch of the Jeep, revealing an enormous amount of fresh fruit, meat and cheese sandwiches, and cans of ice-cold Coca-Cola and bottled water. These provisions were unloaded by a pair of corporals with nothing more than a nod of the head from the major to carry out the task. Eagerly yet orderly, the troops attacked this generous display of South American hospitality. The food, coupled with the warm tropical climate, led the soldiers to believe that they had landed in paradise, rather than a battle ground.

General Krause instructed Guillermo Lossada to return in the morning at 0600 to pick up the major and their most senior NCO, a first sergeant, and himself for their reconnaissance of the ambush site. Lossada said he would also bring civilian clothes for them so they would not appear out of place or draw attention with their military uniforms while reconning the area.

~ * ~

05 May 1993

The sun was not quite over the treetops as the moss green Jeep Grand Cherokee pulled up to the bivouac site. The Spetsnaz soldiers were already conducting quiet calisthenics and stretching exercises led by the general himself.

Lossada looked on and thought how thankful he was to be a civilian. Fifty squat jumps and fifty stomach crunches later, General Krause concluded the morning drill.

Guillermo Lossada had already laid out three stacks of clothing on the hood of the Jeep. Each stack contained denim blue jeans; fashionably faded, colored t-shirts with different graphics or logos; baseball caps of equally different designs; and adjustable leather sandals in a wide range of men's sizes.

Repeating what he had done only a few hours before, Lossada opened the back end of his vehicle. He remembered Patton had once said that an army moves on its stomach, prompting Lossada to deliver a hot breakfast in sealed, insulated containers. The soldiers were elated with the hot meal and commented that the coffee was the best they had ever tasted. Coming from a bunch of Russian soldiers, it was not necessarily saying much, but it did happen to boost the already high level of troop morale.

Lossada drove the general, the major, and the noncom in charge along a narrow, low-lying, winding road that followed a fairly large and fast-moving stream through thick, jungle-like vegetation. The road served as the only access to the Blue Caribbean Beach Resort. On the north side of the road were steep hillsides covered with trees of all shapes and sizes, along with thick tropical underbrush. On the south side of the road was the fast running mountain stream. At some points, the road was no more than a few yards away from the stream, and at other points the stream had carved a rocky gorge that dropped off suddenly beyond the old, decaying wooden guard rail.

Lossada slowed down to a crawl, looking for a specific spot among the trees and scrub to his left. An eighth of a mile farther, just after a bow-shaped curve in the road, he found his spot. He headed the Jeep into the brush about fifteen or twenty yards, well off the road. The four men got out and surveyed the area. Krause nodded his approval after scanning the area, making mental notes as they walked toward the road. One hundred twenty meters ahead, they came to an abrupt, ninety-degree curve to the left. The general stopped, as did the others. He looked up at the trees and then faced the direction from which they had just come.

"Here!" Krause said with complete certainty. "This is it. We use a chain saw to drop these two large trees across the road right here, blocking their advance. We line both sides of the roadway with the antipersonnel mines from here," he said, marking off a spot, "in ten-meter intervals, staggering them from one side to the other, providing overlapping coverage on both sides." Turning toward the hillside, he said, "We space ten men, each with RPG7s, along the embankment to take out each of the vehicles in order."

Krause walked back down the road toward the Jeep and stopped again. "We back the UAZ in first, clear a space up there to give the machine gun a good field of fire over the road. I want the gun taken off its mount until we reach the site. We also back in the KAZ farther down the road and place a road guard, in civilian clothes, down the road about a quarter of a mile to turn back any other unexpected civilian traffic. When the last of their vehicles enters the "kill zone," we simply roll the truck across the road behind them, boxing them in. There is no possible route for escape.

"Major Starikovitch, make sure your men are positioned high enough on the hillside that they will not catch any of the projectiles from the antipersonnel mines facing in their direction. We will be in position just before dawn, so I would suggest you and the first sergeant mark each of the positions for the men and get a good visual concept of the layout now in full daylight. The less shifting around in daylight, the better off we are. We do not want our mole to suspect anything as he drives to the conference site tomorrow morning."

The general took off his baseball cap, ran his hand over his hair, and rotated slowly, a full 360 degrees, giving a last close look over the kill zone. "Once the last of Lossada's men comes through the second curve up there," he said, "we will cut the two trees down behind them, where I had indicated earlier. Any questions?"

~ * ~

06 May 1993

It was expected that the Vargas family would stage their attack on the Lossada group any time between ten o'clock and noon. The private poolside luncheon was designed to put the bait squarely in one central location, with easy access for entry and escape.

Guillermo Lossada waited with a terrific amount of anxiety. He watched all of his men closely, wondering which one of them would betray him. Lossada looked at their eyes, their facial expressions, anything that might give him a clue as to who was playing the role of Judas. Even if he could detect who the insider was, he could not do anything to stop him or even give the impression that anything was suspected. It would only take a quick phone call from the insider to abort the attack. Guillermo Lossada only wished he could personally take care of the person responsible for the murder of his father.

The business meeting began promptly at 9:00 a.m. This was not a typical assembly of corporate executives gathering around a large oval-shaped conference table; it was, nevertheless, a meeting, and it was about business.

Krause and his men had been in place shortly before sunrise. Well-camouflaged MON-50 antipersonnel mines lined both sides of the roadway, and the troops were poised halfway up the hillside, also well-camouflaged and ready to pounce on their prey.

At 8:40 a.m., Guillermo Lossada's black Mazda Miata convertible marked the end of the first procession. This was the predetermined signal to fell the two large Tamarindo trees to barricade the road behind them. The

Spetsnaz first sergeant gave a single hand signal to the corporal with the gas operated chainsaw. The whine of the chainsaw lasted only a couple of minutes before it was followed by a heavy crash and the sound of cracking limbs. The series of noises occurred once more, and then perfect quiet was again restored to the jungle.

With the short business agenda having been completely addressed, Guillermo Lossada glanced again at the clock on the back wall: 11:50 a.m. "Any other topics or problems we need to discuss? If not," he followed quickly, "I believe we have a small feast and plenty of beverages waiting for us in the cabana by the pool."

With that, each of his sixteen men were on their feet and heading out the sliding glass door to the swimming pool area.

Lossada and Hector Maracaibo engaged in small talk as they waited for the others in front to file through the door. "Jefe, if you will please excuse me for just a moment, I need to use the restroom before I begin packing away all of the good food you've provided for us. I'll join you in a couple of minutes." Hector slapped Lossada on the back as friends often do and turned the opposite direction down an interior hallway.

Well, thought Guillermo, *there goes our Judas.* Hector had been with him from the very beginning. Lossada was both surprised and disgusted at learning the identity of the traitor, but he also felt some satisfaction in knowing the truth.

In the hotel restroom, Hector Maracaibo locked the door behind him. From his sport coat pocket he pulled a cellular telephone and pressed a single speed-dial number. Speaking softly into the phone, he relayed a succinct message: "The color is green. I repeat, the color is green." Hector Maracaibo pressed "end" and powered off. His job was done. He leisurely strolled through the entrance foyer of the resort, across the parking lot, and through a beautifully manicured garden of tropical flowers and shrubs which bordered the jungle. This periphery of the jungle would be the safest place for him to sit out the upcoming storm.

Hector did not like the jungle at all. He hated the snakes and everything else that crawled or hung among the vines, but it certainly was better than the alternative. Maracaibo hoped it wouldn't take too long. It was hot and sticky, and he was uncomfortable. He found a clear spot to sit under a tree and waited for the barrage of hand grenades and automatic weapons fire to begin. *Too bad,* he thought. So many of those men standing around the poolside were people he had known since he was a child. But lately the Vargas Family had shown a lot of personal interest in him, made promises to include him in their inner circle of officers, and assured him that this little act of treason that he had just committed would make him a *very* wealthy man. Whatever sorrow and discomfort he felt now would soon pass, he was sure.

Guillermo Lossada was becoming uneasy. The minutes seemed like hours. His men were enjoying the food and drink and the companionship of each other without a care in the world. After all, this was a celebration. In spite of the fresh shrimp, lobster, and other treasures from the Caribbean that were attractively displayed on shaved ice, Lossada had no appetite. He made his way to the bar and asked for a Polar-Solera Cervasa. He needed something to steady his nerves.

Although he trusted his cousin to perform his mission as a professional soldier, he couldn't help but wonder: *What if they came in from the beach? Or what if they have a helicopter?*

The saying "Eat, drink and be merry, for tomorrow you may die," kept echoing in his brain. Being a tethered goat was more than a little unnerving.

The forward observer, stationed three quarters of a mile in front of the designated kill zone, keyed the microphone on his headset. "Lead car is a new model silver Jaguar XJ series, followed by a red pickup truck with four men in the back." The pace suddenly quickened for the observer. "Another two cars, another pickup truck with five or six men, and three more cars following. We have a total of eight vehicles. I repeat, eight vehicles, fairly tight formation. Last vehicle is a white Chevrolet sedan."

Each of Krause's men listened to the radio transmission through their individual headsets.

The first eight men carrying the RPG-7 light antitank weapons brought their tubular fired rockets to their shoulders in a ready position. Now each man knew his target. The remaining antitank weapons would be used as a backup if any of the first volley missed their mark.

The driver of the KamAZ-4310 sat behind the wheel of the perfectly camouflaged truck, waiting for the white Chevrolet sedan to pass the checkpoint. He would simply release the emergency brake and roll the twenty yards onto the narrow road, completely blocking both lanes, sealing off any attempt to escape.

The silver Jaguar, driven by Cesar Vargas, rounded the tight curve at about thirty miles per hour and immediately came to a screeching halt, nearly slamming into the two large Tamarindo trees that blocked the roadway.

Each of the following seven vehicles skidded frantically to stop, nearly ramming into the rear end of the car or truck in front of them.

In a split second, Cesar Vargas knew that they had been ambushed, but it was already too late to react.

Just as the driver of the Russian Army truck positioned his vehicle to span both lanes of the road, he rolled out the passenger-side door and took up a defensive position on the river side.

Eight RPG-7 antitank weapons zeroed in on the fuel tanks of the six cars and two pickup trucks, while the sharpshooters' primary targets were the drivers. General Krause himself transmitted the signal to open fire.

All eight RPG-7s streaked downward on the unassuming Vargas family's soldiers almost simultaneously. The 12.7 machine gun mounted on the back of the ¾-ton truck swept the convoy from the first to the last vehicle, tossing up metal, glass, plastic, and human flesh in its wake.

Cesar Vargas was the first to go, eliminated in a huge ball of flame as the small rocket exploded on impact directly above the gas tank of the silver Jag.

The four men riding in the back of the red pickup truck were scattered into the air by the concussion of the antitank projectile explosion and then engulfed in flame seconds later as the flame followed the fuel line to the thirty-eight gallon fuel tank. The next two cars were also direct hits.

The rocket propelled grenade heading for the fifth vehicle, another pickup truck, was deflected by a tree limb, partially cut down by the machine gun, causing the rocketed projectile to miss its mark. This created a brief reprieve for the occupants of the blue pickup. It took the ninth man armed with the RPG-7 only about four or five seconds to negotiate a tree that was directly in his line of fire, and then to take aim on the target. Three of Vargas's men in the back of the pickup began to return fire. Two of the men were quickly downed, either by the sharpshooters or the machine gunner. The third man jumped from the truck bed, taking cover on the side of the vehicle, and sprayed the steep hillside with a full banana clip from his AK-47. A second later, an antipersonnel mine only six feet away was detonated, and he joined the rest of the burned and gnarled bodies that littered the narrow mountain road.

The last three cars and their passengers had already been successfully destroyed by direct hits from the antitank weapons.

The entire attack took less than two and a half minutes, proving the efficiency of Krause's strike force. There were no cheers, but there were subdued smiles on the faces of many of the soldiers. They had just been tested under live conditions and had done what they had been trained to do, and had done it very well.

The soldiers reassembled on the roadway, now with their weapons slung over their shoulders. The initial feeling was one of total victory amid the burning wreckage, but as the soldiers formed up on the road, they soon realized that Major Starikovitch was not among them. One of the sergeants said he recalled seeing the major no more than a couple of meters behind him on the hillside, just before the fireworks began. He and one of his men walked back to his position on the hillside to find the major, doubting that he was wounded. He had probably just twisted an ankle or something.

A few steps from where he had crouched low in the heavy underbrush only a few minutes before, the sergeant looked down to find his acting CO lying face down in the dark green plastic-looking leaves which prevented blood from being absorbed into the soil. A single round from the wild shooting of the man in the pickup truck had found its target. The bullet had penetrated Major Starikovitch's throat from the front and exited through the back of the neck, creating a ragged hole about two and a half inches in diameter.

One casualty was not a bad price to pay for a mission of such monetary importance, thought Krause. His only regret was that Major Starikovitch was his personal aide whom he had trusted implicitly. Finding a replacement for him would not be an easy task, especially now with so many of his plans to take control of the new communist party just beginning to take shape.

The An-12 cargo plane had been refueled. Preflight checks were completed; engines were idling. The rear cargo doors were folded inward, and the ramp was down to load the troops and equipment. Within forty minutes of the ambush, Krause and his Spetsnaz soldiers lifted off from the Fama de America Coffee Company airstrip for the long journey back to the airfield at Kotelnikovo.

Chapter Nine

Kotelnikovo, Russia
08 May 1993

The young VTA lieutenant hadn't had too much to drink; his voice was just a little too loud for any type of private conversation in the confined quarters of this eatery and drinking establishment on the outskirts of Kotelnikovo, frequented by the Russian soldiers stationed nearby.

"You should have seen me!" he told his three comrades sitting in a high-backed booth along the interior wall. "I was covered with green spray paint from head to toe. I must have looked like some creature from the swamp. I could see the major was smiling, trying very hard not to laugh out loud, but this general, he was a different story altogether. He spoke only a few words, only what was really necessary, and was as stern as anyone I have ever encountered. I guess that's one of the requirements of being a Spetsnaz general," he continued, with the others chuckling and nodding in agreement. "I just wonder why he had us paint over all of the identification markings on the aircraft? And he must have had his men paint over the marks on the two vehicles that were loaded on, as well. These Spetsnaz guys are always so damned secretive, so mysterious."

The others agreed and commented on some of their own experiences with Spetsnaz soldiers.

Major Gerhardt Richter never wore his uniform when he was off base. He often visited this particular little hideaway because it had provided some pretty good information in the past, and the food wasn't too bad either. This evening looked like it could be fairly promising, as well. Richter continued to listen from the booth directly behind the one occupied by the VTA ground crew. The conversation shifted to insignificant shop talk, and Richter figured he should take advantage of this opportunity.

"Excuse me, please," Richter said as he stood up and addressed the four soldiers seated in the adjoining booth. "I couldn't help but overhear you mention someone that sounds a lot like an old acquaintance of mine. Oh, please don't think I was eavesdropping or I have taken offense to the general as being a "hard" person. If it's the person I'm thinking of, you are absolutely correct. The fact of the matter is that this person I'm looking for—a stern, Spetsnaz general—saved my life in Afghanistan a few years ago, and I have unfortunately lost contact with him. Please understand I owe this man my life," Richter said with great sincerity. He could see the expressions on the faces of the four men change from carefree to something much more serious. "Do you recall his name possibly?" asked Richter.

"No, sir, I'm sorry I do not. Spetsnaz do not wear name tags," the lieutenant replied politely.

"Yes, I am aware of that, but do you recall if anyone addressed him by name or would you recognize a name if I mentioned it?"

"Possibly, sir. Now you bring it up, unusual as it may be, I seem to recall that it was not a Russian name.

"Ah," said Richter, showing a degree of satisfaction. "Would it have been Krause?"

"Yes, sir! Exactly right. General Krause," the lieutenant said, pleased to have answered this stranger's request.

"You wouldn't happen to know where he was heading, would you?"

"No, sir, as I told my comrades here, Spetsnaz are generally quite secretive. One thing I do recall is that the flight did originate from VTA headquarters, Moscow, if that's any help." The lieutenant stopped. "Wait...now that I think of it, this morning I did notice an unscheduled refueling of an An-12 listed on the fueling log sometime yesterday evening. I was not on duty. Yesterday was my day off, and I didn't give it a second thought, to be quite honest. But it could possibly be your general on his return leg," said the lieutenant.

"Is there a way we could check on that? Possibly speak with someone who was on duty at that time?" asked Richter, knowing that he could get that information with or without the help of the VTA lieutenant.

"Of course. Lieutenant Melerkhin worked the second shift yesterday, as well as today."

"Ah, very good! I will be in touch with Lieutenant Melerkhin sometime in the near future. You've been extremely helpful."

Richter was astounded at the amount of information this lieutenant had given him without even asking who he was or why he needed to know. *I could have been wearing the uniform of a U.S. Army general and still have gotten the same response!* he thought. So much for tight security in the Red Army Officer Corps.

It took Richter twelve minutes to reach the Kotelnikovo airstrip. A single light burned in the wooden shack that annexed the single hangar building. Gerhardt Richter peered through the uncovered window before entering the cramped room that served as the aviation office.

Two men played cards at a metal table. A pot of tea sat on a hot plate atop of an olive drab, four-drawer file cabinet.

The lieutenant and the private sprang to their feet as the door opened. They were both surprised to see a civilian enter.

"Yes?" asked the lieutenant.

"Lieutenant Melerkhin!" Richter said, immediately setting the junior officer off balance. "My name is Major Richter. I have come to inspect the flight plan log from yesterday. May I see it now, please?"

"Yes, sir, of course. Right away."

Richter was amazed that he only had to *sound* as if he were in authority to obtain military records. No request for any identification. Just bark out an order and sound brash, and he could get whatever he wanted.

A tattered black, three-ring binder was immediately placed on the table, open at the 07 May entries. It was easy enough to locate the flight in question; there had only been a total of four flights logged on the previous day. Major Richter didn't exactly know what he was looking for, but anything possibly involving the elusive General Stephan Krause was worth checking up on.

"Lieutenant Melerkhin, your third entry here on 07 May: 'AN-12 refueled 1845 hours.' What else can you tell me about this flight? Oh, and may I please see a copy of that flight plan?" Richter added to make his investigation appear to be more official.

"Well, Comrade Major, it's highly unusual, but there was no flight plan filed." Lieutenant Melerkhin received a curious look from the major, prompting more of an explanation. "Furthermore, sir, we were ordered to restencil all of the identification numbers and the star back onto the aircraft."

"Who gave those orders, the pilot?" asked Richter.

"No, sir. I believe he was a Spetsnaz officer, possibly a general. I'm not sure. No insignia…"

"Yes, I understand," Richter said impatiently. "Do you recall any name?"

"No, sir, very little was spoken. The pilot gave me orders for refueling, and the other officer, the general, ordered the restenciling and also instructed me to call for a pickup of a body bag."

"A body bag?" responded Richter. *This is proving to be quite interesting.*

"Yes, sir. Evidently they had a fatality on their training mission."

"Who?"

The lieutenant shook his head. "I don't know that either, sir, he only referred to it, the bag, that is, as 'the major's body,' no name. He said the paperwork was in the pouch attached to the bag. I didn't really want anything to do with it. It's actually not my field, if you know what I mean, sir."

Richter nodded. He understood completely. He had just received a wealth of information, unbeknownst to the junior officer who was really not able to completely answer any of his questions.

"Very well. No further questions, Lieutenant." Richter headed for the door before stopping to turn back around. "Lieutenant Melerkhin, do you have anything scheduled going to Moscow tomorrow?"

"I think so, sir. Let me check." Melerkhin picked up a clipboard from a hook on the wall next to the desk. Yes, sir," the lieutenant confirmed. "There is a transport going out at 0720."

"Good. Make a space on that aircraft for me."

~ * ~

Moscow
09 May 1993

"Major Richter, this is an unexpected pleasure," Krause said, rising from behind his desk to greet his visitor. "Please sit down. May I offer you something to drink? Tea or possibly some very good coffee?"

"No, thank you, Comrade General. I appreciate your offer just the same. I won't be taking up much of your time. I know that you're quite busy these days. I came to offer my personal condolences for the loss of Major Starikovitch. I know you and the major had worked together for some time. I am sure that a man of his caliber will be missed."

Krause was astonished. *How in the hell did he know about this already?* This man was *very* well-connected!

"I appreciate your kind gesture, Major Richter. I'm relieved that Major Starikovitch did not have a family. Yes, he will be missed. A good soldier is always difficult to replace."

Bingo! thought Richter. *He's on the right track.* "Which brings me to the point exactly, General. Almost four and a half years ago, you were generous enough to find a place for me in your Army. I have served Mother Russia with the same passion as a natural born citizen; greater in fact, than most, because I can see the potential to turn this country around. You, sir, have the vision and the power necessary to guide the military and political might of this great nation. As I mentioned back then, I would be proud to serve under your direct command."

Richter knew that that was the extent of his petitioning; anything further would be taken as begging or cramming it down the general's throat. That was not the method to use in order to gain this man's acceptance. Krause would need to make it his own idea.

"Thank you, Major Richter. I will certainly consider your offer."

~ * ~

Monday, 14 June 1993

"Major Richter, General Krause here. I've had some time to think about your offer and I believe that I could use someone with your skills and personal commitment on my team. I will personally make sure that all of the paperwork regarding your transfer is processed today. As of tomorrow, at 0730, you will be reporting to me directly. Welcome aboard, Major."

Chapter Ten

Munich, Germany
Friday, July 9, 1993

There was an increasingly obvious buzz circulating throughout the intelligence community in Central and Eastern Europe over the highly publicized activities of the four-star general Aleksey Chesnokov and, conversely, very little chatter over the almost subliminal activities of Lieutenant General Stephan Krause. Erich Mueller was busy following as many leads as he possibly could on both of these men. The core mission of the National Security Agency is to protect U.S. national security and produce foreign signals intelligence information; to collect (often through clandestine means), process, analyze, and disseminate signals, intel information and data for foreign intelligence and counterintelligence purposes, and to support national and departmental missions responsible to the Secretary of Defense.

Mueller loved his position with the NSA Munich office in "free-state" Bavaria, and he liked working for Henry Talbot, but he couldn't help feeling that his boss wasn't letting him work to his full potential. As busy as he was, he didn't feel like Talbot was giving him a free reign on the larger issues.

On the brighter side, totally unrelated to his work, Mueller was eagerly awaiting his aunt's and uncle's fiftieth wedding anniversary celebration that was to be held the next evening at the Hotel Raphael, only a few blocks away. None of his relatives still lived in Munich, but it was the geographic center for the entire family and was easiest to reach by train, plane, or automobile. Munich also had one of the finest five-star hotels in all of Bavaria. It would be nice to see all of the friends and relatives from his mother's side again. It had been a long time, eight or nine years, since the last family gathering at his cousin Karl's wedding.

Mueller was anticipating the normal questions pertaining to what he had been doing with himself, particularly over the past four years. Everyone knew of his scholarship to the University of Wisconsin, but they would be curious about what had happened after those four years. Oddly, even his parents did not know exactly what his occupation was. The best he could do was to downplay things and tell them he had a government job dealing with somewhat sensitive issues that really should not be discussed. He had told them from the start that he would keep them informed about his personal life, as always, that he was healthy and that his employer paid him fairly and treated him well. Hopefully this would satisfy them. It did, but only to a certain extent.

Because he avoided discussing the actual purpose and nature of his work, many blanks were left unfilled for his parents and close family members. Some thought he was working for the Nuclear Power Commission (always under close scrutiny), some assumed he was involved with an underground German political group, and others attributed his secrecy to a possible job with an extension of the Ministry of State Security. He let them think whatever they wanted, as long as they knew that he was okay, but he could never let them know that he was employed by the United States National Security Agency.

~ * ~

Hotel Raphael, Munich
Saturday, July 10, 1993

The Hotel Raphael was the epitome of elegance and old-world charm. Up the wide, curved marble staircase that led from the warm, oak-paneled lobby, adorned with fine oil paintings and large Persian rugs, was a large, lavishly appointed reception hall. White linen table cloths with gold candelabras and crystal chandeliers graced the room for this special event.

As expected, family members gravitated to Erich upon arrival, welcoming him back as somewhat of a celebrity. He felt a bit self-conscious because of this attention. After all, this was a celebration for Aunt Tillie and Uncle Horst, not for him.

Later into the evening, after many toasts to the bride and groom of fifty years and an excellent meal, Erich and his stepbrother, Thomas, were able to break away from the crowd and find a quiet place to talk on the rooftop balcony. Erich had been adopted by the Mueller family at age four and a half, after his parents had been killed in an accident on the autobahn. Thomas was a mere two months younger than Erich. They were raised in the small town of Fussen in the foothills of the Bavarian Alps and in the shadow of King Ludwig's famous Neuschwanstein Castle.

The reunion of the two was long overdue; there was so much to catch up on. They stood at the railing, taking in the picturesque panorama of a starlit Munich, punctuated by the spires of the Frauenkirche, Heiliggeistkirche, and the clock tower of Alta Peter. Erich and Thomas enjoyed several Augustiner Pils as they reminisced about so many events of their youth: playing soccer, hunting with their grandfather, and trout fishing at their own secluded lake. They had vowed at an early age to never brag about the success of their fishing from this beautiful, well-hidden lake for fear others would discover its magic.

The conversation progressed to the brothers' respective occupations. Through necessity, the conversation was tilted more toward Thomas's job.

Thomas wanted to learn more about his brother's career, but was smart enough to realize Erich could not give him direct answers and was obviously evading questions about his work. Thomas did deduce, however, there was some excitement to Erich's job, if not something possibly dangerous at times. He could read that much from his brother's face.

Wanting to direct the conversation back to Thomas so as not to seem rude by not satisfactorily answering his brother's queries, Erich asked, "Tell me more about Rotterdam. How do you like working in Europe's largest port city?"

While attending the Universität München, Thomas had met a girl from Delft whose father was in the shipping business, as are so many people from that region. As the story goes, boy meets girl, gets married, and moves to Rotterdam to pursue his new career in the shipping industry. Thomas was basically content, although he complained mildly about the strange hours he had to work. He explained that the port never closes; ships come and go around the clock.

"Next time you're up north, you'll have to come visit. I'd like to show you around the harbor. I think you would find it rather interesting," Thomas said.

"Yeah, I would like that very much." replied Erich. "I *will* be up to visit you and Maria. I don't know exactly when, but I do promise that I'll come up. It's been too long. We shouldn't let so much time go between visits. I don't want to wait for another family wedding, and I surely don't want to wait for a funeral."

The brothers soon realized it was time to part company. The hour was late, and most of the guests were bidding farewell to Tilley and Horst.

Chapter Eleven

Moscow
Saturday, July 17, 1993

The Lossada/Krause partnership was working out very well. Krause was receiving his hefty percentage of profits in prelaundered U.S. dollars and was taking full advantage of the convenient direct-deposit feature offered by the Banque de Commerce - Genève.

Some of the political and military leaders he had previously been unable to stir were now falling into line. Some influential people who were once staunch backers of the powerful General of the Army Aleksey Chesnokov were now showing significant interest. Krause's well-designed plans for a coup d'état against the current Yeltsin regime were beginning to pay off. Lieutenant General Stephan Krause's name was rapidly becoming well-known throughout the Kremlin. Krause was now more vocal among his peers, stating his opposition to Boris Yeltsin and his followers.

There was also a new openness with his business partner, Guillermo Lossada. Although Krause continued to mainly speak in generalities, it was clear enough to Lossada that his cousin Stephan had higher aspirations than just being a military leader. Recent conversations revealed many of the general's activities over the past four-plus years, making it more obvious that this man was definitely destined for a page in future history books.

Since the massacre of the Vargas clan, Guillermo Lossada had already tripled his cocaine production capacity, increased overall profitability by twenty-five percent, and still could not keep up with the demand. His drug business was just about where he wanted it, at least for the present. Lossada could now devote more of his time to growing his other enterprises.

~ * ~

Killeen, Texas

Prostitution had always been a lucrative business for Lossada in Caracas. He could see that exporting this product—or rather "service"—into the U.S. had great potential, not so much because of the exportation of the beautiful women of Venezuela, for there were plenty of attractive, willing women in the U.S. Rather, it was Lossada's knowledge of the business that would further increase the receivables side of the ledger for Lossada LLC. His target market locations would be the small towns just outside large military installations: a logical choice ever since the days Alexander the Great's legions marched through Asia Minor.

Lossada used two of his more experienced girls, who displayed the discreet business sense required of proper and successful personnel managers, and two others to work as their assistants. These qualities were essential in order to establish profitable new locations in the U.S., along with the necessary strong arms that would protect his investments.

Señora Yolanda San Cristobal had established two new locations within the first month of her arrival in the States.

The Cow Town Motor Lodge was a sleazy little place marked by a neon sign with several of the letters burned out, just outside the main gate of Fort Hood.

At 11:55 p.m., at a table for two in the nearly secluded bar that joined the motel, a late middle-aged man and a very attractive girl with long black hair and a clear dark complexion talked over drinks. The man was obviously military; anyone could tell by the haircut and posture. The scene was all too typical: a soldier and a girl in a bar with rooms to rent directly around the corner.

Guillermo Lossada and Señora San Cristobal talked business at the bar: payroll, physical improvements needed for the building, miscellaneous expenses, etc. A typical agenda for an owner and a manager to discuss.

Lossada had observed and was somewhat distracted by the older guy with the graying flattop sitting with Señorita Camilla Ortiz. He tried to concentrate on his discussion with Yolanda San Cristobal, but there was something about this man. In spite of the quantity of Johnnie Walker Black the man had consumed, he didn't rant and rave, but he was obviously trying to get some point of contention across to Señorita Ortiz. This was not the typical verbal foreplay or haggling over the price of activities included in services about to be rendered. It had considerably more gravity than that.

Although Lossada could not hear enough of the conversation to understand the gist of it, he could tell the man did not slur his speech and maintained a particularly rigid military bearing. *That's it! This guy acts just like Cousin Stephan,* thought Lossada. The man had the same type of military bearing Lossada had observed in his cousin. He was relieved to have solved this minor irritation that had nagged his brain for the last half hour, yet he couldn't help but remain interested in this character.

Just then, Camilla Ortiz came over to the bar, ordered another Johnnie Walker and a glass of orange juice with grenadine—a sort of Tequila Sunrise. As she waited for the drinks, she inched her way over to Lossada and her immediate boss, shaking her head, saying, "This guy is absolutely certifiable. He's a nut case!" Then with a very serious expression she said more quietly, "The man is mad at the world!"

There is nothing at all uncommon about soldiers who are disgruntled with their lives in the military, thought Lossada. If there were, he wouldn't be looking to establish a new business here in Killeen, Texas.

"He keeps telling me how the Army screwed him over, time after time, and how he's going to make those 'sons-a-bitches' in Washington pay," said Camilla.

"What's his beef?" asked Lossada.

"I don't know, exactly," responded Camilla. "Something about an injury in Vietnam, years of dedication, and other technical army stuff that I didn't really understand." Señorita Ortiz glanced back at her table. "But it's that look in his eyes when he says he's gonna 'make them pay' that really kind of scares me, and I don't scare that easy. Señora Yolanda knows that for a fact."

The bartender handed over the Johnnie Walker double and the brightly colored fruity concoction, and Camilla Ortiz returned to the aging warrior.

The gray-haired soldier had now turned silent, as if he had suddenly realized that anyone in the room could have been listening to his conversation. He regretted wagging a loose tongue and allowing a public display of his dirty laundry. Señorita Ortiz actually welcomed the quiet.

Guillermo Lossada, still intrigued by the soldier, also noticed this sudden transformation toward silence. Lossada's curiosity did not want this little game to end, not just yet. As the consummate businessman, Lossada saw this soldier as a possible resource. This internalized anger that Camilla mentioned, *if* it is as serious as she said, could possibly be exploited to their advantage. Lossada was never one to waste a perfectly good character flaw or personal weakness, which could often be manipulated and converted into cash. He wouldn't know if he really had something here or if this guy was just another nut case, unless he put his curiosity to the test.

Lossada instructed Señora San Cristobal to tell Camilla, in Spanish, to bring her customer up to one of the better rooms and to make the man happy, compliments of the management.

"When it's time to settle up the bill, just tell him he's the best you've ever had and that you couldn't possibly ask for any money, but that you'd like to see him again. But most importantly, listen to and remember his conversation. I'd like to know the story behind this guy."

Five minutes later, the soldier paid his bar tab and the beautiful señorita led him out of the bar and up the stairs to a second-floor suite.

Lossada instructed Javier, a very large man compared to most Venezuelans and one of his best enforcers, to watch for the man when he left and to follow him and make damn sure he was not aware he was being tailed. Javier acknowledged the instructions with a simple nod.

At 5:25 a.m. the following morning, the soldier left the motel room, got into his car, and drove onto the military reservation. Fort Hood is an "open post." There are guards posted at the gates, but rarely is anyone stopped for questions. Visitors are just waved through. The sentries are more for show and to give directions rather than to function as true guards.

From a safe distance, Javier observed the soldier pull into a reserved parking space marked "Provost Marshal." Figuring he had been tailing a military policeman, he decided not to press his luck by pursuing the observation any further.

Lossada conducted his debriefing with Camilla Ortiz in the bar turned coffee shop. The smell of cigarette smoke and stale beer still lingered from the night before. Lossada and Ortiz sat at a wobbly table, huddled over mugs of strong black coffee.

"He's an interesting old guy," began Camilla. "His name is Al, no last name. Sorry. He is some kind of officer, a colonel, I think, and he said that he is in charge of the military police at Fort Hood."

That, along with the report from Javier, pretty well confirmed that this man was indeed the base provost marshal.

Damn, this army cop is probably here to shut us down before we really get started, thought Lossada. If he made this place off limits to the soldiers, they were out of business. Period.

On the other hand, why would he have spent all that time with Camilla, pouring his guts out about his personal problems with the Army, and then stay with her until five or later the next morning? He was not your typical MP officer looking to crack down on the local prostitution. It was just plain animal magnetism.

This guy's just another red-blooded American G.I., thought Lossada. *Corporal or colonel, they're all basically the same.*

The rank of full-bird colonel, along with the clout carried by his position as base provost marshal, certainly sparked Guillermo's interest. It also added credence to the idea that this man did in fact hold quite a bit of power, and anybody with all of the status he possessed could very possibly be of some value to him.

But a military cop, of all things! This guy is probably as straight as an arrow.

Ah, maybe I shouldn't even screw around with him, thought Lossada. He didn't want this new business to get off on the wrong foot in the top cop's own back yard.

Twenty minutes had passed, and Lossada was still mulling over the potential value of this officer. The higher the rank, the greater the good—or harm, come to think of it—that could come from it. Guillermo Lossada wondered just how angry this officer was with the U.S. Army, and just how serious he was about 'paying them back' for whatever maltreatment he had endured. He also wondered if it was actually possible for any one man seeking revenge to put a dent in the armor of the U.S. Army?

The thought of messing around with the U.S. Government was a bit unsettling for Lossada, but at the same time, he envisioned the huge profits he could get from selling military hardware. M-16s, semi-automatic pistols, hand grenades, and plastic explosives could all be easily sold for unbelievable sums of cash. The possibilities were almost overwhelming. Maybe he could work out some kind of partnership. It had worked pretty well the last time. But Lossada soon came back to reality and reminded himself not to get too excited. He didn't even know this man's last name! He might still be a nut case, only in a high-ranking position. He chastised himself for playing this little game and daydreaming about this off-the-wall scheme.

Enough wasted time, he thought. *I need to get back to business.*

~ * ~

West of San Antonio, Texas
Friday, July 23, 1993

"Wings," the barmaid answered the phone in a typical Texas drawl. "Sure, wait one." She walked the phone down to the end of the bar. "For you, Mr. Lossada."

The place was packed with airmen from Lackland Air Force Base. It was difficult to hear over the noise and the loud country western music.

"Señor Lossada, it's Camilla Ortiz. I thought you might like to know that our friend, Al, the military police officer, just called and asked if I was available tomorrow night. I said yes. He said he'd be here no later than 2100 hours, whenever that is."

~ * ~

The Cow Town Motor Lodge, Killeen, Texas
Saturday, July 24, 1993

Guillermo Lossada nursed a Budweiser long neck while he waited at the bar with the seductive looking Señorita Ortiz. At 8:56 p.m., a casually dressed (although only vaguely resembling a civilian) Alvin Pallosic strolled into the dimly lit room. He paused for only a moment until he spotted Camilla, then made his way to her side. She afforded him a light kiss on the cheek and held his hand. Señorita Ortiz promptly introduced Guillermo as her boss to make sure her client knew exactly who the players were. Firm handshakes and customary polite greetings were exchanged, but no surnames were offered.

Lossada ordered a Johnnie Walker Black for his guest. After some small talk, Lossada asked Camilla if she wouldn't mind leaving the two of them alone for a short while, that he had some business to discuss with Al. Immediately, Pallosic figured he was going to get hit with the bill for his overnight trip to paradise with the lovely Latina. Whatever the price, he was more than willing to pay.

"Camilla tells me you are unhappy with the Army. Are you possibly looking to resign from the military?" Lossada could think on his feet. He didn't know exactly where this conversation might lead; it might lead nowhere. "Please forgive me if I seem too straightforward. I'm just an honest man who does not believe in beating around the bush. You see, I'm a businessman in a new town, and I could possibly use someone of your background and experience to help me in my operation here. Camilla also mentioned you are with the military police. Is that so?"

"Yes, in fact I am in charge of the entire base security here at Fort Hood. In reply to your first question, I don't exactly know what direction I want to go at this point, but I'll tell you right now that I'm sure as hell not interested in being one of your goons or pimps!" Pallosic responded vehemently.

Lossada checked his anger and disregarded the insult; he would address that at another time. "Oh, please don't take offense. I merely see your experience as an asset. Age tempers one's judgment. A person of your background is much less apt to make mistakes than his younger counterpart who is hot-headed and thinks below the belt."

Pallosic nodded in agreement and said nothing.

Lossada was winning his quest to soothe the savage beast. He needed to hear what was on the soldier's mind. Why the anger? How could Lossada benefit from it? What type of partnership could be established? Surely this man held the keys to the armory and other saleable equipment. Computers would be nice, but not as easy to sell on the street as an M-16 rifle.

"Tell me, Al, if I may be so blunt, what makes you bitter toward the Army? Obviously you are a career man. I thought your Uncle Sam took good care of his faithful leadership corps." He motioned for the bartender. "Another scotch for our guest!"

Pallosic began to explain some of the injustices, painting with a wide brush at first, not getting into too much personal detail. Lossada soon realized the more scotch his companion drank, the more liberal he was with his explanations.

By the third Johnnie Walker, Pallosic began to boast about an M-5 assault vehicle. He explained how he had developed it and how the government had scrapped the project as a cost-saving measure. "The idiots! It was *the* perfect weapon: compact, fast, superior mobility, plus the capacity to deliver tactical nuclear warheads! It beats the shit out of anything the Russians have in their arsenal, and they've got some pretty damn sophisticated equipment in that area."

Lossada's mind quickly flashed to Stephan Krause, wondering if he knew of this U.S. Army "super weapon." *Probably so. That's what generals do.*

Like a proud owner of a brand new car just driven off the dealer's lot, Pallosic offered, "If you'd like to see one of these babies, I'd be happy to show you."

"You've got one here at Fort Hood?" asked Lossada.

"I've got sixteen of the damn things sitting in Motor Pool four, under lock and key, just collecting dust. Tell you what; you come by sometime, and I'll take you for a spin around the block."

"Camilla!" Lossada called. "Come back over here and keep our friend, Al, company. We are finished talking shop. He came here for a good time, not to talk with me, so please make sure he enjoys himself." Lossada smiled broadly and, with a slight bow, said quietly, "With my compliments."

"Oh, and by the way, here's my card. Please give me a call when we can go for a ride in your new 'truck.' I'd like that very much."

"How about tomorrow morning, say ten o'clock?" offered Pallosic.

Surprised by the quick response, Lossada replied, "Perfect! I'll see you then."

"Just ask the guard at the main gate for the provost marshal's office. He'll show you the way."

~ * ~

Fort Hood, Texas
Sunday, 25 July 1993

Colonel Alvin Pallosic provided thrills that Guillermo Lossada had only experienced on roller coaster rides at amusement parks, as they sped up and down the most rugged terrain Texas had to offer. Skidding to a halt back at Motor Pool #4, like a proud father, Pallosic bellowed, "Well what do ya think? Fine piece of equipment, isn't it?"

With his heart still in his throat, Lossada started to breathe a little easier. "Yeah, it is some fine piece of equipment. Now are you going to show me how these rockets work?" joked the passenger, sitting in the Fire Control Officer's seat.

"I only wish I could, Mr. Lossada. I'd point these three darts at the Pentagon and let 'er rip," the colonel said, his smile suddenly replaced with the look of an angry man.

"Understand, also, Mr. Lossada, that these missiles here *are* real, but they are only armed with high-explosive warheads. The heavy-duty stuff, the TNWs, are locked up tighter than a drum back at the armory, for maximum security."

Knocking the dust off his clothing, Guillermo Lossada smiled as the two walked over to Pallosic's car. It was time to cultivate this new alliance and see what it might yield.

"Al, thank you for a most exhilarating ride. I would like to return the favor and have you join me for dinner this evening, but not at the Cow Town, of course. Something a little more refined."

The two men discussed the choices of Killeen's finer dining establishments, which was equivalent to discussing the best hockey players in Ecuador. They agreed upon one and elected to meet at seven.

On his short drive back to the Cow Town Motor Lodge, Guillermo couldn't help but envision his men unloading crate upon crate of M-16 automatic rifles into his mountaintop warehouse in Venezuela. Maybe even some machine guns or possibly some plastic explosives. The street value on this stuff could bring in millions. This guy could be a gold mine! Lossada glanced at his watch: 11:15 a.m., 8:15 p.m. Moscow time.

I think Cousin Stephan would like to hear about my new friend, he thought. *Maybe give me some advice on what I should look for or what to be aware of with this military hardware. He would know.*

Once back in his not so luxurious room at the Cow Town, Guillermo placed a call to Stephan Krause at his Moscow apartment. Krause could detect the excitement in his cousin's voice immediately. Lossada explained briefly how he had come in contact with this "disturbed" U.S. Army officer at a bar in Killeen, Texas.

"...and then I find that this guy is the person in charge of the security and all of the military police for the entire army base! That means he virtually holds the keys to the armory, Stephan; just think of the weapons this man could get for us, if I can persuade him to enter into some kind of partnership."

"If my memory serves me, this would be Fort Hood you speak of, correct? And Fort Hood is an armor center, correct?" said Krause.

"Yeah, tanks and stuff, armor," repeated Lossada.

Humph, thought Krause, *mostly light weapons to accompany the tankers and large-caliber turret-mounted machine guns.* He did not share his cousin's enthusiasm. The general was presently well-supplied with light weapons and machine guns, but the extra cash from the sale of these items would be nice.

"In fact, Stephan," Lossada continued, "I even got to ride in some new vehicle that the colonel helped design."

Still only slightly interested, Krause inquired, "What size gun did this new tank have?" He realized his civilian cousin wouldn't know a cannon from a recoilless rifle, much less the calibration."

"Oh, this vehicle didn't have any gun, Stephan; it had three big-ass rockets on top."

"What did you say?" Krause almost shouted. He couldn't believe what he had just heard.

"I said it had three large rockets. It wasn't a tank, either. It was more like a truck. Four wheels, no tracks. This thing can go anywhere, fast!"

General Stephan Krause was speechless for several seconds. He recalled a brief KGB report he had read about six months before regarding a new quick strike weapon that could deliver a conventional high explosive and/or tactical nuclear warhead.

If I were a religious person, I would think this might be a gift from the gods, he thought.

"My dear cousin Guillermo, I'm afraid you are still thinking like a small-time crook, but that's not at all your fault. I've not given you the full picture. I don't need any small arms or personal weapons, thank you. But you might have stumbled across something I need desperately. In order to achieve my goal, I *must* have a cache of tactical nuclear warheads, along with an appropriate delivery system. I had several SS-A-20 missiles, but they were lost in an explosion."

Lossada had no idea what an SS-A-20 was, but he had certainly captured his cousin Stephan's attention.

"Did this colonel mention if these missiles carried conventional or nuclear warheads?" asked Krause.

"Both, maybe. I know that he said some were high-explosive, and I believe he referred to the other rockets as TNWs, or something like that. I don't know if that answers your question or not, Stephan."

"Tactical Nuclear Weapons. In this case, he was referring to the actual warheads on these missiles. Yes, it answers my question perfectly. Please listen carefully. You must continue to talk with this man and keep his interest. You can*not* let him slip away. The three most important pieces of information I need to find out right away are: how many of these missiles does he have, what kind of kiloton yield do these warheads have, and how many of these launch vehicles are available? Also very important are the technical and operational manuals for both the missiles and the launch vehicles; of course, I will need those, too." Krause was almost out of breath, in his excitement. "I *need* these missiles and the launch vehicles, at any cost. This is critical for my plan to succeed.

"I have no alternative. You have very good organizational skills; you figure out what needs to be done in order to get these weapons to me. Either you steal them from him, or you employ his help to get them. We don't have time to take his technology and develop our own vehicle and the field-ready fire power they are capable of delivering. We need the finished product *now!* You cannot understand the gravity of this mission overall and the impact it will have throughout the world. Please, trust me on this. I will explain it all when we can be face-to-face. As you employed my professional help, I now ask for yours. You will help me?"

"Of course I will. I look forward to this as a real challenge. I will try to form an alliance with the colonel to make our task easier and more efficient, or at least to use him as long as he is useful to us. After that, well, he is expendable," responded Lossada.

"Exactly. Once we have those rockets and launchers, it would be best if as few as possible know anything about this. He would be a potential security risk, and he obviously tends to talk more freely when he drinks, as you have told me. Keep me posted on your progress." With that, Krause signed off.

~ * ~

Lossada realized he should not act too fast. By now, he pretty well had his man hooked on the free sex he provided him, much like a junky hooked on hard drugs. He now needed to test the water.

Over a fine steak dinner and a couple bottles of expensive California Merlot, Guillermo Lossada hinted at buying a few M-16s and some handguns from the Fort Hood armory. A small test. If he balked at this, he would need to forget about any assistance from him and would need to take a different approach—a plan B, whatever it might be.

Pallosic seemed to jump at the suggestion. He said something to the effect that this would help start his own little retirement fund, being that he could not depend on the Army to look after its own.

Guillermo Lossada started off by ordering only ten M-16 automatic rifles and six Colt .45 semi-automatic pistols. A price that seemed very reasonable to Lossada was settled upon, and Pallosic would be paid cash in advance. A small test to see if he was a man of his word.

This was an easy order to fill. Pallosic would be able to acquire these light weapons directly from the military police armory in his own building.

Two days later, Lossada sent one of his men to a given location, at a specified time that Pallosic selected, to pick up the goods. The transaction was made without a hitch. The following day, the colonel made a businesslike follow-up call to thank Lossada for the business and to remind him there was more where that came from.

~ * ~

Thursday, July 29, 1993

At 9:00 a.m., Guillermo Lossada phoned Alvin Pallosic to quickly arrange an early dinner meeting for that evening at six.

The restaurant was not the least bit crowded, yet Lossada requested a table farthest away from any of the other patrons. Pallosic, of course, thought it concerned more small arms. Lossada began the meeting by asking more about the M-5 assault vehicle, along with detailed questions about the XG-777 rocket. If Pallosic was halfway perceptive, he would catch the drift and realize he might have an interested party for his advanced missile launcher. He was indeed perceptive, but also somewhat perplexed. What in the world would somebody like Guillermo Lossada need with an M-5 and a rack full of missiles? He decided to ask the question directly.

Lossada chuckled and replied, "I'm not interested in buying one of your M-5s; I want to buy all sixteen that are sitting in your motor pool, along with the forty-eight XG-777 rockets that go with them."

Pallosic was truly shocked. At first he could hardly comprehend what was taking place. He stared into Lossada's eyes and said, "I appreciate your offer, but quite frankly, neither you nor anyone else has that kind of money."

"Don't be so quick to judge, Alvin. I'm working closely with another party, a very powerful and influential person, who is quite interested in what you have. We don't intend to pay window-sticker prices for these machines and weapons as your government has, but I can assure you that you will be paid most generously for taking this risk. You will never have to wake up at five o'clock in the morning or take an order from your superiors again for the rest of your life. Think about it. If you are interested, let me know. If you are not, forget we ever had this conversation, and we'll just let it drop."

"Yes, I'll consider it, but it will require some serious thought. You've really taken me by surprise," admitted the colonel.

"I'm not trying to rush you," Lossada said, "but we will need to move rather quickly if we really hope to strike a deal."

Pallosic took a long pull from his drink while considering his options. "I could be interested in this venture if two things take place. First, if the money is right, of course, and second, if I will have control of the vehicles and their operators. You see, I'll be forced to leave the country, and I can't run off and hide under a rock and spend the rest of my days counting all my money. I need to be involved. Do you understand what I mean?" he asked, not at all sure Lossada did.

"Of course, I understand, and I can also assure you that you will have command over the vehicles and the troops who will operate them. You are safe to assume that whoever buys this equipment will need someone to instruct the soldiers in all facets of the proper maintenance and operational techniques," Lossada replied. He knew full well that Krause would never agree to those conditions, but nothing could interfere with these negotiations.

"And also, Alvin, something *you* must understand," Lossada continued, looking Pallosic squarely in the eye. "Once you commit to supplying these weapons, we have a binding contract. A contract that *cannot,* I repeat, *cannot* be broken. Quite simply, my associate will expect the goods he has ordered to be delivered as promised, and absolutely nothing less. He *will not* be disappointed. Do I need to elaborate?"

For the first time, Pallosic felt small. He felt the very real vibrations of power coming from this man, who was obviously connected to a very powerful organization. Pallosic now knew what he was up against. No need for elaboration; Lossada's meaning was quite clear.

Krause had given the project to Lossada without any stipulations. The next question would undoubtedly be about money and payment.

I will tell him whatever it is he wants to hear, thought Lossada, *because I really don't believe he will be around long enough to spend a dollar of it once these vehicles and the missiles are delivered.*

"Okay, now for the tough question," he said. "What price would you place on your green trucks with the skinny rockets, along with the technical and operational manuals? Remember, we don't intend to pay retail. Give me a number," Lossada said, enjoying the game.

"Well," said Pallosic, doing some quick calculations in his head about what it would take to live a life of complete luxury for the rest of his years on some remote island. "We've got sixteen M-5s and a total of forty-eight XG-777 missiles; you will no doubt want these with the tactical nuclear warheads. I figure it should be worth about twenty million to you." He watched Lossada's eyes for some reaction.

His statement was answered with a grimace. "I think you may be just a bit too greedy for my partner's liking, Alvin, but let me make a phone call. I will relay your price, and we'll see what he comes back with."

Lossada ordered another round of drinks, excused himself from the table, and walked out of the dining room toward the public phone just outside the men's restroom, toward the back of the building.

Out of sight, Lossada took his time, used the restroom, washed his hands, and stalled in front of the telephone for about five minutes. He did not bother to contact Krause. Checking his watch, he strolled back to the table to join his new partner.

A little back and forth negotiating took place, but Lossada let Pallosic think he had won this game of tug-o-war. A figure of fifteen million was agreed upon: seven and a half million when Lossada took possession of all of the hardware and the remainder upon safe arrival in Europe. Now it was between Lossada and Colonel Pallosic to orchestrate a plan to remove the M-5s, along with their nuclear weapons, from the Fort Hood military reservation and transport them across the Atlantic to their ultimate destination.

A rough game plan was already developing between the two men when the owner of the restaurant began turning off the lights around 2:00 a.m.

The initial plan was that Pallosic would draw up a bogus requisition for the M-5s and the XG-777s to be secretly transferred to another military installation, probably Fort Knox, under top security, thereby creating the need to go through Colonel Pallosic's office with the minimal amount of personnel involved. Sixteen twenty-foot ocean containers would be dropped off by Sea-Land Services at a remote location at Fort Hood. They would eventually be picked up by another carrier and delivered to the port of New Orleans, where Guillermo Lossada would officially take possession.

Chapter Twelve

Fort Hood, Texas
Friday, 30 July 1993
0800 Hours

"Sir!" Major Dennis Edson stood at attention and rendered a crisp hand salute as Colonel Alvin Pallosic entered the office of the main Fort Hood armory. "How may I help you, sir?"

"I need to inspect the XG-777 missiles. Right now, Major."

"Yes, sir. Follow me, please, sir."

Through a maze of vault-like doors and locked steel grid cages, past row upon row of all types of weapons and munitions, the men came to several stacks of long, rectangular OD green fiber shipping cartons, stacked neatly in one of the main aisles. There were about fifty of these cartons, all with white stenciled lettering and yellow markings that indicated "High Explosives." Directly across the aisle from these crated rockets were racks containing forty-eight uncrated XG-777s, minus the nose-cone assemblies, with an array of electrical wires taped and capped and exposed to view. Forty-eight empty nose cones were stacked off to the side.

"Major, where are the warheads for these missiles?" barked Pallosic.

"Sir, originally these were the rockets with the tactical nuclear warheads. We were ordered to dismantle the warheads and—"

"Where the hell are they?" shouted Pallosic, in a near state of panic.

"I'm not exactly sure, sir," Major Edson responded, keeping his cool. "I know for sure they're not here on post, and I would imagine they were sent to Kirtland Air Force Base in New Mexico. That's where a lot of the larger nuclear ordnance is—"

"And where the hell did all of these high explosive missiles come from? They weren't here before!"

"Sir, these were pulled off the M-5s earlier this week, right before they were moved from motor pool four up at North Fort, over to the area they use for storing obsolete vehicles and tracks in West Fort," explained the major.

Pallosic could not believe it. Without further comment, he headed for the door.

~ * ~

The sun was setting as Colonel Pallosic drove out to the western edge of the base, trying to gather his thoughts. There was no way he could retrieve the tactical nuclear warheads from Kirtland Air Force Base, given their tight security. He knew absolutely no one in the Air Force with any authority, much less anyone stationed at Kirtland. Alvin Pallosic knew full well that coming up empty-handed or trying to pass off a conventional high explosive warhead as a TNW would be signing his own death warrant. These people would not accept a "Sorry, we've had a little set back" speech.

Pallosic was relatively close to the compound where the obsolete M-5s were marshaled, so he thought he might as well take a look and make sure the vehicles were still in a secure place, although he didn't know what the hell it would really matter without the nukes.

As he drove the Humvee closer to the M-5s with their empty launch racks, he noticed that about a hundred yards down the row, the old M110A2 tracks with their long-barrel 203-millimeter cannons were silhouetted against a pink sky. *Ironic,* thought Pallosic. *One obsolete weapon parked right next to its obsolete replacement.*

There were thirty or forty of these cumbersome looking vehicles all parked in a tight, orderly formation. He remembered seeing these big guns in Vietnam, and based on the amount of rust formed on the tracks and road wheels, he doubted if any of these had seen service since then. The cogs in Pallosic's brain were beginning to turn, slowly.

~ * ~

Monday, 02 August 1993
0730 Hours

This is definitely not the way I wanted to start my week, thought Major Dennis Edson as he picked up the telephone receiver, tipped off by his first sergeant as to the caller's identity.

"Major Edson speaking. How may I be of assistance, Colonel Pallosic?"

"I need information, Edson. Two things. First, do you have munitions for the 203-millimeter cannon? If so, what types and what quantities do you have on hand? Second, I need to see *all* of the paperwork on the dismantling of the XG-777 warheads."

"Yes, sir. Regarding the munitions for the 203-millimeter cannon, sir, we're dealing with two very different munitions. The most common is the regular high-explosive round. The other is the XM-753, the rocket-assisted projectile with a W-79, low-yield nuclear warhead. I can tell you right off that the XM-753s are no longer stored here." Anticipating the next question, the major continued, "Some were shipped to the Sierra Army Depot in California, and some were shipped to the PW&B Laboratories—"

"PW&B in Amarillo?" interrupted the colonel.

"No, sir. The PW&B Laboratories in Lubbock." Edson waited a moment, expecting to be interrupted again, and then continued. "I do know that we have a pretty large supply of the regular 203-millimeter high-explosive rounds on hand. They're the only artillery rounds we have in this arsenal. I'll have to dig up the file to give you an exact count on those, sir.

Regarding the dismantle orders and worksheets for the 7s, sir, I can have those on your desk by this afternoon."

"Very well, major. Make damn sure it happens, and make sure you include the inventory on those 203-millimeter high-explosive rounds." The line went dead.

Major Edson closed his eyes and shook his head. What was with this guy? What in the world would an MP colonel need with an inventory on old artillery shells? This guy was totally off the wall!

~ * ~

Monday, 02 August 1993
1305 Hours

"Good afternoon, PW&B Laboratories," answered a pleasant female voice on the first ring. "How may I direct your call?"

"This is Colonel Alvin Pallosic, Provost Marshal, Fort Hood. I need to speak with the head of your security section."

"One moment, please." The line was quiet for only a few seconds when a second attractive voice answered, "Security Division, Linda speaking. May I help you?"

"Yes, this is Colonel Alvin Pallosic, Provost Marshal, Fort Hood," he repeated once again. "I need to speak with the person in charge of your plant security section. This is rather urgent, and I hope that I will not be jerked around among a half dozen people before I get the person in charge."

"Yes, sir, allow me to put you on hold for just a moment. I believe you will want to speak with Mr. Meier. His extension is 483, if you happen to be disconnected. Let me see if he's available." There was no elevator music. The next voice was quite a contrast from the first two.

"This is Scott Meier. What can I do for you, Colonel Pallosic?"

"Mr. Meier, first of all, I need to inform you I'm working under the authority of the U.S. Army Criminal Investigation Command out of Quantico, Virginia. We're investigating a very delicate situation taking place down here at Fort Hood that might very well involve some of your personnel at PW&B. Before we go any further, I need to make sure that A, you are the person I need to speak with, and B, this conversation will be treated as classified information and that you understand that this discussion must remain strictly between you and me. Is that correct?"

"Yes sir, you are correct on both A and B. I'll be happy to help in any way I can," replied Meier.

"Good. Now let me give you a little background information as to why I've contacted you," said Pallosic. "My initial investigation began when it was brought to my attention that several of our rocket-propelled grenades were missing. A company commander in the field had an urgent request for twenty-four RPGs. We got a report back the day he received the shipment stating that the RPGs we had shipped him had been replaced with several sections of four-inch lead pipe.

"With this information, very quietly, after hours, my staff and I began looking into the remaining stock of RPGs and all other high-explosive ordnances. When we began inventorying the 203-millimeter shells, we didn't find any missing; the number of pieces counted matched perfectly with the inventory record. But to our surprise, we found one hundred twenty XM-753 *nuclear* projectiles, packed in cases identified as 203-millimeter high-explosive rounds. On very close inspection, these particular cases were marked with a very small yellow triangle on the front, lower-right portion of each case. These were all located on the end of an aisle, with relatively easy access.

"As I understand, most of the XM-753s were to be shipped and stored, and eventually dismantled, at PW&B Labs, with a much smaller portion going to the Sierra Army Depot for storage only. Actually *all* of our obsolete nuclear ordnances will eventually be under your security, is that correct?"

"Affirmative, sir."

"Of course, the XM-753s, marked as standard 203-millimeter shells are in a secure location, as with all of our weapons and munitions at Hood, but probably nothing nearly as secure or sophisticated as your storage facility for nuclear weapons. My thought is that whoever has made this switch will no doubt be back for them at a later date, to move them out of the building at the most opportune time."

"But Colonel, where or how do you figure PW&B personnel to be involved?" asked Meier.

"The parties involved are not interested in an 8-inch artillery shell, unless of course they are planning on stealing one of the 203 Howitzers that fire it. They are *only* interested in extracting the nuke warhead from it. I say 'they,' because one person could not possibly do this alone. I imagine the party we're looking for has plans to sell these nuclear components to some third world country, trying to gain respect as some sort of power that should be reckoned with. PW&B Laboratories is the only nuclear weapons assembly *and* disassembly facility in the country, so I suspect that whoever plans to steal these must have the technical know-how to disassemble and safely remove the W-79 nuke warhead from these shells without creating a small mushroom cloud over the great state of Texas. Think about it; it wouldn't make much sense to try to haul several tons of artillery shells off the base when the only thing of value to them could be stowed away in ten or twelve footlockers that could go undetected in the back of a pickup truck. They could be camouflaged or hidden in just about anything, with other field supplies being shipped out, in file boxes, mixed in with trash, you name it."

"Okay," Meier said to indicate he was following.

"So what I need from you are the personnel files on all of the people who have been involved in either the assembly or the dismantling of the XM-753s over the past five years: present and former employees."

Meier scowled and said, "You're talking about eighty or ninety files, maybe more. Confidential PW&B files. I'm not at liberty to hand these over to you."

"Mr. Meier, you just assured me you were the right person to speak with and that you were willing to help me in any way." Pallosic's voice was noticeably louder now. "Let me remind you, Mr. Meier, this is a federal investigation. Now, am I to understand that you are refusing to cooperate?" Figuring this was the time to end the "Mr. Nice Guy" façade, Pallosic continued, "This is a very time-sensitive issue, so I don't have the luxury of a lot of verbal jousting with you. I'll make it as simple as I can. You give me the information that I just asked for and we get this part of the investigation out of the way quickly and efficiently, or..." Pallosic paused. "...I get a court order to subpoena these personnel files and I put *your* file on top of the heap, subjecting you to the same interrogation as any of the other suspected criminals, along with citing you for the obstruction of a federal investigation. Your call."

After a moment to regain his composure, Meier said flatly, "Give me your mailing address, Colonel Pallosic, and I will overnight the files to you within the next two days." His voice held both defeat and contempt.

"No, Mr. Meier, I plan to come up to Lubbock in the next two days and inspect those files myself. Make yourself available for any questions I might have."

Another flat "Yes, sir," from the Chief of Security, PW&B Laboratories, then a dial tone.

Very pleased with himself, Alvin Pallosic grinned as he rocked back in his chair. He couldn't believe this guy had bought his complete line of bullshit: hook, line, and sinker. What an idiot! It was amazing what a little well-placed intimidation could do. This was going to work out okay after all.

~ * ~

As he read over the actual work order to disarm the XG-777s provided by Major Edson, Colonel Pallosic was specifically interested in the personnel involved in the physical dismantling of the nose cones and warheads from these long, cylindrical rockets. To his surprise, he found there was only one man, a first lieutenant by the name of Darren Hatch, who did the procedure, along with a specialist fourth class who had served as his assistant, basically to hold his screwdriver and carry the tool box. Pallosic accessed Lieutenant Hatch's official military personnel file later that morning. Attached to the OMPF was an additional sheet that contained the lieutenant's civilian education and employment records.

A master's degree in electrical engineering from the University of Delaware, and another master's in nuclear engineering from MIT. Pallosic stared at Hatch's file in amazement. What the hell was this guy doing in an army uniform?

~ * ~

Tuesday, 03 August 1993

Lieutenant Hatch wondered what in the world the provost marshal wanted to see him for. He didn't think he had broken any laws. Hatch had never met the man, but none of the things he had ever heard about the colonel were very charitable.

Just entering the office of the provost marshal caused a mild case of butterflies in Hatch's stomach.

"Take a seat, Lieutenant," said Colonel Pallosic, standing and extending his hand after returning the lieutenant's salute. Pallosic put on his best, most charming smile. This was not the time to be his usual intimidating, abrasive self.

Lieutenant Hatch noticed his official military file squarely centered on the colonel's desk.

"In looking over your file, I was quite impressed with your academic records. Very impressive, but I am also extremely curious. What is a guy like you, with your academic credentials, doing in the U.S. Army? I mean, you could be making a small fortune in the private sector. Don't misunderstand, we're glad to have you, but why the Army?"

"Sir, it's basically because I've always had a genuine interest in nuclear energy. More specifically, I guess, I would define it as a real fascination with nuclear weapons. The U.S. military seemed to be the logical choice for a real hands-on experience and possibly a good secure career. Having visited with each of the four main branches, the Army *seemed* to promise a more 'get-your-hands-dirty' experience than sitting in a laboratory or in an office behind a computer screen. I wanted to put my years of rather exceptional education to some practical application in the actual testing or possibly even the building of tactical nuclear weapons," explained Hatch.

"So you must be fairly satisfied with your position here at Hood." Pallosic had just tossed out a well-placed baited statement to see if Lieutenant Hatch would bite.

"Well, sir," Hatch replied, "to be quite honest, I *was* very satisfied to be assigned to the XG-777 rocket project that was still in the developmental stage. You couldn't find a better learning experience than to be in on the ground floor of this promising XG-777/M-5 project, not to mention the possibility of a fast-track promotion. So, as you can imagine, sir, I was very disappointed when I learned the M-5 project was being scrapped. If you don't have the M-5, there isn't much need for the 7s that were primarily designed for the M-5s. Since that announcement, I've been spending most of my days counting mortar shells or supervising cleanup details in or around the armory building. Pretty damn boring duty, if I may say so, sir. Not exactly applicable to my degrees, sir."

Pallosic could tell by the look on the lieutenant's face that the younger man wondered why he was sitting in the provost marshal's office talking about his education and his present military occupational status. Pallosic decided to curtail the cat and mouse game and get to the point of this meeting. The big question had just been answered. He could definitely work with this.

"Lieutenant Hatch, your boredom problems are about to disappear. Let me start by saying I have applied for a top-secret security clearance for you. With your records, there shouldn't be any hang-ups.

"Okay," Pallosic continued with a bit of theatrical build-up. "Would you be willing to swear to secrecy regarding all aspects of a highly classified mission?"

"Of course, sir." *Anything beats the hell out of counting cases of mortar shells,* Hatch almost said aloud.

"As you know, because it is public knowledge, the M-5 project has been canned. But what I am about to tell you remains right here in this office, between you and me. Agreed?"

"Yes, sir," said Hatch. This was starting to sound kind of interesting.

"Although Congress has canceled funding for the M-5s and the 7s, there is still a specific need for those weapons that have already been manufactured. You don't need to concern yourself with where these weapons will ultimately be used; that's on a need-to-know basis. Your responsibility will be to reassemble some of the same weapons that you recently dismantled, but there's a bit of a twist involved. You won't simply be replacing the same tactical nuke warhead; you'll be installing a lower-yield nuke into the XG-777s to comply with specs coming directly from the Pentagon, for this particular mission. This procedure will basically involve taking the W-79 tactical nuclear warhead from a 203-millimeter artillery shell and transplanting it into the nose cone of the XG-777. Are you familiar with the W-79, Lieutenant?"

"Yes, sir, I am, but the W-79 has a completely different detonation and wiring system than the one in the XG-777. With all due respect, sir, these are not interchangeable," responded Hatch.

"I realize that, Lieutenant!" Colonel Pallosic had no idea what this exchange of warheads entailed. He only knew that he had to come up with some kind of nuclear weapon: low-yield, high-yield, it didn't matter. Something—anything—that would make a Geiger counter chirp. Pallosic was desperate, and this was his only hope for survival. "What I need to know is, can *you* make the exchange work?"

After a moment of hesitation Hatch responded, "Yes, sir, I think I can."

"'I think I can,' is not good enough, Lieutenant!"

"Sir, let me rephrase that, if I may. Yes, it can be done, but until I can *better* familiarize myself with the W-79 warhead—actually handle it—I don't know how much work it will entail or how long it will take. I may need some additional parts and tools to get the job done, sir."

"Don't worry about parts or equipment you might need; I'll take care of that. But understand that time is critical. If you have to work twenty-four hours straight, that's what you'll do. I know I'm not painting a rosy picture

165

for you right now, but I can promise you that if you can get the job done and keep your mouth shut, I will personally see to it that you are rewarded for your commitment to this project. Agreed?"

"Yes, sir. When do I start?"

"I'll get back to you as soon as possible. Hopefully by the end of the week. I still need to work out some details pertaining to the W-79s," Pallosic said.

Chapter Thirteen

PW&B Laboratories, Lubbock, Texas
Wednesday, August 4, 1993

Colonel Alvin Pallosic, dressed in khaki slacks and a salmon-colored knit polo shirt, falling a couple of notches short of business casual, did not want to draw attention by wearing a military uniform. He also understood that if he was actually supposed to be representing the CID, their agents rarely, if ever, worked in uniform. Pallosic expected to find a more lavishly appointed office for the chief of security in a large private firm such as PW&B Laboratories, but instead found the office to be as bland as many generic U.S. Army offices.

Upon meeting Scott Meier, Pallosic flashed his provost marshal's badge and ID, making it perfectly clear from the start he was the person in charge here. With a little less fanfare, the colonel purposely laid down a white, 10x13-inch envelope with two diagonal red stripes, labeled "Eyes Only," on the security chief's desk. The envelope contained some authentic-looking documents, supposedly issued and signed by Major General Robert Graham, Commanding General, United States Army, Criminal Investigation Command.

"Colonel," said Meier, pointing to a side table with two large stacks of manila file folders, "this is the information you requested. This stack," he said, pointing to the larger stack on the left, "contains the personnel files of all those who worked on the assembly or dismantling or on both, for that matter. Keep in mind we have only started the dismantling process; it's been kind of a back-burner project until now, and only a handful of these people have had any experience in this process. The smaller stack here includes personnel who worked on the assembly over the past five years but are no longer employed by PW&B. Is there anything else you need?" asked Meier.

"Yeah, I'd like some space where I can work in private and not be interrupted," demanded Pallosic.

"Yes, sir. Follow me please."

Meier was relieved to hear the colonel's request for privacy. He was not too keen on sharing his office with this guy, for however long this investigation was going to take. Meier picked up the larger stack of files, and Pallosic picked up the remaining smaller stack and followed the PW&B security chief to a vacant private office just two doors down the hallway.

"If you need anything else, just let me know," said Meier.

"Where can I get some coffee around here?" Pallosic barked.

"Down the hall, to your left, is a break room. There should be some in the machine." Meier was not about to act as this man's personal butler and fetch his coffee.

Pallosic returned from the break room and settled behind the desk, sipped from his Styrofoam cup, and took the top file folder from the stack of current employees. The stack of former employees was just a screen, in order to give the impression of conducting a thorough investigation. Personnel no longer employed by the company and not located here on the premises could not be of any real value to him. Once he did find the right person to extract the nukes, he would also need that person to help get the warheads out of the PW&B stronghold, but he would cross that bridge when he came to it.

As Colonel Pallosic reviewed the first personnel folder, he soon realized he had no understanding of the technical jargon in the person's qualifications or job description. It didn't really matter. He was looking for some kind of flaw in the person's character; an Achilles Heel. Some weakness or possibly some unfortunate turn of events that might cause the person to be more vulnerable and, as a result, more willing to accept some kind of payoff or bribe.

About forty files into his search, Pallosic was starting to feel some frustration. So far, each of the files he had reviewed reflected the model employee. Several of these people had glowing recommendations from their supervisors for technical proficiencies and dedication to their work, as well as an excellent attitude toward their job. There were even a couple of employees who had been recognized for their participation in some community service work in downtown Lubbock, representing PW&B Laboratories.

All I need now is to read they also sing in the church choir, Pallosic thought.

By 1500 hours, Pallosic had reviewed only nine more files and was becoming more frustrated. He couldn't find a damn negative thing.

I must be overlooking something obvious, he thought. *They can't all be model employees. Somebody has to be screwed up or have problems.*

The colonel knew that medical files and psychological profiles were tightly guarded. He didn't think it would be wise to demand these under the guise of a federal investigation. This was a pretty good cover, and he didn't want to ruffle someone's feathers enough to have them start questioning his authority. Pallosic was at a loss. He was not making the forward progress he desperately needed to pull this thing off.

Pallosic stared at the four blank walls, as blank as his current imagination, with the exception of a single wall calendar, compliments of Yellow Freight Systems. The calendar had barely caught his attention, but now he casually noticed that the previous occupant of this office had penciled in some ordinary reminders about two months ago: May 3, staff meeting, 10:00 a.m.; May 15, payday/car payment; May 19, Jamie's birthday; May 24–28, vacation; May 30, payday/house payment.

Pallosic reached for the phone and dialed Scott Meier's extension.

"Meier, this is Pallosic. I need the payroll and attendance records on all of these files, starting with the present employees, ASAP!"

"Colonel Pallosic, I don't have access to those files in my computer, but I'll bring up our VP of human resources, and she can help you with this."

"No, Mr. Meier, you don't understand. I don't want anyone else in on this investigation. The fewer who even know I'm here, the better. Have your HR person instruct you, and then you can give me the information I asked for."

Scott Meier decided to take a stand. He was really tired of this guy walking all over him. "Colonel Pallosic, this would be a huge waste of time and energy. For one thing, Ms. Barnett, the VP of human resources, is the one who assembled and organized these files for you. She probably suspects something is going on, or why would I have requested these specific files? Secondly, if and when you do find this person or persons of interest, Reaghn Barnett will be your greatest asset. If you're looking for some insight into these people, Barnett is the person you should be talking with. She hired a lot of these people. In fact, she even plays on the PW&B co-ed softball team. Colonel, she really does know her employees. If you're concerned about keeping this investigation confidential, I can assure you Reaghn is a professional, and she is completely trustworthy."

Pallosic sat for a moment without saying anything. Meier's comments made sense, and he needed all the help he could get on this personnel problem. "Okay, bring her in, but make it perfectly clear to her about the confidentiality."

Twenty minutes later, the vice president of human resources, a delightful woman in her mid-forties, rapped twice on the door frame of Pallosic's temporary office and stepped inside.

"Colonel Pallosic, I'm Reaghn Barnett. Scott has briefed me on the situation. I'll give you access to the payroll records for the people you are reviewing. You'll also have access to their attendance, paid time off/vacation days records. If you'll allow me to sit at the computer for a minute, I'll get you set up."

Pallosic relinquished his chair and stood aside while Barnett entered an administrative access code and, with a few more key strokes, brought up an Excel file labeled "Payroll."

"Colonel, all you need to do is take the employee's ID number from the file folder." Barnett picked one from the large stack of folders. "Type it in here, and bingo, there you have the employee's complete pay history from the day he or she started through the end of the last pay period. You can hit these tabs at the bottom here to view the PTO/Vacation."

Reaghn Barnett stood. "Questions?"

"No. I believe I've got it," replied Pallosic.

"Let me know if you have any questions on any of these people. Off the top of my head, I can't really think of any red flags that jump out at me from this group." Hesitating for a moment and tilting her head, she added, "The only *possible* irregularity I might call to your attention would be Todd Stockton. You'll notice his wages are being garnished. I doubt if it means anything, but he seems to have been having money problems with his ex-wife over the past six months or so. Other than that, it's all pretty straightforward. Call me at extension 456 if you need anything."

"Thank you, Ms. Barnett. That will be all for now."

As soon as Barnett left the doorway, Pallosic began searching the stack of personnel files for Todd Stockton. About two-thirds of the way down, he found it. Stockton, Todd, F. Employee #12654. Following Barnett's instructions, he keyed in the ID number.

There it was. Starting January 15, $435.00 was being deducted from Stockton's check every pay period and transferred to an account at the First Bank and Trust of Lubbock.

Interesting, thought Pallosic. *Looks like ol' Todd has got his butt in a sling. I wonder how that might have happened?*

Pallosic set Stockton's personnel file aside and delved deeper into the computerized payroll file to inspect the vacation days and paid time off. Nothing unusual about Stockton's paid vacation days, most of which were Fridays and Mondays, creating several long weekends in October and November. About ready to shift back to the pay records, he noticed another tab at the bottom of the page labeled "Travel Expense." Pallosic clicked the tab and saw two expenses paid in August of '92 and two more in September, with the notation "Fort Bliss" on all four payments. Pallosic tried to connect the dots between alimony and/or child support paid to the man's ex and long weekends spent somewhere other than Lubbock, Texas.

Naturally, Pallosic's first inclination was to assume there must be some kind of infidelity going on, some out-of-town interest that led Stockton off the reservation. He would need more details before he pursued this angle any further.

"Ms. Barnett, this is Colonel Pallosic. I need to see you as soon as possible. I have some questions pertaining to Mr. Stockton, and I also need to see copies of his expense receipts from each of his trips to Fort Bliss in August and September."

Pallosic was careful in framing his questions to Barnett—routine questions about Stockton's associations with other workers, any previous problems, etc. He worked his way toward questions about details of the divorce. Reaghn Barnett, wanting to give her full cooperation in this federal investigation, answered the questions as honestly as she could, but she was also careful not to give information that could be misconstrued as incriminating evidence against Todd Stockton.

"Does Stockton travel much for the company?" asked Pallosic.

"No, not much at all. These trips to El Paso were a special project he was assigned to down at Fort Bliss, working with the 32nd Army Air and Missile Defense Command. I think he made a total of four trips," answered Barnett.

Methodically scanning several sheets of photocopied hotel, restaurant, and rental car receipts, Pallosic commented, "I'm trying to fit some pieces of this puzzle together as delicately as possible." He paused briefly. "I have a couple of related questions that pertain to Stockton's private life, so bear with me." He read from his ledger pad. "How long has Stockton been divorced? Would you happen to know what brought about the divorce?"

"Well, I know the divorce proceedings went faster than most. Mrs. Stockton hired a top-notch lawyer to represent her, and it was settled out of court in late October last year. Regarding what caused the split, I really have no idea."

"With his four business trips to Fort Bliss that we know of, and possibly some extended weekend trips thrown in, might you suspect that Mr. Stockton was having an extramarital affair in El Paso?"

"Todd Stockton? No way!" replied Barnett, obviously irritated by the question. "No, Mr. Stockton may have other faults, but infidelity would not be one of those."

Still pouring over the expense receipts without looking up, Pallosic asked, "What about drinking or gambling? I see several dinner receipts from the restaurant at Sunland Park Racetrack from each of his four trips to Fort Bliss. Do you think the food served at the racetrack is really that good?"

"If gambling or alcohol is the problem, I don't know anything about it," Barnett replied honestly. "To my knowledge, none of these things have affected his job performance. *You* will have to ask him about that yourself."

Shifting his eyes from the paper-strewn desk to Reaghn Barnett's face, Pallosic responded, "I certainly plan to."

~ * ~

Thursday, August 5, 1993

The slightly built, light-complected thirty-three-year-old from Oklahoma sat across the desk from some old guy with a flattop, wondering what this was all about. He had never been in this part of the building before and wished he could have kept it that way.

"Mr. Stockton, my name is Alvin Pallosic. I am a colonel in the U.S. Army, presently on assignment at Fort Hood, Texas. I'm here to...let's call it a scouting mission for the time being. You come highly recommended by your superiors regarding your work on the XM-753 projectiles with the W-79 nuclear warheads, and I see that you are among the few in this department who have actually worked on dismantling the 753s. Getting straight to the point, I need to recruit someone with technical experience such as yours for a temporary, highly classified project at Fort Hood. This is strictly voluntary, and I can tell you, by the way, that it pays extremely

173

well—above and beyond your normal pay here at PW&B. If you are interested, I would run you through a brief screening process to see if you qualify. We already know some things about your background, but I need a few details. Are you interested?"

"Yes, sir, maybe," Stockton responded with some hesitation. "You say it pays well? Like how much?"

"I'll get to that later. Like I said, I've got some questions before we get into that," replied Pallosic.

"Yes, sir. Sorry."

"Okay, I'm going to get right to it, and I want straight answers. No bullshit, got it?" Pallosic immediately put Stockton on the defensive, as planned.

"Yes, sir."

"Now, I know you made several trips to Fort Bliss and the El Paso area for the company in late summer, early fall of last year."

Stockton nodded.

"And I suspect you've made other weekend trips to El Paso since then. Am I correct?"

Stockton nodded again, skeptical.

"What I need is clarification on what keeps drawing you back to El Paso. *I* think some demon caught hold of you down there, and you can't seem to shake it." Going for broke, Pallosic continued. "I'm thinking you either have a girlfriend—or a boyfriend—or you can't leave the ponies alone at Sunland Park. So what is it?"

Stockton was astonished and angry. "Well it sure as hell isn't a boyfriend, and it isn't a girlfriend, either!"

"So that leaves the ponies, doesn't it? So much into betting on the ponies that it cost you your marriage. Am I right?"

Todd Stockton cast his eyes to the floor in shame, head in his hands.

Pallosic knew he had struck a nerve. *Better strike while the iron is hot,* he thought.

"I'll tell you what; you help me on this project and *swear* to maintain silence about it, and I will personally see to it that you are able to pay off all your debts and get your life back in order again. You might even have enough money left over to buy the former Mrs. Stockton a nice little 'I'm sorry' ring."

Stockton looked up at Pallosic, wondering if this was for real.

"I'm pleased to find out the problem was only with gambling. You see, I couldn't have fixed the other two things." Pallosic locked eyes with Stockton. "Are we on?"

"Yeah. Just tell me what you need."

~ * ~

"As much as I hate to admit it, I was wrong on my initial assessment of Todd Stockton." Pallosic explained to Meier and Barnett, now gathered in Meier's slightly larger office.

"I questioned Stockton this morning and found him to be clean. Actually *squeaky* clean, to be more accurate. I found Todd Stockton to be a very sharp young man, quite interested and eager to cooperate. True, he does have some financial troubles, but that has no bearing on any association with the party stealing nukes from our arsenal at Fort Hood. I'm a hundred percent sure of that, which brings me to the next phase of the investigation. With the assistance of Mr. Stockton, who I feel can be trusted and who has the technical know-how, I plan to set a trap to snare our thief."

This immediately drew quizzical looks from both Meier and Barnett.

Pallosic continued, "I am simply going to make it a heck of a lot easier for him. I'm going to serve these nukes up on a silver platter. I will have Mr. Stockton dismantle about forty-eight warheads from the XM-753s in your storage, in full view of the rest of your workers, and have him casually get the word out that he will be accompanying me on a special assignment, taking these W-79s back to Fort Hood, making it clear as to the exact time and route we will be traveling. I feel that Mr. Stockton's presence will add a great deal of credibility to this whole scenario. I will also get the same word out to the personnel at Hood."

"You can't just drive off with a load of low-yield nuclear warheads. That's absurd!" responded Scott Meier. "You need to file certain forms with the EPA and Nuclear Regulatory Commission to have proper documentation, and that would take weeks. Colonel, I cannot authorize this."

"Mr. Meier, you still don't get it. I don't need your authorization! I take full responsibility for this entire investigation. Win or lose, it's my baby. Understood?"

"So you're basically setting yourself and Todd up to be ambushed somewhere between Lubbock and Fort Hood. Is that correct?" asked Meier.

"I cannot let one of my employees be put in harm's way, to be used as bait!" said Barnett. "No, Colonel Pallosic, that's not an option!"

"Ms. Barnett, let me remind you and Mr. Meier for the *last* time: This is a federal investigation, and I am authorized to use whatever resources I need to break this case. It *is* a matter of national security, and I *will* run this operation as I see fit!" Pallosic stood, glaring down at both of the PW&B execs.

"Colonel Pallosic, regardless of this federal investigation, before I go any further with this, I need to inform Ralph Bishop, our CEO, of what's going on," said Meier. "There's no way in hell that I'm signing off on these W-79s leaving this plant without approval from the top."

Pallosic was caught off-guard with this logical reaction and reluctantly agreed to include the company's CEO in the circle, but first he reconfirmed that this was still his investigation and that he was going to proceed as planned.

Tempers calmed a bit, and the group got back to the business at hand. "What about substituting the real warheads with dummies?" Meier suggested.

"No. If our PW&B accomplice is working in the plant, he or she will be able to see exactly what's going on. Anything other than the real thing will just not work. To put your mind at ease, regarding the safety of Mr. Stockton and the safety of the nukes, I will have our best security detail in plain clothes and unmarked vehicles, with constant radio contact, tailing me the entire distance."

"Colonel Pallosic, Todd Stockton is the only person you interviewed. Aren't there any other people of interest?" inquired Reaghn Barnett.

"No. That part of the investigation is completed. We're moving on." Pallosic was annoyed at being second guessed. "I will speak with Stockton this afternoon, tell him the game plan, and arrange for military transportation from Fort Hood for tomorrow night. That should hopefully wrap it up on this end." As an afterthought, he added, "once we've encountered our bandits, either on the highway or back at Hood—and that might take a few days—I'll make sure you get your W-79 nukes back all in one piece, and I'll have Mr. Stockton back to you by Monday morning. I'm planning on giving him the grand tour of the base and showing him a good time over the weekend. I think he'll really enjoy our Fort Hood hospitality."

~ * ~

"Lieutenant Hatch, this is Colonel Pallosic. Listen up. I want you to be at the motor pool at 0800 tomorrow. Sign out a three-quarter-ton truck with a cover, authorized by the provost marshal's office, and drive straight through to the PW&B Laboratories here in Lubbock. We're talking about at least a six-hour drive, roughly three hundred fifty miles."

"Sir, may I ask what this is all about?" inquired Lieutenant Hatch.

"I've secured forty-eight W-79s from PW&B, and we will be returning them to Fort Hood, along with some extra technical help for you to rebuild the warheads," explained Pallosic.

"Oh, sir, speaking of rebuilding the warheads, I have been studying the schematics and dimensions of the W-79 and looking at the size of the nose-cone assembly on the XG-777. It appears that the W-79 is physically not all that large, and the interior dimensions of the...well, let me start over. In nontechnical terms, if you were looking to add more punch to this weapon, we *might* be able to fit two of these warheads in each of these missiles and double the output."

"In that case, Lieutenant, you had better sign out a deuce and a half."

~ * ~

Friday, August 6, 1993

Scott Meier had consulted with his CEO directly after his last meeting with Colonel Pallosic. Ralph Bishop, of course, was reluctant to release the W-79 warheads, but based on Meier's assessment of the situation, there was nothing that would deter the provost marshal from doing it his way. Meier also had the distinct feeling that Bishop preferred him to deal with the problem himself and not get Bishop involved. If this Army colonel was assuming all responsibility, it seemed futile to stand in the way of a federal investigation.

The race was on to dismantle a minimum of ninety-six XM-753s and safely pack the W-79 nuclear warheads into protective wooden crates before the end of the day. Pallosic explained to Meier and Barnett he had decided to increase the number of warheads basically to "sweeten the pot," and creating a larger payload would make it that much more attractive to the would-be thieves. He also insisted that he would need more help on the plant floor to accomplish this task by no later than 4:30 p.m., claiming this too might catch the attention of the PW&B accomplice.

At this point, Meier and Barnett knew better than to question Pallosic. He was going to do it his way, so why waste the time or the energy?

~ * ~

At 4:35 p.m., the last of the ninety-six wooden crates were being strapped down in the back of a canvas covered 2½-ton U.S. Army truck.

Each person that Colonel Alvin Pallosic had involved in this ever growing charade had been sworn to secrecy, and each person had been told a completely different, contrived story. So far, Pallosic's intimidation tactics had worked perfectly, with each of these characters afraid to speak to anyone or to even question Pallosic's authority.

The road trip back to Fort Hood was arduous for Lieutenant Hatch. No sooner did he back the truck up to the PW&B loading docks and grab a Dr. Pepper and a stale ham and cheese sandwich from a vending machine in the employee lunch room, than he was back behind the wheel with a southeasterly heading on U.S. 84.

The Army "deuce and a half" was no sports car; every mile on the return trip was a struggle. Somewhere between Abilene and Novice, after watching Hatch's head bob several times as he fought off sleep, Pallosic realized his lieutenant had been driving all day—about five hundred twenty-five miles without rest. Stockton, sitting between the two soldiers, had slept most of the journey. It was not out of the kindness of his heart that Pallosic ordered Hatch to pull over and let him take the wheel; it was the thought of crashing this truck into a tree with ninety-six low-yield nuclear warheads in the back and wondering how large a crater it would make.

Slowing down to the speed limit as he passed through the town of Brownwood, Pallosic turned off onto the parking lot of the Ace Hardware store. Leaving the truck running, he hopped out, walked into the store, and came out five minutes later carrying a small ax and two shovels; he tossed them in the back and resumed driving. Both Hatch and Stockton were curious, but said nothing.

A little south of Pidcoke, a small town on the far western edge of Fort Hood, Pallosic turned east off County Road 116 onto an unmarked road leading into the military reservation, then onto another lesser gravel road going northeast that crossed Cowhouse Creek. After crossing the dry creek bed, Pallosic slowed to a crawl. He had found what he was looking for. The previous November, he and some fellow officers had set up a campsite here while deer hunting. He had wondered if he would be able to find this place again. At Fort Hood, the largest army post in the United States with over three hundred forty square miles, it was pretty easy to get lost.

This was a good location. It was a heavily wooded area with the exception of a fifty-by-seventy-five-foot clearing, illuminated by the headlights of the deuce and a half. Pallosic shut off the engine, but left the headlights on.

"Okay men, break's over. Follow me," shouted the colonel as he jumped out of the truck. Letting down the tailgate, he reached in and grabbed the shovels and handed them to Hatch and Stockton.

"I want you to start digging a shallow trench, along that tree line, where we can bury these cases. It doesn't need to be very deep, just deep enough so we can put a thin layer of dirt over the top. I'll cut some brush to use as cover once we've finished digging."

An hour and a half later, Pallosic backed the truck out while Lieutenant Hatch used a piece of brush to sweep over the tire tracks to eliminate any trace that the road had been traveled recently. It was well after 0100 when the men finally passed through the main gate in Killeen.

Colonel Pallosic signed in Stockton at the VIP guest quarters and gave him instructions to "sleep fast," because he would be picking him up promptly at 0700.

"No, on second thought, be ready to go by 0800. Just stay put until I get here," Pallosic said, realizing he couldn't very well have a civilian show up at the armory.

"We'll park the deuce and a half in front of my office for the night, because we'll need it first thing tomorrow," Pallosic told Hatch. "Then, we'll need to go back to the motor pool to pick up a second deuce. There's no possible way we can safely haul all forty-eight missiles in their racks in one truck. Meet me there at 0710, and be sure to bring all of the tools we're going to need."

~ * ~

Central Motor Pool
Saturday, 07 August 1993
0715 Hours

"Wake up, Sergeant! Where the hell do you think you are? You're on duty, soldier! Who's your company commander? I have a good mind to call him right now!" Pallosic shouted, back on his game.

"Sorry, sir. I didn't hear you come in," said the bleary-eyed buck sergeant, scrambling to his feet.

"Obviously not. I don't have time right now to report you to your CO, so make damn sure I never catch you sleeping on duty again. Got it?"

"Yes, sir. Thank you, sir."

"I need to sign out a deuce and a half. Right now. It's for the provost marshal's office, and I just happen to be the provost marshal, so let me sign the sheet, point me to the truck, and I'll be out of here."

Thank God! thought the sergeant. He couldn't move fast enough to get this man out of his motor pool, not even taking the time to ask when he would be returning the vehicle.

~ * ~

Fort Hood Armory
0735 Hours

"Lieutenant, I'm here to pick up the XG-777s," Colonel Pallosic calmly stated as he pulled out several official-looking requisition forms from a manila envelope stamped "Classified Material: U.S. Department Defense, Pentagon." He laid the envelope face up in clear view of the acting officer in charge, in the absence of Major Edson and his second in command.

"Sir, I'm sorry, but I don't know anything about this," explained the young second lieutenant.

"Damn it! I was afraid of that. You're *positive* you do not have a copy of this transfer somewhere in this office?" Pallosic said excitedly, shoving the documents in the second lieutenant's face.

"Sir, we do not have copies of any such order. If they were here, sir, I would know about it."

The colonel did not display the expected anger or hostility, but instead said, with calm authority, "All right; I can't blame you if you never received the paperwork. But believe me, I will get to the bottom of this snafu.

"Okay, this is what we need to do," he said, taking complete control of the situation. "You need to understand that this is all classified information. This order from the Pentagon calls for the forty-eight XG-777s that were dismantled. I'll need all forty-eight of the rockets, along with the nose-cone assemblies, loaded onto the two deuce and a halfs that are waiting at the gate at the back of the building. So if you will please have the gates opened and load these missiles onto my trucks, I'll get out of your hair.

"Oh," Pallosic said as an afterthought, "and I'll be sure to pass along to Major Edson how helpful and cooperative you have been with this extremely important project."

Twenty-five minutes later, after personally making sure the canvas flaps on both trucks were tied down securely, Colonel Pallosic and Lieutenant Hatch were driving away from the armory with a payload of partially dismantled missiles that would soon make Pallosic a very wealthy man. Wealthy beyond his wildest dreams. *A multi-millionaire*, Pallosic reminded himself, grinning inwardly.

After picking up Stockton from the VIP guest quarters, Colonel Pallosic suddenly began to feel the pressure of the next phase of his mission—the most critical. He had successfully duped or intimidated all of his pawns thus far, each enabling him to advance to the next step. He had his key players in place, and now it was time to put it all together. This integration of small nuclear cells and electrical wiring absolutely had to work. Pallosic, foolishly, was not the least bit worried about his technicians making a mistake handling these tactical nuclear warheads and causing a nuclear explosion right in their laps, but he was frightened to death of the repercussions of not delivering the goods he had promised within the time frame they were expected.

Pallosic's mind was swimming with a checklist of details he needed to accomplish, the first of which had already been taken care of. At 0600, a call was made to Guillermo Lossada with an update on Pallosic's progress and instructions for him to arrange for Sea-Land to drop off sixteen empty, twenty-foot containers on chassis as soon as possible, and for the drivers to rendezvous with him at the city-limits sign on the south end of Pidcoke. Lossada would have to be the intermediary, since Pallosic did not have immediate access to a telephone while out in the field.

To better insulate the security of this movement of sixteen commercial overseas containers, Lossada informed Pallosic that he would take advantage of his connections with the Teamsters Union, thanks to his friend and business associate in New Jersey, and call for a select group of sixteen drivers and semi-trucks to make the pickup once the containers were loaded and sealed. No way could they allow the Sea-Land personnel to have any knowledge of the freight being transported or the true destination of the containers.

~ * ~

Guillermo Lossada also had additional details to take care of. Arrangements were made with the owner of two small ocean-going vessels out of the Port of Guairá, just outside of Caracas, a carrier he often used to transport his cocaine into the States. With a few minor modifications to the cargo hold, each of the vessels could carry eight of the twenty-foot containers, four forward and four aft. Once the containers were in place, they would be completely covered with grain—wheat, corn, or possibly soy beans—thus perfectly hiding the actual payload.

The Estrella de Bolivar was presently in port and could be refitted and ready to sail within the next four or five days and be docked in New Orleans by Thursday or Friday the following week. The only minor drawback was that the Margarita Brissa was still out at sea and would not return to the Port of Guairá for approximately another thirty days. No major problem; Lossada would just have to secure the remaining eight containers at the wharf, and he would simply draw up two separate shipping documents with a three-week gap between the two ship dates.

Guillermo Lossada, the ultimate business manager, knew there was not enough time to prepare a cocaine shipment for the States on this first shipment. However, he figured he could certainly take advantage of the delay and quick stop-over in the Port of Guairá for the refitting on the second shipment by sending a payload of cocaine into New Orleans via the Margarita Brissa. *Why waste a perfectly good Caribbean crossing without any cargo?* He would call Carmen DeGraci right away to see if he would accept an unscheduled shipment. Lossada would knock off a little on the price, just to show some good will for his best North American customer.

~ * ~

Carmen DeGraci, at fifty-four years old and with silver-gray wavy hair, was taller than most Sicilians, and not a pound overweight, rather unlikely for most middle-aged Sicilian men. He was the loving father of three daughters and one son.

Lisa, Geana, and Sophia were thirty-two, thirty-one, and twenty-nine. Anthony, twenty-two, was "a belated gift from God," DeGraci would say. "A spoiled brat," most others would say, safely out of earshot of any of the family members. Anthony DeGraci was loud-mouthed and demanding and could not back up anything he said without the muscle of his father or his father's loyal soldiers. It was typical of Anthony to piss someone off to the point of coming after him, only to have one of his father's goons beat the snot out of the unfortunate bastard who didn't realize he was messing with the DeGraci family.

Carmen DeGraci wished that someday Anthony could run the family business, but he was also realistic enough to know Anthony would need to mature a great deal more and gain the respect of his lifelong friends, business associates, and trusted employees. Up until this point, he had protected his youngest as most parents would, but he realized there would come a time to push him out of the nest so he could get a taste of the real life.

Their new supplier from Venezuela, the Lossada family, was working out better than expected. They were now bringing in the larger shipments of cocaine into the Port of New Orleans. Very cost effective; DeGraci liked that. Carmen DeGraci always sent a small team of his own men to oversee the transaction involved in this money for drugs exchange. His men would spot-check the shipment, supervise the unloading, and, lastly, make the cash payment.

"It's time for Anthony to go along to New Orleans on this next trip with Gino and Charley to see how things are done," Carmen told his wife. "Hell, I was eighteen when Dad introduced me to the business."

This would be easy enough stuff for Tony to get his feet wet, DeGraci knew, and it would help his self-esteem to feel like he was actually contributing to something important. *And besides,* DeGraci reassured himself, *Gino and Charley will be right there to look after him, so what's the big deal?*

~ * ~

Fort Hood, Texas
0810 Hours

Pallosic's next stop was the Rental Center in Copperas Cove to lease a forklift for handling and loading the rockets onto the M-5s, a gas-powered electric generator, a set of portable loading ramps to drive the M-5s up into the containers, a large industrial-style canopy to keep the technicians and the sensitive nuclear material out of the hot Texas sun, and a pickup truck with a trailer that Stockton would use to haul all of the equipment. Next was the hardware store for sixteen oversized Master padlocks and any additional tools the lieutenant or Stockton might need. Last was a stop at McDonald's before the men headed to the remote work area on the western edge of Fort Hood.

Hatch and his assistant, Stockton, set up a well-organized workshop under the large gray canopy. Colonel Pallosic, for the most part, was just an observer for this part of the mission and an extra set of hands when necessary. The first conversion of the W-79 warhead to the XG-777 missile took the better part of the day. Pallosic, feeling some anxiety over the amount of time this procedure was taking, knew that he could not rush these men to work any faster. You don't get a second chance to get it right when you're reconstructing a nuclear warhead.

The good news was that the cavity of the XG-777 nose-cone had enough room, in fact, to implant two W-79 warheads, doubling the kiloton power of each missile. All ninety-six W-79 warheads from the PW&B Labs would be used; nothing would be left behind.

Once an assembly system was worked out, the speed and efficiency of the process increased dramatically. The new nuclear-tipped missiles began to roll off their crude production line.

The team of Hatch and Stockton worked steadily through the night. Pallosic praised his two workers and reminded them individually, in private, that he would make good his promise to free them from their present miseries and that life would definitely change for the better just as soon as this project was completed. "Trust me," he said.

At 1120 on Sunday, the last of the W-79 warheads were finally fitted into the remaining XG-777 missile. This highly technical and extremely dangerous task had been accomplished without incident. Stockton and Hatch were exhausted, and Pallosic could see they were about ready to drop in their tracks.

"Well done, men," he said. "Why don't you two grab a couple of hours of shut-eye, and I'll go in to Pidcoke to get us some burgers and a six-pack of cold beer. We'll take a little break then get back at it around 1330. We've only got a little more work left before we can call it a day."

~ * ~

Sunday, 08 August 1993
1330 Hours

"Here's the plan, gentlemen," Pallosic began. "We need to shuttle the M-5s over here and eventually load these rockets onto the launch racks. I've been studying this map," Pallosic said, spreading out a military grid map on the hood of the pickup truck, tracing his finger on a crooked course across the vast western portion of Fort Hood. "It's really not that far from the obsolete vehicles' park to here, as the crow flies, maybe five or six miles. There are no roads, but there is a tank trail that follows the low-lying ground along this creek," he said, pointing the way.

"I'm pretty sure the pickup truck can make it across this terrain; no question about the M-5s. Mr. Stockton, you will shuttle Lieutenant Hatch and me back to the OV park till we've got all sixteen of the M-5s right back here. If we can accomplish this by 1800 hours, I'll see if I can't get you to the airport and get you on the last flight back to Lubbock tonight. So let's mount up and finish this mission."

With no troops training or any helicopters flying over this most desolate sector of the military reservation, the two soldiers driving the M-5s, creating huge plumes of dust, and the civilian behind the wheel of the Rental Center pickup went completely undetected.

At 1740, Pallosic and Hatch pulled the last two Rambo 5s in under the protective cover of a large grove of short, scrubby trees near their work station and the cache of missiles.

The colonel walked over to Stockton, looked at his watch, and said, "Well, Todd, I am a man of my word. It's five forty, and you should hightail it out of here for the Killeen Municipal Airport so you can catch the seven fifteen flight back to Lubbock. Here's a hundred dollars for your ticket. Don't worry about the rental truck; leave it at the airport, and I'll take care of it tomorrow."

Pallosic shook Stockton's hand, thanked him sincerely for his service to his country, and reassured him that he could expect payment in full, wired to his bank on Tuesday morning. He might as well have said, "The check is in the mail." Pallosic figured he would be well on his way to his new life by Tuesday morning.

"Now you keep this agreement between you and me. Understood?" Pallosic said quietly but sternly.

"Yes, sir. No problem."

~ * ~

Pallosic stood looking over the cache of missiles and scattered M-5s. "Lieutenant Hatch, now here's what I want *you* to do."

Hatch was certain that Pallosic was going to have him start the loading process. It was nearly 1800, and the lieutenant was dog tired, having had almost no sleep for the past two days.

"I want you to drop off the truck at the motor pool, go home, get cleaned up, get reacquainted with your wife, and get a good night's sleep," said Pallosic. "And, oh—" he said, reaching into his pocket and pulling out a one-hundred-dollar bill, "here's some money to take your wife out to dinner. I'm sure she's wondering where the hell you've been. Now remember, this is all classified. You're working for me on a special assignment, and that is all you need to explain to anybody. Are we clear on that?"

"Classified," repeated the lieutenant. "Yes, sir, I confirm this is all classified." Hatch was just too damn exhausted to question what this whole mysterious mission was about or to even think about it right now. He just wanted to get home.

"I'll see you back here at 0730 tomorrow."

"Roger that, sir. And thanks a lot."

That night, Alvin Pallosic slept under the gray canopy on seat cushions he had removed from the deuce and a half. It wasn't very comfortable, and it wasn't the first time he had had to improvise some kind of makeshift sleeping arrangement out in the field. It really didn't bother the colonel all that much, because he knew he would never have to be the least bit uncomfortable again for the rest of his life.

~ * ~

Monday, 09 August 1993
0735 Hours

Not willing to leave his valuable property unattended, Pallosic had to wait for his lieutenant to report in. Once Hatch arrived, the colonel drove back to the main fort complex, returned the second deuce and a half, packed a carry-on travel bag, showered and shaved, put on a fresh set of starched fatigues, and made a brief appearance at his office—partly to be seen by his staff, but primarily to make a phone call. Pallosic closed the door to his office.

"Guillermo, this is Alvin Pallosic. Where do we stand on delivery of the twenty-foot containers?"

"Good morning to you, as well, Colonel!" Lossada replied. "Sea-Land tells me these are coming up from Houston and that they will be delivered in Pidcoke sometime around noon tomorrow, so I have arranged to have our trucks and drivers meet you in Pidcoke at 2:00 p.m. Does this give you enough time?"

"Yeah, that should be okay," responded Pallosic, thinking this should give him and Lieutenant Hatch plenty of time to load and secure the 7s into their launch racks, but it also meant another night under the stars standing guard over his own personal nuclear arsenal.

"The nice part about using our Teamster buddies for the shipment to New Orleans is there will be no documents in this transaction, completely paperless. I like to think of it as a gentleman's agreement," boasted Lossada.

"Okay, that's all fine and dandy. Now I need to talk to you about when I get paid. I—"

"Fair enough," Lossada interrupted. "As we briefly discussed before, you will be paid when I take possession of the merchandise. I will have your money when we get to New Orleans. Once we turn the containers over to the ocean carrier at the wharf and they sign off on receiving the freight in good order, you will turn over the keys to the containers and I will pay you the seven and a half million we agreed upon, plus the other half when it arrives overseas. Is that okay with you?"

"I'm going to need the total payment when the containers are delivered to New Orleans. That's when my part of the deal is completed, not when the ship delivers it on the other side."

Lossada thought for a moment. *What difference does it make? Why create waves? We're too far along to have this guy get cold feet and screw things up at the last minute.*

"Well, I can see your point, Alvin. You are completely right; your job is over once we get these containers to New Orleans. I will make arrangements for the total payment to be made as soon as we arrive at the wharf. No problem."

"One other request. I want you to purchase a one-way ticket for me from New Orleans to Atlanta, and then from Atlanta to Paris, departing New Orleans as soon as possible after our business is completed— hopefully by Wednesday afternoon. I want to be 'wheels up' and out of the country before they start looking for me and the M-5s. It's only a short matter of time before the Army and PW&B start connecting the dots. I plan to follow the convoy from here to New Orleans. Call it protecting my interests, but I've got my whole life riding east on I-10 tomorrow night, so I want to make damn sure everything goes smoothly."

"Understood," responded Lossada. "I would do exactly the same."

~ * ~

Colonel Alvin Pallosic took twenty minutes or so to grab a few personal items from his office and throw them in his briefcase, plus a sleeping bag and a couple of MREs from the emergency web gear he kept in a wall locker in the event of some unexpected rapid deployment. He also had some last-minute paperwork to complete.

The official U.S. Government forms that Pallosic prepared, just in case someone of authority should happen to stop him and inquire, stated that the sixteen twenty-foot containers were in transit from Fort Hood to Fort Knox, Kentucky, the U.S. Army's other major armor headquarters, and that he was the ranking officer in charge of this transfer.

Why anyone would travel a southeastern route from Hood to Fort Knox is completely illogical, but I'll cross that bridge if and when I come to it, he thought.

Loading and securing the XG-777 nuclear-equipped missiles onto the powerful launch racks of the M-5 Rambos went uninterrupted and without a hitch. By 1730, the job was complete. Colonel Pallosic thanked First Lieutenant Hatch for his outstanding performance and reassured him of his promises to fast-track his promotion to the rank of captain and to facilitate his transfer to a more prestigious position that would engage his experience and education.

~ * ~

The western edge of Fort Hood, near Pidcoke, Texas
Tuesday, 10 August 1993

Like clockwork, the Sea-Land containers rolled into Pidcoke at 11:50 a.m. Pallosic directed them to be dropped on a vacant Farm & Home Supply parking lot on the south end of town. At approximately 2:15 p.m., sixteen diesel trucks without trailers moved in to connect with the

190

containers and chassis. The colonel guided them on to the military reservation only far enough not to be seen from highway 116. Pallosic had no trouble recruiting several of the drivers to load the M-5s into the large metal boxes. After all, this was pretty cool to be able to drive one of these awesome-looking military vehicles with three very threatening rockets on the back, even if only for a few hundred yards.

By nightfall, the civilian convoy was on the road, heading southeast toward Houston, then to its destination in the Crescent City of New Orleans. Alvin Pallosic, driving his beige 1991 Chevy Impala, followed the convoy with patience at a distance of about a quarter of a mile.

At 0210, heading east on I-10, Pallosic decided to pull into the Welcome Center/Rest Area just within the Louisiana state line. He knew he could rejoin the convoy without any problem after a fast pit stop to relieve himself of the coffee he had been drinking on and off since the beginning of his journey. He was also eager to change out of his fatigues and into more comfortable civvies, but he really didn't want to take the extra time. There would be plenty of time for that when he reached the outskirts of New Orleans.

Also trailing the convoy and Pallosic—by about an eighth of a mile— were Javier and another man, two of Guillermo Lossada's trusted strong arms.

~ * ~

New Orleans, Louisiana
Wednesday, August 11, 1993
6:35 a.m.

The convoy of sixteen twenty-foot ocean containers arrived at the Governor Nicholls Street Wharf in perfect order. The containers were stacked and stored inside the cavernous wharf building, out of sight, per explicit instructions from Mr. Lossada. Eight of the sixteen containers would be loaded into the Estrella de Bolivar in the dark hours of Thursday morning. The remaining eight were scheduled to sail from New Orleans on the fourth of September.

Chapter Fourteen

Office of the Commanding General; Fort Hood, Texas
Wednesday, August 11, 1993
0830 Hours

"General Donovan, this is Jeff Robertson."

"Jeff, good to hear from you. To what do I owe this honor?"

Donovan and Robertson had gotten to known each other rather well after co-lecturing a course on Joint Service/International Operations at the United States Army War College in Carlisle, Pennsylvania, a couple of years ago. Through the course of a conversation over a beer at the "O Club," early in the session, they discovered that Colonel Alvin Pallosic was a common thread for both of them.

"Well, Jim," started Robertson, weighing his words carefully, "it appears your friend Colonel Pallosic has gone AWOL. We received a call from Major Tom Downing, his executive officer over at the provost marshal's office this morning. He claims the colonel was in briefly Monday morning and that he called in yesterday afternoon to check his messages. When he didn't show up at his office this morning, they tried calling his home phone, but there was no—"

"I was afraid something like this might happen," admitted Donovan, "although he might be taking his time getting in this morning. Knowing him as I do, he might be a little—or a lot—hung over."

"I thought of that, too, but Downing also mentioned Pallosic had been acting pretty strange lately, stranger than normal, I should say, and that when he left Monday morning he was carrying out some personal gear and a GI sleeping bag tucked under his arm. Jim, this doesn't look good from where I'm standing. I just wanted to give you a heads-up on your friend's activities before I take any action on this. I am also hoping you might be able to give me a clue, if you know something I don't."

"Jeff, I'm sorry I can't guide you on this. I would recommend you proceed as you would with any other AWOL offense, whether a private E-1 or a full-bird colonel. If he's violating Article 86 of the Uniform Code of Military Justice, he needs to be punished. I would show absolutely no partiality here, friend or no friend; he wears the uniform of a U.S. soldier, same as you and I. Unfortunately, he used to wear that uniform with a great deal more pride back when we served together, so many years ago."

This was precisely the response Robertson had expected from this highly revered warrior.

"Yes, sir, I understand what you're saying. I plan to have the MPs conduct a full-scale search of the post, and I'll also be contacting the judge advocate general's office to draw up the AWOL citation. Is there anything else, General Donovan?"

"No, Jeff. I think that's all you can do at this point. Thanks for keeping me in the loop, and please keep me up to date on your progress, will you?"

"Yes, sir, I certainly will."

~ * ~

0950 Hours

"Wait a minute. Start from the beginning, Major Downing. Tell me exactly what you just told Mr. Bolzenius." Major General Jeffery Robertson could not quite believe what he was hearing.

"Yes, sir. Tuesday afternoon, about 1400 hours, we get a call from a Mr. Stockton at PW&B Laboratories in Lubbock. He asks to speak to Colonel Pallosic. The sergeant at the desk explains that the colonel is out and asks if he can take a message. The man says it's a personal matter and he'll call back later. Mr. Stockton calls again this morning, about ten minutes ago. Sergeant McDevitt goes through the drill as he did before, and the guy comes unglued, so McDevitt sends the call over to me. He starts rattling off about some deal Colonel Pallosic had made with him and said that Pallosic promised him a bunch of money. Then he started rambling on about how he was going to get his life back in order and hung up. The poor guy was about in tears. Sorry, sir, but none of this made much sense to me. I have no idea what he was ranting about, but I'm thinking this could possibly have something to do with the colonel's disappearance."

"I agree, Major. I'm going to need to speak with this Mr. Stockton. Get him back on the horn, and patch him through to my office right away."

~ * ~

"Mr. Stockton, this is General Robertson. I'm the base commander at Fort Hood. I understand you're trying to locate Colonel Pallosic. I might be able to help you with this, but I'm going to need some information from you. You said the colonel owes you a large sum of money? Did he borrow this money and not pay you back?"

"No, nothing like that at all," replied Todd Stockton.

"Then please explain, in detail, how this situation came about," Robertson ordered.

"Well," Stockton hesitated, "this was all supposed to be strictly confidential between me and Colonel Pallosic."

"Mr. Stockton, I sure as hell can't help you if you don't tell me what I need to know. So please start giving me some information, or our conversation is over," said Robertson, becoming agitated.

Realizing he would probably never see a nickel of the money Pallosic promised if he didn't cooperate, Stockton responded, "Okay. For what it's worth, the colonel contacted me last week at work. Said he needed my help on some kind of top-secret mission involving the W-79 nuclear warheads we store here at PW&B."

General Robertson felt a lead weight in his stomach. "Nuclear warhead" was not a term he especially wanted to associate with Alvin Pallosic. "Go on, Mr. Stockton, with as much detail as possible."

"We—myself and some of the other techs at PW&B—had to dismantle about ninety-six XM-735s, the artillery projectile with the nuke warhead, and extract the W-79s. We boxed up the 79s and loaded them into an Army truck and—"

"An Army truck? How did you get an Army truck?" Robertson asked in disbelief, realizing this already bad situation was getting worse by the minute.

"I don't know!" the tech from PW&B shot back, revealing his growing exasperation with the whole bizarre ordeal. "All I know is that some lieutenant, I think his name was Hatch, drove the truck up from Fort Hood. Anyway—"

Robertson, writing all of the details down on a yellow ledger pad, interrupted again, not wanting to miss anything as the questions occurred to him. "Well, where does your money come into play?"

There was a long pause on the other end. Finally, Stockton replied, "This is the difficult part. Colonel Pallosic promised he would help me out of a financial problem—a pretty large gambling debt—if I would provide the technical help he needed for this important secret mission he was working on. He said it had something to do with 'national security' and I couldn't tell *anyone* what I was doing for him."

As Todd Stockton spoke the words, he became conscious of the fact that he had been taken advantage of; there was no money. He had been duped.

Damn! How could I have been so stupid?

Fighting back his emotions, Stockton continued, "General, I am sorry. I was just trying to get my life back. I lost my wife, my house, and whatever savings I had. I trusted what this colonel was telling me. He said he could fix it, and I was stupid enough to believe him. I really am sorry."

General Robertson felt compassion for the young man, as naive and vulnerable as he was, but he needed to get to the bottom of this quickly, knowing there had to be more to this developing nightmare. "Okay, so you loaded these nuclear warheads on the truck; then what?"

"We drove the truck to a small town called Pidcoke, then turned off the highway onto a dirt road. It was dark, but I'm pretty sure we were on the Army base. We crossed a dry creek bed, drove a little further, and stopped near a clearing. We unloaded the truck and then buried all the cases of W-79s."

"You buried them?" Robertson asked, wanting confirmation, hopeful they were still there. "Could you find this exact spot again?"

"Yeah, I'm pretty sure I could find it, but I kind of doubt they're still there."

Stockton continued on with all of the details he could recall from the previous weekend: picking up the rental equipment, reassembling the warheads to each of the missiles, working through the night, and shuttling the M-5s from one point to the other.

Robertson was overwhelmed by this account of Pallosic's outrageous activities. The general believed Stockton's story; he had to. *Nobody* could just make up something like this. It had to be real.

"For God's sake, who the hell authorized these nuclear warheads to leave your facility? Who's in charge of your security?" Robertson blasted the technician, exasperated with the complete lack of responsibility by PW&B in such a critical situation. General Robertson knew full well that Pallosic had simply manipulated this man and used him as a pawn to reach his objective. This guy Stockton was not to blame.

~ * ~

"Mr. Bolzenius, get the PW&B security chief on the horn right away!" General Robertson ordered.

"Major Downing, I want a team of your MPs to take a chopper, go out to Pidcoke, and follow Mr. Stockton's directions to where they worked on these missiles and M-5s. With any kind of luck, they might still be there.

Take some back up. If Pallosic and whoever he has working for him are still there, he's not going to give up without a fight. Take him alive if you can. I want to squeeze him for as much information as I can. There is no way he's in this by himself, so I want to get all of the bad guys involved. Got it?

"Mr. Bolzenius, find out who this Lieutenant Hatch is and bring him in right now."

Chief Warrant Officer Neal Bolzenius masterfully juggled all of these vital duties like a true professional without dropping one. Within three minutes, he said: "Sir, I've got Mr. Meier, head of security at PW&B, on line two."

After listening only five or six minutes to Scott Meier's narrative, Robertson asked, "Did you or your CEO actually read the documents in the 'Eyes Only' folder?"

"Well, I…ah…kind of glanced over the paperwork, and it all appeared to be in order. I mean it was, after all, 'Eyes Only,' and it was signed by some major general from the CID."

"Do you mean to tell me that neither you nor your CEO bothered to authenticate these documents?"

"No, sir."

"So in summary, you let this man who *claimed* to be working with the CID on a federal investigation drive off with a total of *ninety-six* low-yield nuclear warheads, without as much as even checking into the authenticity of this so called 'Eyes Only' document or calling someone at CID Headquarters in Quantico to verify what Colonel Pallosic was doing. Is this correct?"

Clearly seeing his neglect and poor judgment, Meier could not argue. "Yes, sir. I'm afraid that is correct."

"Mr. Meier, I would strongly suggest two things: one, that you seriously pray to God that these warheads are found before they can be used; and two, find yourself the best damn lawyer money can buy, because you are certainly going to need one."

~ * ~

1035 Hours

Reports back to Robertson from the team of airmobile MPs came back negative. The burial place of the warheads had been easily found, and other work had obviously taken place based on the amount of foliage that had been trampled or displaced. The officer in charge of the military police detachment also noted a huge amount of tire tracks from several large trucks. These tracks led them back to the highway and appeared to turn south onto 116. With this information, General Robertson knew his first two priorities were to contact the Texas Highway Patrol and the FBI.

"General Robertson, I've got Lieutenant Hatch on line one. Do you want to talk to him first or just bring him in?" asked the chief warrant officer.

"Bring him in, Neal. I want face time with this guy."

A couple of minutes later, CW2 Bolzenius appeared at Robertson's door with a large mug of coffee for the boss. Setting it on the general's desk, he said, "A hell of a way to start the day, isn't it, sir?"

"Yeah, it sure is, and I don't look for it to improve any time in the near future, either. Thanks for the coffee, Neal."

~ * ~

1105 Hours

General Jeff Robertson had just concluded his interview with Lieutenant Hatch when CW2 Bolzenius knocked twice on the door and stuck his head in, not waiting for a reply. "Sir, I've got the Highway Patrol on line three."

That was fast. Maybe we've caught a break. Lord knows we need it, thought Robertson, feeling a little less pressure now than thirty seconds before. "Put 'em through, please."

"General Robertson, this is Captain Clarke Winkle with the Louisiana State Highway Patrol..."

Louisiana? I didn't contact the Louisiana Highway Patrol, thought Robertson. *Perhaps the Texas Highway Patrol alerted them.*

"Sir, I'm afraid we have one of your men..." continued the Highway Patrol captain.

Thank God they found him, Robertson thought. Pallosic was going to wish he had never joined this man's Army. Robertson hoped they had found the nuke missiles, too.

"That's great news, Captain Winkle. I appreciate your quick work finding him. Did you retrieve the missiles and the vehicles, as well?"

"Excuse me, sir, I'm afraid I have no idea what you are talking about," replied the confused captain. "General, I was calling to tell you we just found the body of Colonel Alvin Pallosic at the eastbound Louisiana Welcome Center on I-10, near the state line. It appears the colonel was strangled to death several hours ago. A cleaning crew found the body early this morning in the men's restroom, propped up in the end toilet stall with an electrical extension cord wrapped around his neck. There were some signs of a struggle; the victim drew some blood from his attackers, but not much. Looks like a robbery. We didn't find any wallet or valuables on the soldier, and there was no car left in the parking area, but we did find his dog tags, ran his name and numbers through the computer, and tracked him back to Fort Hood."

~ * ~

1120 Hours

"General Donovan, Jeff Robertson here. I regret to inform you..."

With those five words Donovan had heard all too often throughout his career as a professional soldier, he knew exactly what to expect. Although his "comrade in arms" had gone rogue and completely over the edge, he couldn't help but feel that for the vast majority of his years, his friend had served his country and the U.S. Army with honor. What a shame it all came down to this at the very end.

"I've already notified the FBI and the Texas and Louisiana State Highway Patrols regarding the M-5s and nukes, but I have not had a chance to contact the brass at the Pentagon, the CIA, or the NSA. Those are my next calls."

Donovan hesitated for just a moment, gathering his thoughts. "Tell you what, Jeff. You've got plenty on your plate right now. I'm going to make those calls for you. I know a lot of these characters personally, and I don't mind being a buffer. This is one time when age and time in grade can be a big advantage. I have the years of experience on my side and can keep these people under control."

"No, Jim, this is my responsibility. I—"

"Jeff, I'm pulling rank on you. I know you can handle the situation; I have no doubt. But I'm taking it from here. That is an order. Understood?

"Yes, sir. Understood. Thank you, Jim."

~ * ~

New Orleans, Louisiana
Saturday, August 21, 1993

The New Orleans Drug Enforcement Administration had received one of those blessings from out of the blue from a guy named Hector; no last name, of course. Hector seemed to know just about everything regarding a shipment of cocaine leaving Caracas to arrive on Friday, September third, in New Orleans. He even knew who the dealer was on the U.S. side who would be receiving the shipment. This gift had everything but a big red bow on it. Senior DEA agent-in-charge, Gerard Boudreau, was licking his chops. To bag the DeGraci family on his home turf, in the act, would be a terrific score, no matter what size shipment they were bringing in.

Evidently someone had crossed Hector somewhere along the line, and now Hector was going to have the last laugh.

Chapter Fifteen

Munich, Germany
Monday, August 30, 1993

Erich Mueller remained busy trying to keep up with the flood of information and leads pouring in from all over Central and Eastern Europe. If only ten percent of the data he routinely collected could be authenticated, he would consider that a pretty fruitful day. Hank Talbot had told him from the beginning, "It's like picking pepper out of fly shit." Unfortunately, when dealing with national—actually global—security, in most cases, emanating out of Eastern Europe, nothing can be discarded until it's been thoroughly analyzed. The rumors of some kind of a communist uprising were ever present. There was a growing feeling of static in the air, but still nothing concrete, nothing they could physically investigate at this time. Not yet, anyhow.

At the end of the day, Mueller checked in with his answering service for any personal calls. Nine times out of ten, his personal calls consisted of someone trying to sell him something or soliciting a charitable contribution. When he was told his brother Thomas had called, a smile appeared on his otherwise deadpan expression. Seven weeks had already passed since the anniversary party at the Hotel Raphael, and Mueller chastised himself for not initiating the phone call to his younger brother.

Erich returned the call from his home phone as soon as he arrived at his apartment. "Thomas, how goes it? Good to hear from you, bro. I hope this is a dinner invitation."

"I'm well, thanks. And yes, it certainly can be a dinner invitation." Thomas's voice was different. Erich could detect something was not quite right.

"Thomas, what's on your mind? Are you okay?"

"I think I need to talk to you. Is your line free from 'bugs,' as you call it?"

"I'll call you back in ten minutes." Mueller was reasonably sure his line was not tapped, but it was always better to be on the safe side. Erich put his shoes back on and walked down to a pay phone off of Sendlinger Strasse. As he walked briskly, he wondered, *What in the world could Thomas have to tell me that would make him concerned about the security of my phone line? Hell, Thomas doesn't even know what I really do!*

The phone rang once. Thomas answered in a low, flat voice.

"Okay," Erich said, "what's with the secret agent stuff?"

"I hope you don't think this is stupid, but I didn't know who else to talk to," Thomas said, sounding mildly embarrassed.

"I'm sure it's not stupid," the older brother said, "but I don't know if I can help you. I'll listen; go ahead."

"About ten days ago, I received a fax at work informing me of a vessel coming in from the Port of Miami in the States, with a load of grain. That's normal, but the person representing this independent vessel said he preferred to do the unloading process with his own crew."

"Is that so unusual?" Erich asked.

"Well, yes and no. It would not be unusual if the cargo was hazardous material or extremely delicate to handle, or if it required some special equipment to off-load it, but this is grain! Nothing special or difficult about off-loading corn or wheat or soy beans."

Thomas paused briefly. "Just so you understand where I'm coming from, Erich, let me explain a little about our operation at Flatworld-Rotterdam. We can receive and off-load almost all shapes and sizes of oceangoing vessels. One of the unique capabilities we have that the larger steamship lines do not is that we have docking facilities and equipment to service the smaller ships, as well. Although it only represents a small percentage of our overall business, we have several of these smaller vessels, say 260-foot to 300-foot, that use us regularly.

"One of these regular clients is A&E Farming Implements GmbH. The guy ships like clockwork fourteen twenty-foot containers of various machine parts to the same consignee in Berlin. These have always shipped freight collect, port to port, from our Flatworld facility in the Port of Miami, on the first and third week of every month for the last two and a half years. Never an exception. These shipments clear Customs every time, no questions. So yesterday, I receive documents for an A&E shipment from some freight forwarder in Miami that I have never heard of before, and I do not receive any of the regular docs for machine parts that I would normally have received by yesterday or today, but—"

"Nothing strange so far;" interrupted Erich. "Could be they have just changed forwarders. Maybe better service or better rates, or—"

"No. They get great service and great rates out of our Miami facility. But here's the odd part; you didn't let me finish. This shipment is not machine parts; its grain. Two hundred forty metric tons of soy beans."

"Is this something that Customs officials or the Ministry of Agriculture would stop or inspect or question?" inquired Erich.

"No, their documentation was perfect. Everything looks completely legitimate and is certified by the U.S. Department of Agriculture. I'd say, except for the rare, random inspection— and they are busy as hell right now—that Customs will probably rubber stamp it, and the shipment will clear the same day as the documents are presented. The only reason *I* question it is because I know the history and the shipping trends of everything received for A&E Farming at the Port of Rotterdam. It just seems kind of abnormal for them. Not necessarily illegal, on the surface, just abnormal, but then that's probably how most contraband slips past the officials. I remember reading some time not too long ago about how bags of heroin have been smuggled in by packing it in with large cases of bulk coffee. Lord knows you could do the same with large quantities of soy beans or any kind of grain, for that matter; or maybe I'm just letting my imagination run wild, trying to find something more exciting in this paper shuffling that I do every day.

"Oh, one more thing that piqued my curiosity: two hundred forty metric tons of grain is not that much. Even a small vessel like this one could probably hold twice that amount. Why would they ship only half the capacity? Their freight charges wouldn't be that much more to fill it to the maximum. It all doesn't make much sense to me. Does it to you?"

Erich was silent for a while, absorbing all of the information his brother Thomas had provided. He didn't think Thomas was creating a story; he just wanted a little more evidence that a banned substance was likely being transported before he jumped into a situation that might embarrass him or his brother.

"Do you normally get grain shipments? Do you have the equipment to off-load it from the ships to trucks or rail or store it in other containers?" asked Erich, searching for more clarification.

"Sure, we get grain shipments fairly regularly, but usually on large vessels like an oceangoing barge, not on a small, conventional cargo boat. We have a huge vacuum system that sucks the bulk grain right out of the hold, or sometimes it's in specially designed containers made specifically for shipping grain," answered Thomas.

"Okay," Erich continued, tossing up any kind of questions that came to his mind, "what would an agricultural implement or farm equipment company need with a load or a half load of soy beans?"

"I don't know. Maybe to test some new piece of equipment? I really don't know," replied the younger brother.

Erich was stumped. There was always the chance illegal narcotics were being brought in by way of a small ocean vessel, hidden within a load of grain. That was actually a pretty good and probably fairly common method used by international drug traffickers but still not enough to go on. Drug control was not in his job description. On the other hand, he could not turn his back on drug smuggling if he happened to stumble across it.

Thomas had never asked Erich for anything. And besides, there *was* a war on drugs. Erich decided he would just keep it a very low profile. His professional conscience would be more at ease now that he had justified his intentions to be of assistance to his younger brother.

"So when does this ship dock?"

"ETA is tomorrow, around 9:00 p.m. Would you like to check it out?" asked Thomas.

"Yeah, I think so. It wouldn't do any harm just to give it a casual look," replied Erich.

"Good. I was starting to feel kind of stupid for even bringing it up. I know it's a long shot, but I'd feel even worse if there was something wrong with this shipment and I didn't even check into it. I'm working days this week, so how about you join Maria and me for dinner at the apartment tomorrow night? Then we can drive over to the harbor together. You see, it was a dinner invitation after all."

~ * ~

The Port of Rotterdam, the Netherlands
Tuesday, August 31, 1993
11:45 p.m.

Erich was simply introduced to the security guard on duty as Thomas's brother, here to see the workings of the harbor and the large ships—nothing more than a personal guided tour.

Both men walked up the narrow staircase to the second floor office that looked out over the docks. Thomas went directly to a gray, four-drawer file cabinet and extracted a thin manila file folder labeled "Estrella de Bolivar, V54E. He turned toward the window and pointed to a navy and white vessel on pier number five, not half as large as any of the other freighters and container ships in port. He turned off the lights in that part of the office so they could get a better view without the glare and light reflection on the plate glass window, but also to avoid looking too conspicuous staring out at the ship sailing under the flag of Venezuela.

The ship had docked at 9:35. Most of the mooring tasks had been taken care of, and only a few of the crew could be seen scampering across the width of the deck. It appeared they were securing the large, double-wide hinged doors in the center of the deck, forward and aft. These were obviously the hatches that the cargo was dumped into and pumped or lifted out of.

"When will they off-load the grain?" asked Erich.

Thomas checked the file again. "Let's see…they have already paid for dock time from 8:00 p.m. today through 8:00 p.m. tomorrow. That is considerably more time than what they should really need for this size vessel. That's a little unusual, too. But to answer your question, I think they would begin off-loading around eight in the morning. They could have the job done by noon or one o'clock if they're efficient."

"Can we get a closer look from the dock?" requested Erich.

"Sure, follow me," responded Thomas enthusiastically.

"Let's first look at some of the other ships farther down the dock," said Erich, "and then come back to the Estrella."

Thomas nodded in agreement and led the way out into the damp night air.

After walking the length of the well-lit dock and casually observing three other vessels, the two brothers came to the Estrella de Bolivar. Erich was somewhat disappointed. He couldn't see anything out of place that even hinted there might be something illegal on board. They couldn't board the ship, and that made it impossible to do a proper search. They walked slowly past the rickety retractable ladder the crew would use to gain access or disembark the ship. Erich wondered just how stable this ladder actually was. It didn't look like it could hold more than two or three men at a time, but that was far from his real concern. Erich also thought that by now the sailors from the ship were out tearing up the city of Rotterdam. If Rotterdam was the least bit similar to any other port cities, the crew would be in no condition to sail by noon tomorrow.

Thomas scowled and shook his head. "I'm sorry to have brought you here on such a wild goose chase, bro."

"Well, I didn't expect to see the crew and dockhands hauling off bails of processed heroin or cocaine in neat little packages wrapped in plastic, did you?"

"No, I suppose not. What now, Erich?"

"We should go back to the apartment, get some sleep, and come back here around 6:00 a.m. to watch them unload this thing. I'd rather be early and have to wait than miss something interesting. Who knows; maybe we'll get lucky," Erich said in an effort to comfort Thomas, who was beginning to feel like a fool.

When they drove out of the yard, they had to wait briefly for a large mobile crane to make the turn into the enormous shipping complex. Erich cursed the driver as he nearly clipped the front bumper of his treasured Mercedes.

~ * ~

Wednesday, September 1, 1993
6:00 a.m

.

Thomas's shift did not start until eight, but he needed and wanted to accompany his brother. By 6:00 a.m., activity around the dock was in full swing. Container trucks were pulling out, and crews and dock workers were busy on the ship's deck, beginning to put equipment in place for off-loading the grain. The trucks to receive the grain were in a marshaling area, waiting for instructions to pull alongside for their cargo.

"It looks like they started earlier than I expected. I hope we didn't miss anything," said Thomas.

Taking up the tail end of a small procession of twenty-foot containers was a mobile crane just like the one they had narrowly avoided the night before, now heading away from the complex.

Mueller parked the car, and they walked immediately toward the Estrella de Bolivar, careful to stay clear of the men and equipment moving about. Thomas pointed out the vacuum mechanism used to off load the grain, which was just now being put in place, so chances were good that nothing had been missed up till this point. As they approached the ship, Erich noticed something at the base of the retractable ladder he had not seen the night before.

Stuck on the navy blue hull was a small vinyl-coated sign that simply read "Jax" in green and gold letters outlined in red. Upon closer inspection, the men realized it was actually a bumper sticker! "This wasn't here last night, was it?" asked Erich.

"No, I don't believe it was. I'm sure we would have noticed it," Thomas responded.

Erich stood on the first step of the ladder, just in front of the light chain that supported the makeshift cardboard sign that read "DO NOT ENTER" in black felt-tip marker. He bent down and rubbed his fingers across the surface of the Jax bumper sticker. It was slimy; a thin coat of oily residue covered the surface of the four-by-nine sticker.

"Jax! What is Jax?" Thomas asked in almost a whisper.

"This is where my college education really pays off. Once on spring break, some of the other soccer players and I went to New Orleans, down in the state of Louisiana. Jax, my dear brother, is a beer. Not a very good-tasting beer, but nevertheless a very popular beer in New Orleans. I even remember seeing a large gray building in the French Quarter with the name Jax in huge red letters near the top. I think it was, at one time, the actual brewery, but it had been converted into a tourist attraction with a lot of shops and restaurants."

"I always knew it was important you went to the States for your university education. Did you major in beer and minor in women?" chided Thomas.

"No, of course not. I carried a double major," responded Erich, causing both men to smile.

"Americans are big on bumper stickers, Thomas. You can often tell their life stories from what is pasted on their car bumpers and in their back windows. You can tell if the person works for a trade union, if he owns a dog, if he believes in Jesus, and who his favorite sports teams are. It's remarkable!"

"Well, then, I suppose you can also tell what kind of beer he drinks, too," replied Thomas.

A puzzled look came across Erich's face. "Hey wait a minute! We might just have something here."

Erich reached down again and felt the hull with a flat hand. He withdrew it with disgust, observing the oily slime on his hand.

"We didn't see this sticker last night because it was under the water line. They *have* off-loaded *something* from this ship! Something heavy enough to displace this much water." Erich demonstrated by extending his arms about three and a half feet from top to bottom.

"If they're just now taking off the grain, what could they have unloaded earlier?" Erich asked himself as well as Thomas, not really expecting an answer.

As if in a movie flashback, Mueller pictured the large yellow mobile crane that had nearly hit him when they were pulling out onto the highway last night. He also vaguely remembered seeing one leave only a few minutes ago. He grabbed Thomas by the arm and said, "That guy in the crane that almost ran into us last night; can they unload large cargo?"

"Yeah, sure. They use them mostly to move twenty-foot containers, nothing larger than that," answered Thomas.

"Let's go! Remember the twenty-footers leaving as we were coming in? And the crane?"

Erich began to sprint across the parking area to the car, with Thomas trying to catch up. He fired up the Mercedes E300 and drove to the main highway, but there was no sign of the small convoy they had passed when heading in. It was a fifty-fifty guess as to which direction they might have gone. Erich turned right, hitting 120 kilometers per hour in no time flat. Then he noticed to his right a fenced-in yard that contained possibly fifteen to twenty yellow mobile cranes. Any one of these could be the crane he was looking for. They were like large insects just coming out of a larva. Mueller slowed down to eighty. This was virtually a dead-end.

He turned the Mercedes around and took off in the opposite direction, hoping to pick up the convoy. Nothing on the road; not yet. Just then he could barely make out what looked like the back end of a container. Mueller slammed on the gas to catch up with the vehicle about one half mile ahead, causing the g-force to press him and his brother firmly to the backs of their seats. It was a container! As he accelerated again to pass it and to see if the others were ahead of him on this perfectly straight stretch of highway, he could clearly see it was a forty-footer, and no other containers were on the road ahead. *Damn!*

Mueller also noticed that in all of the freight yards on both sides of the highway, there were literally tens of thousands of containers: twenty-footers, forty-footers, some on chassis, but most stacked one on top of the other, five or six high. It was now apparent he was looking for the proverbial needle in a haystack.

Thomas could see the disgusted look on Erich's face. It was the same face he'd seen so many times while fishing. It was the "big one that got away" look, but much more serious. Again, Erich geared down dramatically. Thomas said, "You know, Erich, I don't think they would be smuggling drugs in twenty-foot containers."

Once the idea of containers being taken off the ship sometime between one o'clock and five thirty in the morning had sunk in, Erich was no longer thinking about drugs. He was now thinking in terms of heavy equipment; possibly weapons. This was e*xactly* part of his assignment, and he might have stumbled onto something. They cruised back to the Flatworld office.

By this time, it was almost eight o'clock, and Thomas needed to take his post at the large metal desk. Erich pulled an old straight back wooden chair next to the desk. He couldn't tell his brother he was looking for weapons for a possible communist uprising. He had to pursue this under the auspices of hunting for smuggled drugs.

"I'm wondering about that Jax sticker," he told Thomas. "If this ship sailed from Miami, Florida, why would it have a Jax Beer bumper sticker slapped on its hull? To my knowledge, Jax is only sold in the New Orleans market these days."

Erich sat quietly for a while, contemplating his only clue up to this point. His thoughts kept returning to the scene he recalled in the French

Quarter, standing opposite Jackson Square, between Café Du Monde and the Jax Brewery building. Freighters plied this wide part of the Mississippi River, and a calliope blasted its shrill notes in puffs of white steam. Crowds of people clogged the street and sidewalks, carrying their drinks in their hands, most having had more than enough to drink and some even having trouble negotiating the curb and other obstacles like benches and light posts. *People having fun, enjoying their holiday. Jax Brewery, a tourist spot right there on the river. Restaurants, bars, souvenir shops with all sorts of trinkets and trash. Bumper stickers?* Erich thought to himself, *Sure, why not?*

Now Mueller could begin to picture a ship's crew arriving in the port after a lengthy voyage across the Atlantic, or possibly just up from the Caribbean or the Gulf of Mexico. *Hmm...possibilities. Would these sailors spend their pay and precious limited time on women and booze?* Well that was a given, ever since the first vessel had crossed a body of water. Sailors also probably blew their money on useless little souvenirs in the ports they visited, something of a reminder of the city. *Jax Beer? Jax Brewery? Yeah, sure, why not?* This could make sense.

After a long silence, Erich asked Thomas, "You're sure this ship sailed from the Port of Miami and not from somewhere else?"

"Yeah, of course, it's written right here on all of the documents," Thomas said, tapping the manila folder with his finger. "Why do you ask?"

"I'm thinking this boat sailed from New Orleans, not Miami."

Now it was Thomas's turn to pause and rock back in his swivel chair, cradling his chin in his left hand. "Two obvious possibilities come to mind. A: their previous port of call was New Orleans; or B: the documents were altered, which might explain why the documents were in such perfect order."

"Or there might even be a possible C: both of the above," Erich added.

"Yes, that's a possibility, too. A little 'misdirection' to throw someone off track."

Erich Mueller merely nodded his head in agreement.

~ * ~

By 10:45, the Estrella de Bolivar was completely void of its cargo of grain. This was indicated by the water displacement level on the side of the vessel. Thomas and Erich looked on from the second-story window.

"We need to board that ship and give it a firsthand inspection," Erich said in a low voice. "Any suggestions?"

Before Thomas could reply, Erich asked, "What about a safety inspection? Surely there must be some provisions for things like that."

Thomas stepped quickly to the nearest phone on an unoccupied desk. Taped to the phone, next to the speed dial numbers, were several typewritten phone numbers. Near the top of the list was the number for the Harbor Environmental Safety Agency. He tapped out the numbers on the push-button phone and held up one finger, indicating Erich should wait a moment.

Upon hearing the greeting from the other end, Thomas introduced himself properly to the authorities and said he had noticed what appeared to be an oil leak coming from one of the ships at their docking facility. He suggested politely that it would probably be wise to have someone come straight away, if possible, to have a look at this potential environmental hazard, because the vessel was scheduled to sail some time before sundown. Thomas knew full well they would be there within the hour to check out the water near the ship and basically snoop around and make a fuss in the name of world ecology.

"Next," he said, "we have to create a little oil slick of our own. Give the harbor safety people something to look at. Follow me."

After dashing down the steps, they slowed their pace when exiting the door, careful of attracting any unnecessary attention. Thomas appropriated a hand truck with two small forks and a concave back. Now a man with a mission, Thomas guided the two-wheeler to an area with several thirty-gallon drums. Asking his brother for some assistance in tilting the edge of one of the drums slightly off the surface of the concrete dock, he slid the forks under the drum and cradled it in the contour of the hand truck.

Thomas wheeled it with ease between a small dockside fire station and a large coil of fire hose affixed to a sturdy light standard. This gave just enough cover to avoid being seen from the office building or either end of the dock. The only real threat was possible observation from the deck of the Estrella de Bolivar, which only afforded a limited view, or from someone traversing the dock directly behind them. Those were good enough odds.

Pushing the drum almost to the edge, Thomas said to his brother, "Wait here."

He returned in a few moments with a wrench-type apparatus. Bending down to the bottom of the drum, he fitted the hex wrench around the plug screw and applied some pressure. Immediately, black lubricating oil poured out and over the edge of the dock and into the harbor.

"I *really* hate to do it this way. This water here is bad enough as it is, but I can't think of any other better options right now."

They stood there leaning against the fire shed, talking and acting as casual as they could, hoping no one would notice this flagrant violation against Mother Nature.

Five minutes later, the drum was drained. Again, Thomas tilted back on the handles and wheeled the empty drum back to its original location. He returned with several large shop rags to mop what little oil had dripped onto the dock. No sooner had Thomas and Erich disposed of the oily shop rags and gone back to the Flatworld office, than a twenty-six-foot craft that could have been mistaken for a police boat pulled alongside. An overly energetic young officer who looked like the pride of the Dutch Navy stepped smartly from the deck in the direction of the office structure. Thomas intercepted him just before he reached the door.

"I am the person who called in to report the oil leak. It seems it's gotten worse. If you'll come with me, please, I'll show you. Oh, excuse me, this is my supervisor, Mr. Van Hooten."

Erich, picking up on Thomas's lead, smiled and extended his hand to the harbor safety officer saying, "We are *very* concerned about our harbor. Thanks to good people like Mueller here, maybe we can help solve this appalling violation of our waterways. We would like to accompany you on your inspection of this vessel." Erich paused. "After all, this is our docking facility."

"Of course, Mr. Van Hooten, let's proceed without further delay," said the uniformed young man.

The three walked briskly over to the Estrella de Bolivar and bounded up the weather- worn retractable ladder. They were met at the top by the ship's first mate.

The HESA officer explained the suspected infraction and pointed over the starboard side to the narrow space between the ship's hull and the dock, to the black and rainbow effect the oil played on the surface of the water.

The first mate was reluctant to have them board, much less inspect his vessel. He explained that the captain had gone ashore and he was not at liberty to let them inspect the ship without him. But on second thought, he reasoned it might be better to go along with the wishes of these harbor officials to minimize the present and any future hassles he and his crew would encounter while in the confines of the Port of Rotterdam. And besides, the secret cargo, whatever it was, was gone now, so why not?

"Okay, I'll take you below, and you can see for yourself there are no oil leaks coming from this ship."

He led them to the large hatch in the forward portion of the ship and proceeded down a removable ladder into the main cargo hold. A terrific amount of dust and residue from the hulls of the soy beans had settled on the floor. Nothing looked outwardly suspicious to Thomas in this spacious, empty cargo hold. Two teams of three men were sweeping and shoveling the remaining grain that could not be sucked up by the vacuums into two large wooden boxes.

"We run a very clean ship, as you can see," said the first mate to his three visitors.

"I am primarily interested in your fuel supply at this time, not the cleanliness of your cargo holds," the safety officer said, making a weak attempt to sound like the voice of authority. "I assume it is amid ship?"

"Yes, sir, it is. This way, please."

Back up the ladder they climbed to the main deck, and then they descended fewer steps on a permanent ladder into the engine room. The first mate indicated that the fuel was contained in large storage tanks fore and aft, with another directly below the grating they were standing on.

"There is no direct access to the fuel from here, of course, but you can inspect the fuel intake valve here." The seasoned sailor pointed to a conglomeration of pipes, valves, and hoses.

"The fuel is fed from here into these diesel engines here and here," he said, pointing port and starboard. He took a flashlight from a bulkhead rack and shone the beam in all of the dark areas between the tightly fitted machinery.

The HESA officer peered eagerly, following the light. He shook his head, almost seemingly disappointed in not finding even a trace of leaking oil.

"Outside of ordering a complete hull inspection from the exterior, your ship seems to be quite fit," the officer said. "I will make note to follow in your wake as you leave the harbor in order to determine if in fact the oil is trailing from this vessel. When do you plan to shove off?"

"Before 1800 hours, I would suspect. We're waiting to take on more provisions, which should arrive any time now," answered the first mate.

The young officer, satisfied with the interior inspection, thanked the first mate for his cooperation and moved back up the ladder to the main deck. He took a quick look over the port side of the ship and made his way back down the retractable ladder to the dock. Erich and Thomas followed.

"We will follow up on this," the officer said, "and thank you for alerting us to this problem."

With something that resembled a hand salute, he bounded gracefully back to the deck of the cruiser that carefully and immediately pulled away.

As the brothers walked back toward the entrance of Flatworld-Rotterdam, Thomas grumbled, "Damn. Nothing!"

"Not necessarily so, my bro." Erich allowed a little smile. "Did you notice the pieces of angle iron welded to the floor of the forward cargo hold? Did you notice the welds looked to be newer and a lot less rusty than the rest of the fittings on the walls and the overhead?"

Not waiting for Thomas to answer, he said, "And did you notice those angle iron brackets were placed at exactly ninety-degree angles to one another?"

Erich flopped down on the wooden chair next to Thomas's desk. He closed his eyes to allow his brain to process what few bits and pieces of information he felt were of any consequence.

"What are you telling me, Erich?" Thomas shook his head.

The older brother got up and walked over to the window. He studied the Estrella de Bolivar for a minute or two and then replied, "I'm saying that I think those sections of angle iron were placed there for a specific reason: to keep twenty-foot containers from shifting from side to side and front to back while in transit. When we were in that forward cargo hold, I tried to visualize the space it would take for four twenty-footers, grouped together two by two, and I think they would fit. They could be lifted out through the overhead hatches easily enough with one of those mobile cranes we saw. Right?"

"Right."

"And can we assume that the aft cargo hold could be fitted similarly to the forward hold?"

"Yeah, I'd say that's a pretty safe bet," responded Thomas as he watched one of the office clerks lay some paperwork in his "incoming" tray.

Thomas smiled and thanked the young girl, then casually reached across his desk for the new file and began to read.

"Will you look at this!" he exclaimed, as he walked to the window and handed the documents over to his brother. "Looks like we've got an identical shipment to the Estrella."

Thomas immediately went to the file cabinet and pulled out V54E.

The two compared the docs side by side. Sure enough, every detail of the second shipment was identical to the first. Only the name of the vessel—the Margarita Brissa —along with the voyage number and the ship dates were different. Tonnage, cargo, and special off-loading instructions were exactly the same.

"Well now, this *is* interesting," Erich said as he digested this latest information. These new shipping documents seemed to bring it all together. He recalled a "flash report" from NSA-HQ sometime last month about some nuke-tipped weapons missing from an Army base in the States, but he couldn't remember all of the details. He'd need to check this out with Talbot as soon as possible.

One part of him wanted to share his ideas with Thomas, but he knew professionally that he needed to leave his brother in the dark from this point forward. He could have no further involvement. All of a sudden, in Erich Mueller's mind, the stakes had just been increased exponentially. If this tip netted any big fish, he would have his brother to thank.

"Thomas, whether you realize it or not, you've given me a great deal of information that I'll need to follow up on right away. Sorry to leave in such a hurry, but this stuff never waits."

As they walked back out to Erich's car, the older Mueller said, "I'm going to report what we've seen to my supervisors and wait for further instructions."

Erich extended his right hand, saying, "Thanks for your help, Thomas. Who knows, maybe we might be able to break something up. It might be something big, and then again it might not be anything at all. But you never know until you track it down, right?"

The brothers embraced, patting each other firmly on the back. As Thomas bounded back up the stairway, two steps at a time, a smile of satisfaction crossed his face. He felt he had certainly done his good deed for mankind today. Shuffling documents was definitely going to seem dull from here on out.

Chapter Sixteen

Once out of the Flatworld facility, Erich Mueller drove directly to the NSA's Benelux listening post, fortunately also in Rotterdam, and placed a call to Henry Talbot. Mueller gave a detailed report, leaving nothing out.

"So, Hank, what do you think? Can you find the copy of that 'flash report' about the missing weapons from a military base? Do you think we might have something here?"

Talbot, who was already sorting through a thick stack of fax messages beginning August first, responded, "You might, Erich; you just might. Hold on a second; I'm looking. I also recall that same report just a few weeks ago about some nuke-tipped missiles and several prototype Army vehicles reported missing from Fort Hood. Ah, here we go. This one dated August 11, 1993, says 'Sixteen M-5 launch vehicles and forty-eight XG-777 missiles missing from Fort Hood, Texas; believed to be armed with W-79 low-yield nuclear warheads. No further details available at this time.' I'm thinking one of these launch vehicles could possibly fit in a twenty-foot container. I have no real reason to believe these M-5s and the XG-777s were on this boat in Rotterdam or that there might be an additional shipment of the same weapons preparing to ship, but I think the whole thing smells like dead fish. I think it could possibly be too big to ignore, don't you?"

"That's exactly what I'm thinking."

"Do you feel your hunch about New Orleans is strong enough to pursue it?" asked Talbot.

"Yeah, I do."

"Okay, then. Drive on up to Amsterdam, stay the night, book yourself on the first flight to New Orleans, and check it out. We'll probably be blasted for wasting man hours and money, but I'd rather be criticized for that than have General Chesnokov show up with a bunch of U.S.-made nukes and their high-tech delivery systems. Call me when you get to New Orleans, all right?"

~ * ~

Thursday, September 2, 1993

Delta Airlines flight #239 from Amsterdam's Schiphol International Airport flew nonstop to Hartsfield International in Atlanta. Mueller had an hour and a half layover before his connecting flight to New Orleans, certainly plenty of time for a cold beer and a hot dog. He wasn't really hungry or in need of a drink; he just needed to kill some time and to think.

He rehashed again in his mind, making notes on a cocktail napkin, the little information he had to go on and reconfirmed to himself he had to follow his gut feeling and pursue this investigation instinctively. If he waited for all of the facts, nine times out of ten, the bad guys would be long gone. He had explained everything to Talbot by means of a secure phone line that linked their Amsterdam counterpart to Munich. Mueller had left with Talbot's approval and a cooperative attitude adjustment from the Dutch sector, once he had explained how this situation came about through his brother and not wanting to call alarm to something that did not appear to be of much significance at the time. The fact that Talbot's jurisdiction also covered the Netherlands and that Mueller seemed to be his fair-haired boy weighed heavily upon the relatively light tongue-lashing he received from the Dutch section chief for infringing on their turf. They agreed to watch for the convoy of a possible eight twenty-foot containers (although according to the section chief, this would be a complete exercise in futility in an area that depends on about ninety percent of its income from the transportation of oceangoing cargo) and to track the whereabouts of the Estrella de Bolivar.

The announcement was made for Delta flight #1033 to New Orleans. Boarding the aircraft, Mueller was pumped up and eager to get into this assignment. There was just something about New Orleans. Was it the perpetual party atmosphere or was it the European flavor that set it apart from other American cities? He settled back in window seat 18A and enjoyed the moment, for he knew from experience this could well be the quiet before the storm.

~ * ~

New Orleans, Louisiana
Thursday, September 2, 1993

The Crescent City was predictably hot and sticky. After a quick change in the Delta Sky Club, from his one piece of carry-on luggage, Mueller was dressed for the climate. He did not have the appearance of a businessman nor did he ever wish to look like a government agent. If any label could be pinned to him, it would be that of a typical twenty-seven-year-old American, young successful professional: sun glasses, a yellow oxford shirt with sleeves slightly rolled at the cuff, Dockers khaki shorts, and brown Birkenstock sandals.

Immediately after his brief visit to the Sky Club, Mueller found his way to the airport security office to claim a small package about the size of a flattened shoe box, wrapped in plain brown paper. He said nothing to the officer behind the counter, but simply produced his government ID, his gun permit, and the claim check with the corresponding numbers to the package. Receiving the package about ten minutes later, because no one is in a hurry in New Orleans, he thanked the officer, tossed the parcel into his carry-on bag, and was on his way.

"The French Quarter, please," he told the taxi driver.

As the taxi was exiting I10/Hwy 90 onto South Claiborne near the Superdome, the driver inquired politely, "To what hotel, sir?"

Mueller had purposely not made a reservation, wanting to find the best vantage point near the Mississippi to observe as much river traffic as possible.

"Ah, the Royal Sonesta," was his delayed response.

From the Royal Sonesta on Bourbon Street, he would check his bag with the bell captain and proceed on foot to locate the best room with a view. Erich Mueller tipped the bell captain well to help ensure his belongings would be held in safe keeping, even for just this short period.

"Well, thank you, sir. I'll take real good care of this for you," said the white-haired black man.

Mueller turned right from the front entrance, then down St. Louis Street and past Pat O'Brien's toward the river. *Yes, this is definitely New Orleans,* he thought. He smiled inwardly as he recognized that distinct, unmistakable aroma which seemed to be unique to the Vieux Carré. It was nice to be back, even if only on business.

Just upstream from the old, historic French Market area was the Governor Nicholls Street Wharf. Mueller walked along the red brick "Moon Walk" parallel to the Mississippi. He paid more attention to the string of old French buildings laced with black wrought iron balconies that lined Decatur Street than he did to the traffic on the river. There would be plenty of time for that later.

Mueller noticed a four-story building that had good potential, but there was no indication it was a hotel. Upon closer inspection, he could see heavy velvet curtains on the windows and modest glass or crystal chandeliers. He rounded the corner at Ursuline and Chartres and saw the vertical sign that read "Hotel Provincial." *Now let's hope they have an upper-story room facing the river,* he thought as he lightly tapped the bell on the registrar's counter.

Luck was with him so far. Indeed a room on the fourth floor would be ideal, perfect for his observations. This particular building, one of about four that constituted the Provincial, was probably well over one hundred fifty years old, with twelve-foot ceilings and heavy wood-framed windows that lifted open, unlike most modern hotel windows. The most important advantage was that one could see clearly from the Governor Nicholls Street Wharf all the way to the Trade Mart building about a mile downstream. This would not be a textbook stakeout by any means. *No,* thought Mueller, *this will be more of a scavenger hunt for clues.*

On his way back to the Royal Sonesta, Mueller decided he might as well treat himself to at least one good meal before he assumed his position at his observation post at the Hotel Provincial; a fabric-upholstered chair near the window. There would be a steady diet of room service food for the duration of this project. He could always call out for pizza, of course, but that would be a crime in a city which claims fame for so many of its world-renowned restaurants.

An early dinner at Tujague's was undeniably one of the best culinary pleasures to be found in the French Quarter, with six courses of the finest traditional Creole food Erich Mueller had ever experienced, capped off with several cups of chicory coffee. Mueller figured he could use plenty of this high-octane stuff to keep him alert during his vigil.

The elderly bell captain, still on duty at the Royal Sonesta, greeted Mueller with a smile and retrieved his bag without ever asking for a claim ticket. He seemed puzzled when Mueller refused his offer to take the luggage to the room and instead headed for the door and hopped into a waiting taxi. *Better take a cab, even though it's only a few blocks,* he thought. *Nobody walks down Bourbon Street carrying their luggage.*

Mueller unpacked his bag, took a cool shower to rejuvenate, and pulled up the padded chair to the window. A pair of Bushnell 20x50 binoculars and a 35mm Nikon F90 equipped with a 35-70mm f/2.8AF zoom lens were placed on the small wooden table at his right side. Before Mueller got settled into position, he brought the telephone within reach and unwrapped his brown paper package. His Beretta 92F was nestled in the neatly cut foam rubber, along with three fully loaded 9mm magazines, also fitted into cut-out sections. Picking out one magazine and inspecting it briefly, he tapped it home into the handle of the gun, chambered the first round, and double-checked that the safety was on. Mueller added this to the other tools of his trade on the small mahogany table. He didn't really expect anything to happen that would warrant the use of the 9mm, but he knew he had to be prepared for anything at any time.

Mueller picked up the phone to check in with his boss, Hank Talbot. It was the middle of the night in Munich, but his instructions were to report in when he was set up. Mueller also wanted to know if the Amsterdam office had found out any more info on the Estrella and if any of the containers had shown up.

A groggy Talbot answered his personal line, and it took a few seconds before he could clear out the cobwebs. "This better be good," Talbot answered, skipping the conventional "Hello."

"Mueller here, Chief." The crisp voice was almost more than Talbot could bear at three thirty in the morning. Talbot cringed and forced himself to sit upright, gradually regaining his faculties.

"Did I wake you?" Mueller was enjoying this.

"Oh, hell no; I always get up at oh-three-something for no good reason." Talbot's voice quickly became all business. "What's up? Find anything?"

"No, not yet. I just got set up. I'm at the Hotel Provincial, with a room overlooking the Mississippi River." Mueller gave Talbot a few more details: room number, phone number, etc.

"Did you hear anything from Holland yet?" Mueller asked, knowing this would be much too soon for any answers unless they just happened to locate the containers.

"No news here. I'll call if I hear anything," said Talbot.

"Thanks. You can go back to sleep now."

"Yeah, right," grumbled Talbot, "and thanks for the wake-up call. I might have overslept till five." He hung up and headed for the shower, shaking his head.

~ * ~

The Governor Nicholls Street Wharf was not equipped for the largest ocean vessels, but then again, it would certainly be accessible by the Estrella de Bolivar or a ship similar in size, within the parameters set by the industrial port authority.

The late evening and early morning hours passed quickly enough. Erich Mueller sat comfortably in his ornately decorated padded chair, feet propped up on a matching ottoman, watching people stroll up and down Decatur Street. *Such a wide variety of people*, he thought, from teenagers to the elderly "blue hairs," tourists, conventioneers, locals, and, of course, plenty of "women of the evening" working the street corners.

The one specific group of people he was looking for—civilian sailors—was not among the throng that plied the street below. Erich began to question his hunch, but soon reminded himself that nothing ever happens right away, at least not on the first night. He almost felt guilty for creating such a cushy assignment for himself. He sat back and listened to the enjoyable variety of sounds coming through the open window. The open-air street-side club directly across the street featured a typical Dixieland jazz band with a male vocalist who tried to sound like Louis Armstrong and did a pretty good job of it. One of the excursion boats coming back from a late-night outing, probably a charter cruise, was blasting away on a steam calliope. The clip-clop of horse-drawn carriages was also a very familiar sound within the Vieux Carré.

As the sun began to rise, Mueller called for room service: coffee with chicory, two scrambled eggs, fried potatoes, country ham, rye toast with butter on the side, and an order of grits. Not the typical German breakfast he was brought up on, but what the hell. *When in Rome, do as the Romans, right?*

Over breakfast, he decided it would be wise to take advantage of a little modern technology for the surveillance aspect of his mission. Reaching for the yellow pages, he looked under "camera equipment." One ad read, "All the latest in VCR and mini camcorders in stock. 515 Canal Street. Open 9:00 AM – 6:00 PM. *That'll work for me,* Mueller thought.

He preferred working alone, but realized it did have its drawbacks. There was no way he could stay at the window around the clock to watch and wait. Leaving Europe in a hurry, without any real preparation for the mission, was going to present some problems. Mueller had anticipated that. He had not had the option of bringing some of the company-owned high-tech video and surveillance equipment. He would just have to get creative and do the best with the materials available to him.

Canal Street was within easy walking distance from the Hotel Provincial. Erich Mueller strolled leisurely along the Riverwalk and turned right. Several blocks up on Canal, he found the camera store and had to wait a couple of minutes for the nine o'clock opening. Once inside, he made his selections quickly: the latest offering from Sony, a VCR camcorder with built-in digital display, instant replay features, and a fast forward/fast rewind system with excellent clarity and a wide angle lens setting; a tripod; carrying cases for both the camera and the tripod; and two blank VCR tapes of the best quality.

Only a few doors down from the camera store stood the New Orleans landmark, Maison Blanche Department Store. Erich decided it might be wise to add a few articles of clothing that would benefit his mission. Nothing fancy, just a few things to help him blend into his surroundings, and definitely some dark and flexible clothing for his late-night reconnaissance.

Mueller was back at the Provincial by 9:55 a.m. and had all of the new equipment set up within fifteen minutes. With the camcorder set on the slowest speed, he could record six hours of activity, or four hours with better clarity. *Better to go with the higher level of clarity*, he reasoned. It would be much easier to watch in fast-forward mode when reviewing the tape. He sure couldn't afford to miss anything.

Erich stood by the window, watching and thinking. Some river traffic, mostly barges, one huge freighter sailing under the flag of Japan, and an automobile ferry that was perpetually traversing the wide Mississippi. He looked toward the left at the Governor Nicholls Street Wharf. Still not a soul around he could see from his vantage point. *Might as well see if I can get a little closer and take a better look while I have the time.*

Under the watchful eye of the video camera with its wide angle lens, nothing would be missed. The camcorder was set on the intermediate speed; that gave Mueller four hours. He checked his watch, stuck the semi-automatic in the small nylon holster concealed inside the waistband of his trousers, and left his shirt untucked to drape over the bulge of the 9mm. He would need to be back by about one fifty. He hung the "Do Not Disturb" sign on the knob and closed the door behind him.

Approaching the wharf, Mueller noticed a few people coming and going from the northeast entrance of this colossal warehouse building. There were four or five empty flatbed cars sitting idly on the railroad siding running along the eastern edge of the building. His vision was limited on the river side of the warehouse. An eight-foot cyclone fence with barbed wire strung across the top halted his progress.

Mid-morning was hardly the best time to jump the fence and clip the barbed strands of wire. Mueller decided to take advantage of the daylight for reconnaissance and get in as close as possible. He needed to know positioning of doors and windows, types of locks, blind spots to hide in, surveillance equipment, traces of guard dogs, and especially an escape route if things got out of hand. He knew he should be prepared for any and all things. Tonight, he thought, he would definitely be back to check things out more thoroughly.

Mueller casually approached an unattended guard shack, observing the surrounding area the whole time, taking it all in and committing it to memory. Once in front of the guard shack and the locked gate, he sensed he was being watched. He pulled out a small slip of paper from his pocket, as if to check the address. He looked up at the number above the door on the building, shook his head in mock disgust, shrugged his shoulders slightly, and turned and walked in the opposite direction. The only thing he didn't do was smile and wave for the surveillance cameras.

Once back on Decatur Street, Erich Mueller felt the urge to reconfirm his original idea that only hinted New Orleans was the port of origin for the

Estrella de Bolivar. He was basically betting the farm on the one small hunch: the Jax Beer bumper sticker affixed to the hull of the small cargo ship. If he could just find a sticker like the one he saw in Rotterdam, he could be rid of this nagging negative feeling he had regarding chasing ghosts that didn't exist. Naturally, Mueller headed directly toward the large gray Jax building, catty-corner from Jackson Square. *One of the more obvious havens for visitors and tourists,* he reasoned.

As expected, Mueller found snack bars, restaurants, a lot of souvenir shops, and several clothing boutiques. He worked his way down from the top floor, exhausting every shop that could possibly sell bumper stickers. He literally found hundreds of various stickers, commenting on everything imaginable. Some were pretty clever, but none of them even suggested Jax Beer. He left, disgusted with himself for even traveling to this city. The term "wild goose chase" kept creeping back into his head. He knew full well that's what he would hear repeatedly from Talbot. He also anticipated bearing the brunt of choosing this popular, colorful travel destination as a mini vacation, a few days of R&R. Mueller wasn't like that, and he would very much resent any such innuendo to that effect.

Walking back to the Hotel Provincial, Mueller was lured into a shop on Decatur Street called "Aunt Sally's" by the fantastic aroma of molasses, brown sugar, butter, vanilla, and pecans all melded together and poured onto a long, marble cooling slab. Mueller found it too hard to resist in his present state of funk. *What did they call those things?* It took a few seconds for him to remember. *Pralines!* The sweet smell of this confection had to be the best form of advertising to attract customers in from the street, he thought. Although terribly fattening and of very little nutritional value, Erich Mueller succumbed to the temptation and ordered a box of three of these little New Orleans delicacies.

While waiting for the shop clerk to ring up the sale, Mueller was struck by a bolt from out of the blue. Directly behind the counter he saw them: a whole stack of green and gold bumper stickers with the single word "Jax" outlined in red. Without looking up, the young woman behind the counter asked, "Will that be all for you, sir?" She received no response, because the man was already out the door, forgetting completely about the pralines lying on the counter top.

The bounce had returned to Erich's step as he crossed Decatur to the Provincial. Still not enough to get excited about or to bother Talbot with, but it was enough to rekindle his own interest. *Still nothing more than a hunch,* he kept reminding himself.

In his room overlooking the riverscape of New Orleans, Mueller first took a quick glance out the window to see if anything was happening on the waterfront. Nothing new or unusual. He then sat down, rewound the tape in the video camera to the beginning, and started to watch it on fast forward. He saw himself dash over to the large green metal warehouse building, round the corner, and, within seconds, come scampering back along the moonwalk and out of the picture again. About one minute later, still on the fast-forward setting, a relatively small navy blue and white cargo ship came into view, entering from the right side of the display screen. "Whoa, what is *this*?" the NSA investigator exclaimed out loud, jumping up to set the speed back to normal. If a ship could have a twin, this was it: identical in size, shape, and color to the Estrella de Bolivar!

He watched with great intensity as the vessel moved from the right side of the wide channel in a sweeping motion, like a big U-turn, just beyond the Governor Nicholls Street Wharf. At that point, the view of the ship was obscured by the warehouse, to where only the two gantry towers protruded above the building. Mueller looked away from the video again and looked out toward the wharf, and this time he did indeed notice the tips of the gantry towers. He rewound the tape and watched it again, this time on the slow setting. It was impossible to read the name painted on the bow or the stern. Erich figured he must have just missed seeing the ship as he entered the Jax building.

Now he felt he was gaining some ground. Time for another walk. Not intending to have a perfect disguise or to become invisible, Mueller changed from the navy blue collared shirt he had worn in the morning to a white Nike T-shirt, and from long trousers to khaki shorts and sandals. He added sunglasses and a Cleveland Indians baseball cap, hoping to not be recognized as the same person who had been snooping around earlier in the day.

Ever so casually, he made his way through the old French Market toward the wharf. He purchased an apple from one of the open-air market vendors and polished it on his shirt as he walked north of the wharf building. Mueller could now confirm the ship was, in fact, the Margarita Brissa, sailing under the flag of Venezuela. *This means nothing,* he told himself. *There have to be several hundred of these ships registered through the Venezuelan government.*

Okay, maybe that was something.

He noticed the empty flatbed cars on the rail siding were still in the same position as before, and now four barges were moored directly upstream from the wharf. Nothing unusual about this. Barges were scattered all up and down the river. Erich found a park bench with part of the morning paper folded neatly at the end. Chomping away at his apple, he sat down, picked up the newspaper, and gave every impression he was actually reading it. His attention went back to the nearby barges. Hundreds of birds—probably some type of gull—were congregating all around the domed fiberglass coverings that protected the cargo. *The barges must be full, based on their waterline. And the cargo?* The question didn't linger very long. Since it was attracting all of these birds, it had to be grain. *Of course.*

Water levels seemed to be the key. Mueller observed that the Margarita Brissa sat high in the water, obviously empty or containing no significant amount of cargo.

From across this widest part of the Mississippi, in a section called "Algiers," a pair of high-powered binoculars was also trained on the activities surrounding the arrival of the Margarita Brissa.

Chapter Seventeen

Algiers, New Orleans, Louisiana
Saturday, September 4, 1993
1:40 a.m.

Six New Orleans DEA agents occupied the unmarked twenty-one foot Chris-Craft Concept, alongside the Cobalt 223 with another six agents, all watching the Margarita Brissa through binoculars from the far side of the river, waiting for the first glimpse of the buyers to meet the sellers. It had been a long, tedious vigil since about midday. An unmarked Bell Jet Ranger 206B-3 with a sharpshooter positioned in both the port and starboard hatch sat on a nearby parking lot of a vacant discount store with its engines cut to idle speed, waiting for the call to action from Senior Agent Gerard Boudreau, Chief of the N.O. DEA office.

~ * ~

Erich Mueller had done his daylight recon as efficiently as possible, but he could not manage to enter the wharf warehouse in broad daylight for obvious reasons. Once the activity around the Margarita Brissa settled down, he would find a way over the fence and take a firsthand look at the cargo the ship's crew may be preparing to put on board.

At 1:45 a.m., most of the crew clanged down the ship's retractable metal ladder and out of the wharf building, then proceeded out onto Decatur Street, almost exactly as Mueller had originally envisioned it back in Rotterdam with his brother Thomas.

Mueller noticed a dark brown Crown Victoria pull up to the gate; it was immediately waved through by an ununiformed guard. He couldn't see who or how many were in the car through the dark tinted windows. Mueller was *not* planning on any visitors tonight.

Finding a blind spot from the surveillance cameras was impossible, so Mueller had to manufacture a blind spot. He was directly underneath the camera as it slowly swiveled from side to side, taking in 180 degrees as it panned. Mueller looked for a rod or stick or something to impede the semicircular rotation of the camera. He saw a discarded shipping pallet and managed to break off an already split piece of pine from it. Mueller took the narrow, thirteen-inch piece of wood and stuck it through the top three or four openings of the eight-foot-high chain link fence. It only cut off an inch or two of the rotation, but that's all he needed to work on cutting the coiled barbed wire across the top of the fence. With a pair of wire cutters from his back pocket, he began to snip and move the cut wire carefully to the side. Once over the fence, an open ventilation window at eye level made entry totally accessible.

As soon as he was inside the wharf warehouse, he spotted them immediately. There, on the side of the building nearest the river, were four stacks, two high, of twenty-foot Sea-Land containers. *Hallelujah!*

Each of the containers were locked tight with huge Master padlocks. There did not appear to be any easy way to get into these containers to see if, in fact, they held any of the military hardware he suspected would soon be *en route* to Rotterdam. Mueller reasoned that someone must have possession of the eight keys that would unlock these metal boxes.

The only light came from a few red "Exit" signs and a Coca-Cola vending machine in a small, half-glassed office situated at the top of the second level, overlooking the entire dark warehouse.

No one around…where are the Crown Vic and its passengers? Mueller wondered. He also considered again the problem at hand of being able to inspect the containers. Without a bolt cutter, he really needed to find the damned keys! After a brief moment, he dashed up the straight flight of dimly lit steps, two at a time, taking the risk of being spotted. Once in the office, Mueller could move about on his hands and knees and not be seen from below. He groped through the top desk drawers of two old wooden desks and came up with one set of car keys, a house key, and the turnkey for the Coke machine. No key hooks or key box were on the wall; the office search proved to be no help.

Mueller dashed downstairs and took cover behind some large, corrugated cardboard cartons to plan his next move. From this new vantage point, he noticed a thin strand of light coming from a partially open freight door on the river side of the warehouse. Very little outside light penetrated the darkness of Governor Nicholls Street Wharf from that far end, but enough light existed to guide him down a narrow aisle toward the obviously unlocked door. He considered moving directly toward the open door, but instead opted to look for an alternative exit.

Guided by the nearest illuminated Exit sign, Mueller found and tried a small side door along the same side of the building. It was unlocked from the inside, with no emergency exit alarm. He slowly opened it and immediately felt the heavy, humid air and smelled the unmistakable scent of the Mississippi at its southern most port. Forty yards down the dock, he saw four men standing near the Crown Vic, talking and laughing. Two of the men appeared to be drinking from thirty-two-ounce beer cans.

The four continued to talk for a short time and then climbed the metal retractable ladder and boarded the vessel. Lights went on in a passageway about mid ship, possibly leading toward the galley. Erich Mueller also climbed the ladder once the four disappeared down the passageway. Wearing all dark clothing to blend in with the night, his 9mm held at the ready in a two-hand grip, he moved across the front portion of the deck, just below the bridge, with a low, smooth movement that would make it difficult for anyone to detect his presence on the Margarita Brissa.

~ * ~

"Who in the *hell* is that?" muttered Gerard Boudreau, lowering his night vision binoculars and handing them to his second in command.

"Ahh, shit, Gerry! He doesn't look like he's one of their players, and he sure as hell isn't one of ours," said his lieutenant. With the night vision optics still to his eyes, he calmly announced, "Hey, this is it. They're starting to take some large equipment bags out of the boat, and they're walking toward the ladder. This is it! What about our mystery guest?"

"Screw it. We'll ask questions later; we gotta go, *now!*" Boudreau said. With one quick signal from his radio, everything was set into motion.

The Jet Ranger helicopter took off and was hovering above the bow of the Margarita Brissa in about fifty-five seconds. A powerful single beam of light illuminated the entire forward section of the ship. "Everybody freeze! Drop your weapons! Drop the bags!" came the amplified command from the helicopter. Stunned by the blinding light and the booming voice from above, everyone on the deck froze in place, including Erich Mueller, who was more surprised than anyone.

"What the—?" Mueller said under his breath. He could see two large pleasure craft approaching rapidly, spotlights fixed on the Margarita Brissa and encompassing the other three men, all who had been carrying large nylon equipment bags along the starboard side of the deck. The three had dropped the bags at their feet, as they had been commanded to do. It was now obvious to Mueller that the men in the boats and the chopper were drug enforcement officers and he was smack dab in the middle of a full scale drug bust!

"You there! Center deck," the loudspeaker addressed Mueller. "I said drop your—" Just then a hatch flew open about ten feet to the left of Mueller, and a young man opened fire on the hovering helicopter with a .45 semi-automatic. Mueller had been about to drop his handgun when the first shot struck one of the DEA sharpshooters, dropping him from the helicopter into the river below. The gunman quickly turned toward Mueller, who was already in a crouched firing position and instinctively let off two quick well-placed blasts from his 9mm. Both rounds caught Anthony DeGraci squarely in the chest, throwing him up against a blood-splattered bulkhead.

Only moments later, the deck of the Margarita Brissa was swarming with DEA agents in flak jackets, weapons drawn. One of their men was down, and they were all operating on a short fuse. None of these guys were in the mood for any bullshit from wiseass drug runners.

Once the dust had settled on the highly successful drug bust, Boudreau was able to authenticate Mueller's identity as a Special Operations Investigator for the National Security Agency and get his detailed explanation concerning his reason for being there.

Keys for the eight remaining locked containers were found in a strong box in the main warehouse office, along with documents to accompany the shipment to Rotterdam. Now, finally, Mueller had solid proof of the sophisticated weaponry being stolen from the U.S. Government, which, in all probability, would have been turned around and used against U.S. troops or their European allies.

For obvious reasons of national security, every effort was made by the NSA to keep the news of the retrieved XG-777 missiles and M-5s as far from the media as possible. Fortunately, this was achieved by the diversion created by the simultaneous drug bust involving the notorious DeGraci family, which generated an enormous amount of publicity.

As far as the press and the public were concerned, at this point, Erich Mueller was just another member of the large DEA team that had made the bust.

~ * ~

U.S. District Court
Eastern District of Louisiana, New Orleans

The preliminary hearings were expedited and completed in record time, allowing the case to move right into the trial. The office of the deputy director of the National Security Agency hired Robert Rauh, a prominent and trusted attorney from New Orleans, to represent the interest of the NSA regarding Erich Mueller's involvement in the trial of Carmen DeGraci.

Rauh came highly recommended by the DEA, having recently been involved in a similar situation with the FBI up in Baton Rouge. He was briefed on the details by Mike Agnussi and reminded of the necessity of strict confidentiality.

Anne Avery removed her judicial lace collar, folded it neatly, and laid it on the credenza. She hung her robe in the closet behind her desk in the spacious oak paneled chambers of the senior U.S. District Court judge.

"Please have a seat, Mr. Rauh," she said, nodding toward a chair.

Judge Avery took a folded piece of paper from her black leather brief case, sat behind her enormous mahogany desk, donned her bifocals, and began to read.

"The director of the National Security Agency, General Jeschke, has requested rather adamantly that we somehow withhold Mr. Mueller's true identity as an NSA inspector for the upcoming trial because this would in some way jeopardize our national security. Can you please explain this to me?"

Bob Rauh explained in detail what had led Erich Mueller to New Orleans in search of the weapons that the NSA anticipated would somehow be used against President Boris Yeltsin in a possible coup d'état, thus jeopardizing the newfound democracy in Russia and promoting a reinstatement of communism.

"I see," said Avery, pondering what Rauh had just told her. "Foremost, I insist this be a fair trial. There is no alternative. Secondly, I find it appalling to think that communism could find its way back as the governing body of Russia. I've read about some of the unrest there, but I had no idea we were this close to Yeltsin actually being overthrown.

"This is what I can do and still remain within the parameters of our legal system. I will meet with both the defense team and the prosecuting attorney prior to the trial and explain that Mr. Mueller is, in fact, a federal law enforcement agent on a government-sanctioned assignment not directly related to the DEA. Furthermore, I will warn them I will not permit any questioning addressed to Mr. Mueller regarding his position or the specific organization that he belongs to, due to the interest of national security. Noncompliance will result in a charge of Contempt of Court, along with a hefty fine. That should pretty well keep these monkeys off his back and keep his real assignment under wraps, but bear in mind that he is a key witness and he will be on the stand up against some of *the* sharpest and most ruthless defense attorneys Carmen DeGraci can buy.

"And as you know, Mr. DeGraci has mighty deep pockets. They *will* beat him up—I see it every day—but rest assured I will not allow them to press him for any of this confidential information that could end up hurting our country, either directly or indirectly. After all, Mr. Mueller is not the one on trial for importation, wholesale distribution, and the sale of cocaine; the DeGraci family is."

Coming directly from the chambers of Judge Avery, Rauh met with Erich Mueller to relay all that had been discussed and to go over some much needed pretrial preparation.

Mueller and Rauh were both relieved and grateful to have such a reasonable, fair-minded, and patriotic person like Judge Anne Avery presiding over this district court.

Another thing Mueller was obviously grateful for, all credit given to Gerard Boudreau, the tight-lipped Cajun DEA boss, was the fact that none of the press ever caught wind of the eight twenty-foot containers that were about to be loaded onto the vessel moored to the dock at Governor Nichols Street Wharf. For all anyone else knew, this Venezuelan cargo ship had made its delivery and was headed back to South America. The media folk had totally missed the larger of these two huge stories, but the smell of blood in the water with the DeGraci drug bust was intoxicating and more than enough to keep these sharks occupied with only one of them.

Even though he was occupied with the trial proceedings, Mueller continued to work from New Orleans, trying to find the whereabouts and the rightful owner of the first eight containers.

"Thomas, how's it going? Have things calmed down a little at Flatworld-Rotterdam since my visit?"

"Erich, I must admit I rather miss the excitement that you bring. Are you doing okay?"

"I'm doing fine, thanks, but I need a little more of your professional help. Can you run down more information from the consignee? I think it was a company called A&E Farming Implements. We never had much of a chance to discuss this, but how could—or how did—a legitimate company like this get involved with importing contraband from the United States? Any ideas?" Mueller was careful not to reveal the fact that the shipment had contained nuclear weapons.

"Well, Erich, I'm happy to say I've already checked into this, but disappointed to tell you I don't have a very good answer for you. After you left, I immediately called A&E and asked to speak with the person who signed the Shipper's Letter of Instruction. After the person I was speaking to checked into this, I was told no one had ever heard of this person and that A&E has never used this carrier. Furthermore, they claimed they had never ordered any grain of any kind from the U.S.!"

"Does this sound reasonable to you? Is it possible?"

"It's very possible. First of all, it was a prepaid shipment, which eliminates a lot of questions right from the start. If it's all paid for, nobody aside from the customs officials really cares where it came from or where it's going. All anyone had to do is look to see who is a regular importer—that's a matter of public record—and just forge the shipping documents in the name of A&E Farming Implements GmbH. Simple as that."

"Okay, that all seems pretty logical. One other question. Do you happen to have the name of the person who signed this Shipper's Letter of Instruction?"

"Yeah, as a matter of fact I do. It's here somewhere," said Thomas as he flipped through the file folder. "Ah, here we are. It was a person by the name of Alvin Pallosic."

~ * ~

Erich Mueller, with the help of Mike Agnussi, was able to coordinate with Major General Jeff Robertson and make arrangements for the eight containers and their valuable contents to be quickly and quietly removed from Governor Nichols Street Wharf. The Sea-Land containers would then be transported back to Fort Hood by a select team of plainclothes Louisiana State Highway Patrol officers headed by Captain Clarke Winkle. At the Louisiana/Texas state line, Winkle's people would turn control of the convoy of eight over to another covert team of military police from Fort Hood, now headed by Major Tom Downing.

Mike Agnussi had begun to conduct his own investigation of all parties responsible for the stolen weapons. He was also investigating who was to have been the recipient of the weapons on the other end. Finding this information would be critical in locating the first eight containers that were somewhere on the European continent. General Robertson was able to provide Agnussi with all of the information he needed about Colonel Pallosic, but unfortunately that was a moot issue, since dead people can't answer any questions.

Agnussi contacted Sea-Land and found out sixteen twenty-foot containers had been ordered by Colonel Alvin Pallosic, Provost Marshal, with an official government requisition, then dropped at a location on the western edge of the Fort Hood Military Reservation at the city limits marker of a town called Pidcoke. Payment was to be made per usual government contract with the carrier. This was obviously a dead end.

~ * ~

As the trial went into the second day, the jury heard the sworn testimony of two key witnesses: the operations manager of Governor Nichols Street Wharf warehouse and the captain of the Margarita Brissa.

Mueller listened intently, hoping to pick up some clues regarding the operations manager's involvement with accepting the military hardware. On the other hand, he hoped to God this guy would not volunteer any information about the containers and stick to the questions specifically related to the drug transfer.

Although he had testified under oath, it didn't seem to bother the operations manager at all that he was committing outright perjury while on the witness stand. Mueller wondered if everyone else in the courtroom was so completely blind as to not recognize these blatant lies—lies designed to protect and insulate the DeGraci family and the cocaine supplier, whoever he might be. But when Erich Mueller stopped to realize the punishment for lying under oath wasn't near as bad as what the DeGraci organization would do to the man if he testified against the mob boss from New Jersey, Mueller completely understood the reason for these lies.

When the captain of the Margarita Brissa took the stand, it was all the same. One lie after another. He was not able to recall anything of any importance and implicated Colonel Pallosic whenever the opportunity presented itself, careful not to divulge any information whatsoever about his communications with the Venezuelan drug lord. It was clear to Mueller that both of these men had been coached extremely well on how to deflect certain types of questions and then just flat out lie about those they could not deflect.

The fear of guaranteed reprisal from the DeGraci or Lossada organizations was more than enough to keep both of these witnesses comfortable with the idea of prison time as opposed to the alternative.

~ * ~

One would have expected a figure as influential as Carmen DeGraci to battle the prosecution with the strength and confidence he had always displayed, but this was not the case. With the loss of his only son, he felt as if someone had cut out his very heart. There was no fight left in this powerful man the media referred to as "Don Carmen." Even his defense team did not fight with the same vigor and voracity they normally did without DeGraci behind them, pushing them hard every inch of the way.

To add to his anguish, DeGraci blamed himself for suggesting Anthony make the trip to New Orleans to get involved in the business. He believed he had condemned his own son's soul to hell, not much different from the dozens of faceless people he had killed by a mere suggestion to his loyal henchmen. As influential and powerful as he was, he could not bring Tony back among the living. No, Carmen DeGraci could not bring life, but he sure as hell could bring death.

Within his subconscious, DeGraci reasoned that by eliminating the one who actually brought about his son's death, he could take vengeance and possibly find some kind of peace. Death by the hand of DeGraci had never been a personal thing; it had always been a business decision. Now it was personal, as personal as anything could ever possibly be.

Immediately following the emotional trial and just before being hauled away in shackles in the custody of the State of Louisiana, Carmen DeGraci was able to briefly meet with his two remaining trusted captains, Joey Castelletti and Nino Falcone. DeGraci took Castelletti by his broad shoulders and tried to pass along his sense of strength and leadership through this embrace with his favored godson. Without a spoken word, it was understood the torch had been passed. It was also very clear to Joey Castelletti that it was now *his* responsibility to avenge the death of Anthony DeGraci, which he accepted as a great honor, no questions asked.

Chapter Eighteen

Moscow
Monday, September 6, 1993

"How could Lossada be so *damned stupid?* So greedy, to jeopardize the success of this entire operation, just for the price of one lousy shipment of cocaine!" shouted General Stephan Krause upon receiving the faxed message from Guillermo Lossada informing him that his second shipment of XG-777s and M-5s had been seized by drug enforcement officers in New Orleans. Lossada hadn't had the guts to contact him by phone. Krause was absolutely furious.

Major Gerhardt Richter was on hand for this display of rage that had erupted from the normally cool and calculated Spetsnaz general. He poured Krause a tall glass of Stoli and did his best to calm the man down and position himself, hopefully, for a more coherent and comprehensive accounting of what had just taken place by asking a few well-placed, relevant questions. A wise move on the major's part, because at present, he could gain nothing from the ranting and raving of this newly created madman.

Once the general finally sat down with vodka in hand, Richter almost immediately started collecting a wealth of new information regarding some of the past activities involving the appropriation of weapons, equipment, and troops prior to his new position and, even more importantly, learning exactly what Krause intended to do with them in the very near future.

As the Stoli began to take its desired effect on General Krause, Richter helped reason with him that the eight M-5s and the twenty-four XG-777s should certainly be adequate to carry out his mission. Sure, sixteen vehicles and forty-eight missiles would have been better, but because of the high-speed mobility the M-5s possessed and the range of the XG-777 missiles, there should be no trouble deploying the rockets in any direction, at any targets.

Krause walked over to the large wall map of Europe. He stood there for several minutes, jiggling eight red map pins in his left hand, studying the map. He looked over at Richter for a moment, looked back at the map, and then put the map pins back in the top desk drawer.

What was that all about? wondered Gerhardt Richter.

As much as Richter had wanted to be close to the source of all that was going on with Krause when he was stationed in Kotelnikovo, he had not fully anticipated how extremely tight everything was in Moscow. His life was under a high-powered microscope every minute of every day. It seemed to Richter that about one in every four people on the street in Moscow was KGB or another brand of secret police. Constantly being watched because of his military position and close association with the general made everything Richter did a risk to his secret identity, thus making it increasingly difficult, sometimes impossible, to get any kind of message back to Talbot in a timely fashion. He knew the risks involved and always had to weigh them against the benefits. Worst case scenario always seemed to be the same: getting caught, being executed, and consequently ending the flow of vital information he was able to provide to the NSA. It was actually the third part of the scenario that troubled Richter the most.

~ * ~

The general was a highly determined individual. He had not given up hope; he just hated to be shortchanged and did not want anything to disrupt his master plan. He needed to move forward in order to stay on pace with his schedule, to continue to coordinate his activities with his Moscow staff, and most important of all, to stay a full length and a half ahead of General of the Army Aleksey Chesnokov.

A conference was to be held within the next three weeks in a remote area of the Czech Republic slightly north of Linz, Austria, and just east of the German border near the town of Cesky Krumlov. Krause was assembling his senior officers, along with two regimental generals who had only three weeks earlier allied their troops and equipment for the common cause under the direction of Lieutenant General Stephan Krause.

In spite of his most recent setback, Krause was well pleased with the data being received from the "faulty" communications satellite. He continued to feed more nonsense information into the satellite computer while also maintaining a separate disc with all of the accurate data on western troop movements and their defensive postures and other essential strategic information. Krause also controlled a sophisticated jamming device from the Cosmos 1813C satellite that could foul television and radio microwaves being relayed from other communications satellites.

The most important key to derailing the coupe, considered Richter, was to somehow take possession of the original *accurate* disc and the backup discs that were stored in locked, safe-like metal boxes in two separate locations. If the original and two backups were found missing, Krause would most likely suspect Richter, simply because he was among the most recent insertion into his inner circle.

If he was to be successful in acquiring the three discs, he needed to find a way to buy some time in order to stay in his position, a vantage point of extreme importance, especially at this critical juncture.

If the discs could somehow be substituted with other similar discs that were slightly altered—key items changed only enough to cause the end result to be incorrect—it could work. A single digit could keep a nuclear warhead from being fired automatically from a remote control center and/or rendering their jamming device inoperable.

The problem was not so much in actually stealing the discs, but finding time when they would not be in use. When the opportunity came, Major Richter would definitely need to act without hesitation.

~ * ~

September 21, 1993

21 September – Russian President Boris Yeltsin announces in a television address his decision to disband the hostile Soviet-era parliament that has blocked economic reforms. In his address, Yeltsin declares his intent to rule by decree until the election of the new parliament and a referendum on a new constitution.

22 September – The Supreme Soviet declares Yeltsin be removed from presidency, by virtue of his breaching the constitution, and Vice President Alexander Rutskoy is sworn in as acting president. The decision is ineffective as the members of parliament have already been dismissed from office.

23-24 September – Yeltsin is confronted by significant popular unrest, encouraging the defenders of the parliament. Moscow witnesses what amounts to a spontaneous mass uprising of anti-Yeltsin demonstrators, numbering in the tens of thousands, marching in the streets, resolutely seeking to aid forces defending the parliament building. Demonstrators are protesting the new and terrible living conditions under Yeltsin. Since 1989, the GDP has declined by half. Corruption is rampant, violent crimes are skyrocketing, medical services are collapsing, food and fuel are increasingly scarce and life expectancy is falling for all but a small handful of the population. All of these factors are being attributed to Yeltsin's leadership, or lack thereof.

Chapter Nineteen

Munich, Germany
Thursday, September 23, 1993

"Congratulations, Hot Shot! Well done!" Hank Talbot praised his top field investigator. "Now I suppose you'll wanna go to work for the DEA."

Mueller was still in New Orleans at the Hotel Provincial where it had all begun only twenty-one days before. It seemed like a year.

The Hotel Adria Garni was home for Henry Talbot: a nice, unassuming little hotel on Liebig Strasse, a relatively quiet street away from the hustle and bustle of the center of Munich. In Talbot's position, he never felt comfortable living in a house or an apartment. *Too easy to nail you down,* he had always believed. *Always better to travel light .You never know when you might have to pick up and go.*

Erich Mueller sounded exhausted to his boss over the phone. Talbot knew all of the signs, even though Mueller said he was fine and that he would be back in Munich the day after tomorrow. As much as Talbot needed him back on home turf, he knew it was best for Mueller's safety, primarily, to give him a few days of R&R before returning him to the field. *No good trying to cut wood with a dull ax,* reasoned Talbot.

"Tell you what, Erich, how about you take a few days off once you get back to Germany? Get a little rest before coming back to work. It might do you some good. What do you think?"

"Yeah, maybe you're right. A couple of days of serious trout fishing might be just what I need. I'll take you up on that offer. Thanks."

"Good. Just be ready to jump back into the thick of it again on Tuesday," Talbot said. "Now for some good news from this side of the pond: I just received a communiqué late last night from Richter in Moscow. You'll be happy to know that shipment of M-5s along with the nukes that arrived in Rotterdam *are*, in fact, the property of General Stephan Krause! This was a very brief and very sketchy report, and we have no idea where these weapons are right now. Richter seems to think that Krause is planning some kind of 'show of force,' but doesn't exactly know where or when. If we continue to get this kind of information from our man in Moscow, we're both gonna be busy as hell just trying to keep up with the flow."

"Fine by me, boss. I'll be ready. See you Tuesday." Mueller signed off.

~ * ~

Moscow
Monday, September 27, 1993

Waiting for the most opportune time—with time being a rare and valuable commodity lately, based on the pace and activities of Lieutenant General Stephan Krause—Major Gerhardt Richter carefully framed the question that had needed to be answered for the past two weeks. "Comrade General, respectfully speaking as your aide de camp, in order to better serve you, I think I should be made aware of the targets you have selected for these tactical nuclear warheads you've recently acquired, and of how you plan to use them."

No sooner did the words leave his mouth, than Richter felt certain he had over stepped his boundaries.

Krause raised an eyebrow, and Richter knew he was in for a severe reprimand. But much to his surprise, Krause offered him a seat, folded his hands on the top of his desk, and replied calmly, "Major, I have eight trusted officers in the field who will be controlling their own individual launch units separately; each of these officers has no idea where the other launch units are, or how many other launch units there might be for that matter. General Romokovitch, my second in command, and Captain Karpinov, our computer guru, know these locations. A total of two men, other than myself, know everything about the operation, and eight men have their own individual assignments; that is all. The wider the circle, the greater the possibility these highly guarded locations would somehow be disclosed. Understand, Major Richter, it's not that I don't trust you; that's not it at all. I do trust you, or you wouldn't be here working for me. It's purely the time-tested military practice of 'need to know.' In your particular job function, at this point, you do not need to know. Period.

"What I *can* tell you is this: my main objective in using these nuclear-tipped missiles is to attract attention to the fact that I am—or rather will be—the new, uncontested president, restoring a new world order of communism back to Mother Russia," Krause said with great pride, "and to accomplish this, I need the military might to make it perfectly clear I am serious about my demands to be recognized by the world, more specifically by the United States and all European countries that belong to the United Nations. If I need to flex my muscle and use some force, I am completely prepared for that. In fact, I think it would add to my credibility; they'll know early in the game not to screw with Stephan Krause."

~ * ~

Munich
Tuesday, September 28, 1993
8:35 a.m.

Hank Talbot sat in the small, cozy lobby of the Hotel Adria, reading a copy of the *International Herald Tribune*. He was feeling rather content right now; information regarding General Krause and the planned coup continued to trickle in from Richter, and it completely dovetailed with the reports Mueller had provided. No major discrepancies from either source, and that allowed Talbot to breathe a little easier.

The latest word from Richter was news of a conference that *might* take place somewhere in the southern part of the Czech Republic and would probably happen pretty soon. Could be something big. His ace right-hand reliever would be returning to duty today, thank God. Talbot desperately needed some help from the bullpen right about now.

Talbot glanced up from his paper to notice a couple stepping up to the chest-high reception desk. Man and wife, he automatically assumed. Both seemed to be in their early forties, the wife maybe a little younger. They both looked fit and had healthy, natural-looking tans.

The man spoke in German to the clerk behind the desk, but it was obvious German was not his native tongue. Based on the couple's clothes and his pronunciation of certain words, Talbot determined they were probably Americans. When the man said a few words to his companion in English, Talbot knew they were indeed from the U.S. He had always seemed to analyze people in his idle moments, a kind of pastime for him, a bit of a carryover from his professional training.

Just then his vibrating pager took life in his side pocket. He removed it and noted it was from the Moscow phone number. *This must be something hot for Richter to not be using a cut-out,* he thought. Talbot went back up to his room immediately to return the call.

It was hot, all right. Red hot! Richter spoke quickly and with an economy of words. "I'm going to be traveling with Krause tomorrow to an old monastery in the southernmost part of the Czech Republic, near the town of Cesky Krumlov, for a high-level planning conference with his newly formed 'joint chiefs of staff.' I have acquired three floppy discs that contain the access codes needed to communicate and control the Cosmos 1813C satellite, Krause's basic control tool. From what I gather, and this is not firsthand, he plans to use this satellite to jam all TV and radio waves coming out of Moscow, thus cutting off mass communications to the people from Yeltsin or possibly General Chesnokov. He would also have the capability to broadcast his message, whatever or whenever that might be, to the rest of the world via *his* satellite. Krause would be the only voice the Russian citizens could hear. But here's the real kicker: most important of all, he can use the Cosmos 1813C to launch the XG-7s remotely, from anywhere, by loading target codes and firing sequence codes for each one of his twenty-four rockets.

"Unfortunately, I could only locate the firing sequence codes, so we still don't know where the hell he plans to stage these missiles. I'm still working on that, and with any luck I'll be able to have this information within the next few days. For the time being, I've replaced these three discs with blank ones, and I hope like hell no one tries to use them. That's highly unlikely, because we are now packing up all of the headquarters office for our move: files, computers, everything, and the next opportunity for these control discs to be used will be once the computers are installed and hooked up in the monastery, at the earliest three or four days from now. The discs have already been passed off to my cut-out last night and are on the way to you right now. You should have delivery no later than noon today, providing nothing catastrophic happened to the courier," promised Richter.

"What we need," continued Richter, "are the three discs to be copied, then the originals to be slightly altered, say changing one digit up or down in each one of these twenty-four firing sequence codes, along with the access code for the satellite. Then the altered discs need to be delivered back to me. That's the tricky part. The borders are all being watched very closely right now. In fact, they have actually doubled the number of border guards, and these guards are being assisted by regular Russian Army troops—Krause's men, for sure, in most areas. You *cannot* risk driving or taking a train. Can we use Erich Mueller as our courier?"

"Yes, of course," said Talbot.

"I ask that because Mueller is fluent in German, naturally, and I seem to remember he also speaks some Czech. Because I do not speak a word of Czech, and Mueller does not speak Russian, we will need to converse in German. In this part of the Czech Republic, so close to both Germany and Austria, it's not uncommon at all to hear German spoken in these rural areas. Speaking English would be totally out of the question.

"I don't have time for a lot of details," Richter continued. "I'm leaving most of that up to you and Mueller to figure out. So here is the basic strategy: I have arranged for a local grocery man, a man by the name of Jakub Dvorak, to make early morning deliveries to the monastery only twice a week, on Saturdays and Wednesdays. I want Mueller to find Dvorak and hitch a ride up with him, because he will be the only one allowed up the road to the monastery. I want you to put the altered discs back in the bottom of a cigar box, where I've taken out a few so the box appears to be full. I'm the only cigar smoker in the group, so I'll be sure to receive them. I'll inform the quartermaster to be on the lookout for the cigars with the grocery shipment.

"I will also need Mueller to take back any new information I have for you. Most likely I will have at least some kind of updated battle plan, and hopefully the information we need on the positions of the 7s and M-5s by that time, and I'll need to get this back to you in the safest, most capable hands possible. That would be Erich Mueller. Do you agree?"

"Yes, I agree completely," confirmed Talbot, "and Mueller *is* our best man. He's my only field ops inspector capable of pulling this kind of mission off with any chance of success."

"Good. Then take this down. I'm looking at map edition 5-TPC, series V782, sheet 6446-IV. The grid coordinate for the monastery is AC61550889. Got it? How you get those three discs back to me is entirely up to you. Just make damn sure I'm not caught with my pants down."

"That's a tall order, but we can do it. You can take that to the bank. Keep up the good work, Richter, and keep your butt covered, okay?"

Major Gerhardt Richter closed the line.

Henry Talbot immediately shot off a secure fax to Mike Agnussi at the NSA Headquarters at Fort Mead and explained in detail this latest development. Agnussi came back right away. His reply was brief and not at all enthusiastic, but that was his way of tempering his own enthusiasm and remaining cautiously optimistic:

Good job, Hank. Go get 'em. The ball is in your court. Use whatever means you have at your disposal. M.A.

Reading between the few short lines, Talbot understood Agnussi's cool response. He still required more exact and specific information. They now knew that General Krause had control of the missing M-5s and XG-777s, along with the firing code sequence, and that was very big. They also knew the access codes to the satellite. They had a meeting site, and there would be an exchange of floppy discs. That was all great, but it was still not enough. Those were three necessary pieces of a very large and complex puzzle, but how could they effectively defend against this guy if they didn't have any idea where these weapons were?

The ball is in my court. Work with it, Talbot thought, his creative genius thrown into high gear. *How do I get Mueller in with the altered discs and then out, hopefully with the M-5 locations, with all of the additional security around?* It would be quite a challenge, but not an impossible task.

Forty-five minutes later, after a short walk to the peaceful confines of the Hofgarten and about a half hour of sitting on a park bench in perfect solitude, Henry Talbot had developed a rough plan.

After six or seven attempts to contact General John Bussen, Commander in Chief, United States European Command, headquartered in Stuttgart, Talbot finally broke through the protective red tape that surrounded the four-star leader of all U.S. Military throughout Europe, Turkey, and Greenland.

"Bussen," came the strong voice from the other end of the connection.

"General Bussen, this is Senior Special Ops Investigator Henry Talbot. I'm in charge of the National Security Agency station in Munich. I—"

Bussen interrupted. "Mr. Talbot, if this is official government business, which I assume it is, I would expect to be notified by your boss, General Jeschke, or by the Deputy Director... what's his name, ah..."

"Agnussi, sir, Michael Agnussi."

"Yes. Agnussi. Thank you. You do know, Talbot, that we follow the chain of command here, don't you? You seem to have missed a couple of links."

"Yes, sir, I realize that, but I just spoke with Mr. Agnussi earlier today, and he instructed me to use whatever means necessary to accomplish my mission. I believe Mr. Agnussi is rather swamped with the information and activities of General Chesnokov right now, and I seem to be adding another front to that battle, so I felt it was my responsibility to take the initiative and contact you directly."

Talbot had already captured the general's complete attention with his first sentence. As a professional soldier, Bussen fully understood the importance of accomplishing the mission and following his superior's orders.

"Okay, Mr. Talbot, I'm listening."

Hank Talbot went on to explain the tight border security, the importance of making contact with his inside man, Spetsnaz officer Major Gerhardt Richter, and the tentative plans to have his second in command, Erich Mueller, be dropped by parachute just east of the German/Czech Republic border.

"I'm with you on this, Talbot, and I think you've got a workable game plan. My only concern is that we've already allocated all of our ground troops, Airborne, and Military Airlift Command, along with reserve troops and equipment on high alert status, targeting all of the probable hot spots General Chesnokov is capable of igniting. This ranges as far north as Kaliningrad on the Baltic and as far south as the Bosporus on the Aegean Sea, so you see we're talking about twenty-five hundred to three thousand miles of turf to cover, spreading us pretty thin in a lot of sensitive places.

"Off hand, I don't know where we can scare up the personnel or the transportation to pull this off on such short notice, but I'm sure I can find at least one aircraft and a platoon of jumpers somewhere here on the continent. This *is* an important mission regardless of what your higher-ups might think, so I'll get you what you need to carry out your mission. Where can you be reached?"

~ * ~

Hank Talbot picked up his phone on the first ring.

"Mr. Talbot, this is Captain Cronan Cleary, Commander of Company F, Ranger, 425th Infantry, Michigan Army National Guard. I just received a call from European Command, 7th Army in Stuttgart, General Bussen's office, about some sort of covert jump into the Czech Republic. Is this correct?"

Talbot was confused. *Michigan National Guard? How the hell do they figure into this picture? I finally reach the head honcho who commands the entire U.S. Seventh Army, the Sixth Fleet, and the Third Air Force, and I end up with a lousy NG unit from Michigan? What gives?*

"That's correct, Captain Cleary, but I'm not so sure my request reached the appropriate party. Michigan is not exactly just around the corner from Munich, and not to look a gift horse in the mouth, but how is a 'straight leg' NG unit gonna help me jump into the Czech Republic?"

With feathers only somewhat ruffled, Captain Cleary responded in an appropriately sharp tone. "Actually, Mr. Talbot, we *are* just around the corner from you. I'm calling you from Ramstein Air Base near Kaiserslautern. We're here for our two weeks of annual training, working on a joint NATO training mission along with the 166th Airlift Wing, Delaware Air National Guard, and a couple of companies of Belgian paratroopers. And for your information, sir, Company F, 425th Infantry, is *not* 'straight leg.' We are *not* one of your 'run of the mill' National Guard units. We are, in fact, the Long Range Reconnaissance Patrol Company for the VII U.S. Corps. Not to belabor the point, but we have been in existence longer than any other such unit in the entire U.S. Army, active or reserve component. Each one of us is Airborne, and all of us are Rangers and damn proud of it. Do you have any further questions regarding our qualifications, Mr. Talbot?"

"No. I'm sorry I was not aware that the Army had such a STRAC National Guard outfit such as your 425th, and I do appreciate your assistance," Talbot responded graciously, realizing he did not want to further insult the guy he was now relying on to help carry out his mission. "What about an aircraft to drop us in? Who would I need to contact about transportation?"

"I've already contacted our Air Force counterpart, the 142nd Airlift Squadron, part of the 166th Delaware ANG. The squadron commander,

Colonel Tom Germaine, will be making all of the flight arrangements. When I explained this was a covert operation, he said he actually wants to pilot the aircraft himself for this mission—evidently a real hands-on guy. I'll need to know exactly when you plan to begin this mission, and you'll need to brief me and Colonel Germaine on all of the details."

"For planning purposes, I can tell you I'm looking at a night jump, Friday night," said Talbot. "I'll have more details when we meet. I plan on driving up with my second, Erich Mueller, the man who will be making the jump, as soon as I can wrap up a few loose ends down here in Munich. How about we meet Friday morning in Stuttgart at the Seventh Army HQ? That's about half way for both parties, with you and Colonel Germaine coming from Ramstein. That should save us some travel time. Oh, and while I'm thinking of it, Mueller will need to get a military ID, a set of BDUs, and a pair of jump boots while we're at the Seventh."

"Three things," said Cleary. "Don't worry about driving up; I've got a chopper here at my disposal, and I'll send it down whenever you're ready. Second, we might be a little less conspicuous if we just flew out of Ramstein: fewer questions to answer and easier to keep a low profile. We can also get the ID, the uniform, and any other equipment he might need here at Ramstein without any fanfare. Third and most important, your man Mueller *is* jump-qualified, correct?"

"Yes, sir, he is. About six months ago, we ran him through a special ten-day crash course at Fort Benning. He has made his five, including a night jump, no problems. Actually he enjoyed the hell out of it. And yes, keeping a low profile is essential to this mission, so we'll make it as simple as possible and keep it all within Ramstein. Good suggestion."

"I'm glad to hear Mueller is comfortable with a night jump. I don't want anybody wetting his pants when we open the jump door and the light turns green. Call me at this number whenever you're ready." Cleary relayed his personal phone number, and the two signed off.

Hank Talbot was genuinely impressed and very grateful for the newfound cooperation he had received from General Bussen, obviously a man who follows up on his commitments. And this guy Captain Cleary was extremely well-suited and experienced for the job that lay before him, an essential guy to have on your team going up against the opposition.

Talbot had thought out all of the basics for Mueller's entry over the line into   the Czech Republic, but he still needed to work on how to get him back out into Austria or Germany. *One step at a time. I'll think about that tonight.*

~ * ~

11:50 a.m.

No sooner than Henry Talbot had hung up the phone after ordering a light lunch from the hotel kitchen than he was notified by the front desk that a courier was waiting for him in the lobby with a small package wrapped in brown craft paper, a special delivery that required his signature.

Talbot immediately hustled down the stairs, signed for the parcel, forgot all about his tuna salad sandwich and cottage cheese, and bounded back up the flight of steps as fast as his large frame could make it. Once inside his room, with the door locked behind him, he carefully unwrapped his package: a box of fifty wood-tipped Hav-A-Tampa Jewels cigars, with about six or seven missing. In their place across the bottom of the box were three blue floppy discs. Talbot smiled. This guy Richter was good! Before noon, Richter had promised, and here it was. He tore the cellophane wrapper from one of the wood-tipped cigars and went looking for a book of matches. *He won't miss just one of these little jewels.*

As the bells from St. Anne's Church tolled twelve times announcing the Angelus, Talbot sat back in his chair, enjoyed the taste and aroma of his Hav-A-Tampa Jewel, and marveled at the accuracy of the delivery.

The NSA chief was enjoying a brief moment of relaxation when the phone rang. *This better be Mueller calling from the airport or the train station asking to be picked up*, he thought. *We've got a lot of work to do!*

The voice on the other end was not Mueller.

"Hank, this is Agnussi. You'd better be sitting down, because I've got some terrible news. Erich Mueller has just been found shot to death. One round from a high powered rifle, right through the head."

There was silence on the other end as Henry Talbot gathered himself. "Oh, God. How the hell did this happen?"

"Details are still very sketchy at this point. Evidently, according to the German police, two love birds found Mueller's Mercedes parked in their usual 'parking spot' out in the boonies near a small lake outside of Fussen last night. They notified the local police because they couldn't see anyone in or near the car. The police went to check it out early this morning and found Mueller floating face down in the lake. They figure he had been dead for approximately forty-eight hours. They also found his Beretta and traced the serial number on their computer, which brought it back here to Fort Mead.

"The locals," Agnussi continued, "along with German State Police, are running an investigation and interviewing people right now. I'll have to keep you posted from this end. You can't risk showing your hand. Understood?"

"Yeah, I'm afraid so. Call me back at the office as soon as you can, okay?"

"Sorry, Hank. I know Erich was a friend, as well." Agnussi told Talbot to "hang in there" and closed the line.

Son of a bitch! thought Talbot, slamming the receiver down. *Now what?* It didn't take him long to figure it out. He would have to do the mission on his own. "Damn; I'm getting too old for this crap, much less jumping out of airplanes!" he mumbled to himself.

Just before 4:00 p.m., Munich time, Talbot received another call from the deputy director of the NSA.

"Just found out the German police have some leads and a pretty fair description of two possible shooters. They picked up some undisturbed tread marks from the dirt road leading to the lake where Mueller was shot. They're in the process of trying to get a make on the car from those prints, but nothing yet."

256

"Yeah, well what about the shooters?" asked Talbot anxiously. "I don't care about the damn car!"

"I'm getting to that, Hank. Just try to hold on, okay?" Agnussi said, doing his best to keep Talbot reasonably calm. "The police first checked the hotels in the area, a good move on their part, asking about any suspicious or unusual looking guests, non-tourist types. Right off the bat, the elderly proprietor of a small hotel in Fussen told them of two American men traveling together: one short and kind of muscular who spoke some German she said was not easy for her to understand, and the other tall and slim who didn't say anything. Passports were checked upon registration. U.S. passports, but undoubtedly forged if these guys are the shooters, so not much help there. They drove a minivan, she recalled, because they had trouble finding a large enough parking space. The tire prints could possibly help us on that. The old woman at the hotel said she saw them in 'American' clothes when they checked in, and later they were both in traditional Bavarian-type clothes. She said they looked 'funny.' Oh, she also said the shorter man had darker skin, but not like a black person, and the tall one had a very light complexion, for whatever that's worth."

Agnussi continued. "Obviously this was a hit on Mueller, not a random shooting or an accident. This is Germany, not LA. You should stay on your toes, Hank. We don't know what brand of kooks are out there, and we'd still like to get a few more good years out of you, all right?"

"Yeah, I'll watch my backside. Thanks for the heads up."

Talbot wanted to fill his boss in on the plans to link up with Major Richter and the conversation he had had with the CICEUCOM earlier in the day, but this did not seem to be the right time. Talbot realized neither he nor Agnussi were exactly in the proper frame of mind to debate the issues regarding General Stephan Krause and the twenty-four 'loose' nuclear-tipped missiles wandering around somewhere in Europe. *Not right now,* Talbot thought. *I'll talk to him about it tomorrow.*

It was past seven o'clock when Talbot left the office and chose to walk home. He could use some fresh air, and he always thought better as he walked. In his present mood, he preferred not to do battle with the crowd on the U-Bahn; someone might get hurt.

Talbot stopped at the front desk of the Hotel Adria to pick up his room key and exchange greetings with Moritz Hatke, the hotel manager. Coming down the steps into the lobby, he could not help but notice the same couple he had watched check in earlier that morning.

Wow! Talbot nearly said out loud. The woman was dressed in a form-fitting, floor-length black evening dress, cut low enough to expose a modest amount of cleavage, suspended by two thin spaghetti straps. Her light brown hair, almost blond, was very neatly coiffed and accented with a single delicate white rose. She carried a black evening clutch in one hand and a nosegay of small white roses on her other wrist. She looked absolutely stunning.

The gentleman wore a plain black tuxedo with a black cummerbund and a black butterfly bowtie. A single white rose boutonniere was pinned to his left lapel. Because Talbot had an eye for detail, he noticed the gentleman was wearing very highly polished, 'spit-shined' military low quarters, rather than the patent leather dress shoes typically worn with a tux.

"My, my," exclaimed Moritz, "you both look quite handsome!"

The woman blushed slightly, knowing all eyes were upon her and not her mate. She responded with a humble, "Thank you."

"It is Strauss's 'Gypsy Baron,' correct?" asked Herr Hatke, genuinely interested, "performed by the Zurich Symphony Orchestra?"

The couple acknowledged that the hotel manager was correct on both counts.

"Enjoy your evening!" Hatke said pleasantly.

"Vielen Dank. Tschuss!" responded the male, and off the two strolled toward the waiting taxi engaged for a short fare to the Bavarian Opera House.

"They seem to be very nice people, although I have to admit I only met them this morning as they checked in," said the hotel manager, who seemed compelled to share with his long-time guest, Henry Talbot. Moritz Hatke always made it a point, as part of his job, to know his clientele, not in a nosy or intrusive way, but more as a true professional seeking to better serve his valued guests.

Chapter Twenty

Munich, Germany
Wednesday, September 29, 1993
6:55 a.m.

Talbot was up early this morning. He hadn't slept well for several reasons. First, he'd been thinking a lot about the murder of his partner; second, he was anxious about all that needed to be done today; and third, being a firm believer in Murphy's Law, he couldn't help but worry about what else that might possibly go wrong.

As he sat along the window side of the Hotel Adria's breakfast room, drenched in the early morning sunlight and sipping his second cup of strong coffee, Talbot observed "the couple," as he'd come to think of them. They were obviously returning from an invigorating early morning run, more than likely through the nearby Englisher Garten.

Sweat glistened off the exposed tanned skin of both runners. The man was short, no more than five-seven, but he appeared fit. He wore a gray sweat-soaked WIU t-shirt, black nylon running shorts, and New Balance running shoes. The woman was the personification of fitness. She was dressed in a navy Lycra running top and matching shorts with high-cut side vents. Talbot never quite got to the shoes.

The NSA chief did his best to try not to stare as the couple stopped to quench their thirst with a quick fix of orange juice from the beverage bar. The runners tossed down a second round of OJ and went back up the stairs toward their room. No fanfare or flash about them; they were just going about what seemed to be a normal routine.

Talbot was bothered by something, but he didn't know what or why. He poured a third cup of coffee. He could almost feel he was within reach of some kind of epiphany, like having someone's name on the tip of your tongue and groping desperately until something triggers the brain to release that information. *What the hell is it?* he wondered.

A telephone rang some distance away, probably at the front desk. Suddenly the memory hit him like a brick, causing him to spit out his coffee as if it had burned his mouth. *The call yesterday from Mike Agnussi. Of course!* Agnussi had said the old lady the police had interviewed—the one who ran the hotel in Fussen—had described one of the possible shooters as being short, kind of muscular, dark-skinned and German-speaking. *Holy shit! That's the exact description of this guy!*

Now Talbot's mind was racing. *Why would the shooter be here at the Adria when there are hundreds of other hotels in Munich? Why would he even be here in Munich?* He mulled this around in his head for a time and came to a startling conclusion: *Oh my God, it must be me! Somebody is working from the inside and is trying to pick us off one at a time. What else could it be?*

Talbot had to control himself before he did anything stupid or irrational. He first set his coffee down, realizing he certainly didn't need any more caffeine. He began to place what few bits of information he had about the man in some kind of logical order. Talbot had only seen this guy on three very short occasions: The first time was yesterday morning while he was checking in and spoke German quite adequately to inquire about his room reservation, confirm the cost of the room, and determine what time breakfast was served. The second was yesterday evening when he was decked out to the nines in a tux to go to the opera. Short hair, some gray.

Talbot had also noted military low quarters, highly polished. Had the woman been the one in question, Talbot could have recalled a great more detail of her physical characteristics and dress. The third time he'd seen the man was just now in the breakfast room. The man was tan and trim, relatively short, somewhere between five-six and five-eight. WIU T-shirt. *What is WIU? Western Indiana U? Western Iowa, Illinois, Idaho? Could be something, maybe nothing at all.* What about his companion? Was she his wife, girlfriend, accomplice? She was attractive, also very physically fit; that's about all he knew.

Not much to go on. Talbot briefly considered asking Hatke to see their registration card. He could get a wealth of information from it, including a passport number, name, and address, if any of that contained even a shred of truth. Henry Talbot, of course, had never disclosed *his* true occupation to the hotel manager. He was just another American businessman working for a company that produced widgets used in the manufacturing of quality automobiles. He even carried a few samples around in his briefcase. Talbot drummed the tabletop with his fingertips, staring blankly in the direction of the beverage bar. A girl was cleaning off the tables at the far side of the dining room, hustling back and forth from the kitchen.

Talbot began to review what he knew again in his mind. Suddenly, he realized: it was the shoes! If the man had ever been in the military, his fingerprints would be on file at the Military Personnel Record Center. If he had ever been arrested, his prints would also be on some file with some central law enforcement agency somewhere back in the States. Talbot waited for the girl to go back into the kitchen with a full tray of dishes. He got up and casually strolled over to the end of the beverage bar where the runners had set down their empty fluted juice glasses. Swiftly, but very carefully, he picked up the glass the man had used, with thumb and forefinger only on the rim, and dropped it into his suit coat side pocket. He headed directly to the public phone in the small, unoccupied hotel lobby.

"Captain Heinsz, speaking," responded the other party.

"Johann, Hank Talbot here. I hope you're not too busy right now."

"Herr Talbot! Good to hear your voice. Never too busy for an old friend. How may I help you, Henry?" the captain of the Munich Police Department, Third District, cheerfully replied.

Talbot appreciated the straight-to-the point approach, no waste of time and no bullshit. "Can you take a set of prints from a juice glass, like right away? You see, I've got a bit of an emergency going on, and I don't have time to go through my normal channels."

"Of course we can do that; no problem! I'll be happy to assist in any way I can."

"Can I meet you somewhere to hand over the glass?" asked Talbot.

"I'll meet you in five minutes at the Odeonsplatz, on the right side, closest to the Theatinerkirche."

"Great. Thanks very much, John. I appreciate it. See you in five."

Talbot transferred his handkerchief from his hip pocket to the side coat pocket and loosely wrapped the glass, taking great care not to smudge the prints.

The hand off took place as planned at precisely the given time. Heinsz said he would fax a copy of the prints to his office within the hour. Truly a man to Talbot's liking, Johann Heinsz asked no further questions. He clearly understood the nature of Talbot's business.

The NSA chief strode briskly back to the hotel. He slowed down considerably before entering the lobby. There they were. The couple was standing at the reception desk speaking with Moritz Hatke. Talbot gave a weak, forced smile as he, too, stepped up to the counter.

Mr. Hatke continued talking with the couple. "… just down the street to your right, till you reach the Isar, then only a few blocks down to your left. You can't miss it, and I'm sure you'll enjoy it. The Deutsches Museum is my favorite one in the entire city."

The couple thanked Hatke, and the man did exactly as Talbot had anticipated. He reached in his pocket and laid their room key, attached to the large metal fob, on top of the counter for the hotel manager to return to the proper hook on the board behind the front desk. The room number was plainly stamped onto both sides of the fob: 221. Moritz handed Talbot his room key without asking, hanging the other key on the board in almost the same motion.

The couple exited the Hotel Adria to the right as instructed. They were dressed in casual, but proper summer clothing, and the woman had an expensive-looking Pentex 35mm camera slung over her shoulder. *So, off to visit the Deutsches Museum,* thought Talbot. That could easily consume the rest of the day.

Talbot wasted no time in retrieving the lock-picking tool from the briefcase in his room, along with a pair of latex surgical gloves.

Reaching the second floor, Talbot noticed the housekeeper had evidently just finished her rounds on that floor. The linen cart was parked in its designated spot in the supply closet with the light off and the door slightly ajar. This was probably the most opportune time to break in, Talbot considered. He didn't want the housekeeper walking in on him in someone else's room.

He knew he needed to work fast. Standing in the hallway in full view, he worked the small, drill-like tool proficiently. It took less than thirty seconds to crack the door lock. Once inside the room, he began looking for any clues pertaining to this couple's true identity. Who was this man? What opposition force was he working for? Who else might be working with him? Was he in fact the trigger man who had killed Erich Mueller? If he was, and the description certainly seemed to fit, this guy would pay the full price. Justice would be served quickly!

Talbot was realistic and knew he would not likely find the high-powered rifle used in the murder, nor did he expect to find any personal weapons in the room; it was much too risky for a professional to leave a weapon lying around a hotel room. Paper clues were about the best he could hope for: receipts, used airline or train tickets, boarding passes, anything that would link this guy to being in the area at the approximate time of the shooting.

If I'm next on his hit list, he should have some sort of dossier on me, thought Talbot as he began looking through the top dresser drawer. "Hmph, socks and underwear. Big help," he grumbled. The second drawer contained a couple of neatly folded lightweight sweaters. Nothing. Talbot then noticed four pieces of luggage on the floor of the inset closet, directly to the left of the door.

~ * ~

"Oh, darn it," said Laura Bucher mildly.

"What's wrong, hon?" asked her husband Mark.

"I forgot my camera bag," she said, shaking her head in disgust.

"Do you need it? I mean, we're just going to the museum."

"Just the museum! This is the Deutsches Museum we're talking about," Laura said, realizing the museum didn't hold quite the value for her husband as it did for her. "I want to take plenty of pictures, and I don't have any extra film for my camera or any of my other lenses. Tell you what; you stay right here, do some people watching, and I'll run back to the room and get the bag. It'll only take me a couple of minutes."

"No, no, I'll go back and get it. You can stay here and take some pictures of the bridge and the river. I'll be right back," he responded dutifully as she had hoped he would.

"Well, okay; if you insist. Hurry back," she said.

Mark Bucher took off at a quick jog in the direction of the Hotel Adria.

Bucher bounded up the steps to the hotel foyer two at a time. "*Zimmer Nummer zwei zwei eines, bitte,*" he requested of the desk clerk.

"*Jawohl, Herr Bucher,*" the clerk responded and handed him the key to room 221.

~ * ~

Henry Talbot heard the key enter the lock and the rubber-edged metal fob buffet the door. *Ah shit!* He instinctively reached back for the Model 64 Smith & Wesson 38 Special tucked away in his waistband holster. He hoped like hell it was just the housekeeper. If it was *the man*....Talbot positioned himself in the open closet area next to the door, but he would be only partially concealed. No other choice. No time. The senior NSA investigator held the revolver near his right ear, ready to spring his arm forward at any instant. The door opened with a quick, hurried movement. He already knew it wasn't the housekeeper.

Did I leave the door unlocked? wondered Mark Bucher. *I don't think so.* Upon stepping through the threshold, Bucher felt the presence of someone else in the room. He tried to stay calm and walked toward the dresser, knowing full well the camera bag was in the closet area with the other luggage. Bucher's first thought was that he had interrupted a burglar in the act. The initial fear grew more into anger at the thought of their personal privacy and belongings being violated. Worst yet, the thought that it could have just as well been Laura coming back to the room and finding the intruder, putting *her* in immediate danger, really fanned the flames of anger that were mounting rapidly.

Bucher then moved toward the desk, giving the impression he was looking for a pen, a key, something. He was stalling, trying to figure out his next move. Bucher needed to collect his thoughts and his courage quickly. He stalled, fumbling around at the desk, wanting to give the thief an opportunity to get out. Thoughts of a cornered animal raced through his head. If he could possibly avoid a conflict, so much the better.

The moment the man stepped toward the desk, Talbot was just out of view. It was his only chance to move from the open closet, where the man would plainly see him as soon as he came toward the door. His only option was to duck into the dark bathroom, directly on the opposite side of the closet area, no more than four or five feet away. Taking a deep breath and with his weapon at the ready, he darted from daylight to darkness in a split second.

Now with his back to the desk, Bucher was looking in the direction of the window and the small television standing on a pedestal. He caught the reflection of something white streak across the blank, dark gray TV screen. Alarmed and growing more angry, Bucher actually now felt he might have the upper hand. He figured he had a slight edge with the element of surprise, because the guy could not have anticipated that his movement was detected. Bucher also considered that this intruder had to be some sort of lowlife two-bit burglar who lived in the shadows and preyed on innocent, unsuspecting people.

Bucher had the option to walk past the bathroom door and out of the hotel room and hope the police could respond quickly enough to catch this guy, or he could confront the intruder who had violated his space and had suddenly sparked a fury he had never felt before. He kept thinking: *This could have been Laura up here instead of me! What then?*

Walking toward the door, he could see through the thin crack between the hinged door jamb and the bathroom door. A figure was standing behind the partially closed door in the dark. Bucher's senses seemed to suddenly be more acute; he could actually hear the intruder breathing and smell his perspiration.

Talbot stood perfectly still in the dark, again holding his pistol at the ready near the right side of his head, hoping the other man would soon make his exit so he would remain undetected.

Bucher was never one to start a fight, although he had never backed away when threatened, either. With the adrenalin pounding through his veins, Bucher stopped in front of the door as if he were ready to turn the handle and leave, but instead, he pivoted on his left foot, bent at the waist to his left, gave a side kick with his right foot, and hit the partially open bathroom door with all his strength. Talbot caught the full impact of the solid wooden door squarely on the nose and mouth.

Dazed by the crushing impact, Henry Talbot dropped to his knees. Bucher flipped on the light to find a large man, blood streaming from a smashed nose and a mouth full of blood and broken teeth, kneeling on his bathroom floor. Still struggling to maintain consciousness, Talbot began to level his S&W 38 Special in Bucher's direction. Bucher lashed out with his left foot, which came straight up under his enemy's right hand and connected at the wrist, causing the weapon to leap from Talbot's hand and clatter toward the tiled shower floor.

Talbot, now in even greater pain, seemed to reach back and find a reserve of strength. He sprang to his feet and in one fast motion grabbed Bucher, lifting him five or six inches off the ground, slamming and pinning him against the wall so that his much smaller opponent was now eyeball to eyeball with him. Talbot was like a wounded bear. The big man's battered face was close enough for Bucher to feel the blood spraying from his nostrils. Bucher's legs and arms were immobilized by the weight and pressure of Talbot's body.

In this position, Mark Bucher had only one option to break free. He drew his head back slightly and with lightning speed, he rammed his forehead down onto Talbot's already broken nose. Talbot's knees buckled and fell backward, striking his head against the porcelain wash basin.

Sprawled in a pool of his own blood, Hank Talbot lay spread-eagle across the tiled floor. Bucher wondered if he had killed the man. His heart was pounding. It took a minute or so for Bucher to regain a degree of composure. He had never had to actually fight for his life before. The thought of possibly having killed the intruder made Bucher nauseous. He knelt down, putting his index and middle finger together and placed them on the common carotid artery that was easily found on the man's neck. Without any problem, he was able to pick up the man's somewhat irregular pulse. That's all Bucher really cared about. He didn't mind that the trespasser lying on the floor was severely battered and bleeding; he just did not want to have to deal with having killed someone, even in self-defense, on his conscience for the rest of his life.

Satisfied with a more steady pulse now, he picked up the Smith & Wesson revolver and walked to the phone on the desk. "Mr. Hatke, this is Bucher in 221. You had better first call an ambulance, then call the police, and then get up here right away. I found someone snooping around in my room, one of your guests I believe, and you'd also better send up housekeeping with a mop and a bucket, because there's a lot of his blood in my bathroom which needs to be cleaned up!"

"Oh, my God!" exclaimed the hotel proprietor, as he looked at the sprawled body. "This is Mr. Talbot! What have you done to him?"

"He was in *my* room, pointing *this* at me!" He held up the handgun for Moritz Hatke to see.

"I...I don't understand," said the bewildered Hatke.

"Well, neither do I, but I will definitely find out as soon as he comes around," said Bucher with conviction as he could feel the wrath starting to build again.

A middle-aged police lieutenant was the first to arrive on the scene. Upon seeing the grotesque sight and also checking Talbot's pulse and making sure the "victim" was breathing all right, he looked up at Bucher and shook his head. "Sir, this is probably not your lucky day. You see, you have just beat up a close friend and associate of the captain of Munich's Third District Police Department, Johann Heinsz. You'll need to come with me to answer some questions."

Bucher had anticipated that, but was disturbed by the thought that, although he was the victim of this intrusion, he was the one to be interrogated. *Who the hell is this guy?*

Talbot was now coming out of unconsciousness. The paramedics were arriving, followed directly by Laura Bucher, who was almost in a state of panic at this point after seeing the emergency vehicles with lights flashing just outside the hotel entrance. A sick feeling developed instantly as she followed them up the stairs to room number 221.

Seeing Mark standing next to the policeman—in a blood-stained shirt, but without any obvious injuries—she sighed with relief. "Thank God! Are you all right?"

Bucher gave his wife a reassuring half smile and said, "Yeah, I'm okay." They embraced for a long moment.

"I got concerned when you didn't come back right away. I figured something had to be wrong. Then when I saw the police car and the ambulance outside, I prayed a "Hail Mary" that it wasn't you."

Genuinely confused, she asked, "What is going on here, and who is that?" She looked toward the man being placed on a rolling stretcher.

"*I* don't even know what happened. I came up here and found this guy snooping around in our room when I came back for the camera bag. He pulled a gun on me, and the next thing I know, he's lying on the bathroom floor with blood pouring out of his mouth and the back of his head."

"Are you telling me *you* did this? I can't believe it!" said Laura, amazed.

"Yeah, well, I guess I did. That's a little out of character for me, isn't it?"

"Just a *little* out of character for you?" she said with a subtle grin, shaking her head. "What in the world got into you, Mark? I don't get it."

"Hon, I was scared, and then I was angry. It's hard to explain. A lot of thoughts rushed through my head in a matter of seconds. One thing that really bothered me was it could have been you walking in on this guy, and I thought of what he might have done to you. It's more than just knowing someone wanted to steal our belongings. Besides, I don't think he was here to do that, but something more sinister. I wondered, too, if he might possibly be stalking us or, more specifically, stalking *you*. It *is* possible. I seem to recall the look he gave you last night as we were in the lobby leaving for the opera. It's still bothering me, and I plan to find out exactly who this man is and what he was doing in our room. I promise you that," vowed Bucher.

"Now I've got to go with this policeman and explain what happened. Seems this guy is a friend of a precinct captain or something, so maybe it won't take too long to get to the bottom of this, I hope."

Mark Bucher was driven directly to the office of the captain of the Third District at Central Police Headquarters. He would need to answer a few brief questions for their "accident report," the lieutenant told him.

Seems a bit of an overkill, thought Bucher, *to be questioned by a police captain for just protecting myself in my hotel room! Something is definitely not right with this picture.*

Captain Johann Heinsz had been briefed on the situation and personally conducted the private questioning, realizing this was probably connected in some way with Talbot's investigation and requests from earlier in the morning. Heinsz would certainly keep this information confidential until he had the opportunity to speak with Talbot at greater length.

Once Captain Heinsz was satisfied with the responses given by Mr. Bucher, who appeared to be quite normal and who had apparently just been in the wrong place at the wrong time, Heinsz politely told Bucher he was free to go. No further questions at this time.

"Not so fast, Mr. Heinsz. I'm not leaving until I find out who this man is and what he was doing in my room. Now it's your turn to answer some questions!" The fury was once again starting to boil.

"Very well, Mr. Bucher. You are entitled to an explanation, I suppose. I'll give you as much as I am permitted to tell you," replied Heinsz. "Mr. Henry Talbot works for your government in, let's say, some sort of police capacity. He told us, after regaining full consciousness, that he was pursuing official government business. That is all I can tell you at this point."

"And where is he now?" asked Bucher calmly.

"Well, Mr. Bucher, you have broken his nose, fractured his right wrist, knocked out or broken five teeth, and given him a mild concussion to the back of his head. Mr. Talbot is, of course, in a hospital," replied Heinsz with exasperation.

"What hospital?"

"I cannot give you that information," the captain responded without any hesitation.

"Okay. Then I'll be leaving now. Thank you," said Bucher coldly.

"Thank you for your cooperation, Mr. Bucher," responded Captain Heinsz in a professional tone.

~ * ~

Bucher did not go directly back to the Hotel Adria. He first stopped at a flower shop near the hotel. "I'd like to send some flowers to a friend of mine who was recently in an accident, but I don't know exactly which hospital he was sent to. Could you call the nearest hospital and ask if he has been admitted?"

"Of course, I'll be happy to. His name, please?" asked the clerk.

Three minutes later: "Yes, a Mr. Henry Talbot was just released from the emergency room and was admitted just a short time ago," replied the information desk receptionist at Our Lady of Victory Hospital. "Room number 314."

Bucher paid cash for the bouquet of flowers and, as if it were an afterthought, said, "Instead of you sending the flowers, I think I'll just deliver them myself."

"That would be a *very* kind gesture!" agreed the shop keeper.

Maybe not so kind, thought Bucher.

~ * ~

Captain Johann Heinsz had no idea what his American friend had up his sleeve, but he knew Talbot should not be bothered by this man who had administered such a beating at the hotel. Heinsz understood this was possibly—no, *probably*—the man Talbot was interested in, for whatever unknown reason. Now finding himself in the game, the Munich Third District police captain took a proactive stance and dispatched four plainclothes officers to keep tabs on Mr. Bucher: two to watch the front door of the Adria and the other two to keep a watchful eye for any suspicious activities at Our Lady of Victory Hospital and protect his colleague, if necessary. It was a good idea, although initiated a little too late.

Bucher received friendly smiles as he passed through the halls of the hospital; it was amazing what a handful of flowers could add to one's character.

Room 314. A single room. No staff around at this time. Talbot was propped up in bed and appeared to be sleeping. Probably pretty well-sedated, thought Bucher. Talbot's head was bandaged like a turban, and white tape made a large X across the bridge of his nose. His eyes were surrounded by pools of deep purple discolored skin.

Bucher knew what he was about to do would be considered cruel and inhumane, but he had to find out this guy's true identity, supposedly highly revered, and get to the bottom of what had provoked the assault. The terms "government business" and "police capacity" kept coming back to him. No one ever said the U.S. Government was devoid of corruption, and cops who have used their badges for all the wrong reasons was unfortunately not unheard of, either.

Bucher approached quietly and removed the nurse call button from the bedside, placing it out of reach. He retrieved a clean washcloth from the adjoining lavatory. Very gently, Bucher took the sets of restraining straps that hung over the sides of the hospital bed and quietly clicked the upper set together across Talbot's chest and upper arms and clicked the lower set across his knees.

Grabbing Talbot by the lower jaw, Mark Bucher pulled down firmly and stuffed the open mouth with the washcloth, and then quickly drew the straps down as tightly as he could. Now Talbot was fully awake, trying to yell and struggling like a person in a straightjacket.

Bucher leaned over the bed, face-to-face with his adversary, keeping his voice low but firm. "You can make this a completely painless conversation, or you can try to endure more pain than you experienced this morning. Just nod if you can understand what I'm saying."

Talbot growled through the gag stuffed in his mouth, and his eyes raged with anger. He obviously understood.

"All I want from you is to find out who you are and why you were rummaging through my hotel room. Were you possibly stalking me? Or my wife? I need to know. Just a straight answer, that's all."

Talbot began to settle down. When he had first gained consciousness, his initial thought was that this man must indeed be Erich Mueller's killer. As savage of a beating as he had taken, it had to be him. It had all added up.

The NSA chief was thoroughly disgusted with himself for letting this cold-blooded assassin get the best of him and, worst of all, for letting him get away. But now, this man had come back for him, blowing Talbot's original theory that he was next on this guy's hit list.

He could have put me away back in the hotel room, but he didn't. Now he's had a second chance to kill me, but instead, he's asking me who I am. If he's not Mueller's killer, then just who the hell is he? Talbot wondered.

Hank Talbot grumbled something with a mouthful of cloth.

"Now, if you want to talk, I'll take this washcloth out. But I'm warning you," Bucher said as he took a small Swiss Army knife from his pocket and opened the fingernail file. "I don't do manicures very well, and I'd hate to drive this nail file too far up behind your fingernail. Just cooperate and tell me what I need to know."

Bucher took the file and placed it under the fingernail on Talbot's left index finger, applying just enough pressure to cause a slight amount of pain. "Are you ready to talk?"

Talbot squinted his eyes shut and nodded. Bucher removed the gag with his left hand while keeping the file in its sensitive location.

"Just who the hell *are you,* mister?" snarled Talbot.

Ignoring the question completely, Bucher continued his interrogation. "People seem to know *you,* Mr. Talbot, but that doesn't answer why you were going through my wife's and my belongings. Or were you waiting for *us*?" He paused a moment. "All right, I'll answer your question first. My name is Mark Bucher. I'm a businessman from St. Louis, and my wife and I are here on holiday. It was supposed to be more of a second honeymoon, but I'm afraid you may have pretty well screwed that up for us. Your turn, Mr. Talbot."

"Hank Talbot. I can't say it's been a pleasure to meet you. You got lucky back there in the hotel room, Mr. Bucher, if that's your real name. Nobody has *ever* caught me off guard like you just did. You're lucky you're not dead! I'll tell you that I work for the U.S. Government, and that's about all. Right now, you're under twenty-four hour surveillance" Which was a lie, but it would have been an excellent idea, if he had any manpower at all. "You are under suspicion for a particular crime that involved another government inspe—I mean, employee. Consider yourself under house arrest until further notice. Don't leave the city."

"Under house arrest! That's absurd. For what? Beating the crap out of an intruder?"

"No, for the interference of...an official government action." Talbot continued to struggle for words to support his unfounded suspicions. "And possibly—no, *probably*—endangering the lives of millions of Europeans."

273

The NSA chief immediately regretted saying that and the previous remarks. The influence of the pain-killing drugs may have just jeopardized a national security issue. *This whole ordeal should never have happened.*

"Until I find out exactly what authority you have, Mr. Talbot, you can go to hell!" Bucher shot back defiantly as he walked out the door.

Talbot's mind was racing, searching for answers. He realized he could no longer carry out his covert airborne mission over the Czech border in his present condition, and the clock was running out. He had to get out and get back to his office or to the hotel to contact Fort Mead and relay the latest events of the day. *I've gotta get some help. Fast!*

In a matter of seconds, as if someone had turned off the lights, Talbot succumbed to the rest his body craved.

He awoke an hour and fifteen minutes later when a nurse came in to check his vital signs. Looking at the wall clock, Talbot could see that the possibilities of the crucial linkup with Richter were beginning to evaporate. *Damn!*

Just then, Captain Johann Heinsz came in carrying a large manila envelope. Taking the side chair and skipping the normal greeting, he immediately got down to business. "I've put a tail on the man who did this to you, Henry. He—"

"Well, you're a day late and a dollar short, John. He's already been by to visit, and he brought me these nice flowers," Talbot said, scowling.

Heinsz looked perplexed. "Tell me what's going on, and maybe I can help."

"Thanks, but I'm afraid it's my game at the present. You can call off your watch dogs, too. I think I was chasing the wrong guy. If he was who I thought he was, you'd be at the morgue right now, identifying my body."

"I guess you don't need these prints then?" Heinsz asked, holding up the manila envelope.

"No, I suppose not. Wait, on second thought, I will take them. They might possibly be of some help, but I doubt it. Thanks, John."

As soon as Captain Heinsz left the room, Talbot sat up in bed. He had double vision and his head was splitting, but he began to unwrap his bandages. He could not afford to waste any more time. Before shedding the flimsy hospital gown, Talbot located a white lab coat from a supply cabinet near the nurse's station. His dark trousers were bloodstained but useable, and the newly acquired lab coat would have to do, since he figured the emergency room personnel must have discarded his once-white dress shirt.

Wearing the white lab coat, Talbot walked undetected out the front entrance of the hospital with the manila envelope serving as a shield to mask his battered face when oncoming pedestrians came his way.

The office was closer to the hospital than the hotel, and it provided more of the communication equipment he needed. Talbot opened the manila envelope as he closed his office door behind him. He immediately placed the very clear and enlarged copy of three fingerprints on the fax machine: right thumb, right forefinger, and right middle, established by the positioning on the juice glass. He attached a handwritten note, requesting the identity of the fingerprints immediately, along with a strong suggestion to check the military database first.

The one-button speed dial connected Munich to Fort Mead within seconds, and Talbot watched as the single sheet slid through. The fax confirmed that the message was received on the other end, so Talbot waited about five minutes and then picked up the phone to call the deputy director of the NSA.

In less than nine minutes, the computers at the National Security Agency matched the fingerprints Talbot had forwarded to those of Mark A. Bucher, found in the U.S. Military personnel archives.

Mike Agnussi relayed the data from the green-bar printout. "It says this guy's name is Mark Bucher. Served six years in the U.S. Army National Guard, Missouri, 138th Mech. Infantry. Sworn in on 06 June 1970. Basic Training: Fort Polk, Louisiana. Infantry AIT, North Fort Polk, Louisiana. Qualified as an expert with the .45 semi-automatic and as a sharp shooter with the M-16. Last military position held was Squad Leader/Track Commander. Highest rank achieved: Sergeant, E-5. Honorable Discharge: 06 June 1976."

"What about college? Anything about a 'WIU?'" Talbot asked.

"This only shows thirty credit hours from the University of Missouri-St. Louis prior to his enlistment. Education records were seldom kept up-to-date back then after active duty was completed. Great-looking military record, never a problem. Always scored high on intelligence and leadership tests, and maxed out on all of the physical training scores. That's about all I have on this guy, Hank," said Agnussi.

"That's good enough," replied Talbot, now a hundred percent convinced he had been stalking the wrong person. He chastised himself for going off half-cocked on what now seemed to be a pretty weak description of the person who *might* have killed Erich Mueller. But time was short, and Talbot was under terrific pressure to make contact with his man Richter. As overwhelming as it might seem, the safety of as many as eight major European cities were in his hands.

"Now here's the downside, Mike," Talbot said. Embarrassing as it was, he explained in detail what had taken place regarding his suspicion of Bucher as Erich Mueller's assassin and what had resulted in Talbot's rearranged face, broken wrist, and mild concussion.

"Good Lord, Hank. I can't believe it!" exclaimed Agnussi. "Let me get this straight; you let some American businessman on vacation kick your ass, in *his* hotel room, because you thought he fit the description of one of Mueller's possible shooters? Hank, do you realize we probably have at least five people in this building alone who would fit that description? Just what the hell where you thinking? I guess we can expect a call from his guy's attorney any minute now. Well that's just *great*! Now, how effective do you expect to be with a concussion, double vision, and a broken wrist? How do you plan to carry out your duties in that condition?"

Henry Talbot knew he deserved a severe chewing out from his boss, and he also figured this would not be the end of it, either.

"That brings up my second point: the mission." Talbot took a deep breath and exhaled slowly, anticipating Agnussi's response. "Do you remember telling me in your fax yesterday morning that the ball was in my court and to use whatever means I had at my disposal?"

"Yes, I remember. Go on," Agnussi confirmed, fearful of what might come next.

"Well, I worked out a plan to rendezvous with Richter to get more information on General Krause's activities, by jumping into the Czech Republic just over the Germany/Czech border—"

"You worked out a plan with whom?"

Talbot had dreaded the question. "With General Bussen."

"General Bussen! The CIC of the European Command? You're not really talking about a military jump are you?"

"Yes, sir, I am." Talbot quickly added, "And interestingly enough, General Bussen approved my plan and told me he would provide me with whatever I needed to carry out the mission."

Mike Agnussi was dumbfounded. "Henry, you *know* you have absolutely no authority to request assistance from the military, especially from the four-star who happens to command every soldier, sailor, marine, and airman throughout Europe and then some! All of a sudden, I can envision the two of us standing in front of a congressional hearing on Capitol Hill."

Although Agnussi was appalled by his subordinate's conduct, he marveled at the fact that Talbot was able to get to the man who could actually get it done. This plan, however lame or ingenious it might be, would have been mired down in the normal bureaucratic channels of the Pentagon for weeks. He had given Talbot free reign to get the job done; he just didn't think he would use these extraordinary measures to accomplish it.

"Henry, I'm telling you: use the military for your transportation *only*. It ends right there. No further involvement with the military! Got it?

"Yes, sir. Understood."

Now sensing that Agnussi had cooled off a little, Talbot continued, "As you know, Mike, Mueller was going to be my link with Richter, so when you told me about the killing, I planned to do it myself. I *cannot* pull any of my other assets from their present assignments now, because they are potentially as crucial to the overall security of this European sector—and

Moscow, I might add—as our commitment to stop General Krause in his tracks before it's too late. Also keep in mind that Krause now has twenty-four XG-777 missiles and eight M-5 launch vehicles at his disposal, and Lord knows what other sophisticated weaponry he may have stashed away somewhere. He is a dangerous man; you can see that. Mike, I need some help! Being banged up the way I am, I can't do this mission myself. I know it's a lot to ask, but I need somebody who's jump-qualified, can speak German, and can operate in an unfriendly environment. Can't you draft some able body there at the fort or pull somebody off the street?"

Agnussi stayed calm. Composure was a necessary attribute for the person who sat behind the deputy director's desk. "I'll see what I can scare up for you and try to have that person on the next plane to Munich."

Talbot looked at his watch. It was near two o'clock in the afternoon Munich time, which meant it was only eight o'clock on the East Coast. This was somewhat encouraging. It would give Agnussi ample time to find somebody within the organization with the skills needed for the mission, with time enough to catch an evening commercial flight to arrive in Munich early the next morning. If worse came to worst, there were always military flights into Rhein-Main or Ramstein Air Force Base as an alternate possibility.

"Well, do the best you can, Mike. And Mike, please be quick about it, okay?"

"I'll call when and if I find somebody for you. In the meantime, stop snooping around where you don't belong. You're too old for that kind of crap, Hank. Got it?"

The fact was that Fort Mead did not regard this particular threat with the same fervor Talbot did. Of course this was highly important, but Agnussi was busy putting out other larger fires in Moscow and the Middle East that could have an instant impact on the U.S. if not checked immediately. Agnussi was not going to be sucked in by the "squeaky wheel" syndrome.

Another contributing factor in prioritizing efforts was that the twenty-four missing XG-777 missiles and the eight M-5 vehicles had not yet been physically spotted anywhere in Europe—not by satellite photos nor by a single observer. They needed something more solid. Agnussi was looking for "hard evidence."

~ * ~

2:00 p.m.

"Luke, this is Mark."

"I thought you were in Germany!"

"I am. Hey, I'm calling from a pay phone, and I don't have a lot of time. I've got a problem, and I need your help—"

"Is Laura all right?" the veteran policeman interrupted.

"Yeah, she's fine, but I've run into a very unusual situation." Bucher explained how he had found the intruder in his hotel room and had proceeded to render him unconscious on the bathroom floor, in a pool of his own blood.

Luke Yacovelli was laughing out loud, picturing the scene.

"Luke, this isn't funny! I don't know who this person is. Says his name is Henry Talbot, and the German police revere this guy as if he were something sacred. Claims he works for the U.S. Government, possibly in some sort of law enforcement capacity. Can you check in your police databank to see if there is in fact a Henry Talbot in a federal or state department job over here?"

"I can't access that information myself, but I have some friends in high places who can probably find out for us. Personnel records are extremely secure for obvious reasons, but just simple verification shouldn't be too much to ask," replied Yacovelli.

Bucher gave a brief physical description of Talbot and the phone number at the Hotel Adria so that Yacovelli could get back to him. He was pleased to be able to have at least some kind of indirect information to help level the playing field. He smiled, thinking it was always nice to live across the street from the deputy commander, Division of Criminal Investigation,

St. Louis County Police Department, even if Luke could beat him at tennis consistently.

Laura Bucher laid across the bed atop the white, down-filled comforter, trying to read the latest John Grisham novel and keep her mind off the threat to their safety and Mark's violent encounter with the intruder. After all of the police and paramedics had left, the woman from housekeeping moved in and sanitized the ravaged bathroom. Laura welcomed the fresh, antiseptic scent of the soap and cleaning solvents to help wash away any trace of the gruesome events that had taken place right there in their room.

Moritz Hatke had promptly sent up an abundant fruit basket and a large bunch of freshly cut flowers, along with a sincere note of apology for the "mishap" that had occurred that morning. Laura was totally perplexed by the violence that somehow included her husband. He had been whisked away by the local police before he could tell her any details of what had really transpired. Naturally, she was worried about him and felt very alone and unsafe without him.

The sound of the key entering the lock and the door handle turning caused an instant anxiety attack for a second or two. It was Mark, thank God, and he was okay. They held each other tight for a long time, enjoying the security they felt in each other's arms. Sitting on the bed, Mark explained again, this time to Laura, everything that had taken place, omitting not even the most minute detail, because he wanted her input into this to help make some sense of it all.

As Bucher was finishing up the saga, the phone rang. It was Luke Yacovelli.

"I've got the lowdown on Henry Talbot for you," he began. "He is exactly who he said he is, Mark. He has nineteen years with the Department of Defense, sixteen years of which have been with the National Security Agency. The last seven years, he's held the position of Sector Chief-Munich. This 'history recap' was a little extra bonus they threw in just because I was such a charming guy to work with. Listen, Mark, this is absolutely strictly confidential information. You did *not* hear any of this from me. I do not want to jeopardize this source!"

"Understood, Lukey, and thanks very much."

Mark Bucher sat down at the desk and massaged the bridge of his nose with his thumb and forefinger. He should have felt relief, but he didn't. He actually felt guilty for roughing up somebody who was just trying to do his job, a job the security of the United States had entrusted to people like Henry Talbot.

It hit him like a slap in the face: "interference in an official government action and probably endangering the lives of millions of Europeans." *Talbot's anger was real!* He hadn't just been snooping around for no good reason. He had been here for a legitimate purpose.

Have I possibly jeopardized some important mission, Bucher wondered, *or have I just been reading too much Tom Clancy lately?*

Bucher left a message with the front desk for Talbot to contact him as soon as he returned. Hours passed, and the phone did not ring. He wondered if Talbot would bother to call him back. Bucher went down to the lobby to check if his key was still on the hook. It was there, so he decided to wait for Talbot to pass through the lobby to retrieve his key. Not more than twenty minutes had passed before the battered body of Henry Talbot strolled up to the desk.

Seeing Bucher get up from the smartly upholstered lobby chair, Talbot grumbled in a low voice, "Ah shit, not you again. I had enough of you this morning."

Bucher walked up to Talbot. "Yeah, I know, and I found out who you are and what you do," he said quietly. "Can we talk in private?"

Talbot pointed toward the dimly lit, unoccupied breakfast room. He pulled out a chair from a table for four and simply said, "Speak."

"I know you are in fact Henry Talbot, employed by the Department of Defense since 1974, and that you have been the NSA section chief here in Munich since 1986," Bucher said, to add to his much needed credibility. "And don't bother to ask how I got this information."

Talbot tilted back in his chair and almost smiled, revealing several empty spaces where teeth used to be. "All right, I won't ask, but that's pretty good. So what is it *you* want?" he said flatly.

"I want to apologize for what I did to you this morning. I didn't—"

"You couldn't have known," Talbot broke in, "and I'm sorry I mistook you for one of the bad guys. I'm afraid that was pretty unprofessional on my part."

"I hope I didn't really screw things up for you, I mean operation-wise," Bucher said with genuine sincerity.

"You did, but that can't be helped now. Hindsight is 20/20, isn't it?"

"Well, I wanted to get that off my chest. I am terribly sorry." Bucher extended his hand. Talbot accepted it with an equally firm left-handed grip.

Chapter Twenty-one

Munich, Germany
Thursday, September 30, 1993
6:15 a.m.

Mark and Laura occupied a small table toward the rear of the Adria's breakfast room. They were the only guests until Hank Talbot came through the doorway. Mark immediately stood up and motioned for Talbot to join them.

Talbot looked worse this morning than he did the day before. His blackened eyes made him look like something out of a horror movie: a walking zombie. Mark introduced Talbot to Laura, and she openly expressed her sympathy for the mishap of the day before.

Including Talbot in their conversation as they enjoyed their morning coffee, Laura explained they were having a friendly disagreement over the activities they had planned for that day.

"We've rented a car and agreed today would be an excellent day to drive down to visit the Neuswanstien Castle, and then my crazy husband gets this wild idea from *Fromer's Travel Guide* that he would like to try his luck at hang gliding from the neighboring mountain slopes! He's done some wild and outlandish things before, but this is the limit. I'm not going to let him ruin *my* vacation by doing his impersonation of Icarus flying too close to the sun. Tell him he's ridiculous, will you?"

Talbot grinned in response, only half listening, his mind preoccupied. He felt as miserable as he had ever felt in his life. *Agnussi damn well better have some warm body for me today, or we're all screwed,* he thought. He felt the familiar vibration in his pocket again and removed the pager, then saw it was a call from Agnussi. *Well, speak of the devil!*

Henry Talbot excused himself, explaining he had to respond to this call, and quickly went back to his room. *Holy crap; it's twelve thirty in the morning, and Agnussi is still at it,* he realized as he punched in the numbers.

"What do you got, Mike?"

"Hank, you're asking for the impossible right now. Someone who is jump-qualified, speaks German, and can get around behind enemy lines. But here's what I came up with: A. Inspector Jack Murphree, age thirty-four, speaks German and Czech like a native, very smart young guy, also worked as a PT instructor for the FBI down at Quantico before joining the NSA—"

"That's great; how soon can you get him over?" Talbot asked impatiently.

"You didn't let me finish, Hank. His only flaw is that every time he gets on an airplane, he has a tendency to toss his cookies. Obviously no jump experience." Agnussi quickly moved on to his next alternative.

"B. Inspector Brian Dalaney, age thirty-seven, served six years with the 82nd Airborne. He's jumped out of more planes than most people have flown in, good security clearance, but—"

"Yeah, but..." repeated Talbot in anticipation.

"But the only German he knows is 'Lowenbrau.' Not exactly the linguist you had hoped for."

"Mike, why the hell did you even bother to call?"

"Henry, I'll tell you why I called!" The tension in Agnussi's voice was becoming very clear. "I called hoping you might be able to find *some* flexibility in your plan. You've got to be able to work with the tools and conditions you are given! This is not a textbook case; none of them are. You know that."

Talbot was obviously frustrated with the perceived lack of support from the home office and chose not to listen to his supervisor's explanation regarding a flexible plan. Besides, at this stage of the game, it really was too late to make any major changes.

"Damn it, Mike, I'll do it myself!"

"Henry, get a grip! Like I've tried to explain to you before," Agnussi paused, trying very hard not to lose his patience with the Munich sector chief, "you know how thin we're spread right now. Let me spell it out for you; this is why we can't afford the extra manpower to chase after the people *you* presume to be our worst threat. What you may not be aware of is the recent build up in troop strength backing General Chesnokov, on two separate fronts. This guy is smart and extremely cunning. For the most part, his military activities have managed to stay under the radar, at least up till a short time ago.

"Chesnokov has a very large percentage of the troop support from both the Russian Army, which was pretty much a given, and surprisingly from the Russian Navy, as well. He now has the unquestioned support of Admiral Yakushkin, commanding the Baltic Fleet, and Admiral Dyachenko, who commands the Russian Navy in the Black Sea. The key element in both of these locations—and I know this personally from my time at the Pentagon—are the military factories and support facilities in these areas that they would have complete control over.

"In the north," Agnussi went on, "they've got two missile assembly plants, one huge tank factory, two electronics assembly plants, and a grand total of *seven* shipyards, all centered around Leningrad and Kaliningrad! Just south of Moscow, they have three nuclear weapons facilities and at least five chemical/biological warfare plants that we know of. There could be more. And if that's not enough to impress you, to the extreme south near the Black Sea port of Sevastopol, centered around the main Naval Aviation Headquarters, General Chesnokov has assembly plants in Rostov and Taganrog producing Russia's newest, most high-tech fighter aircraft, already rolling off the production line. That, my friend, is the very *real* threat to our global security.

"Hank, the best intel I have leads me to believe General Chesnokov's first move will be to invade Turkish soil and quickly secure the Bosporus Straits and, in doing so, control all shipping lanes from the Black Sea all the way into the Mediterranean and at the same time also control a huge amount of crude oil to be brought in for all of the refineries on the Black Sea coast. *Or* there is the possibility of a strike on Yeltsin directly in Moscow, but that's rather improbable. I've discussed these possibilities with General Bussen at Euro Command, and he agrees this troop buildup appears to be more than just casual saber rattling.

"Consider this, Hank, Chesnokov undoubtedly has a lot more nuclear capabilities than Krause's twenty-four *tactical* nuclear warheads. Correct? And furthermore, we don't even know at this point if Krause really intends to use these nukes, or if he just plans to stash these away in some hidden armory somewhere, just to add to his war chest." The deputy director of the NSA let his Munich station chief absorb this information for a minute. "Do you see where I'm coming from now? Do you know how important it is to stop Chesnokov's coup from taking place?"

"Mike, I understand a lot more now than I did five minutes ago, but I want *you* to understand, also, that we've got an additional threat—"

"*Possible* additional threat," interrupted Agnussi.

"Okay, possible additional threat," conceded Talbot, "coming from General Krause, in several different directions; eight to be exact."

"Understood, Hank, and we will monitor that. I only wish we had more available, qualified resources to help you out. Until we have some absolute concrete evidence as to *where* these threats are and that this guy genuinely plans on hurting us, I have to follow the director's orders and stay focused on General Chesnokov's activities around Leningrad and Sevastopol and all the spaces in between. If that's all you've got right now, I've gotta run. Somebody forgot to drain the swamp. But do keep me posted on this, okay?"

Disappointed, but not at all surprised, Talbot signed off and hung up the phone.

For a few moments he had forgotten about the persistent double vision problem and his terrifically disfigured face, not to mention his broken right wrist. *Damn, I stick out like a neon sign,* Talbot said to himself as he looked at his reflection in the window overlooking Liebigstrasse. He stood and looked out impassively. His mind was almost a blank at this point, as he watched the light morning traffic on the narrow street below and an intermittent flow of pedestrians, mostly businessmen and women making their way to the nearby U-Bahn station.

Talbot noticed the figures of Mark and Laura Bucher walking toward their rental car parked halfway down the block. *Hmph, off for a visit to the castle and—wait a minute!*

Talbot raced down the stairs; the tiny elevator was too slow. He ran down the street to meet the Buchers, just as they had adjusted and fastened their seat belts.

"I've gotta talk with you, Mr. Bucher. It's *very* important!" said Talbot, panting.

Bucher's first inclination was to say, "Sorry, not now," but there was such a sense of urgency in his voice and in the expression on his face that he could not ignore the other man's plea.

"I'm sorry, Mrs. Bucher, but I need to speak with him alone."

Mark got out of the car, and Talbot led him a few yards down the street. "The plan I mentioned that you had screwed up, well, you might be able to help after all. I need you to deliver a small package—"

"Sure, no problem. Where?"

"Hold on; I have to ask you a few questions. It's not as easy as it sounds. I'll explain later." Talbot was not making any sense to Bucher, who was doing his best to understand what the other man wanted to tell him or ask him.

"Slow down, Mr. Talbot. Take a breath. What are you trying to say?"

"Okay. Sorry about that." Talbot now started to take a few deep breaths. "First, I need to know if you were really serious about the hang gliding you mentioned at breakfast."

Wondering how in the world his plans to go hang gliding could possibly be of interest to Mr. Talbot, Mark responded honestly, "Oh yeah. I actually convinced Laura to let me try it, with her stipulation that I'll take the four-hour introduction course, and I'll only be doing it one time, from one of the beginner slopes. Her conditions, so we compromised. She agreed this wasn't nearly as bad as when I tried my hand at skydiving a few years ago."

"Skydiving! You're kidding! You've actually jumped out of a plane?" Talbot could not quite believe what he was hearing and wondered if his luck was about to change.

"Yeah, just once. Hunter Field, Sparta, Illinois. A twenty-eight-hundred-foot static line jump from a little Cessna 172. It was fantastic! What a rush." The excitement was evident on Mark Bucher's face. "Have you ever jumped?"

Ignoring the question, Talbot asked, "So you really enjoy this kind of thing?"

"Yeah, I really do. Laura calls it 'flirting with death,' but I don't look at it that way. It's just good, wholesome adventure to me. I don't do as much of the adventure stuff as I did in my twenties and thirties, unfortunately. Maybe I'm just getting older. Years ago, back when I was on active duty in the Army, I even requested to go to jump school at Fort Bragg, but my NG unit back home shot it down. They said it wasn't in their budget, and furthermore, there were no slots for any Airborne troops in a mechanized infantry battalion. Too bad; Airborne really appealed to me, but it would have been pretty difficult to stay jump-qualified in a 'straight leg' Guard unit. Oh well, life goes on, right?"

"Yes, it sure does, and this might be your lucky day," responded Talbot. *Mine too, I hope,* he thought, trying to suppress a smile.

"Okay, here's the story in a nutshell, but I have to warn you this is considered highly classified information. I wouldn't be asking for your help, as a civilian, if I had any other alternatives. And I don't. You are basically my last hope, and millions of lives could actually depend upon your decision. I can't make you do this."

Mark Bucher's curiosity was more than a little piqued.

~ * ~

Henry Talbot had verbally laid out the entire plan for Bucher. The businessman from St. Louis stood there in amazement, shaking his head. "Hey, Mr. Talbot, I'm really flattered, but I'm not James Bond."

"I'm not asking for James Bond. I just need a courier, that's all. Somebody who can pick up and deliver."

"Then why not call UPS?" shot back Mark Bucher, making both men smile slightly.

"You've got what it takes. I figured if you were crazy enough to try hang gliding, jumping out of a plane with a real parachute would be a piece of cake for you! I've seen your military records. You're in great physical shape, your German is pretty good, and now I learn you're jump-qualified as a civilian. And in addition to all of those attributes, I think you've got guts! You have all the bases covered. So what's your answer?" Talbot waited just a moment. "Not trying to sound overly dramatic, but your country is really depending on you. What do you say? Yes or no? If it's affirmative, we need to get moving on it *now*. The clock is ticking, Mark."

Bucher said nothing; he seemed to be in another world at the moment.

~ * ~

St. Thomas Aquinas High School
Florissant, Missouri
September 1968

Mark Bucher considered himself to be patriotic. As unusual as it was for a seventeen-year-old high school senior, he was terrifically proud of his country, but he rarely expressed these deeply rooted feelings about being an American.

He understood, as well as believed in, the old maxim: "Freedom is not free." He looked up to men like his father, his uncle, and his grandfather who *chose* to fight for their country in a time of war.

Most kids going into their senior year of high school really didn't know what career path they wanted to follow. Most knew they wanted to go to college; some knew exactly where they would go or hoped to attend and the curriculum they would follow, while others put off making decisions like that till the eleventh hour. Not Mark Bucher. He planned on enlisting for a three-year hitch in the Army, probably infantry, maybe even go Airborne. College would have to wait. The plus side to that plan was that after his enlistment was up, Uncle Sam would pick up the tab for his college education through the GI Bill.

All aspects of serving in the U.S. Army appealed to young Bucher. He even welcomed the physical and psychological challenges that basic training would present. The rugged life of an infantry soldier, along with an underlying sense of adventure, was precisely what he was looking forward to.

Mark Bucher sincerely wanted to do his part to serve his country as his father and grandfather and so many great Americans had before him, but this Vietnam War was quite different from World War I and World War II.

Although stopping the "Red Tide" of communism in Vietnam was of paramount importance, it didn't begin to measure up to the direct acts of aggression that incited World War II. Why was this conflict in Vietnam so unpopular? Why wasn't this conflict a rallying point for other good Americans to get behind and promote their patriotism? Why were all these left-wing liberal hippies protesting the war? Mark Bucher looked for legitimate answers, but couldn't quite find any that fit his own personal beliefs and principles. He was convinced the freaked-out, pot-smoking hippies were just a bunch of spineless wimps who were afraid to put on a uniform to defend their country.

Father Denny Anderhalter taught religion to the senior boys at Aquinas High School. He felt an obligation to make the young men in his class aware of current events and to encourage them to really think about what was going on in Southeast Asia.

The good Father was by no means a pacifist, nor was he a "hawk." He was, however, a historian with a steady moral compass, and he had been keeping a close eye on the conflict in Vietnam, with all of its political, social, and spiritual ramifications. Father Anderhalter also understood the necessity of stopping the aggressive/atheistic communists whenever and wherever possible. He felt that fighting the spread of communism was like fighting a brush fire on a windy day; you work hard to stop it at one point, but the flames kick back up in two or three other places.

Considering the escalation of the war in Vietnam and realizing the impact it could have on these boys, the priest completely revamped his lesson plan for the first semester. He scrubbed the "Religions of the World" syllabus he normally taught through the first ten weeks, replacing it with "Christian Ethics & the Southeast Asian Conflict."

In order for his students to draw their own conclusions about the present conflict, Father Anderhalter assigned his seniors to several tasks:

Read at least the front page article every day in either the *St. Louis Globe Democrat* or the *St. Louis Post-Dispatch* covering the war in Vietnam, for class discussion the next day.

Read *The Seeds of Destruction*, by Thomas Merton. Give particular attention to Part 2, Chapter I: "The Christian in World Crisis," regarding Pope John XXIII's encyclical *Pacem in Terris* ("Peace on Earth") and St. Augustine's views on "A Just War." Be prepared for daily, ongoing discussions on these topics.

Extra credit can be earned by doing additional reading in *Newsweek*, *Time*, and any other major news publications. Additional reading on the "Just War" topic can also be found by our very own St. Thomas Aquinas in the school library (hopefully by now you know where that is).

Father Anderhalter recognized that this was a very weighty assignment and was prepared to walk these kids through it, but he wanted to take advantage of the opportunity to teach the young men how to think on their own, express their thoughts verbally in front of their peers, and come up with a mature conclusion to what was right and what was wrong. It would be a lesson on morality in our world today. More importantly, Father Anderhalter hoped to teach his students the value of applying Catholic teachings and Gospel values to the issues of the day.

Midway through the first semester, Mark Bucher stopped by Father A's classroom at the end of the day, hoping to catch him before he left for the rectory.

"Hey, Father, do you have a minute?"

Father Anderhalter looked up from the papers he was grading, took off his glasses, and smiled. "Sure, Mark. What's on your mind?"

"Father, I'm really having a difficult time with this course," Bucher said, mildly apologetic.

Anderhalter was surprised to hear this. "What do you mean? You're doing great! You're coming up with better observations and more intelligent questions than anyone else in this class."

"That's not the problem, Father."

"Then what *is* the problem, Mark?"

"Quite honestly, Father, the more I read and the more I listen in class, the more confused I get."

Perplexed, the middle-aged clergyman listened attentively.

"You see, Father, the one thing that has been most important to me for the last three years or so is to join the Army after graduation. An important part of my family heritage is the military. My dad enlisted in the U.S. Navy directly after the Japanese attack on Pearl Harbor, and he fought in North Africa during World War II. My Uncle Paul was a Navy Seabee, landed on Iwo Jima with the Marines and actually watched them raise the flag on Mount Suribachi. My grandfather was an infantryman in the U.S. Army and fought the Germans in the trenches of Compiegne, France, during World War I. These things were without question *the* patriotic thing to do. Father, these men are *my* heroes, and I also want to do my part to preserve our freedom, our form of democracy, and protect our country. "

Anderhalter nodded, somewhat taken aback.

"But I'm very confused about Vietnam being a 'just war.' I really do want to serve my country as a soldier, but the more I learn about the war in Vietnam, the more I question the morality of *why* we're fighting over there. I've been studying the 'Seven Principles of the Just War,' and all of the other stuff written by Augustine and Aquinas and the rest of them. I can find valid arguments on both sides. I mean, communism is basically atheistic and aggressive, and I have a very strong feeling it needs to be stopped. So Father, for me it's a personal thing, and I really would appreciate your advice as to whether I should pursue my dream and enlist in the Army after graduation, or if that would be morally wrong in the eyes of the Church."

Father Anderhalter was astonished at the maturity and sincerity of this young man's concern about doing the right thing. "Mark, that's a good question. I can tell you, first of all, that the Catholic Church would never condemn you for joining the military. After all, where would our country be without a national army to defend it? Saint Augustine was all in favor of keeping the peace; in fact he said it is our obligation as Christians to work toward peace. And in the Gospel, we find Jesus telling a soldier to be content with his pay. He didn't tell him to desert or that he was doing something immoral, did he?"

Mark nodded in solemn agreement.

"But it all boils down to your own conscience," continued Anderhalter. "If you truly believe there is *no* legitimate merit for the U.S. to be in this fight, then change your plan; adjust your sights and choose another dream.

"Conversely, if you truly believe you *can* help bring about peace on earth—remember *Pacem in Terris*—and stop or at least slow down this domino theory of one nation after another falling under communist oppression, then go for it! Although if you are still on the fence and don't have a one-hundred-percent rock-solid conviction one way or the other, I might have a suggestion."

"Sure. I'm definitely open for suggestions," said Mark. "That's pretty much what I came here for."

"Okay, then, what would you think about joining the National Guard or Reserves?"

Father A could read on Bucher's face that the idea had never crossed his mind. "I'm not an authority on the subject, but in my younger years, I did serve as a chaplain for the Missouri Army National Guard. So I know a little about it."

"Yeah, but that's not like the *real* Army, is it? And besides, I'm looking for a little adventure in my life, too," said Bucher.

"Yes, Mark. It actually *is* the real Army, and depending on the type of unit you join, you could see plenty of adventure. I probably sound like a real National Guard recruiter, so bear with me. You take the oath to defend the United States of America and to obey your superiors, just as any soldier does. You go through the very same basic training and advanced individual training along with all of the regular troops. Nothing is different except that you come back home to serve with your NG unit after six months of active duty instead of being shipped to Vietnam for twelve months like most soldiers who come out of basic and AIT. It's the busiest six months of your life, and it *is* challenging. Trust me.

"Chances are you would never be activated to serve in Vietnam," explained Anderhalter. "It is a gamble, of course, and you have to be prepared to go—to be activated, that is—and to go anywhere you might be needed like Vietnam or any other hot spot. The Red Tide is not just contained in Southeast Asia.

"In addition to that," he continued, "I'm sure you're aware that the Army National Guard is often called upon to assist in natural disasters: situations like tornados, floods, hurricanes, and things like that. Sometimes they're called out for civil disturbances such as riots or protest marches, but even that's pretty rare. And you know something, Mark, these are all very honorable ways you can serve your country and your fellow citizens, too. It doesn't necessarily mean you have to pick up a rifle to be a soldier; it might be a shovel, a sandbag, or a riot baton."

Anderhalter hoped he hadn't overwhelmed the high school senior with too much information, but it was all true, and he wouldn't be doing his job or doing Bucher any favors by sugarcoating things, thus increasing the possibilities of the student making a bad decision.

"So, what do you think, Mark?"

"You know, Father, it is an option that I will certainly consider. It's not exactly perfect, but then again, not many things are. I guess that's really why I'm here asking for your advice in the first place."

"Then I would further suggest you pray about this decision. You need prayerful discernment. Offer this up during your prayers at Mass. Ask the Lord to send you a sign of His will. If you submit entirely to His will in this matter, you can't go wrong.

"Obviously, this is a matter that you've not taken lightly," Father Anderhalter continued. "Two important questions you need to ask yourself, Mark. First: is your conscience willing to accept taking a life in the process of defending your country, yourself, or your fellow soldiers *if* you are called upon to do so? Second: will *you* be satisfied personally with this decision? Will the National Guard present the challenge you're looking for, and will this satisfy that burning desire you have to serve your country in the military? Is there enough *adventure* in it for you? It's a six-year commitment, and there is no turning back, unless you choose to go active. Like I said before, the only thing I can tell you, Mark, is to think about it, pray about it."

Father Anderhalter smiled with genuine understanding and compassion, rose to his feet, and extended a hand. Bucher followed his lead.

"Thanks, Father Anderhalter. You've been a big help."

"My pleasure, Mark. That's what I'm here for."

As Bucher left the classroom, Anderhalter was reminded that times like these, even though few and far between, made his job as an educator truly gratifying. The clergyman closed his grade book and headed for the chapel to pray for Mark and his decision.

~ * ~

Munich, Germany
Thursday, September 30, 1993

Was this the opportunity Bucher had been looking for all these years? An opportunity to finally come through for his country in a critical time of need that had never presented itself during his six-year enlistment in the National Guard? This might be his only chance to perform the patriotic duty he had dreamed of many years ago: a duty that no one else, at this time and place, could do.

Looking back up at Talbot's bruised and bandaged face, he finally said in a clear and confident voice, "Sure, I'll do it. I can't afford to gamble the lives of millions of Europeans, can I? Now I've gotta go back and break it to Laura. She'll probably think you're trying to get even with me," replied Bucher reluctantly.

"Remember, Mark. You *cannot* tell her what you're doing. Tell her something else, tell her anything else, but you cannot divulge any information about this mission."

"I'll simply tell her the truth. It's something I *need* to do. I'll leave it at that and hope she understands. When will I get back?"

"You should be back safe and sound by Saturday afternoon. You can also tell her this 'activity' is a paying job. I don't expect you to do this for free. I'll explain the benefits package when you get back," Talbot said with a toothless smile.

The NSA chief looked at his watch and said, "Okay, we've both got things we need to accomplish. You know that gold statue on the tall pedestal in the middle of the Marienplatz? Meet me there at eleven."

Talbot headed toward his office to work on the task of copying and altering the three blue discs as Richter had instructed him to do. Slight, periodic changes were implanted into the program, throwing off the calculations just enough to cause the Cosmos 1813C communications satellite not to function properly and render the XG-777s' remote, automatic firing sequence inoperable.

Mark Bucher returned to his patiently waiting wife who was flipping through the travel guide describing King Ludwig II's Neuschwanstein Castle and the surrounding attractions. He would certainly honor Talbot's instructions by keeping this mission strictly classified and not explaining what he would be doing for the next two and a half days. Still, it bothered him, because he had always been upfront with Laura on all matters, large or small. Mark told her he was sorry he couldn't tell her everything right now, but he had very important business to attend to, and he would explain the whole story when he got back. He also promised he would make up for the lost time as soon as he returned.

Laura, of course, could not possibly understand what was going on and didn't like it one bit. But their marriage was built on trust. She would trust Mark, as always.

~ * ~

10:50 a.m.

As he walked through the quaint side streets of Munich to meet with his new NSA boss (which sounded extremely weird in Bucher's mind), he wondered if his sense of adventure had possibly gotten in the way of plain ol' common sense. Sure, he craved adventure, and yes, there was this genuine desire to be an unsung hero for the country he loved so dearly, but had he gone a little over the edge this time?

Bucher vividly recalled an article he had read years ago in a prominent psychology publication. The article had stated that psychologists have long contemplated what causes some people to take physical risks by doing something dangerous just for the excitement. Some people take it to an extreme by earning their living as stunt men or race car drivers, while others engage in death-defying activities like sky diving and hang gliding just for the hell of it. But they all take great pleasure and satisfaction by knocking on Satan's door and then dashing away at the last minute.

The article also had gone on to say that adventurers have always been society's heroes, be they real or fictional: Christopher Columbus, Charles Lindbergh, Neil Armstrong, or Indiana Jones.

For some reason, the article's words had stayed with Bucher and seemed to be especially in the forefront of his memory today.

At 10:58 a.m., Henry Talbot emerged through the crowd to meet Mark Bucher at the base of the statue. Tourists gathered here every day at this time in the Marienplatz to watch and listen to the famous Rathaus-Glockenspiel. Talbot, completely immune to all tourist activities, literally pulled Bucher through the crowd in the direction of his nearby office. Located just around the corner from the Rathaus (City Hall), three stories above the Donsil Restaurant (considered by Talbot to be another tourist trap, though it served pretty good traditional Bavarian food) was the nondescript, unidentified office of NSA Listening Post-Munich.

Once inside the office, Talbot extracted a large-scale military grid map from the shelf above his desk. Spreading it out over the scattered papers on the desk, he jabbed his finger in the center of the map near the converging boundary lines of Germany, Austria, and the Czech Republic, which resembled a shaky, inverted Y.

"You know how to read one of these things?" asked Talbot.

"Sure. What do you need to know?"

"Okay, here's a little test. Find grid coordinate AC61550889."

"No sweat."

There was a brief pause while Bucher intersected the lines with his right and left index fingers. "That coordinate brings you right on top of this ridge, right here," he said, punctuating it with his right index finger. He then checked the legend in the corner of the map to verify the elevation. "Let's see, twenty feet for each contour line. You've got one, two, three, four, five lines, so that point is roughly one hundred feet up from this river or creek at the base."

Obviously pleased he had handled the quiz so easily, Bucher commented, "I did pretty well in my land navigation classes."

"Yeah, I can tell," replied Talbot, impressed with Bucher's ability. "Well, that's your objective, an old monastery on top of that ridge line. We'll be using an Air Force C-130H for the insertion, compliments of the Delaware Air National Guard. They will drop Captain Cleary's Company F Rangers right here, a mile or less west of the German line. By the way, these guys are National Guard, too, so you'll have a little something in common with these troopers."

Yeah, very little, thought Bucher, starting to feel like a Little Leaguer stepping out onto the field at Busch Stadium to play with the Cardinals.

Henry Talbot pressed on with the briefing. "You, however, will remain on board for a short time as the aircraft climbs and veers south. You will then jump and drift, hopefully undetected by their radar outposts, over the Czech border—here—while all of the attention will be on the sixty-two Airborne troops and the C-130 and what will look like a bunch of snowflakes floating down onto German soil. They will do a static line jump at a fairly high altitude, giving them the maximum hang time, whereas you are going to do a little free falling and a lot of drifting. I should correctly refer to it as 'flying,' as the pros do. They call it a 'High Altitude High Opening' or HAHO jump. We ruled out the HALO 'Low Opening' jump for you; it is definitely too dangerous for a less-experienced paratrooper like yourself. If the wind conditions are favorable tomorrow night, we'll have you fly closer to your objective with the aircraft barely crossing the Czech border. We're banking on these Russian radar operators not to pick up this single stray snowflake."

Reading the concerned look on Bucher's face, Talbot decided to change the subject. "Hopefully tomorrow we'll have some time for the jumpmaster to run you through a crash course, pardon the phraseology, in some of the basics of military skydiving and familiarize you with the equipment you'll be using.

"You'll have a military ID with the name Major Mark Smith on it, just in case you are detected on the way down and the Russian Army has a welcoming committee come out to greet you. We will explain that you simply just veered off course a little and apologize profusely. Oh, and while I'm thinking of it…"

Talbot reached into his lower left desk drawer and pulled out a Browning 9mm Hi-Power Standard, laying it on top of the map.

"I thought you said I was just a messenger boy," said Bucher flatly.

"This is just to be on the safe side," responded Talbot.

"Well you can put it right back in the drawer, because I don't want it. I wouldn't use it anyway, and it would just weigh me down."

"No, you bring it with you," insisted Talbot, "it's part of the uniform. We'll issue you a shoulder holster like the tankers wear, a couple of magazines, and some ammunition when we get to Ramstein. You know how to use this thing?" he asked, remembering from Bucher's Army records that he had qualified as an expert.

"It looks a lot like the old Colt .45 semi-automatic, but somewhat smaller and a little lighter, I think," said Bucher as he drew back the slide, inspected the chamber for any rounds, and popped the empty magazine from the handle. Satisfied the weapon was empty and safe, he let the slide glide forward with a metallic snap, tapped the magazine home, and thumbed the safety into the on position. Once again, Talbot was impressed.

"Now, back to the briefing. It's imperative you get all of this right," said the NSA officer. "As soon as you touch down, you quickly stash the chute, your helmet, and web gear. You *keep* the handgun and holster with you. If nobody has found you by this time and if your leg isn't broken, you get out of the uniform, stash that, too, and turn into a civilian again with some outdoor clothes that will be in your rucksack just as soon as you possibly can. Are we clear?"

"Crystal, sir!" Bucher loved that response from Tom Cruise in the movie, *A Few Good Men*, and couldn't pass up the opportunity to use it. It sailed right over the top of Henry Talbot's head.

"How proficient are you with your German?" Talbot asked, turning away from the map. "You will need to communicate with Richter *auf Deutsch*. You sounded pretty good with what little I've heard you speak back at the hotel."

"I get by okay. I've had a few college credits of conversational German, but I'm mostly self-taught. I try to keep up with it. You know, the old 'use it or lose it' thing."

Talbot understood completely.

"Okay, let's try to put this together for you," Talbot said. He wanted Bucher to have an overall understanding without overwhelming him and especially without giving him pertinent classified information, just in case he was apprehended by the bad guys.

"Our inside man is Major Gerhardt Richter, a former NVA officer, now part of the Russian Army, specifically a Spetsnaz officer now. He is basically the 'aide-de-camp' for General Stephan Krause, also former NVA, the man leading this particular coup d'état. There is at least one other coup building up steam that we know of right now, but Krause is the ringleader of this one, with a rapidly growing following from the Russian Army Officer Corps and several of the old Politburo members. You are to make contact with Richter to personally hand over the discs, in this cigar box, and receive any updated information, written or verbal, that he can give you to bring back to me. Understand he is expecting our Special Ops Investigator, Erich Mueller, who was murdered four days ago."

Bucher said nothing, but his face expressed instant anxiety.

"What's wrong?" asked Talbot. "You look like you've just seen a ghost!"

"No, I'm okay. Go on."

"Richter will immediately consider you a foe, and you will quickly need to convince him otherwise, or I guarantee he will be your newest, largest threat."

"Any suggestions?" inquired Bucher.

"None at the present. We can think more about that later. Let's concentrate on reviewing some of the other details right now." Talbot paused briefly, organizing his thoughts and looking at the grid map. "You will be dropped just to the east of this bridge, in this open area, and once you pass this road junction, you will need to keep an eye out for the grocery truck and link up with Mr. Dvorak delivering the monastery's food supplies and other necessities. He only delivers to the monastery on Wednesdays and Saturdays, coming up this road here, sometime in the very early hours of the morning, I would imagine. Again, it's up to you to find a way to intercept him; use whatever plan is workable as long as the exchange is made. Use your resources.

"I'll put the cigar box together with the discs in the bottom, as if it were a fresh box. Richter is the only cigar smoker in the group, by the way, so he'll be the one looking for the cigars. Once the exchange is made, get the hell out as quickly as you can."

Pointing to the map again, Talbot said, "Head south to the Austrian border. It will be much easier going out than it was coming in. We'll also have a civilian passport made up for you, an Austrian passport. Shouldn't be any problem getting you back into Austria. Catch the train in Linz for Salzburg, then from Salzburg back to Munich. Nothing to it!" exclaimed Talbot. "Any questions?"

"So I'll be traveling through this open area," said Bucher, pointing to the appropriate place on the map, "then along this thin broken line, probably an unpaved road, for approximately four to six miles from my drop zone, here, to my objective, here. Correct?"

Talbot nodded affirmatively.

"What about jump boots?" asked Bucher.

"We'll get you some. That's no problem."

"Well it's the four to six miles in brand new boots that concerns me," said Bucher, remembering very well the blisters that formed at the reception station prior to basic training at Fort Polk. "It sounds petty, but it could create a problem," he said, thinking through each detail.

"I can't very well have you jump in white sneakers, can I?"

"No, I know that. The jump boots are necessary for the jump, but I'd like to bring a pair of my own Adidas hiking shoes for my midnight stroll through the Czech countryside, and I think it would add to my civilian ensemble better than the U.S. Army jump boots. Any objections?"

"If they'll fit in your field pack, go for it. Just stash the GI boots with the other stuff as soon as you come down. And hide it well, Mr. Bucher. We can't afford for them to find any of this gear with U.S. Army stamped all over it, right? Oh, and speaking of civilian attire, do you have an outdoor jacket, something you'd go hiking in? And do you have a civilian-style backpack?"

"Yeah, I've got a medium-weight Columbia jacket and a fairly small Padagonia day pack."

"Small is good in this case. Bring these items plus your hiking shoes with you."

Bucher nodded and made a mental note to also throw in a toothbrush and a small tube of toothpaste.

"I figure you'll have roughly five hours from the time you hit the ground till you rendezvous with Mr. Dvorak in the delivery truck. That should be ample time to get rid of the gear and find the objective, even in the dark. Oh, and speaking of darkness..." Talbot reached in his top left-hand drawer and took out a small pen light with a red lens cover. "You'll need this to read the map tomorrow night. Use the red light so you don't ruin your visual purple, and also so you don't stick out like a beacon in the night."

"Let's see your watch," Talbot said as he reached for Mark's wrist to see his simple, but functional Timex Marathon. "Luminous dial?"

"Yup."

"Good piece of equipment. Hang on to it. You're gonna be traveling light," remarked Talbot as he gathered the 9mm, the pen light, and the folded grid map and placed them in a dark blue nylon carry-on bag. "We'll get your passport, shoulder holster, lensatic compass, web gear, jump boots, and uniform tomorrow on base. Oh, and you should also have some cash in your pocket."

From a metal four-drawer file cabinet, Talbot removed a wad of blue one-hundred Deutsche Mark bills, equal to about one thousand U.S. dollars, and a smaller stack of Austrian shillings. "I don't have any Czech Korunas for you, because their currency is smack dab in the middle of a big transition phase. It's a huge mess right now, but anybody will be happy to take your DMs, so don't hesitate to use them as needed. I've thrown in enough Austrian shillings to buy your train ticket back and whatever food, drinks, or other incidentals you need for your trip back to Munich."

Leading Bucher to the door, Talbot said, "I suggest you go back to the hotel now, get some rest, and take Mrs. Bucher out somewhere for a good, Bavarian dinner tonight. Remember to get a receipt. You are now a contract employee, working for the National Security Agency/Department of Defense, so we will, of course, be picking up the tab for your meals and hotel from this point forward." Henry Talbot smiled. "Get a good night's sleep tonight, because you won't get a wink of sleep tomorrow. That's for sure.

"As soon as you leave, I'll be calling Captain Cleary to arrange for our transportation to Ramstein early tomorrow morning. Meet me for breakfast at six o'clock and be ready to go."

Chapter Twenty-two

Macomb, Illinois
Spring 1973

Much to his dismay, with his busy schedule, Mark just did not have the time to throw himself into any traditionally adventurous situations outside of his monthly weekend drills and annual two weeks' training with the 138th (Mech.) Infantry, Missouri Army National Guard.

Sometime during the second semester of his junior year at Western Illinois University, Mark Bucher fell in love with a girl in his English lit class. This was a new kind of adventure. Laura Kapels made his heart rate increase just by entering the room. Later he would find she could actually make his heart pound and cause him to sweat as if he had just repelled off a two-hundred-foot cliff on a hot day.

About a month and a half after graduation, Mark and Laura were married. Mark was happier than he could have ever dreamed. They both wanted children, but that was apparently not in God's plans right then.

~ * ~

Fall 1983

Life was great, and Laura was the love of his life. Work was great, too, in the international sales department of a midsize sporting goods importer/manufacturer in St. Louis. Occasionally, Mark traveled to trade shows in Europe. He had it all. What more could he want?

Then suddenly, Mark's world changed from "Life is great; we don't have a care in the world," to "The test results came back positive, Mr. Bucher. I'm sorry to say you have been diagnosed with a very aggressive cancer in your right kidney."

Only a week before, Mark had gone to a urologist after observing what appeared to be blood in his urine. *Probably nothing, but it's best to have it checked out,* he thought.

There are no words to adequately describe the sensation one feels upon hearing those cold, hard words: "You have cancer."

Mark and Laura Bucher had each other, and they had their faith in God. For them, these were the most essential elements they needed to endure—to survive the next minute, the next day, the next week. Together, they repeated a single comforting prayer over and over, like the chorus of a song that played deep in their hearts: "Jesus, I trust in you."

The urological surgeon was cautiously optimistic after the cancerous kidney was removed. There had been no apparent complications, although this type of procedure was never a slam dunk. There was always the looming threat that the cancer may have spread to other organs, along with the pressing challenge of a long road to recovery. Being confined to a hospital bed for a week and to his home for another week was going to be pure hell, but Mark realized he had to follow his doctor's orders and do everything he could to restore his health and to protect the remaining kidney.

While Mark was recovering in his private room at DePaul Hospital, Mitchell J. Davies, Mark's lifelong best friend, stopped by for an evening visit, his third in as many days. Mitch and Mark had grown up together since grade school, had gone to high school together, and had attended two semesters at the University of Missouri-St. Louis together. They had even served together in the same National Guard unit. They were indeed closer than most brothers.

306

It was difficult for Mitch to see his friend so pale and weak, with a tube that pumped bile from his stomach up through his nose and several other tubes and wires hanging from his left arm. He would do his best to not show concern.

"Hey, what'd you bring me, Mitch?" asked Mark, attempting to show more strength than he felt.

"I brought you a book, but I'm afraid it doesn't have any pictures," Mitch replied, "so I don't know if you'll be able to enjoy it very much." He flopped down a dog-eared paperback entitled, *You Only Live Twice*, by Ian Fleming.

Mark had read all of the Ian Fleming spy adventures years ago and had recently embarked upon reading the works of John Gardner, the author who picked up the James Bond character after Fleming passed away and took credit for bringing Bond into the '80s.

Mitch had a reason for selecting this particular master spy novel. Toward the middle of page eighty-six was a simple Haiku, a short Japanese poem from which the book's title had been derived. It read:

You only live twice
Once when you're born
And once when you look death in the face.

Mitch had underlined the Haiku in red ink. As with so many of the male gender, Davies found it difficult to come right out and tell his lifelong buddy and confidant just how much he cared for him.

Mitch had wanted to give Mark the book before the surgery but couldn't quite muster the courage. His unspoken message was "Don't give up. There is still a hell of a lot more life to live out there, more mountains to climb, more dragons to slay. Don't regress into some shell; come out swinging. Most important of all, don't leave us. We all love you too much to bear that pain." Mitch Davies hoped Mark could read between the lines to find his message.

In the weeks following the surgery, people close to Mark began to notice a difference in him other than the normal healing process. It was as if he had been born again. Not in the way of a "born-again Christian," because his faith had never wavered the slightest bit. But now his spirit, his outlook on life, and his energy and ambition seemed to have skyrocketed. Mitch joked to Laura that if he thought he could acquire some of this newfound enthusiasm and energy by having a kidney removed, he'd go to see the doctor tomorrow.

Laura was concerned that Mark was pushing it too hard with the physical reconditioning. Laura ran every day. She had been running now for several years. Mark had only been a weekend runner before the operation, but now he was running every day, too, trying to keep up with his wife. He also returned to a regimented program of calisthenics consisting of push-ups, sit-ups, and chin-ups. He even talked about someday running a marathon.

Chapter Twenty-three

Munich, Germany
Friday, October 1, 1993
6:00 a.m.

Mark Bucher and Henry Talbot met in the breakfast room of the Adria. Not much was said; no idle chit-chat this morning. Mark filled his plate with a couple of hard rolls, mild cheeses, and thinly sliced ham and sausage; later he went back to the white linen-covered buffet table for fresh fruit, granola, and yogurt. The young girl attending to the hotel patrons knew to bring the small pots of black coffee to the two Americans without even asking. As the two men finished their breakfast, Talbot got up and fetched two fluted champagne glasses and poured from a chilled magnum resting in a silver ice bucket at the end of the beverage table.

Returning to the table, he handed Bucher a glass and raised another, whispering, "Here's to you, Mark. Godspeed. Your country is sincerely grateful for you answering this call to duty."

Bucher raised the glass to his lips and took a small, symbolic sip. With a slight smile, he said, "Okay, let's get this show on the road before I regain my senses and change my mind."

Quickly, he picked up his backpack and headed for the door, as Talbot picked up the blue nylon bag with the 9mm Browning, penlight, map, and box of cigars and followed him out of the building.

Expecting to find a taxi waiting in front of the hotel, Bucher turned to Talbot and impatiently asked, "So where's our ride?"

"It'll be there. This way," he said, as he stepped out at a quick pace in the direction of the English Garden, a few short blocks away.

As they walked, the NSA chief reviewed several key points he wanted to drill into Bucher's head so they would be second nature to him when he hit the ground. The harsh reality was that the second he stepped out of the Air Force C-130H, Bucher would be completely on his own. No one to confer with or to receive instructions from, no lines of communication. So Talbot had to cram as much information into the rookie's head as he possibly could. A successful mission was paramount. Failure was not an option. There was just too much at stake here. Bucher would have to use *all* of his tools to get this job done.

For the second time, Henry Talbot went over the issue of Gerhardt Richter expecting to see Erich Mueller. Bucher would need to give him a pass phrase to ensure his credibility.

"My code name is 'Buckeye.' Mueller's was 'Badger.' We never really gave a name to this mission, so no need to concern yourself with that, but it would be wise to do a little discreet name-dropping as soon as you have the major to yourself."

Talbot described all of Richter's physical charac-teristics for a second time: height, weight, build, hair color, eyes, almost down to the size of his shoes.

They walked the next half block in silence. Waiting for the traffic light at Prinzregenten Strasse and Letchenfeld, Talbot took out a note pad, scribbled some numbers down, and handed it to Bucher.

"Now commit this number to memory; it's the number to my secure line."

He gave Bucher a minute to digest the numbers, then tore off the top sheet, wadded up the paper, and shoved it in his pocket.

"Got it?"

Bucher acknowledged and repeated the number back in fast order.

"You call me when it's safe, after you've completed the job. If all goes well, your first opportunity to call will probably be when you reach the train station in Linz."

Entering Munich's largest city park, still very sparsely populated with only a few runners at this early hour, they walked along the wide path leading to the flat open area below the Monopteros.

When they heard the sound of an approaching helicopter, Talbot glanced at his watch without looking up. "Right on time."

Before the skids of the U.S. Army UH-1D Huey touched the ground, Captain Cronan Cleary was out and trotted over to greet the two NSA agents. Cleary, in his late thirties, stood five-feet-ten and was built like a running back—probably had been one in his days at the U.S. Military Academy at West Point. He administered a genuine "vice-grip" handshake as the introductions were made, with no intention to impress. The three then climbed into the Huey for the flight back to Ramstein Air Base.

The captain donned a flight helmet so he could communicate with the pilot and copilot while Talbot and Bucher strapped themselves in, sat back, and prepared to enjoy the ride. As the UH-1D lifted off, Bucher once again felt that distantly familiar, unique sensation of flight only experienced in a helicopter. The adrenalin was beginning to flow.

The Army chopper pilot cut speed and descended quickly as they entered the tightly controlled air space surrounding the U.S. Military compound at Ramstein. Cleary's jeep was waiting, with a middle-aged sergeant first class dressed in a freshly starched battle dress uniform and black beret, sitting behind the wheel.

As the three walked toward the jeep, Cleary conferred with the senior NSA inspector as to what the priorities of the day would be. They both agreed that the detailed briefing was most important, but the C-130H and crew would not be available till 1300 hours.

"We've got a lot of work ahead of us, don't we?" said Cleary, addressing Talbot.

The conversation was suspended during the brief ride to the corrugated metal Quonset hut that served as temporary headquarters for the visiting Rangers of the 425th Infantry, Michigan Army National Guard.

Once inside, with the door closed behind them, Captain Cronan Cleary resumed the conversation where he had left off.

"Okay, so we're going to need a military ID, an Austrian passport, BDU, jump boots, helmet, web gear, and what about weapons?"

"He's got a 9mm Browning, but he needs a shoulder holster and probably a couple of extra magazines," responded Talbot.

"Okay, what about a KA-BAR?" asked Cleary. "I've got a couple that were given to me by the CO of a Marine Force Recon group that jumped with us last year. Mr. Bucher should really take one; it's a hell of a nice knife, and it is considerably quieter than that 9mm Hi-Power he's packing."

Bucher managed to keep his mouth shut, but shot Talbot an icy stare. Talbot knew where Bucher was coming from, remembering his "I'm not James Bond!" line and his immediate aversion to carrying the 9mm back at the office.

Cleary immediately picked up on the nonverbal, although he didn't quite know how to translate it.

"You have a problem with the KA-BAR, Mr. Bucher? If you do, we have other commando knives you can use: larger, smaller, double-edged daggers, you name it!"

Before Talbot could jump in and say anything, Mark Bucher sounded off. "No, sir, that's not the issue. I don't intend to use the gun *or* the knife. I understand my mission is to deliver some floppy discs in a cigar box, take whatever information Major Richter has for me, and get my ass back to Munich as quickly as possible, not to wage war singlehandedly with a 9mm and a commando knife. Captain Cleary, I am *not* a commando; I'm just a courier."

Cleary scowled and looked at Talbot in total disbelief, waiting for the senior NSA officer to voice his outrage over such a premeditated dereliction of duty. In Cleary's Army, a soldier takes his orders and carries them out to the best of his ability; he doesn't just do the minimum required. *This guy is not a team player,* thought Cleary. *I'd kick his ass out of this outfit so fast his head would spin.*

Henry Talbot had wondered if he could pass Bucher off as an NSA Special Ops Investigator without revealing his true identity and without going into a long dissertation on how this man happened to come to fill this position. Here was the moment of truth; he could see it in the expression on the seasoned Ranger's face. No point in even trying to bullshit this guy. He'd see right through it in a second. *Better for Bucher's safety and for the success of the mission that I lay all the cards on the table now,* Talbot thought.

"Well, it's like this, Captain Cleary. My second in command was murdered this past Sunday. I accidently got a little banged up, as you can see, and became incapacitated to the point that I could not make the jump myself. I had to scramble to find someone to fill the slot ASAP. Our friend Mr. Bucher, here, just happened to enter the picture in the nick of time with all of the essential qualifications I required for this particular mission. Long story short, I've signed him on basically as a temporary National Security Agency contract worker. You may not like it, but he's our man."

"You're telling me that Bucher is a *civilian*, not affiliated with the NSA up until yesterday, and you're going to have him do a night jump into the Czech Republic to meet with our contact, a Russian Spetsnaz officer, in the immediate area of General Stephan Krause? With all due respect, Mr. Talbot, I totally disagree with your plan. And you're right; I don't like it. I don't like it one little bit."

Feeling the need to defend his strategy, Talbot offered, "Bucher has jumped as a civilian, speaks German, and is familiar with the semi-automatic, if necessary," he interjected quickly. "He served six years in a mechanized infantry National Guard unit and is very proficient with land navigation. Mr. Bucher *is* perfectly capable of pulling this off. As far as his reluctance to carry the Browning and the KA-BAR, he probably won't actually *need* them; it's just better to err on the side of caution, that's all."

"Then consider this, Talbot," Cleary said, in a reasonable tone. "Why not let *me* make the jump? I've got everything but the German, and I'm sure I could work around that. Let *me* do it. It's a no-brainer."

"No. I can't do that."

"Well, here's another alternative. Let's say all sixty-two of us Rangers jump with Bucher into a common drop zone on the Czech side. This would definitely catch the Russian's attention and create a huge distraction away from Bucher. Once on the ground, we'd proceed in five-man patrols to separate recon targets, evading enemy detection, back to a designated friendly location on the German side. I know for damn sure we could outrun 'em and outmaneuver 'em all the way to the Czech border. You see, Mr. Talbot, we'd have the Russians chasing us instead of looking for Bucher, and he'd be well on his way to his objective without ever being detected." Cleary paused a moment. "This is a *real* plan! We've practiced this evasion drill dozens of times throughout the Cold War. My men know this like the back of their hands; they could do it in their sleep. It'll work; nobody gets hurt, and you become a hero. What'd you say, Talbot?"

Henry Talbot stood quietly, contemplating Cleary's plan for a couple of minutes. It was an excellent plan, no question.

"No. Can't do it. I have specific orders *not* to get the military involved, other than the transportation to our objective. There is no bending of the rules on this one. Thanks, but no."

Captain Cleary shrugged his shoulders. He had done what he could. He knew this mission was completely Talbot's responsibility, and he called all the shots. He also knew his orders came directly from General Bussen, the CICEUCOM, so he, of course, would follow those orders, whether he agreed with them or not.

More important than that, Cleary's primary concern was for Bucher's personal safety. Talbot was sending a novice to do the work of a pro. He envisioned this rookie operative as a lamb being led to the slaughter. There was just something about Bucher that didn't strike this seasoned Airborne Ranger as the type who would be able to aggressively confront an enemy combatant if the situation were to present itself.

Cleary had seen all types of warriors throughout his military career and considered himself to be a qualified judge of more than just strengths and weaknesses, but also of men's capabilities—their capacity to perform in certain situations. Some men had it; some did not. One could have all the mechanics of a good soldier—be an expert marksman or a skilled parachutist—but nothing tested the true mettle of a soldier like actual combat experience. Up till that point, everything else was just another training exercise.

As much as Talbot wanted to downplay any danger that might be involved, this was not going to be a walk in the park. No two ways about it, in Cleary's estimation, this was indeed a high-risk assignment.

~ * ~

St. Thomas Aquinas High School
Florissant, Missouri
Friday, August 25, 1967

Head coach Jerry Hurlbert stood on the sidelines near the fifty, holding his clipboard, making a few notes as he watched the players go through their final set of drills for the day. These "two-a-days" were tough, especially in the hot, humid conditions typical of late August in this part of the Midwest.

The normally jovial Hurlbert had his game face on. This was the last workout before he made the final cuts. When it came down to the final cut, he knew all of these kids had worked hard to make it this far, and they all truly wanted to make varsity. He wished he could give each one of them a slot on the roster, but that was not the real world. Hurlbert had to make some hard decisions this afternoon.

Richard Tadlock, a first year assistant coach and offensive coordinator for the Aquinas Falcons, was being groomed for the job of head coach, possibly as soon as next season. It really just depended on when Jerry Hurlbert would decide to finally hang up his whistle. Tadlock trotted across the practice field to join his mentor.

"Hey, Coach, how's your list coming along?"

"Well, Richard, I think I've narrowed it down pretty well, just a few more to go. But I'd like your input on some of these guys. I'd like to see if your evaluation agrees with mine, or if you're seeing something I might be missing."

Handing Tadlock the clipboard, Coach Hurlbert said, "Here, take a look and give me your honest assessment."

Tadlock took the well-worn clipboard and surveyed the list.

"Coach, I don't mean to be difficult, but I really don't know what I'm looking at."

The stat sheet was divided into six narrow columns: Name, Assigned #, Height, Weight, Best time 40 yds, and Comments.

"I'm with you on all the stats, but I don't understand your Comments code."

Hurlbert chuckled and responded, "No, I guess not. Sorry. That's just my brand of shorthand. Here, I'll show you."

Picking players' names randomly, he explained, "Okay, here we have Burkhart. I've got him down as GS/GA. That means he has good speed and good agility. Okay? And here we have Kirwan: GtH/QR. That means he has great hands and quick reflexes."

Tadlock was trying not to laugh, because he could see the old coach was totally serious about his coding system and that to interrupt this coaching lesson would be a huge mistake.

"Now let's look at Davies. I've got him down as VAg/KS: very aggressive, but kind of slow. I think his aggressive play overrides his lack of speed. Aggressive trumps speed every time in my book."

Richard Tadlock agreed completely. So far, each of these players had a plus sign behind their names, and Tadlock was actually starting to catch on to Hurlbert's code.

"Now, here we have Bucher. I've got him down as GS/NKI." Hurlbert began to explain, but Tadlock jumped in.

"All right, I've got the good speed part down, but you've got me stumped with the NKI."

316

"Well," started Hurlbert, taking off his sunglasses and studying Tadlock. "I think Mark Bucher has the *potential* to be a great little athlete: good speed, physically fit, pretty good skills, and overall, a really nice kid. The problem is that he has no killer instinct. Would you agree, Richard?"

Tadlock had to ponder this evaluation for a minute but finally said, "Yeah, Coach, I suppose you're right."

Coach Hurlbert uncapped his felt-tip pen and lined out Mark Bucher.

Chapter Twenty-four

Ramstein Air Base, Germany
01 October 1993
0815 Hours

For the next couple of hours, the morning was occupied with getting the passport and visiting the quartermaster for Bucher's camo BDU, jump boots, web gear, and Kevlar helmet.

The issuance of the personal gear was somewhat reminiscent to Bucher of the reception station at Fort Polk—up to the point when the quartermaster began to sew on the gold oak leaf and the crossed rifles of an infantry officer on the collar. But it was the badge of a senior parachutist over the left pocket and the Ranger tab on the upper portion of the sleeve, just above the 101st Airborne Screaming Eagle patch, that made Bucher feel unworthy. He recognized the hard work, dedication, and courage it took to earn the Airborne winged parachute and the sheer strength, stamina, and determination required to achieve the distinction of Ranger. All of these elements together described the proud tradition of the 101st Airborne. Bucher had read enough history to know that the men who wore the Screaming Eagle insignia had been consistently regarded as members of the best fighting forces of any nation since 1942. Although he felt completely undeserving to wear these badges of honor on a borrowed uniform, they instilled a real sense of pride and a stronger desire to see this mission through to the best of his ability.

Unfortunately, there was no time for a practice jump, which would have put Cleary's mind a lot more at ease. The next best thing was to run Bucher through some basic parachute instructions for the next hour and a half, consisting of a little classroom work, some very basic familiarization of equipment, and some jump and roll techniques from a four-foot practice platform. Cleary concluded the brief, but extremely necessary review and training session with asking Bucher to take several jumps from the platform dressed out under the full weight of his combat load: helmet, rucksack, two canteens, jump boots, web gear, weapon, and parachute harness. The captain was satisfied with the mechanics of the dry run, but still had doubts that he couldn't quite shake.

Back in Cleary's office, Bucher began to shed the heavy equipment and stack it neatly in the corner. He marveled that these were the everyday tools of the trade for the modern Airborne soldier. Cronan Cleary approached the NSA operative with the leather sheathed KA-BAR.

Extending the knife to Mark Bucher, he said, "Here, take this. This is *not* a weapon. It's a gift. Every one of my paratroopers carries a knife when he jumps. It comes in pretty handy if your chute gets caught up in a tree or if the cords get wrapped around your leg and you're hanging upside down looking like a piñata. It does *not* have to be used solely for sneaking up behind a bad guy and slitting his throat. It might come in handy. Trust me."

"Thank you, sir," said Bucher with a smile. "With that colorful explanation, I will accept your gift and wear it in good health."

"I think we need a little break," Cleary announced to Talbot, checking his watch. "Bucher's been working pretty hard. We've got time to grab lunch over at the Officers Club before we meet with our flight crew. And besides, the Air Force chow is not like Army chow; it's more like eating at a nice restaurant. I'd rather Mr. Bucher have a full meal in his belly now with plenty of time to digest it instead of waiting for an evening meal. Jumping on a full stomach doesn't always work so well with inexperienced jumpers."

"Lunch" resembled a meal suitable for the Joint Chiefs of Staff. The three were served roast turkey with all of the trimmings. It could have been the picture of a traditional Thanksgiving meal, minus the wine.

"Eat up, Mark. You're going to need all the carbs you can pack away for your hike through the Czech countryside tonight."

Talbot had had his doubts in the beginning about the capabilities of an NG unit coming to his aid—doubts that were quickly dispelled once he learned from their CO just how qualified the Rangers from Michigan really were. Similar questions regarding the readiness of the Delaware Air National Guard were also on his mind.

Rather than embarrass himself or insult the unit commander of the 142nd Airlift Squadron, Talbot broke the silence among the three as they were finishing their meal with a question for Cleary. "So what about this Air Guard unit you've been working with? Are they any good?"

Now that sure is a stupid question! thought Cleary, chuckling. "Well, considering I've been flying with them for the last six or seven days and we haven't gone down in a huge ball of flame yet, I'd say they're pretty good. Seriously, though, they've also supported several of our operations back in the States and we've developed a kind of unofficial relationship with these guys."

"I do know a little about Colonel Germaine, the Squadron commander who has volunteered to fly the mission himself, and also a little about the lieutenant colonel who will be in the right seat tonight. Earlier this week I had dinner with Tom Germaine and Jake Byrnes, who is normally in the driver's seat. Both of these guys are exceptional aviators with a ton of hours in the C-130H. Tom Germaine was brought up in a family of fliers. He told me his dad was actually an Army Air Corps 'Ace' in World War II. Tom earned a PhD in Aviation Technology from Purdue University some years ago, and presently in his civilian job, he runs the Delaware Aviation Center, a highly accredited flight training center in the New Castle area. Doctor Germaine started there as a certified flight instructor; now he owns the place.

"Jake Byrnes, our other pilot, has been flying since he was sixteen. He claims he was piloting a Beechcraft Bonanza before he was driving the family Ford station wagon. He's used to flying big planes. In his real job, he flies a 747 for a charter air cargo firm, so flying the C-130 is no big deal for him. I don't know about the rest of the flight crew, but I know Bucher will be in good hands with these two fellas at the controls."

~ * ~

In a private preflight briefing room directly off the Ramstein AB flight line, Captain Cronan Cleary began the briefing precisely at 1300 hours. He made the introductions between the Army and Air Force personnel quickly and without any fanfare.

"I'll start by telling you men the obvious. This mission we are taking on this evening is classified as Top Secret NOFORN [No Dissemination to Other Foreign Countries]. What is discussed here in this briefing room stays right here. The only people who have the need to know are the other seven men sitting at this table. Aside from Colonel Germaine, you have been selected for this mission based on your ability and previous performance in your specialized field. We need to be completely thorough, so I'm now going to let Senior NSA Special Ops Investigator Henry Talbot give you the basics of the operation, and then we can dissect the plan as we go along."

From an overhead projector, a grid map was projected on the front wall. The map covered eastern Germany, western Czech Republic, and northern Austria.

Hank Talbot stood and cleared his throat and began. "Very basically, gentlemen, we have an urgent political situation that requires us to drop one of our operatives, Mr. Bucher, into the Czech Republic, just a few miles east of the German/Czech border, right about here," he said, pointing to the right center of the projected map with an old rubber-tip wooden pointer. "The exact grid coordinate is AC61550889. Because of heightened border security and time constraints, a night jump seems to be the best method of reaching our objective. Captain Cleary?"

Cleary picked up. "Because the Russian Army is now manning all of the radar outposts along the border, we need to create a diversion. Tonight we will take up two platoons (twelve five-man patrols) and deploy them at a relatively high altitude, not requiring supplemental oxygen, within a mile or less of the border. This should be a pretty good distraction for radar operators on the ground. It will give them plenty of tiny white dots to watch on their radar screens as the aircraft continues to fly east for about nine or ten miles while sharply increasing altitude and banking to the south, apparently just making a wide turn for their return. The Russians are already uptight about the possibility of outside interference from U.S. ground troops, so they're going to be more interested in watching where all these jumpers are landing than watching the precise flight pattern of the C-130 that will already be turning back toward Germany. At this point, Mr. Bucher—who will have been pre-breathing one hundred percent oxygen for the previous thirty to forty-five minutes—will deploy at approximately twenty-one thousand feet, making a 'High Altitude, High Opening' jump to allow him maximum flying time toward his target drop zone. I want Bucher on the ground at 0130 hours, so Colonel Germaine, please let me know what time we need to be wheels up."

"No problem, Captain Cleary. I'll have that for you within the half hour," replied Germaine.

Cleary continued, "Captain Gibbons, I understand you will be acting as the navigator/flight engineer for this mission, so you will need to coordinate closely with your loadmasters and our jumpmaster, Sergeant First Class Juston, to ensure we drop our Rangers just west of the line, not over it, and to make damn sure we have Mr. Bucher hit his target, as well."

"If I may interrupt for just a minute, Captain Cleary," interjected Lieutenant Colonel Jake Byrnes. "Last I looked at the weather map about twenty minutes ago, it looked like the wind speed was picking up pretty good in the higher altitudes over most of the western and southwestern parts of Germany, so Captain Gibbons, I want you to pay particular attention to any changes and update your calculations accordingly. Understood?"

Captain Harry Gibbons responded with an almost inaudible, "Yes, sir."

Gibbons was new to the 142nd team, having recently transferred in from the 109th Airlift Wing, New York Air National Guard that also flew the C-130s. His record was clean, and he came with plenty of hours in the third seat, along with good recommendations from his CO back at Stratton. Byrnes would have liked a sharper, more enthusiastic response, but he let it slide, not wanting to make a scene with the others present in the room. Byrnes did, however, make a mental note of it.

The Army Ranger officer continued, "We have given Mr. Bucher the identity of 'Major Smith.' Captain Roesel, I want you to explain to the troops that Major Smith is an observer from the 101st and that he will be evaluating our jump tonight. No other explanation is necessary. Sergeant Juston, after you get your gear together, I want you to personally prep Mr. Bucher for the jump tonight. Mr. Bucher is not a seasoned jumper, and this will be his first HAHO, so take him under your wing and spend the remainder of the afternoon and evening coaching him on all aspects of the jump. Cram as much instruction into this time as you possibly can. He's going to need it. If you need to get back out on the platform for more dry jumps, then do it. Whatever it takes for him to make a successful jump and walk away under his own power. Understood?"

"Yes, sir!" SFC Gabriel Juston responded with enthusiasm.

"Questions? If not, I'm sure Colonel Germaine and his men will need this time to go over their charts and flight plan. Captain Roesel, Sergeant Juston, you know the drill, so let's get crackin'."

Near the temporary HQ of Company F (Ranger) 425th Infantry, Michigan Army National Guard stood another corrugated metal building, several times the length of the adjacent CO's lair. Inside, Cleary, Talbot, and Bucher observed several parachute riggers working diligently over two terrifically long tables lining the north and south walls of the elongated Quonset hut, stretching the parachute lines and precisely folding the silky nylon MC1-1D static-line parachutes into their deployment bags.

Captain Cleary went to a separate locker at the far end of the building to retrieve his own parachute and his personal gear.

"You going up with the troops, too, Captain?" asked Talbot, somewhat surprised.

"Are you kidding? Of course I'm going up, but coming back down is always the tricky part. You didn't think I'd pass up an opportunity to jump into the black sky, did you? Night jumps are fantastic! It's still fun for me, Mr. Talbot. It's what keeps me young." That part was fairly obvious to both Talbot and Bucher.

In the distance, they could hear the cadence chant of Company F, 425th, coming closer. Led by Operations Officer Captain Marcus Roesel, they double-timed directly through the open, extra-wide garage-like doors on the west end. They continued to double-time in place for a minute or so, with their cadence song amplified tenfold in the confines of the aluminum building. *Impressive,* thought Talbot. The pride was obvious on the face of their commanding officer, who seemed to have added an extra couple of inches to his chest.

"Captain Roesel!" boomed Cleary, acknowledging his presence.

"Sir!" responded the captain with equal volume before turning to give the command to his Airborne Rangers: "Halt!"

Roesel stepped off smartly toward his superior officer and asked, "Issue the chutes, sir?" Long Range Reconnaissance Patrol Companies are different in their organizational structure from traditional infantry companies in that both the commander and the operations officer hold the rank of captain, although the commanding officer is clearly in charge.

"Yes, Marcus, that's an excellent idea; it makes for a much softer landing. The chutes always seem to come in handy when we jump out of an aircraft at high altitudes. A lot fewer injuries, too, I might add," responded Cleary, pleased with his own humor.

Roesel oversaw the distribution of the chutes and harnesses, as the atmosphere in the elongated Quonset hut rose to the intensity of a locker room just prior to the big game with the home field advantage.

Bucher envied these soldiers who had really captured the spirit. The adrenalin was already pumping. Getting caught up in the excitement, he briefly wondered, *Why didn't I do this?* But of course, it had been because of Vietnam. He'd almost forgotten.

The jumpmaster for this mission, identified by the star and wreath atop the silver-winged canopy of a master parachutist along with the bright red armband, came over and saluted the rank of major worn on Bucher's uniform.

"Sir, I am Sergeant First Class Gabriel Juston, although you can call me 'Gabe' or 'Justo' if you'd like. I'm the jumpmaster tonight, and I will be here to assist you in any way I can and explain anything you might not be familiar with. Let's first go back to the CO's office and collect your personal gear, then we'll go through the whole procedure and whatever freefall procedures you might need work on. Then we'll get you set up with a parachute and some of the other interesting equipment you'll be using tonight."

Among all of the activity, Captain Cleary turned to the NSA chief and said: "Mr. Talbot, we've got it under control now. You're free to bug out. I'll personally take responsibility for Mr. Bucher from this point. Unless you have further instructions, we've got a plane to catch."

"Thank you, Captain Cleary. I really do appreciate all of your help. I hope we can talk about this over a beer sometime real soon."

Seeing Bucher and the jumpmaster at a distance on their way back into the shed as he was leaving, Talbot hollered, "See ya, Major Smith. Good luck with your evaluation!"

Bucher understood completely.

"Okay, Mr. Bucher, I'm going to get you set up with everything you will definitely need, and a few things you *might* need," said SFC Juston.

Juston had immediately set Bucher at ease, and that is exactly what was needed at the moment. The middle-aged sergeant first class exuded confidence and was obviously a real professional at his trade.

"First, your rig," he said, holding up the bulky apparatus for Bucher to inspect. "This is the MC-4 standard military free fall parachute system. It's used by the U.S. Army Special Forces and Rangers, Marine Corps Force

Recon, and the Navy Seals, just so you know this is the finest parachute system in the U.S. Armed Forces today. It's designed to meet the full range of free fall parachute operations, including HALO and HAHO. The MC-4 system is built around a 370-square-foot rectangular gliding canopy design used for both the main and reserve canopies. The harness is adjustable at seven points, so we can make it fit comfortably. It has a belly band and four equipment rings that will accept oxygen bottles, weapon, rucksack, whatever. And this is a FF2, your automatic ripcord release; it is for assured activation of the main parachute. I will set it to activate your chute at 20,000 feet.

"Now this little gadget here is your MA2-30 altimeter. It has a luminous face, and the revolving pointer indicates 12,000 feet per revolution, with a red and black warning sector. You do not want to go there. *If* for some reason you notice your altimeter reads 15,000 and your main parachute has *not* activated, go ahead and manually deploy the main by pulling the ripcord, here, that will be located on the right front chest area. I don't want you to wait until it becomes critical, okay? This altimeter comes in very handy for night jumps because it's very difficult to tell exactly when you are about to make contact with mother earth when it's pitch black out there, like it's going to be tonight."

Juston paused, going over a mental checklist of what else the rookie paratrooper might need. He concluded, "…and I'll need to get you a knife out of the arms room. We all carry a straight blade when we jump."

"Yeah, I know. I just happen to have one right here, Sergeant. Captain Cleary gave it to me," said Bucher, pulling the sheathed KA-BAR from his rucksack.

"Perfect!" said Juston, "I've got just the thing for that."

Two minutes later, he returned with a leg scabbard that would allow the knife to be strapped snugly to the outside of Bucher's right calf.

"Best place for it: out of the way, but easy enough to get to when you need it."

~ * ~

Ramstein Air Base
2330 Hours

Cleary approached his jumpmaster and Mark Bucher, with Captain Roesel three paces behind. "Sergeant Juston, is Mr. Bucher ready?"

"Yes, sir. Equipment-wise, he has everything he needs."

"Mr. Bucher, are *you* ready?"

"Yes, sir, as ready as I'll ever be."

"Then let's get at it! Captain Roesel, get the men formed up out on the tarmac."

~ * ~

Monastery–Southern Czech Republic near Cesky Krumlov
2330 Hours

The long awaited general staff meeting had gone on considerably longer than Richter had expected. Finally, he now had the eight target cities he had been waiting for: London, Rome, Amsterdam, Brussels, Paris, Munich, Frankfurt, and Zurich. This was exactly what he needed to pass along to Talbot through Erich Mueller. Damn, the time was short! They couldn't afford even the slightest hiccup, or there would be no time to stop this maniac from destroying half of Europe. There were no limits to what a narcissist like Krause would do to gain recognition and power.

"Gentlemen, thank you for your attention," the general said in closing. "I trust that all of your assignments are now clear. You are dismissed. Sleep in tomorrow. Get some rest, because Sunday could very well be an extremely busy day. We will see."

"Oh, Captain Karpinov, Colonel Zotkin, and General Romokovitch, I need to see you for just a moment," Krause said as an afterthought while the others were leaving the room.

"Captain Karpinov, what is the status of number eight, slated for Zurich?" inquired Krause.

"Comrade General, only minutes before the meeting began, Lieutenant Charkovonly reported they had completed a makeshift repair to the radio, and it is working, but not a hundred percent functional. They are now almost halfway to Zurich."

General Krause looked at his watch, scowled, and pondered this update for only a moment. Turning to his operations officer, he inquired, "Colonel Zotkin, what alternate sites do we have within reach with time enough to get set up?" Because Krause had originally figured he would have sixteen sites, he had several alternatives available.

Referring to his hand written notes, the colonel replied, "Sir, we have Milan; the site is due south of a town called Albavilla, not terribly far from the southern edge of Lake Como. We also have a very small mountain community called Kahlenberg on a hillside overlooking Vienna, elevation 484 meters. These, sir, are the only two sites we could possibly reach within the next few hours and be assured of enough time to have the men and equipment in place. I personally think Milan would be a bit of a stretch, sir."

"Very well. Vienna it is. We need to redirect team eight immediately. Colonel Zotkin, radio the team leader, provided their damn radio is working, and give him all of the details regarding the Vienna site. Now!"

Krause marched out of his temporary office, leaving General Romokovitch, Colonel Zotkin, and Captain Karpinov looking at each other. Obviously the general had other things to attend to. But just prior to attending to these other engagements, Krause went into the computer center—forgetting for a moment that the damn computer was still down—grabbed a piece of paper, made a handwritten note, and taped it to the CRT screen. It simply read: "Line out #8" in big, bold letters.

Richter had had the foresight to recruit a semi-attractive woman about thirty-eight years old and with about twenty years of experience to keep the general company for the night; plus he had sacrificed his only bottle of Martell VSOP Medaillon Cognac to ensure that Krause would sleep well into the morning, or at least be occupied with other activities. Richter had paid the woman twice the normal fee for an overnight appointment.

Later that evening, checking on his investment, Richter walked past the closed heavy wood door of the general's bedroom and heard muted tones of Mozart wafting through the space between the floor and the door, along with an occasional giggle. Gerhardt Richter smiled. His commander was being well taken care of.

~ * ~

Ramstein Air Base
2340 Hours

Up until now, the whole idea of dropping into the former Iron Curtain country once known as Czechoslovakia could only have been described as exhilarating to the ultimate adventure seeker in Mark Bucher. Now—seeing the open aft section of the large troop transport with its four Allison T56-A-15 turboprop engines running at idle speed and its gray metal ramp extended to receive its cargo of paratroopers—reality began to set in.

He had much more than a mild case of the butterflies. Bucher could not permit himself to toss his lunch. After all, he was the "evaluator" on this exercise, a seasoned jumper, at least according to the embroidered badge with wings and a star above an open canopy on his left chest. *What the hell did I get myself into?* he pondered, looking up to the heavens. Bucher happened to notice how quickly the clouds were moving now and how the sky had turned from clear to gray since earlier in the afternoon.

"You all right, Bucher?" asked Captain Cleary.

"Yes, sir, I'm okay. It's just that it's been about twenty some years since I've jumped out of a plane, that's all."

Cleary chuckled and slapped Bucher on the back. "Don't sweat it, Mark. We haven't lost a man yet. Not on my watch, anyhow."

Two Air Force crew members, pilot and navigator, in OD green flight coveralls and blue garrison caps, made their way down the ramp of the C-130H and walked toward Cleary and Bucher. The copilot, Lieutenant Colonel Jake Byrnes, stayed on the flight deck so as not to leave a completely fueled aircraft unattended with engines running.

"We're ready to load whenever you are, Captain Cleary," said Colonel Tom Germaine.

Also noticing the changing sky, the veteran Air Force pilot turned to his navigator/flight engineer. "Captain Gibbons, are you up to date on the weather over our two drop zones?"

"Yes, sir. I'll check again as we approach the weather station at Regensburg."

"Well, make darn sure that you do, Captain!" Germaine said, mildly leery of his new flight engineer/navigator's attitude.

Yeah, right, thought Gibbons, becoming increasingly irritated. What was this crap, anyway? Everybody was so concerned about the damn weather. This was basically just a stinking training exercise! It was not like they were on a real combat mission, for God's sake! And these idiots were acting like this was his first ride in the third seat. But what really pissed him off was wasting a perfectly good Friday night on some stupid night jump that probably could have been done any other night of the week. Gibbons could have been at the O Club or a dozen other beer halls in Kaiserlautern.

This is the last damned time I get talked into volunteering for extra duty just to earn a few brownie points with the CO! he thought.

"Sergeant Juston, get yourself and Mr. Bucher situated up front on the starboard side, and save me a space," ordered Captain Cleary. "Captain Roesel, load 'em up!"

Company F marched from the tarmac and up the ramp. These guys knew the drill and enjoyed every minute of it. The only thing missing, thought Bucher, was the helmet butting and the slapping of shoulder pads. These guys were pumped!

Once the ramp was raised, the troops settled into their semi-comfortable, webbed bench seats that lined the port and starboard bulkheads and ran down the center. Juston walked up and back down the center of the aircraft, quickly inspecting each of the paratroopers, including the operations officer and the commander. They were *all* his responsibility at this point.

With the four Allison turboprops torqued to maximum power, the C-130H transport lifted off the main runway at Ramstein Air Base at precisely 2350 hours and set its easterly course toward the border of the Czech Republic. The whine of the landing gear retracting was audible and ended with a metallic click. The troops were now totally quiet, most contemplating the mission at hand. A few tried to grab a few minutes of sleep. They knew it would be a long night.

~ * ~

2434 Hours

The master sergeant, one of the two Air Force loadmasters, emerged from the flight deck and walked down the four or five metal steps into the cargo bay, clipboard in hand. He stepped up to SFC Juston, put his head close to the jumpmaster's ear, and told him they were about twenty-one minutes out from the drop zone.

Juston squatted down in front of Bucher, flanked by Cleary and Roesel, and relayed the information. He explained loudly enough for just the three to hear, trying to put the novice paratrooper as much at ease as possible. "Mr. Bucher, Captain Gibbons has made the calculations for your jump, taking into consideration all of the weather-related factors: wind currents, wind speed at the higher altitudes, and surface wind speed. We have factored in your exit altitude, free fall time, and glide time, and put it all together to have you land as close to your target drop zone as possible. Right now, it looks like you will jump at 21,000 feet, about nine or ten minutes after the other troopers have deployed. I figure you will only have about a ten to twelve-second free fall, giving you plenty of time to fly with the much slower surface winds, according to Captain Gibbons."

Now addressing Cleary and Roesel in a more hurried delivery, he said, "Sirs, it's just about show time. It's pretty breezy out there tonight; we have surface winds at eight knots, gusting to twelve. Winds at jump altitude are twenty knots, gusting to thirty with thick cloud cover, but no rain at this point. Good luck, sirs!"

SFC Juston got to his feet and positioned himself in between the jump doors at the rear of the aircraft and shouted over the noise of the engines: "Twenty minutes!"

The Rangers started to readjust their equipment and get ready for the jump. There was no screwing around. This was all serious business. *Game time!*

About ten minutes later, SFC Juston hooked up his static line to the anchor-line cable, faced forward in the aircraft, stomped his foot on the floor, held his hands in front of him with the palms facing the Rangers and shouted, "Get ready!"

The Rangers stomped their feet to acknowledge the command. The safety NCOs on each jump door hooked up and passed their static lines to the two Air Force loadmasters.

SFC Juston then pointed his hands to the outside rows of seats and shouted, "Outboard personnel, stand up!"

The outboard rows, thirty-one Rangers including Cleary and Roesel, stood up and faced the rear of the C-130. Those closest to the jump doors raised and stowed their web seats.

SFC Juston pointed his hands at the inside rows of Rangers and shouted, "Inboard personnel, stand up!"

The inside rows, the remaining thirty-one Rangers, stood up and faced the rear of the C-130.

Juston raised his hands with his palms facing each other and his index fingers forming hooks. Pumping his fingers up and down, he shouted: "Hook up!"

Almost simultaneously, sixty-two Rangers clicked their static lines to the overhead steel anchor line cables that ran the length of the aircraft, inserted the safety wire, and tugged to test them.

SFC Juston then formed an O with his index fingers and thumbs, sliding them forward and back and shouting, "Check static lines!"

Each Ranger ran his fingers down his own static line, making sure it was properly attached. Juston checked the static lines of his safety NCOs, and they checked his.

Next Juston pumped his open hands to his chest and sounded off: "Check equipment!"

Each Ranger ran his hands over his front to make sure all of his equipment was properly fastened and then checked the back of the Ranger in front of him.

Juston cupped his hands behind his ears and shouted: "Sound off with equipment check!"

Starting at the rear of the line of jumpers, each Ranger slapped the back of the man in front of him, shouting, "OK!"

The last man in line looked at the jumpmaster and sounded off: "All OK, Jumpmaster!"

Juston gave his two safety NCOs an OK signal, and the loadmasters opened the jump doors. An immediate rush of frigid night air at 3,500 feet slapped each of the Airborne troops in the face: a not-so-subtle "wake up call," as if their senses were not already on high alert.

Once the doors were locked in place, the safety NCOs ran their hands along the leading edges of the doors, checking for anything sharp, and stomped on the jump platform to make sure it was firmly locked in place. Bracing themselves in the doorway, they leaned out into the 125- knot wind stream. Normally they would do this to look for the drop zone, but tonight they saw nothing but black.

The safety NCO on the starboard door came back in and gave a thumbs up to Juston, who tapped the other safety NCO on the shoulder.

With both safety NCOs ready, Juston turned to the Rangers and called out, "DZ coming up! Stand in the door!"

SFC Juston and his safety NCOs kept an eye on both of the jump doors and the red jump caution light. When it turned from red to green, Juston shouted, "Go!"

Without any hesitation, the Rangers in both doors thrust themselves into the darkness of space, and each one followed the next at one-second intervals. Sergeant First Class Juston kept his eyes on the operation, looking for problems. Each safety NCO ensured the static lines were kept clear of the jump door and remaining jumpers.

When the planeload had exited the aircraft, the safety NCOs stepped back into the jump doors to confirm all jumpers had cleared the aircraft and that there were no "hung jumpers." Both came back in calling, "Clear!"

The port jump door was closed and secured by the Air Force tech sergeant, while the starboard door remained open. Now it was just Jumpmaster SFC Gabe Juston, Mark Bucher, the two safety NCOs, and the two loadmasters who occupied the vast cargo space of the C-130H. Bucher was on his feet, but had not moved any closer to the rear of the fuselage, per the jumpmaster's instructions directly after the last of the paratroopers had left the plane.

In the excitement of the jump, especially at night, no one saw that Bucher did not "hook up," and no one would miss the outsider once they were on the ground, primarily because no one was assigned to him as a buddy. His absence would not be questioned. Besides, the general consensus among the soldiers was that these evaluators "moved in mysterious ways."

Now each of the six men left in the cargo space were pre-breathing oxygen from the console. Juston signaled Bucher to join him in the rear of the aircraft. The air seemed even colder to Bucher as he approached the starboard jump door. The strong wind charged in, enveloping the interior of the transport with all of the harsh elements found outside at an altitude of 21,000 feet.

Standing two feet from the edge, Bucher kept his head and eyes straight forward, looking into the black night sky. No stars, no moon. His heart was now pounding so hard he wondered if the jumpmaster might be able to hear it.

SFC Juston disconnected the oxygen feed from the console, quickly switching to the bail-out bottle, and began a thorough inspection of his last jumper. Everything was secured and in place. Lastly he switched Bucher from the console to the bail-out bottles and gave the NSA rookie a thumbs up.

"Okay, Mr. Bucher, you're lookin' good. Relax. Enjoy it! Savor the moment, because the trip down doesn't last very long." Juston paused for a moment. "Are you ready?"

Bucher nodded affirmatively.

The two men both stood waiting, eyes trained on the overhead red light. Green. A quick, "Good luck, sir!" followed by a sharp salute and a subtle push from behind propelled Bucher into the darkness.

Chapter Twenty-five

Western Czech Republic
Saturday, October 2, 1993
1:15 a.m.

Free falling face down in pitch blackness has to be the strangest sensation one could ever experience without the aid of a hallucinogenic drug. No reference points can be seen on the ground. The sensation is more of flying than falling—passing through the atmosphere at a terminal velocity of 120 miles per hour, air gushing all around, and no natural clues to indicate how much distance has been covered on the fast journey toward earth.

Bucher had begun counting immediately after leaving the starboard jump door of the C-130. There was no reason to question the performance of the oversized watch-like altimeter strapped to his wrist, but he found a degree of comfort in the simple counting exercise ("one thousand one, one thousand two…"), all the while waiting for the FF2 to automatically deploy his main chute. At about "one thousand five," the initial shock of leaving the aircraft had worn off and Bucher was beginning to enjoy the free-fall sensation. At about "one thousand twelve," he could feel a slight tug from behind as the spring-loaded guide chute sprang free, leading the main canopy. In a few short seconds the main canopy popped open, snapping Bucher into an upright position.

Ah, the moment of truth! All was well, so far. Bucher did a quick parachute-function check as SFC Juston had instructed him to do, just to make sure everything was working properly.

For now, all Bucher could do was just enjoy the ride. He could make out the charcoal clouds below him in the overall darkness because they were moving fast. As he made his gradual descent into the next level of clouds, he could feel a damp chill. He wondered if the powerful wind coming from the west had altered his downward progress. He felt as if he were being propelled into a parallel flight with the surface.

Bucher checked his altimeter. The luminous dial indicated six hundred feet, but it seemed he was not dropping nearly as quickly as before.

Bucher could now see a few scattered lights from farmhouses and a small village a couple of miles away. Finally, with these lights as a reference point, he could tell that he was in fact moving *very* fast. He also realized this strong surface wind did not make for good landing conditions. How far was he blown by the wind from his targeted drop zone? His mind began to race, imagining the dangers of trees and possible power lines. Buildings were not much of a threat out here.

Bucher could make out what appeared to be a tree line coming up fast in front of him. He was over a small open field or meadow right now, but not for long. The ground was racing below him, and the trees in his flight path grew larger and larger with every second. He suddenly remembered the quick-release buckle that would separate him from the parachute, dropping him into the open area. Dropping from ten or twenty feet seemed a better option than dealing with the oncoming forest. He groped for the release for a second or two and could not find it. Too late! Bucher was now being hurled through the branches of what seemed to be hundreds of pine trees. It was like running the gauntlet, being pummeled by thousands of arms lashing out at his face and upper body. The real danger was meeting up with the trunk of a tree or possibly being impaled on some broken limb. Bucher had no control.

Finally Bucher's feet hit the ground. It was a hard landing since his canopy had been fouled by the treetops and the supple pine branches had not offered much resistance against his weight on the way down.

He lay there in a crumpled heap for a full minute before moving, afraid he may have broken or badly sprained something. Slowly, he rose to his knees and then to his feet. He unstrapped his chin strap and tossed down his helmet, stretching and testing his back, arms, and shoulders. Legs and feet seemed to be working all right. Surprisingly, he was okay; only a few scratches and some bruises would surface later. One deep vertical scratch on his right cheek, about three inches long, was deep enough to draw blood. Bucher took out his handkerchief and dabbed the wound with water from his canteen, hoping the bleeding would stop soon. Oh well; the toughest part was over. He had survived the jump, and so far, no Russian soldiers were there to greet him! Looking up to the dark sky, he offered a quiet, but very sincere, "Thank you, God." Now he'd better get on with the job. Lots to do.

With two good tugs on the parachute risers, Bucher was able to free the chute from the overhead tree branches. The olive green nylon chute slithered to the ground like a snake. He quickly changed out of the uniform into his civvies and went to work immediately trying to find a place to stash the chute, helmet, uniform, boots, and web gear, keeping one of his canteens and getting rid of the other. An entrenching tool had not been issued because of the extra weight, so he couldn't dig a hole. He did, however, spot a half-decayed, fallen tree nearby. Bucher turned it over, branches crumbling in his hand, and managed to scratch out a hole with his KA-BAR in the soft soil, large enough to cram in the contraband. He rolled the worm eaten log back over the equipment and spread out some of the loose underbrush to help camouflage the disturbed area.

Once the task of concealing all of his gear was completed, Bucher strapped the KA-BAR back on his calf, but this time under his trouser leg, against the skin. He also readjusted and tightened his shoulder holster with a nylon Velcro strap and closure to a more comfortable position now under his dark brown nylon Columbia jacket. He laced up his Adidas high-top hiking shoes to complete his new civilian identity. *Now to figure out where the heck I am*, he thought.

There were no stars visible through the cloud cover to help in navigating tonight. He would have to rely on his lensatic compass and any physical features he could identify on the map. The only thing he knew for sure at this point was that he was not in the large open flat area they had designated as the drop zone. He would simply need to head south and east until he ran into a road, a town, a creek—anything that would show up on the map.

Bucher recalled the open field he had passed over just before hitting the trees. He would start from there and not attempt to fight his way through the forest. The area was certainly dark and secluded enough for him to be in the open; along the tree line would be ideal. He moved at a quick pace, knowing the clock was ticking. *Better to reach my objective early and lay low for a while, maybe even rest up a little*, he thought.

Trotting about a half mile in a southeast direction along the edge of the open field, Bucher ran into a narrow gravel road running due north and south according to his compass. He headed south, still looking for a landmark to establish his exact location with something on the map on this dark, windy October night. One note he logged in his mind was that he was heading up a very slight incline, almost undetectable to a casual observer.

Off in the distance, to his "one o'clock," he could see a single light twinkling. He stayed on the road and picked up his pace to a trot again, eager to get his bearings so he could continue his journey confident he was heading in the right direction.

Now a few more lights were visible, and he could see the headlights of a car on a road that probably intersected with the gravel road he was on, maybe another three quarters of a mile away. *A main road possibly?* he wondered. Bucher could now make out a steeple or a clock tower rising above a dozen scattered buildings, plus another car going in the opposite direction of the first. Now he needed to become invisible. He could not allow anyone to spot him and take a chance of notifying the local police of a stranger prowling about in the dark.

He edged closer to the village and came upon a small stream no more than three or four meters wide. He heard the gurgling water before he saw it and then noticed the low, flat bridge that spanned the brook. The bridge was part of the paved road where the cars had traveled a couple of minutes earlier. Bucher decided to take refuge on the other side of some hedges where he could study his map. He could now plot the stream, the bridge, the paved road, all just south of a small unnamed village, sitting on a slight elevation.

Bucher studied the center of the map closely, taking all of the physical clues into consideration. He found nothing. After what seemed to be a long time, but was probably no more than three or four minutes, he found it. Following widely spaced contour lines from the upper right-hand corner of the map, he was able to pinpoint his location.

Oh, shit! Looking at the scale at the bottom of the map, he made a quick visual calculation that caused a cold sweat and put a large knot in the pit of his stomach. He was approximately thirteen miles away from his objective! He had been blown off course five or six miles by the strong low-level southwesterly winds—or had the navigator miscalculated? Probably both. He would now need to trek through the countryside more than twice the distance they had originally figured in order to find the monastery.

How in the hell can I make it by sunrise, he thought, and in the next breath: *Suck it up.*

The Army called it double time. He would need to run to his destination in order to rendezvous with the early morning delivery truck. *Possible or impossible?* The luminous dial of his Timex read two o'clock. *Yeah, I can do it,* he tried to convince himself, but he knew that, although the additional distance wasn't so bad, the extra weight of the backpack, canteen, 9mm with extra ammo, and survival knife would be the killer. Running in blue jeans and high-top hiking shoes wouldn't help matters either.

The paved road would be his best route for about the first six or seven miles, more than half the journey. This would bring him to an intersection with a lesser road that angled off in a southeast direction. No more than a quarter of a mile down that road would be a bridge that crossed the Vltava River. It was just on the other side of this river by half a mile or so that the Air Force captain had promised to deliver him. Crossing the river had never entered into the plans. For now, his main concern was to cover as much ground as he could. In the dark hours he could make better time on the road than he could do running cross country and taking the additional risk of getting lost or bogged down in the woods. He would take his chances on the road and jump off into a ditch or head into fields or forest whenever he saw any oncoming headlights from either direction.

Having been a distance runner, Mark Bucher knew the importance of pacing his speed in order to make it to the finish line. Not too fast, to ensure not burning out too early, but fast enough to reach his destination on time. He set his rhythm slightly faster than a typical Airborne shuffle. Only time would tell if this would be sufficient. He would check the time and miles at the next physical landmark down the road.

Sporadic road traffic caused Bucher to dive for cover more often than he had anticipated, wasting more time and energy than he could afford, during the first hour of his trek. At about 3:05 a.m., traffic settled down to almost none. The run was beginning to wear him down. Somewhat discouraged in his premature fatigue, he considered the energy consumed by making the jump, the mental stress of the whole ordeal and no sleep for the past twenty-two hours, several extra pounds on his back, and the chore of running in jeans, a long-sleeve shirt, and a jacket that was now absorbing large amounts of sweat. *No wonder I feel like I've gone ten rounds with George Foreman,* he thought. So much time to think. Quiet, no stars or moon to watch, no scenery to occupy his time, just him and the road.

He had to stay focused and alert, keep his mind occupied, and not worry about obstacles that might lie ahead. He had to keep convincing himself he could do it. He didn't have Laura to reassure him as she normally did. To kill time and occupy his mind, he began to think of all of the different, interesting, challenging, and beautiful places he and Laura had run together: along the sugar-white sand beaches of Destin, Florida; through the grassy meadowlands surrounded by snow-capped peaks in Rocky Mountain National Park near Estes Park, Colorado; down the long stretches of running and biking paths parallel to Lake Michigan along Lake Shore Drive in Chicago; and of course their most recent run through the English Garden in Munich. Mark recalled that he had run thirteen miles or more at least a half dozen times while training for the St. Louis Marathon about this same time last year.

All of these great memories and many more crossed his mind as he continued to run. He soon realized that somewhere within the last fifteen minutes he had found his second wind. His pace had quickened and, more importantly, he had renewed spirit and confidence, derived from the powerful, positive feelings and memories of pleasant experiences and mental and physical victories he had achieved only through the help of God. *Let's give credit where credit is due*, he had often thought.

"Looks like it's time to ask for another small miracle, Lord," he said softly, looking up into the black sky.

Bucher had become so wrapped up in his thoughts that he almost over ran the narrow road that joined the pavement to his left. He allowed himself a break and stopped briefly for a drink from his canteen and half of a Power Bar. He knew his body required the fuel to continue the trek. He also took a minute to review the map. Better than three-fourths of the way, he noted with satisfaction, glancing at his watch. He was meeting his required pace, but not by a very wide margin. *About a quarter of a mile to the bridge, and then it's all up hill from there.* Not a very pleasant thought.

It was tough getting the legs started again, once he had stowed the penlight and map back in the Padagonia backpack. He felt a little stiff, but no cramping. The new direction led him into another heavily wooded area on both sides of the narrow road.

Bucher turned a sharp bend on the partially gravel-covered road toward the bridge and froze in his tracks. The orange glow of the fire burning in a short cylinder—half an oil drum— clearly illuminated three figures huddled closely around it: soldiers. Rifles were slung over their shoulders as they stood talking and laughing and passing a clear bottle.

Obviously they had not heard him approach, and it was much too dark for them to see anything outside of the perimeter of light cast from their fire pit. Bucher could see the framework of an old metal bridge just beyond the armed sentries. He could barely make out the faded letters on the sign on the right-hand side: "Vltava."

The issue now was how to circumvent these three armed men controlling the passage of any travel across the river. Had the soldiers been alert and quiet and without a fire, Bucher would have jogged right into their hands. End of mission.

Surveying the situation, Bucher figured he would angle through the woods to his right and head downstream, then simply wade across the stream twenty or thirty yards down from the bridge and work his way back to the road once on the other side.

Inching his way closer to the stream, within the protective cover of the thick trees, he began to hear a different sound: the roar of rushing water. Immediately Bucher had his doubts about simply wading across. The noise of the rushing water grew louder. Within a few yards of the river he could see the torrent of white water crashing over and around huge, half-submerged boulders. This was no little stream. Attempting to ford this river on foot would be suicide.

Bucher had no other choice but to somehow use the bridge. He cursed the fact that if he had been dropped on the other side of this bridge like he was supposed to have been, this problem would not have existed. The NSA rookie made his way quietly along the riverbank with the aid of the rushing water that camouflaged what little sound he created.

When he reached the bridge abutment, he noticed no change in the guard's activities. That was good news. The circle of light from the fire extended almost halfway across the bridge. Bucher quickly surveyed the structure from underneath, then stepped back to view the superstructure of the bridge. Old and rusty; he would hardly trust driving his car across for fear it would collapse.

He noticed that two-inch metal support rods for the decking, spaced about eighteen inches apart, were exposed on the underside where time and weather had caused the concrete to crumble away. These extended about ten or twelve feet out over the water and then stopped where the rusted metal was then again encased by the concrete which was still intact. Jumping up about twelve or thirteen inches, Bucher grabbed onto one of the exposed support rods and began to move hand-over-hand out over the torrent of water below, praying the next rod would continue to hold his weight and not be rusting to the breaking point. His shoulders ached under the extra weight he carried, and his bulky clothing impaired his mobility. *Only three more feet; I can do this.*

In front of the last two rungs, an extension of the superstructure—reinforced metal lattice—angled downward to where it connected with the decking and extended another few inches beyond the underside of the bridge. Bucher was able to get a good handhold at the bottom of the metal beam and pull himself up onto the deck of the bridge, exposing himself for a second or two within the shadowy firelight. Without hesitation, he climbed the lattice work as one would climb a ladder, inserting hand and foot into the diamond-shaped openings. At the top of the structure he was about twenty feet above the deck and an additional thirty feet or so above the boulders and raging waters below.

The vertical climb was not difficult, although when it leveled out across the top of the bridge, it required something of an unnatural movement. He did not dare stand upright and attempt to walk across the ten-inch wide metal beam. He instead continued in a crawling manner at a snail's pace. Bucher could not take his eyes off of his hands reaching one in front of the other, concentrating on maintaining his balance. *Don't look down. Do not look down!* At the point where the horizontal beams angled back down at a forty-five degree angle, Bucher was forced to pivot around and head back down feet first.

As he made the pivot and resumed a more natural, vertical position for the climb back down, he looked toward the fire to confirm the Russian soldiers had not changed their relaxed posture. *No change; thank you, God!*

What did alarm Bucher, from this elevated lookout, was the sky starting to become pink to the east. *How much time did I burn up trying to cross this damned river?* he wondered. Frustration was setting in, causing him to again doubt he'd be able to pull this off. He truly felt the weight of the world on his shoulders.

Once back on the ground, he slipped into the protective cover of the trees for another twenty or thirty yards, just enough to remain out of sight and out of hearing range of the three posted sentries. Back on the road, Bucher broke into a flat-out run; no longer could he afford an "Airborne shuffle."

The original plan that had been discussed with Henry Talbot called for him to attract the attention of Gerhardt Richter near the rear entry of the monastery while the delivery truck was unloading. Hopefully, Richter would be outside smoking a cigar and overseeing the delivery of the provisions. Richter had assured Talbot that none of the ranking officers, especially General Krause, would be awake at that early hour on a Saturday morning. This was the only day of the week he allowed himself and his staff an extra hour or so of some much needed sleep.

From the river, the road became increasingly steep as the contour lines on his map had indicated. The road required several switchbacks to make the climb. Bucher had run two miles from the bridge. The sky was beginning to brighten slightly over his left shoulder. With four miles to go, Mark Bucher knew the chances of successfully completing this vitally important mission were now all but lost.

Just then, Bucher heard the sound of grinding gravel and the low growl of a truck struggling with the steep grade, only seconds before he saw the headlights. He had no time to dive for cover; the old truck had made the turn and he was instantly in full view.

~ * ~

Richter paced around in the back garden area of the eighteenth-century monastery, puffing on a cigar, pretending to be enjoying the morning air and the first smoke of the day. *Where the hell is he, damn it! And where the hell is the truck,* he grumbled.

The down-computer ploy would not hold up any longer. It *would* be fixed by today—by this morning, in fact! Krause's schedule called for his ultimatum announcement to be made at noon today. This entailed the process of entering the encrypted access code from the disc into the computer to link him to the 1813C Cosmos satellite by which he planned to transmit his communiqué to the leaders of the western world.

Krause had already deployed the eight teams who manned his new mobile nuclear-armed rockets from a central marshaling point in a deserted warehouse building on the outskirts of the old Dutch city of Maastricht into their designated locations. In some cases, depending on the distance to be traveled, these teams had been dispatched as much as two days ago. Richter now had all of this vital information and was anxious to send it back with the NSA courier, Eric Mueller.

All eight rocket launchers were set up in remote locations, within easy striking distance of eight major European cities. Because of their mobile capability, they could go anywhere and not be restricted to launch only from behind boundaries of the countries that once embraced communism. The individual XG-777 missile armed with two W-79 tactical nuclear warheads could not wipe out an entire large city, but it could certainly inflict a great deal of death and destruction and create panic with its pinpoint accuracy, annihilating the country's government centers, key military installations, or densely populated areas. Three of these XG-777s concentrated on one target city could certainly destroy a very large portion of any one of these metropolitan areas. Eight mobile launch vehicles, each loaded with three of these nuclear-tipped rockets represented one hell of a lot of fire power spread out over Western Europe.

According to the plans, at exactly twelve o'clock noon, Krause would announce to the world via his communication satellite, from a prepared statement, his intentions—or rather *demands*—to be recognized as the new leader of Communist Russia, along with a threat of "severe repercussions" if his demands were not met by a given time.

Stephan Krause would hold the selected eight major metropolitan cities as hostages. If his new communist order was to succeed, he would need to catch the attention and respect of the rest of the world by some show of force. If it meant launching one or two missiles into any one of these highly populated cities to open the world's eyes to the new world power, then so be it. He was prepared to go twenty-four rounds with these prominent European leaders if necessary.

The only possible defense against a threat like this was to find and destroy the mobile missile launcher and its payload before orders were given to strike. This was a highly unlikely scenario, considering these M-5s and their rockets would probably be kept buttoned up in their original shipping cartons—the twenty-foot containers—which made them virtually invisible. One could hide a twenty-foot container anywhere a small delivery truck could be parked, then move it to another location within minutes without leaving a trace.

Richter had never really expected this type of devious, unconventional warfare from General Krause. He had only been alerted to the "city hostage" plan the night before at Krause's senior staff meeting. If only he could have gotten the word out sooner. But he had faith in the seasoned NSA station chief. If anyone could get the job done, it was Henry Talbot.

~ * ~

Bucher froze. The truck driver slammed on the brakes to avoid hitting him. Suddenly, with an instinctive reaction that surprised even Bucher himself, he drew his semi-automatic pistol from the shoulder holster under the Columbia nylon jacket and pointed it directly at the driver's head. Bucher wasn't sure who was more nervous, the driver or him. The driver's eyes were wide with astonishment.

Bucher stepped quickly around to the passenger side, opened the door, and got in. He hoped like hell the driver spoke German; after all, even though they were only a few miles from the German border, they were still in the Czech Republic.

He didn't bother to ask but just began speaking in his best German. "I do not intend to hurt you. Please just do exactly what I tell you to do. If you help me, I will pay you a large sum of money." Bucher waited a second and said, "Now please give me your wallet."

Trembling, the man reached back and handed Bucher an old brown leather billfold.

Bucher took out the driver's license, gave it a glance, and then shoved the wallet into his jacket pocket.

"And if you do not cooperate, I will cause great harm to you and your family. You see, now I have your name, and I know where you live."

What a lie! thought Bucher, knowing he was totally incapable of harming this man or his family, but he also knew he had to make an impression on this guy in order for the mission to succeed.

Jakub Dvorak, according to his Czech driver's license, responded in perfect German with utmost sincerity. "Yes, sir, of course I will cooperate."

"What is your business here?" Bucher asked flatly.

"I'm delivering food and supplies to the soldiers at the monastery at the top of the hill."

That was exactly the answer Bucher had hoped for.

"Good. I will help you unload the truck."

Understandably, the driver was perplexed. *Here's a man who puts a gun to my head, offers to pay me big money, and now volunteers to help unload my truck. I don't get it!* Jakub Dvorak just nodded his head in agreement.

The two drove in silence for the remaining next couple of miles until the road straightened out and provided a full view of the castle-like monastery in the distance. From a quarter of a mile away, Bucher could see two guards on the road directly in front of the stately old building.

"Slow down," commanded Bucher, trying to buy a few seconds, racking his brain as to what to do next.

Dvorak slowed and reached down under the driver's seat (luckily not for a gun, or Bucher would be dead) and pulled out a large green bottle of Pilsner Urquell. He popped off the cap with an opener that was bolted to the underside of the dashboard and quickly handed it to Bucher.

"Here, take this. Act like you're drunk or passed out or something."

Mark Bucher took the bottle, poured some of the beer into his hands and splashed it onto his face as you would apply after shaving lotion. He managed to spill some on the floor of the truck, as well. He laid his head back and slouched in the corner of the cab as if he were sleeping off the alcohol. Dvorak came to a complete stop as one of the road guards approached the truck on his side. The guard had recognized the truck and the driver from the previous visit, but he was curious about the passenger.

With an air of complete authority, the Russian sergeant shouted in Czech, "You are supposed to come alone! Those are the rules! Who is this?"

"This is my uncle. He is totally drunk, as you can see. I brought him with me to save his life," Dvorak said with a straight face. "My aunt said if she *ever* found him drunk like this again she would kill him." He grinned good-naturedly. "And I believe she would!"

Receiving the curious reaction he'd hoped for, Dvorak continued, "I know she's physically capable of it. She's actually slightly larger than you are, Sergeant."

They both chuckled a little, and the guard waved them through.

Once away from the guard post, Bucher rose from his slouched position, opened his eyes, and smiled. "Excellent job, Mr. Dvorak, whatever it was you said!" He handed the driver a one-hundred Deutsche mark bill. "Keep up the good work, and there's more where that came from."

They rounded the gravel drive to the back of the monastery. There was Bucher's man, puffing away at a now stubby cigar. He could see the doubt on Richter's face when he realized Bucher was not his prearranged contact, Erich Mueller. Mark Bucher returned a look he hoped might possibly convey a message of alliance, but he knew it would not be enough.

Bucher immediately dug out the box of cigars from his backpack and approached the Russian major. To a casual observer, he might have been making a peace offering of sorts.

"Sir, I'm sure you will enjoy these fine cigars," he said in German in a very low tone.

Richter accepted the box as if he had been handed a snake, still very unsure of the visitor. Sensing this skepticism, Bucher had to think of something quickly that would tie him to Mueller or Talbot, something to indicate his association to the NSA.

A few long seconds later, in almost a whisper, he blurted out, "I enjoy Badger football, but I think the Buckeyes will win."

"I suppose you are probably correct," responded Richter, without changing his expression.

Richter was still not completely sold on the stranger's true identity. This man could very well be a plant, and he wasn't about to hand over any of this strategic information on rocket placements and target sites without first testing these hopefully altered discs. He would run a fast check, testing two or three important elements in the XG-777 remote firing code sequence and the access code to go live with the Cosmos 1813C satellite, and then return the discs back to the cigar box, which he would put away in his room until he could safely place them back in the metal storage boxes without being detected.

Richter needed about fifteen minutes to replace the switch on the computer, boot up, and run the test. Unloading the truck would not take more than five or six minutes.

"Corporal, make sure you give these men something to eat after they have unloaded the provisions, and put on a fresh pot of coffee for them, too," Richter said to the enlisted man in charge of the kitchen, before he disappeared down the stairs to the computer room set-up in the cellar. *Pray God no one should wake up and wander down into the nerve center at this time of the morning,* he thought.

The dark bread, fresh from the oven, with rich, homemade butter was equal to a feast in Bucher's estimation. It had been yesterday at noon since he had eaten a full meal. He had been running on two Power Bars, a canteen of water, and pure adrenalin since then.

As the two men sat in silence, enjoying their bread and coffee, a distinguished-looking, middle-aged man wearing a bulky knit sweater and casual trousers entered the kitchen.

The startled corporal snapped to attention and said, "Good morning, General. Coffee, sir?"

Obviously knowing his commander's morning ritual, he grabbed a large mug and filled it with the black liquid, adding just a touch of sugar.

Bucher's eyes met Krause's. It was unavoidable on Bucher's part, but completely intentional on the part of the Spetsnaz general. Bucher could feel the icy stare. He nodded cordially to his host and resumed eating the dark bread. The general took his coffee and stepped out of the kitchen without speaking a word.

Five minutes later, while Bucher on his second large cup of coffee, as was Mr. Dvorak, the major came into the kitchen wearing a subdued smile.

"You've eaten well, I take it? Good! I will not cause you further delay. Because our general is a most kind and appreciative man, he would like to give you each a little memento for the wonderful food you have brought to us." He handed the driver a small jewelry box. "And I appreciate the fine cigars, as well," he added, handing another small box to Bucher.

Dvorak opened the lid to find an imitation gold lapel pin with the encrusted Hammer and Sickle symbol of the Communist Party.

"Take good care of these small gifts," Richter said, making direct eye contact with Bucher. "This symbol will become a very important designation again in the near future. Wear it with pride."

Major Richter walked the men out to the truck. While Mr. Dvorak secured the canvas across the top of the truck bed, Richter pulled Bucher to the side, out of view from the building and the driver.

"I don't know who you are, but I'm forced to trust you, and we have no time to talk about it. I have given you *the* most important information that directly affects the safety and well-being of the greater part of Europe, on microfilm in your pin box. It is essential you deliver this to Talbot immediately! If you made it here, you can certainly make it back to Munich. Millions of lives are at stake, and the burden is now your responsibility to make sure the information is delivered. No more time. Talbot *must* receive this today, absolutely as soon as possible, without fail. Understood?"

Some delivery boy! thought Mark Bucher. *No pressure; just pick up and deliver. No problem!*

~ * ~

Richter returned to the computer center and literally tore the place up as if he had been searching for the spare switch. He would give Captain Karpinov a tongue lashing for not being able to find the part, which oddly enough, Richter was able to find so he could make the necessary repairs.

Chapter Twenty-six

Southwestern Czech Republic
Saturday, October 2, 1993
6:53 a.m.

As Dvorak was backing the truck out to leave the monastery, Bucher asked if there were any other roads that led out, rather than the one they'd driven in on, explaining he wanted to avoid the guards at the bridge.

"There's an old logging road, but I doubt you would want to take it. It's in terrible condition with deep ruts and potholes and a wooden bridge that's in even worse shape than the one you crossed earlier this morning, and it goes a few miles out of my way to get back home."

"Good, we'll take it. Even if there are guards posted, they couldn't know I wasn't with you coming in this morning."

"Very well," responded Jakub Dvorak. "We'll take the logging road."

"Here's another hundred DM for your excellent cooperation," Bucher said, peeling off a blue-colored bank note. "Do you have children?"

"Yes, two little girls, ages six and four."

Bucher, feeling deeply indebted to the man, peeled off two more hundred Deutsche mark bills. "Here, these are for your daughters. Buy them something special."

353

Dvorak was amazed. This was actually turning out to be his lucky day. He thanked the stranger nonchalantly as if this happened every day.

Looking in his rear view mirror to make sure they were no longer in view of the monastery, Dvorak rolled down the window and heaved the small box containing the Hammer and Sickle pin as far as he could into the woods.

"I will have no such trash lying around in my truck, much less pin it on my coat!" the driver exclaimed.

"So you don't agree with the major's prediction concerning a return of communist power?" asked Bucher.

"I will not have my daughters brought up under a communist government as I was. I will leave this country and go as far west as I have to, to avoid that kind of oppression."

This display of unsolicited national pride was comforting to Bucher. At least the man next to him was working with him rather than against him, even though the driver had no idea what this whole ordeal was all about. As far as Dvorak was concerned, this foreigner—an American or possibly an Englishman; he always had trouble distinguishing between the two—delivered a box of cigars to a Russian major, and that was all that took place. *Those must be some pretty damn good cigars to go to that much trouble to deliver them,* thought Dvorak, knowing there must be more to it than that.

~ * ~

6:55 a.m.

Richter had not liked sending off the microfilm with the stranger, even though he did have the proper code words associated with Talbot and Mueller, but the major had no other alternatives. There would be no other opportunities to get this critical information back to Henry Talbot. Major Richter hustled back down to the computer center to further inspect the new backup discs and also scatter and generally make a mess of the spare parts inventory before the rest of the staff was up and about.

Gerhardt Richter had just finished replacing the two backup discs in their designated slots in the metal safe-like boxes and then trashing the cartons that the spare computer components were stored in. He sat down at the console and began booting up a program containing some nonessential light weapons inventory information, while waiting for the right opportunity to retrieve the original altered disc he had taken from the cigar box and temporarily stashed in the drawer of his night stand.

General Stephan Krause stood in the doorway. "Major Richter, I'm surprised to see you working so diligently at the computer so early on a Saturday morning, and this is not even your area of responsibility!"

"Sir, *it is* my responsibility, as your *aide-de-camp*, to ensure this operation runs smoothly. The computer has been down due to a broken part, threatening the success of your mission. I, sir, am happy to report that I have found the spare part and have made the necessary repairs. We are now back up and running, as we speak, sir."

"Very good, Major Richter. You are extremely industrious, but don't you think you should alert Captain Karpinov of your breakthrough?"

"Of course, Comrade General. I was about to send for him. I just wanted to make sure everything is running properly first. I will have the sergeant wake him up at once."

"Very well. Keep me informed of your progress. *Now* we will be able to inform the world via satellite, on time and as planned, that the New Communist Order will be a force to be reckoned with. They *will* listen to me."

While Krause was still within earshot, Richter summonsed the sergeant to "get Captain Karpinov's ass out of bed and down here to the computer center at once!" This was strictly for show. Richter had no need for the captain, nor would the computer geek get in the way now. The foot dragging was now over.

Within ten minutes, Captain Anatoly Karpinov joined Richter at the console. The major reprimanded Captain Karpinov one more time for his inability to find and repair the broken switch, but not as severely as before, much to the captain's surprise. Richter finished with the, "If you want something done correctly around here, you have to do it yourself" routine.

~ * ~

7:10 a.m.

Five minutes later, General Krause appeared at the door with a sergeant and another soldier, both with their automatic rifles held at their chests in the ready position.

"Richter, you amaze me!" said the general in a friendly voice. "You are smart enough to somehow infiltrate my ranks and might possibly have done something with this computer disc without my knowledge—at least up till now. Hiding this disc in your nightstand was rather foolish, wouldn't you agree?" he said, holding it up in his left hand.

"Trying to sabotage my *coupe d'état*!" The anger was now evident in his voice. "I can only assume you have sent all of our strategic information back with the delivery man. A very clever plan, but obviously not clever enough. I'm actually embarrassed to say I didn't suspect you of anything until this morning! Now it's quite easy to fit all of the pieces together. Your miraculous repair of the computer without the aid of Captain Karpinov so early on this Saturday morning, along with your overly generous efforts to provide me with such professional entertainment last night and throughout the early morning hours, was just a little too much.

"Oh! And once my curiosity was aroused, I checked with our road guards to see if they had noticed anything unusual. Sergeant Belenki said there were two men in the delivery truck this morning rather than one. Then I brought this up to the guards posted at the bridge, and they told me there was only the driver. Furthermore, none of the three men could recall seeing the truck return back over the bridge!

"Karpinov!" shouted the general. "Run this disc and compare it with the backup discs to see what Richter might have deleted or if there is anything at all left on the disc."

356

Although Richter was extremely disappointed that his luck and his career as a spy had just run out, as he had been squarely caught in the act of duplicity, he managed to smile inwardly, grateful Krause did not suspect that the main disc or the two backups had ever left the premises. There was still hope.

"Well, we will catch up with your accomplice who drives the truck soon enough, and I can assure you we will deal with him properly, but not in nearly as agonizing a way as what I have in store for you. Sergeant! Take this traitor bastard out of my sight. I'd like to kill him now, but that would be rushing it. I want to savor the experience when I have a little more time. It's like taking the time to enjoy the aroma of a good Cognac or a captivating woman, eh, Richter? Make sure he is chained up securely and out of my sight!

"And now we'll need to find another headquarters location immediately, thanks to Major Richter, and move out as quickly as possible."

Krause turned on his heels, leaving Richter to the guards who suddenly took on the characteristics of two rabid Dobermans.

~ * ~

Yorkshire, England
Saturday, October 2, 1993
7:12 a.m.

Menwith Hill Station provides communication and intelligence support service to the United Kingdom and to the United States, specifically to the National Security Agency. It is an interesting sight to see from the air, resembling a couple of dozen golf balls scattered around the green countryside of North Yorkshire. These "golf balls" are the spherical domes that house some of the largest electronic satellite monitoring devices in the world, along with a large number of vertical mast antennae to monitor high-frequency radio transmissions.

Elizabeth Emerson, a civilian attached to the U.S. Army's 713th Military Intelligence Group, monitored the gray screen on her desk in B Compound. She would be the first to admit this had become a pretty dull assignment, although it hadn't always been that way. A couple of years ago, the NSA crew at Menwith Hill Station had their hands full with an important role in the Gulf War. The only other notable high points had been space shuttle flights and a few international activities that had happened much too infrequently. At times, the monotony of watching the repetitive blips was almost unbearable.

Emerson stepped away from her monitor for a few minutes to refresh her cup of tea. When she returned, she didn't notice anything specific at first, but she had a feeling—almost subliminal—that something was a little different. She couldn't quite put a finger on it.

Active satellites glowed red on her monitor; inactive satellites and other space junk were greenish yellow. The feeling annoyed Elizabeth enough to call up the active list on her CRT. This listing gave basic information on whose satellite it was, the date it was sent into orbit, its approximate size and primary function, such as weather satellite, communications satellite, or classified (basically a spy satellite), and a few other labels of lesser concern. This screen also noted any deactivation dates with another column for any rare reactivation dates. These were highly uncommon.

Scrolling down the activity log on her CRT, Emerson found the source of her annoyance immediately. A Russian Cosmos satellite labeled #3679B had been brought back to life. *Very interesting indeed!* Now she could focus her attention on this new red dot. She knew the exact location it occupied in the heavens, and she even had the sophisticated electronic equipment to pick up a signal when the orbiting satellite was transmitting. Although the satellite-to-earth transmissions were scrambled and could not be deciphered within her block, friends at the U.S. National Reconnaissance Office could determine a fairly specific area, within a radius of about two square miles, of where the microwave messages were being sent. This activity was not in any way part of the responsibility of the tracking station; in fact, it fringed on the international regulations regarding electronic eavesdropping. But it certainly helped while away some of that dull time parked in front of the monitor.

Elle Emerson reported the rebirth of this Russian satellite to NSA headquarters at Fort Mead immediately, as she had always been instructed to do with anything out of the ordinary. After her brief communication with Fort Mead, she set about the task of triangulating the location of the transmission beam receiver in relation to the satellite and back to her location, a simple exercise in geometry.

~ * ~

7:15 a.m.

"So, Captain Karpinov, did Richter manage to delete all of the data on the disc?" inquired Lieutenant General Krause.

"No, sir, I've compared the original with both of the backups, and they are all identical. I can't see there are any changes. I think he was probably preparing to make changes or delete all of the data once the system was back up. It appears you must have caught him just in time, Comrade General."

Krause breathed a sigh of relief, giving himself full credit for having prevented this traitor from throwing a wrench into his well-laid plans to restore communism under his control.

It seemed strange the general was not throwing a fit of anger. He actually displayed the air of a conquering warrior, strutting around with his chest puffed out like a Bantam rooster. Krause had just dispatched a team of his best guards, under the supervision of Lieutenant Pavel Sluskaya, to drive to the house and store of his grocery supplier to force whatever information they could out of the driver about his part in this spy mission and to find the other party, as well.

As a precaution, General Krause ordered Karpinov to instruct each of the eight commanders of the mobile launch units to manually reset the ten-digit target coordinates by changing only the last number in both sets. This would only alter the pinpoint accuracy of the missile by no more than fifty to sixty meters. For example, the missile would now strike the guard shack to the left of the main entrance to Buckingham Palace instead of going straight through the front door. Krause could no longer leave any of the satellite or missile (target) data completely in its original form for fear this critical information had been passed along from Richter to the spy.

He was now confident that even with the information the spy may have, he would not be able to interfere with Krause's master plan. Sure, they probably knew the cities to be targeted; anyone could have guessed most of those key locations anyhow. But finding a twenty-foot container outside these huge metropolitan areas would be next to impossible.

Krause called his remaining officers together to inform them of his early morning discovery. He first wanted to illustrate to his officer corps that *nothing* could escape his watchful eye and that punishment would be forthcoming.

"I'll give the traitor plenty of time to think about it," he informed his cadre.

Second on his agenda was the problem of relocation. Because this headquarters location had been compromised, it had to be moved to another secure site not terribly far away; there was no time for a lengthy road trip. Tomorrow he was scheduled to proclaim the New World Communist Order. He would carry out his ultimatum and demonstrate his strength by a show of force, if necessary.

The third order of business was a report from Colonel Zotkin regarding the placement of his eight launchers and crews; he would need to run a check on the computerized target acquisitions. The colonel began by running down the list of target cities: "Our Rome, Munich, Brussels, Amsterdam, London, Paris, Frankfort, and Vienna crews are all..."

"Stop," said Krause. "Colonel Zotkin, tell me again, in detail, the type of site we have secured for our Vienna crew."

Again, referring to his handwritten notes, the colonel replied as he had the night before. "They are located in a very small, secluded, mountain community called Kahlenberg, on a hillside overlooking Vienna, elevation 484 meters. The nearest town is Grinzing, five and a half kilometers down the road. They have an excellent observation post, as well as kitchen facilities and more than enough space to billet the men."

"Well, it's obvious Vienna is by far the closest and easiest site to reach from here. The logistics appear to be more than adequate for our needs. They have already secured this site, correct?"

"Yes, sir. No problems have been reported. This is Captain Bakhvalova's team, so you can be sure he has prepared the site very well."

"Good. We need to put our rapid deployment plan into effect now, with Kahlenberg as our objective. I expect you to be on the road in forty-five minutes." Krause checked his watch, as did all of his officers. "As soon as you arrive, I want the radio equipment set up first. I will need to broadcast my ultimatum at noon sharp, so make sure you are on the first truck to depart, and make damn sure you have everything set up and operational as soon as I get there, Captain Karpinov. Colonel Zotkin, and I will leave after the last truck has moved out, and we'll make a quick inspection to make sure nothing of any value has been left behind. Move quickly, gentlemen! We are racing against the clock." The men were dismissed.

~ * ~

7:29 a.m.

Twenty minutes after Emerson's discovery of the resurrected Russian Cosmos satellite, a radar technician watching his monitor at the National Aeronautics and Space Administration on Cooper's Island, Bermuda, noticed an almost identical happening, only from a much greater distance. He picked up a signal emanating from a new, unknown satellite somewhere over the North Atlantic and connecting with a receiver directly on the coastline of Italy, in very close proximity to Rome.

361

~ * ~

7:31 a.m.

Elizabeth Emerson, now intently watching her recently discovered live satellite, saw the new red light change back to greenish yellow before her very eyes. *What the…? Can't these Russians make up their minds?*

Within five seconds, the light turned to red again. For the second time within about thirty minutes, Emerson picked up the phone and punched the direct dial to her boss at Fort Mead.

~ * ~

"General Bussen, I have Deputy Director Agnussi, NSA, on line three for you, sir," announced Chief Warrant Officer Jerome Quin, manning the desk outside of the CICEUCOM's office.

"Thank you, Mr. Quin. I'll take it." The Commander in Chief of the European Command punched the flashing button to connect. "Admiral, it's been a long time since we've spoken. I hope all is well at Fort Mead."

"General Bussen, Fort Mead is fine. It's the rest of the world I'm concerned about. Sir, we've got some additional intel that will require your top priority. It appears we have the rebirth of a Russian Cosmos series 1800 satellite sending radio signals to locations near London and Rome," reported Mike Agnussi. "I have strong feelings this is directly linked to General Krause's activities that Hank Talbot has been tracking."

"I concur, Mike. You seem to have a much broader scope on this situation than I do at this time, so I defer to you; what do you think is the best way to approach this?"

"Well, sir, we only have an approximate coordinate, but with some low-level reconnaissance, I'm hopeful you'll be able to quickly locate and then eventually engage what might be two of the Russian outposts equipped with the missing missiles and launch vehicles."

Agnussi gave Bussen all of the details he had gathered from Menwith Hill Station and the NASA station on Cooper's Island, Bermuda.

~ * ~

7th Army Headquarters, Stuttgart, Germany

"Mr. Quin, I need to know what Air Force assets we have available to us in Italy and the UK," commanded General John Bussen, "to pinpoint the exact location of a small unit of Russian soldiers and at least one or maybe two vehicles about the size of a three-quarter ton truck in both of these areas. We don't need high and fast; we need something low and slow enough to get a visual on their locations, given approximate grid coordinates. I want to be close enough to get some long-range photos, but it's imperative we not scare these Russians off. Make it clear we are *not*, I repeat, *not* to engage. Once we have their exact location, I'll send in some Airborne troops to take care of business."

"Sir, I can tell you off the top of my head that we have the 510th Fighter Squadron at Aviano AB in northern Italy, and we've got the 48th Fighter Wing out of RAF Lakenheath in Suffolk, Eng—"

"Mr. Quin, F-16s and F-15s are not what I would consider 'low and slow.' We need observation and recon, not an air strike, at least not at this point."

"Yes, sir, I know. What I was going to suggest, sir," he said, "was that the 510th has both Search and Rescue and Close Air Support teams they've been utilizing in the Bosnian conflict, and there's a Rescue Squadron that flies HH-60G choppers—I think it's the 56th—that's attached to the Fighter Wing at Lakenheath."

"Excellent, Mr. Quin. That's exactly what I had in mind. Get it started right now. The clock is running down."

Director Jeschke personally knew the head of MI6, the British Secret Intelligence Service, whom he called to "strongly encourage" the evac of the royal family and Prime Minister John Major to a secure location outside of London. Simultaneously, Agnussi made the call to General Cesare Pucci, the Director of SISMI, Italy's Military Intelligence and Security Service, informing him to take all necessary precautions for the safety of President Oscar Luigi Scalfaro, Prime Minister Carlo Ciampi, and Pope John Paul II.

The simplistic solution to this dilemma would be to give in to the wishes of the new communist party to be heard, at least until the fanatic could be disarmed. But any security or law enforcement agency with a real backbone would not give in to terrorists' demands. Every nut job with a bomb or a method to deliver one could disrupt the General Assembly every day otherwise.

~ * ~

Bucher and Dvorak bounced down the logging road for the better part of fifteen minutes. Bucher checked his map and confirmed with the driver their exact location. Having made a large "horseshoe" curve through the forest, they had ended up back on a paved road well away from the bridge Bucher had crossed only a couple of hours before. Dvorak stopped the truck and looked to Bucher for further instruction.

"I need you to take me to Linz," Bucher said politely.

Linz, Austria, was another hour and ten minutes due south. Based on Talbot's intel reports, the Czech-Austrian border would not be very well patrolled. Bucher hoped like hell Talbot's information was accurate.

"Do you know of any back roads or less traveled routes to get us into Austria?" Bucher asked.

"Yes, I believe so, but I think it would be wise to bring a little something for the border guards, just to assure our safe passage if we are stopped. We can go by my store to pick up these items, fill up the gas tank, and then head to the border."

This sounded like a workable plan, and Bucher didn't have a better one. The rookie NSA operative realized he was facing a new danger. He was beginning to become fatigued. With the smooth paved surface and the warm sun coming through the windshield, he could barely keep his eyes open. He knew he had to stay alert. *Can't let down my guard. Too much at stake.* Even though Jakub Dvorak seemed almost too good to be true, he knew he had to keep him on a short leash to ensure his control.

In five minutes, they pulled up to a small country store. The driver opened the storage room on the side of the one-level wooden building and instructed Bucher to wait there. He returned a couple of minutes later carrying a case of beer in green bottles, a thick, foot-long smoked sausage, and a bottle of clear liquid with no label.

"This should work," Dvorak said with confidence.

He filled the gas tank from a large, elevated tank around the back of his store and then proceeded out onto the main road heading south. Two or three miles farther down, he turned onto a road not much better than the logging road, but which led to scattered houses and farms. The closer they came to the Austrian border, the more the quality of the road continued to diminish.

Directly ahead on the road that had now become a dirt and gravel path were two soldiers. This was the border.

"Be passed out again," said Dvorak. "It worked pretty well the last time. You speak good German, but you still sound too much English."

Bucher hoped this act would work just one more time. Both Russian soldiers stood steadfast in the middle of the road. One unshouldered his rifle and held it at port arms; the ranking guard advanced to the truck.

In Czech, the guard yelled out loudly, "What is your business out here where only God could find you?"

"Sir, I am delivering my uncle to a friend's house to sleep off a long night of serious drinking. His place is in the village on the other side of that hill," Dvorak said, pointing toward the border. He did in fact know the area fairly well.

"What's in the truck?" barked the sentry.

"Nothing much, sir. Just some beer, a bottle of vodka, and some smoked deer sausage. If you would like a couple of beers, sir, you are welcome to them," Dvorak responded, hoping the guard would take the bait.

The sergeant walked around the rear of the covered truck; pulled out the full case of beer, the bottle of vodka, and the large rope of venison sausage; and set them on the ground near the other Russian soldier.

"You won't be needing these anymore," he laughed. "Consider this the toll for using my road. Now get out of here!"

"Yes, sir," the driver said sheepishly and drove on.

"Hook, line, and sinker," Bucher muttered, realizing the idiom meant nothing to Mr. Dvorak.

Once they were in the village and on a main road, Linz was not far away.

"To the train station, please," Bucher said, sounding more like a friendly directive to a taxi driver. He was very pleased with his performance as a rookie "cut-out" for the NSA. He could hardly believe what he'd just accomplished. But he was also fully aware that a great deal of credit belonged to his adopted assistant, the grocery driver, for the success of the mission.

Bucher looked forward to a relaxing train ride back to Munich and a well-deserved breakfast in the dining car. Eggs and sausage—no, maybe Eggs Benedict and some fried potatoes and a large glass of tomato juice—sounded awfully good right about now.

The truck stopped at the entrance to the main train station.

"Oh," said Bucher, "I almost forgot. Here's your wallet back. Thank you very much for your tremendous cooperation. Here's a little more for your services," he said, handing over another two hundred Deutsche Marks.

To Dvorak, this was by far the easiest money he had made in his life.

Mark Bucher grabbed his backpack, gave Dvorak a genuine smile, and headed to the ticket counter of the old railway station.

The train station resembled a set in a 1940s movie. According to the timetable under the shed, the next train to Munich would depart in twenty minutes. Bucher paid cash in Austrian shillings and found a public phone. Oddly enough, the memorized phone number came back easily to him. He had never been good with phone numbers or street addresses before.

The phone rang. While Bucher waited for Henry Talbot to answer, he smiled, anticipating the opportunity to hold Laura in his arms again. It seemed like a week since he'd told her goodbye in their room at the Hotel Adria. Three more rings. He was also eager to tell Talbot he had not only delivered "the cigars" but was transporting back some very critical information from Major Richter. *Three more rings; what gives?*

Finally, on the eighth ring, Henry Talbot picked up the phone.

"Mission accomplished!" said Bucher, immediately wishing it had not sounded so much like a line from a low-budget war movie.

"Great!" Getting straight to business, Talbot asked calmly, "Do you have anything for me?"

"Sure do. I've brought you a little something from my trip to the Czech Republic."

"That's great. A few things are starting to open up now. I've been on the phone and fax all morning, but can't really tell you anything at this time." Hank Talbot hesitated for just a second, gathering his thoughts. "There is one very important thing I need to tell you, so listen up. There's been a slight change in plans…"

Damn! thought Bucher. *I knew it couldn't just end like this.*

"Laura and I have come up with a plan—"

"Laura!" Bucher was alarmed. No way did he want Laura involved in this mess.

"Hey, I've already bought my ticket for Munich. I'm here at the Linz train station, and *I am* on my way back home in fifteen minutes!" Bucher was emphatic.

"Settle down, Mark. Here's the deal; just listen. Hang on to your ticket for Munich and get on the next train, as you had planned, but I want you to get off in Salzburg. Laura and I are taking the next train to Salzburg where the three of us will link up. You and Laura will catch the next eastbound train going to Vienna, for some well-deserved R&R, compliments of 'the company.' According to the timetable, you'll only have about six or seven minutes to catch the train to Vienna. We meet, you give me my souvenir from the Czech Republic, and I turn around and get on the next westbound train and head back to Munich to do *my* job. Your job will be finished when you make the drop to me at the station. Laura has your bags packed and ready to go. Okay?"

"Yeah, sure, but explain; I don't quite understand why we're doing all this. Seems like a lot of extra work to me."

"Well, Mark, it's like this. Salzburg is about halfway between Munich and Linz. Laura doesn't feel entirely safe here in Munich without you, with all of the crap that went on back at the hotel. Can't say I really blame her on that score, and the weather here has turned cold and rainy. It really is kind of miserable here, and besides, I think she would really like to visit Vienna on a U.S. Government expense account. You both deserve it. You did an exceptional service for your country. Take a week; take two weeks. I don't care. Relax and enjoy. Take time to smell the strudel."

"You're right. I guess we do deserve a little break. Okay, it's a good plan. I'll see you in about—what? Three hours?"

~ * ~

Grinzing, Austria
8:50 a.m.

"Yes, Father. Of course, Father. I'll send someone up as soon as possible," replied Robert Schmidt, Chief of Police, Grinzing, Austria, a tiny little touristy wine village halfway up the mountain that overlooked Vienna.

Father Ebersbach was concerned about the intrusion of a group of eight or nine men who had come up to Josefskirche (Joseph's Church) and the historic Sobieski Chapel late the night before and dropped off a large container, the kind overseas cargo is shipped in, explained the priest. It wasn't so much that they placed this "ugly metal box" behind his beautiful church as it was their attitude: "Rude, obnoxious, and some were even downright sacrilegious!" he told Schmidt.

The police chief explained that he could not very well arrest anyone for being rude or obnoxious, or even sacrilegious, although he wished he could at times. "We wouldn't have nearly enough jail space if that were the case," he said, trying to lighten the mood of the white-haired cleric. "I will, however, look into these people leaving their container on the church grounds without your permission. I'll get this taken care of, Father."

9:10 a.m.

The grocer was easily located. Lieutenant Leonid Sluskaya, in charge of this special guard detachment, chose to take the "nice guy" approach for starters. He asked Mr. Dvorak to please sit down and tell him all of the events from this morning regarding his delivery to the monastery. The lieutenant was extremely polite.

The grocer explained exactly what had happened. A man had hijacked his truck at gun point. A complete, detailed description of the man was discreetly coerced from Dvorak, along with the observation that the man spoke German fairly well, but with an American or English accent which was difficult to conceal. Jakub Dvorak finally got around to the end of his tale, telling Lieutenant Sluskaya that he had dropped the stranger off at the train station in Linz.

"Do you honestly expect me to believe all that nonsense? You are more stupid than you look!" The lieutenant backhanded the grocer across the face, drawing a thin stream of blood from the corner of his mouth. Dvorak sprang to his feet to retaliate, only to catch the butt of an AK-47 from one of the soldiers across the side of the head, dropping him to the floor.

Quite dazed, struggling to retain consciousness, the grocer managed to shout, "That *is* the truth! There's nothing more!"

The only thing he did not mention in his account of the morning's events was the six hundred D Marks paid to him by the stranger. Now with his head pounding, feeling as if it could explode, he realized the six hundred Marks was definitely *not* the easiest money he had ever earned after all.

With a vicious kick to the ribs, Sluskaya assured Mr. Dvorak he would return and talk some more. The team of Russian guards were now in pursuit of the stranger. He was their true adversary, not the grocer. The lieutenant actually did believe Dvorak's story; it was all quite feasible, but he needed to make an impact on this commoner to achieve this perceived position of authority. *Let the man tell his neighbors how he received a fractured skull and bruised ribs! That will certainly illustrate who is back in control!*

At the ticket window of the Linz rail station, Lieutenant Sluskaya stepped in front of three people standing in line to purchase tickets.

"Excuse me, please," he said with a forced smile to the woman on the opposite side of the glass. "Do you recall selling a ticket earlier this morning to a gentleman about this tall?" He held his hand up to about his eye level. "He was wearing a brown nylon jacket and blue jeans."

The woman looked up and squinted her eyes, as if that would help jog her memory.

"He spoke German, but with a strong American accent..." the lieutenant said.

"Ah, yes. Now I know!" she said, quite pleased with herself. "Yes, he purchased a ticket to Munich, as I recall."

"Which train did he take?" asked Sluskaya more sternly.

"It was most likely the 8:27 train," she responded pleasantly. "Oh, and one more thing, sir. It was a one-way ticket to Munich."

Now confident this was the man he was looking for, the lieutenant immediately phoned the critical information back to General Krause. It was possible they would be able to apprehend the spy before he could do more damage.

Stephan Krause immediately notified his allies in Munich of the "spy." The leader of Krause's Bavarian alliance assured him he had it covered. "Don't worry, Comrade General. He will *not* get away!"

~ * ~

10:37 a.m.

The two hour and ten minute journey on the Austrian train to Salzburg was extremely comfortable. Mark felt his appearance must resemble a woodsman just emerging from a long hunt in the forest: a two-day growth of beard and dirty outdoor clothing that smelled like beer. He longed for a hot shower and a shave. He sensed the other passengers were looking at him. The Austrians are a very proper people, always dressing appropriately for the occasion and always neat as a pin. No wonder Bucher felt so out of place.

Before going to the dining car, Bucher stopped in the water closet to wash his face, brush his teeth, and comb his fingers through his short-cropped hair, for whatever comfort this would allow.

The breakfast menu offered on the Austrian Railroad was equal to most four-star hotel restaurants in the States, thought Bucher as he cut into an Austrian version of Eggs Benedict with his fork. Trying not to appear as ravenous as he actually was, he devoured the two poached eggs and a generous slice of ham covered in rich Hollandaise sauce atop lightly toasted bread, similar to an English muffin. He capped it off with a tall Bloody Mary that sported a stalk of celery and a couple of large green olives. Bucher sat back, took a deep breath, closed his eyes, and savored the first moments of true relaxation he'd had since Thursday morning. After a few minutes, he flagged down the waiter, paid the bill, and ordered a black coffee to go.

Mark Bucher had just returned to his cabin as the announcement for Salzburg was made by the conductor. As the train began to slow down in the rail yard, his thoughts were entirely of Laura and how much he missed her, even though it had only been two days. The trip to Vienna now seemed like a wonderfully romantic idea. *Thank you, Mr. Talbot!*

Mark wondered whose train would arrive first.

Chapter Twenty-seven

Salzburg, Austria
Saturday, October 2, 1993
11:13 a.m.

Mark Bucher was waiting track side at the Salzburg station when the train from Munich rolled to a noisy stop. Laura and Henry Talbot were the first passengers to step off the train. Laura darted out to meet Mark as if it had been weeks since they had seen one another. She did not know what her husband had been asked to do over the past two days, other than to deliver a very important message. She could see he looked tattered and tired, and he had a nasty cut on his right cheek, but at least he was safe and they were together again.

"I hate to break this up," Talbot said as the couple embraced, "but we've got some business to take care of, and your train leaves in exactly five minutes and mine in seven! I *cannot* miss my train and then have to wait an hour for the next one. Time is critical, so let's get going, okay?"

"Sure, of course," said Bucher as he slipped his left hand into the deep, side cargo pocket of his jacket, carefully palming the jewelry box that contained the valuable microfilm.

Like a pro, he extended both hands and grasped Talbot's left—since his right was still in a cast—to suggest a warm greeting.

Hank Talbot smiled as he felt the plastic box pressed into his hand and casually thanked Bucher, for this was neither the time nor the place to express his true gratitude for the mission this total stranger had performed for him. As Talbot turned and headed for track five—Munchen 11:20—he couldn't help but think of how lucky he had been to run across this unique character. He chuckled to himself at the irony. He could still feel the pain from his broken nose and broken hand, yet still felt fortunate to have met this skillful and courageous individual.

Talbot chose a window seat and finally settled back to relax for the trip back to Munich. As soon as he was comfortable in his seat, he reached into his left coat pocket and felt the small plastic box. He wondered exactly what type of critical information it might contain, and then suddenly regretted he had not made an arrangement for a charter helicopter or plane to fly back to Munich. A genuinely disgusted Talbot reluctantly admitted to himself that he just wasn't thinking as clearly as he had before his concussion. He hoped he hadn't overlooked any other details that could later prove to be critical.

~ * ~

At exactly 11:18 a.m., the eastbound train for Linz and Vienna departed from the Salzburg Hauptbahnhof. The train was fairly crowded, so Mark and Laura claimed the first two seats they could find together. Not until the conductor came by to punch their tickets did the Buchers realize Talbot had purchased first-class accommodations for their trip to Vienna. The conductor somewhat begrudgingly directed the American couple to one of the cars near the front of the train. While digging out the Eurorail tickets from a thick envelope stuffed with other travel documents, Mark discovered Henry Talbot had also made arrangements for them to stay at the crown jewel of Austria, the five-star Grand Hotel Wien.

Once the Buchers were settled into their first-class cabin, Mark looked through his luggage for some clean, comfortable clothes to change into. It wasn't until he was in the WC removing his nylon jacket he remembered he was still heavily armed. The shoulder holster carrying the 9mm Browning had fit so comfortably that it now felt quite natural—a second skin. He felt the loss of the additional two and a half pounds as he shed the semi-automatic and nylon holster and placed it gently on the floor. Now he was acutely aware of the KA-BAR knife strapped to his right calf, concealed under his trouser leg. He unstrapped the knife and stared at the weapons on the floor for a moment. Maybe he should throw them out the lavatory window, he thought, while the train sped down the track. He surely didn't need them anymore; he never did think he would. Bucher opened the window and bent down to pick up the weapons, before realizing they could be found by anyone. These weapons could very well fall into the hands of the wrong person or some kid, and someone could get seriously hurt or killed. He did not want to have to think about that. He tucked them into the clothes he had just removed and crammed them into the Samsonite carry-all bag Laura had brought for him.

Mark washed, shaved, and applied deodorant and aftershave lotion, careful to avoid the cut on his right cheek. He felt like a new man in his clean clothes. He returned to the cabin, taking the window seat. Laura snuggled up against him without saying a word. She didn't need to. Laying her head on his chest, she seemed almost as tired as Mark was. Neither of them had slept a wink the night before.

"Get some sleep if you can, hon," he said softly.

"I will, if you will."

"No problem there," Mark replied, as the motion and the muffled rhythm of the steel wheels crossing every half inch gap of the polished metal track began to lull them both to sleep.

"One thing before I doze off," Laura whispered. "I've got a surprise for you tonight."

"Oh? I love your surprises! Hmmm, what could it be? Something white with pink ribbons or maybe black lace?"

"No, silly, but that, too, if you have the energy. I have tickets for two balcony seats at the Vienna State Opera House tonight!"

"No way! Really?"

"Yep, and you'll never guess what's playing."

Mark shrugged.

"Tonight is the final performance of 'Die Fledermaus,' your all-time favorite Strauss II, right here in his very own backyard."

"That's fantastic! How'd you pull this off? These tickets must be like gold."

"Well, actually Mr. Talbot called someone and had them arrange to get these tickets for us. Whoever it is must be extremely influential to have gotten these at the last minute."

Mark was indeed thrilled at the prospect of seeing the famed performance, especially at the legendary Vienna State Opera, but he wondered if he could stay awake for it. Normally these productions didn't start until nine o'clock and didn't finish much before midnight.

Bucher posted the Eurorail ticket stubs on the clip above the glass door to indicate their final destination was Vienna and to lessen the possibility of a conductor bothering them before their arrival. They both fell into a deep, restful sleep huddled in each other's arms, as a gentle rain diagonally streaked the windows.

~ * ~

Kahlenberg, Austria
11:15 a.m.

What in the world are all of these military trucks doing up here in the church parking lot? What's going on? Father Ebersbach wondered cynically as he looked out the window of his study in the old parish rectory. Slipping on his favorite well-worn black cardigan sweater, the clergyman decided to investigate this incursion for himself. Out the door quickly, he crossed the lot and headed directly for the church. *I'll find the person in charge of this menagerie and get to the bottom of this!*

~ * ~

11:50 a.m.

The move from the remote monastery in the southern Czech Republic to the mountain overlooking the capital city of Austria moved with the precision of a fine Swiss watch. The only surprise for Krause upon his arrival was the news that an old priest had gotten in the way and threatened to call the authorities. Captain Bakhvalova decided it was easier to eliminate him than take a chance he might interfere with the mission. Krause was not upset; he had anticipated some resistance and a few obstacles along the way. His launch commander had handled the situation as he would have himself.

"Captain Bakhvalova," Krause addressed his site commander, "you will find Major Richter in shackles; he is a prisoner found guilty of high treason. Treat him accordingly. Put him in a secure place out of my sight, and I'll deal with him later. I actually want Richter to sweat blood as he waits for his execution, so I'm not in a hurry to kill him. He should suffer until I feel it is the right time for him to die."

Looking at his watch, the general summoned his communications officer.

"Lieutenant Charkov, show me to the communications center. We have about five minutes before the announcement. I assume everything is in place and ready to broadcast?"

"Yes, Comrade General. Everything is in place, but we've not had a chance to test it yet."

Ready to jump all over his communications officer for not being completely prepared, Krause suddenly realized the communications team had only arrived less than an hour before. "Okay, then let's put it to the test right now. Captain Karpinov, you have the access code ready?"

"Yes, sir!" Karpinov responded, inserting the disc into the computer and waiting for it to boot up.

376

The access code for the Cosmos 1813C appeared on the screen; the connection was successful. All eyes were on Captain Karpinov as he entered the next command. Nothing happened; the communication code was not accepted. He tried it again. Nothing!

What's wrong with this damn thing? Karpinov thought. He took a spiral notebook from a drawer on the console to confirm what he believed to be the correct sequence and then tried another set of coded numbers. Still nothing! Sweat began forming on the communications officer's forehead as he frantically tried another set of codes.

"Captain Karpinov, is there a problem?" asked Krause.

"I—I don't know what it could be! We are connected, but it's not accepting any other commands! I don't understand what—"

"Well, you damn well better understand something very soon!" shouted Kraus. "You have five minutes." The general stormed out of the room.

~ * ~

11:59 a.m.

"Tell me you've solved the problem, Captain Karpinov," Krause said calmly.

"Comrade General, I have still not determined what's wrong with our satellite connection, but I do have an alternative plan we can put in place immediately."

"And?" Krause said impatiently, coaxing his subordinate's response. "Come on, Captain, we don't have all day! It *is* twelve o'clock."

"Sir, I suggest we send a fax message to each of the heads of state and the secretary general of the UN."

"You are kidding, right? We have one of the most sophisticated communication satellites in existence, and you tell me to send a fax? That's like writing a letter to Santa Claus, for God's sake! We're telling the world we are the new world power to be reckoned with, and we send a fax message? This is pathetic! You may be joining Major Richter if you can't come up with a better solution than that, Captain Karpinov."

377

"Comrade General, if I may comment," interjected Major General Romokovitch, Krause's second in command, a quiet, intellectual man who always weighed his words before he spoke. "I don't see we have any other options at this point, sir. Actually, contacting *only* these people in authority, in a more clandestine manner, might be a better way than causing mass hysteria. We want these key people to concentrate on your proposal and understand the full weight of your ultimatum, giving it their undivided attention, and not to be distracted by their citizens going crazy in the streets."

Krause pondered this new concept for a moment and reluctantly agreed this was actually the better way to go.

"Very well, Captain Karpinov, have it typed up and I will sign it. You have all of the necessary fax numbers, I take it?"

"Of course, Comrade General!"

~ * ~

12:10 p.m.

Mrs. Gerste, the housekeeper for Josephskircke, had never known Father Ebersbach to be late for his noon meal unless he was on a sick call or some other parish emergency.

If it were an emergency, he would have told me he was leaving, she thought. He was probably just over in the chapel having a little quiet prayer time, God bless him! She would walk over to remind him that dinner was ready. He hated it when his soup got cold.

~ * ~

Mike Agnussi's phone began to ring off the hook. First the White House communications chief and then the office of Secretary of State J. Duncan Pomeroy. Because the National Security Agency monitors all incoming communications to the president and the secretary of state, Agnussi already had a jump on the situation. Now he had it in black and white, right in front of him.

"I, Lieutenant General Stephan Krause, have assumed the power of the New World Communist Order of Russia, replacing President Boris Yeltsin. I demand to be recognized as the uncontested president of Russia. I will require the written confirmation of this change of power from the president of the United States and all European heads of state, along with the secretary general of the United Nations. Upon receiving this confirmation from the UN and the other western powers, I will immediately claim my rightful position in the United Nations General Assembly. It is important to understand that failure to comply with these instructions will result in grave consequences throughout Europe. I have set a non-negotiable deadline for twelve o'clock noon, tomorrow, Sunday, October 3, exactly twenty-four hours from now. There will be no exceptions."

So this is the threat Talbot had warned us about. Sounds pretty real to me!

Agnussi immediately linked this with the strange rebirth of the Cosmos satellite he had just recently learned of from Menwith Hill and the NASA station in Bermuda.

Reports of the ultimatum came pouring in from Germany, France, the UK, Italy, Belgium, Austria, the Netherlands, and the Security Council of the United Nations. All were the same. All wanted to know if this was a confirmed, legitimate threat or if it was just some crackpot trying to scare people and make the next TV news lead story. There was never any shortage of those nut cases to go around.

Agnussi's message was the same to each of these countries as he had just relayed to the Brits and the Italians only a short time ago: Lay low, don't create a panic, don't respond to the threat, and secretly move your key people to a safe house somewhere away from any of the large metropolitan areas.

Okay, so we know what countries Krause has sent his list of demands— his 'ransom note'—to, but we still don't know any other exact target cities other than London and Rome, Agnussi thought. *We've just gotta hope and pray Henry can come through with these details soon enough to do something about it.*

~ * ~

Vienna
1:51 p.m.

"Excuse me, Herr Bucher," said a very attractive blonde female conductor, gently shaking Mark on the shoulder. "Vienna Hauptbahnhof in ten minutes."

Opening his eyes to the pleasant vision, Bucher thought the Vienna Chamber of Commerce could not have chosen a better spokesperson for their welcoming committee.

"Oh, okay. Thank you," he replied groggily.

"That was a fast three hours," muttered Laura in a sleepy voice.

While Laura touched up her makeup, Mark went and splashed some cold water on his face and brushed his teeth again in an effort to chase the lingering cob webs from his head after such a sound sleep. Both of the Buchers now felt refreshed and almost well-rested after their much needed siesta.

~ * ~

Munich
1:57 p.m.

It was quite obvious to the trained eye of the chief NSA inspector in charge of Station M that something was up as the train rolled to a stop at the Ost Bahnhof on the outskirts of central Munich. Men in leather coats and sunglasses spaced evenly across the platform appeared to be watching and waiting for someone. *Who? Couldn't be me*, reasoned Henry Talbot. One of the men boarded Talbot's car from the front and walked slowly and purposely down the aisle, looking, studying each male passenger, some closer than others.

Damn this hideous nose! Talbot grumbled to himself, knowing the blackened eyes and bandaged nose had to stick out like a neon sign. No agent or inspector, covert or not, ever wanted to show any outstanding characteristics in his appearance. To blend into the wallpaper was the goal.

Oddly enough, when one of the leather-coated men walked by, he didn't seem terribly interested in the large, bruised, and battered man, but instead asked a middle-aged, short-to-average-sized man a few rows behind Talbot to stand up and produce some identification and answer a few basic questions. He was not the man they were looking for, but he probably fit their general description. Talbot had observed several other of these Gestapo types loitering around the Grafing station that preceded the East rail station and the final stop at the Munich Hauptbahnhof.

As Talbot exited the train at Munich's main rail station, he noticed an even larger contingency of these leather-coated goons, but they were only watching this train and none of the other more than twenty tracks leading in and out of the huge shed. *What the hell is up with this?*

One of these plainclothes policemen, Russian Army soldiers, or possibly even KGB officers seemed to look straight through him as if he were invisible. The NSA chief saw he held a sheet of white paper in his hand, as most of the other goons did, too. Straining to see what was on the sheet without being conspicuous, Talbot cautiously moved in a little closer. The paper didn't seem to have text but rather some kind of illustration. He hesitated to move in any closer to get a better look, then realized he could probably get as close as he wanted with little risk of being noticed because the man and the rest of the "goon squad," were all so intent on observing the people coming off the train. In the man's hand was a computer-generated composite sketch of a male face. There was now no mistaking who they were looking for. The likeness of Mark Bucher was incredibly accurate.

~ * ~

2:20 p.m.

Talbot remained outwardly calm, in spite of his stomach becoming one giant-sized knot. Whatever vital information the microfilm from Richter contained, it was almost surely changed in some way, now that the Russian general's plans had been exposed. Hank Talbot told himself not to jump to conclusions until he could view all of the information contained on the microfilm. *One good thing,* thought Talbot, as he walked at a steady pace down Neuhauserstrasse back to his office, was the Russian general obviously didn't know where Mark Bucher was. They had his description, but they wouldn't be looking for him in Vienna. He was almost sure of that.

The National Security Agency chief had not taken the plastic jewelry box out of his pocket—had not even looked at it while on the train—taking no unnecessary risks.

He sat down in front of the television-like display and watched the information light up the screen. The first data to appear was a series of eight major European cities listed under the heading "Targets": Amsterdam, Brussels, Frankfurt, London, Munich, Paris, Rome, and Zurich. Behind each city named was a ten-digit code in two groups of five numbers each. These code numbers had been the key, but now that Krause knew the mission had been compromised, certainly he would have changed the target codes and the satellite access code.

Second, Talbot learned of Krause's ultimatum. It was now 2:20 p.m.; the general would have tried to make his broadcast two hours and twenty minutes ago. Talbot hoped like hell he had altered the control disc enough to inhibit the message from going through, or they had one hell of a lot of panic throughout the continent to deal with.

Talbot didn't even need to look at his watch. All this was set to take place exactly twenty-two and a half hours from now. He had felt that with Bucher's work accomplished, they had a pretty good shot at being able to derail the rebel Spetsnaz general without the use of conventional military force and without the loss of any U.S. military lives. This, he had hoped, could be done by basically jamming the signal to the Cosmos satellite that controlled the XG-777 missiles and changing firing sequence codes that would eliminate the chance of a manual over-ride by the fire control officer in each of the eight M-5 missile launchers. Now there was little hope to hang on to and very little time.

One small consolation was that with such little time, even Krause would probably not change his target cities; there just wasn't enough time to move their equipment and set up new sites. Talbot reached for his secure line to Fort Mead. It was definitely time to call in the cavalry.

~ * ~

"What do you mean he was *not* on the train? You let him get away? You *idiot!*"

"Comrade General, I checked it myself. No one on that train matched the description of the man you are looking for."

"Did you check the previous stops before the main station?"

"Yes, sir; the East Bahnhof and Grafing Station. Nothing."

"Well what about the stops *between* Linz and Munich?" The general's patience was wearing very thin. "Salzburg, Traunstein, Rosenheim, any of the others?"

"No, sir," the officer said sheepishly, realizing this could have been his big mistake.

"Did you know passengers *are* permitted to get off the train whenever it stops at a station, you *imbecile?* Did it ever occur to you the American spy could very well buy a ticket for one destination, then get off and head north or south instead of west, just to throw us off? Do you think for one moment the American CIA or some other agency would simply stroll in and stroll back out, unconcerned about covering his tracks? They are bold, but they certainly are not stupid! You, Comrade Redick, you are the stupid one. I will deal with you later." The line went dead.

~ * ~

Vienna
2:31 p.m.

The rain was pouring down. Even in the relatively short time it took to hail a taxi and to throw their luggage in the trunk, Mark and Laura were soaked.

It was a short taxi ride from the main rail station to the Grand Hotel Wien. Mark and Laura sat in the back seat of the taxi, looking at each other and laughing. Ostensibly they held each other for warmth, but the embrace evolved into a deep kiss that lasted until the doorman opened the rear taxi door as they pulled up to the Grand Hotel Wien.

The opulence of the hotel lobby was breathtaking; a far cry from the cozy little lobby of the Hotel Adria Garni in Munich. The check-in process was painless. The hotel manager was summoned when the desk clerk learned their new guests were the Buchers. The manager expressed his profound gratitude they had chosen the Grand Hotel Wien while in Vienna, and if there was anything at all he could do to make their stay more comfortable, they should not hesitate to contact him directly.

As the porter carted their bags up to the room and opened the double-wide doors, Mark couldn't help but think the nicest part was this was all compliments of Uncle Sam. He enjoyed seeing his hard-earned tax dollars at work this way! If their room wasn't the presidential suite, it had to be a close second. A basket of fresh fruit, a bottle of 1982 Bordeaux (from the Pomerol appellation), and a selection of excellent Austrian cheese sat on a small round table in the entrance foyer, framed by two large vases of freshly cut flowers.

"Oh, my God, Mark, can you believe this? Whatever you did for Mr. Talbot, you must have done it extremely well. Honey, isn't this fantastic?" Laura hugged her husband and kissed him passionately.

"The first thing we need to do is get out of these wet clothes," he said. "Why don't you see if they have a couple of those nice plush bath robes, the kind you won't find at the Holiday Inn?"

Wrapped in their extra-plush white robes adorned with the Grand Hotel Wien crest, they sat on a comfortable love seat and sampled the cheeses, grapes, and strawberries, along with the best red wine either of them had ever tasted. Then, without speaking, Mark took Laura by the hand and led her to the comfort of a hot shower.

Twelve minutes later, now wrapped in huge white fluffy bath towels, Mark and Laura flopped on the bed and began to let their pent-up emotions take control. This *was* indeed the second honeymoon they had hoped for in Munich. Neither one noticed the small red message light on the phone was blinking.

~ * ~

2:35 p.m.

Mike Agnussi had briefed his boss, General James Jeschke, director of the National Security Agency, and was now attempting to contact the secretary of defense to explain the recent breakthrough of solid information.

The SEC DEF, Charles McCasky, had of course insisted on being apprised of all potentially volatile situations like this, but yet was often inaccessible for these most critical events. Agnussi could not believe the political "foot-dragging" that occurred so often in this present administration.

Our nation's security is nothing to screw around with, Agnussi thought, *yet some of these appointed cabinet members seem to think they're still in campaign mode for the commander in chief!* No big surprise to Agnussi, though, who felt most of these presidential lackeys never did have the best interest of the military at heart, or national security, for that matter. It was all about politics! As the former rear admiral—now deputy director of the NSA— he found this frustrating.

There was no time to spare. Jeschke had to make a decision based on Agnussi's intel. The big danger lied with creating a panic throughout the eight major European cities. Just the hint of a nuclear threat would cause total chaos. Contacting the metropolitan police forces and each of the affected countries' military would be a last resort. These M-5 rocket launchers had to be taken out covertly, by an inconspicuous surgical strike by U.S. special ops teams—eight of them to be exact.

~ * ~

"Sir, I have Deputy Director Agnussi on the line for you again," called Chief Warrant Officer Quin.

"Thanks, Jerry, put him through."

"General Bussen, I need to get right to it. We've got a very critical situation involving what appears to be about half of the population of Western Europe..."

Agnussi explained in detail their extremely delicate objective.

"I understand you were able to insert one of our people into the Czech Republic who helped get us this intel. What kind of surgical strike might you suggest to knock out these mobile missile launchers, understanding that time is working against us?"

"Well, Mr. Agnussi, we don't have a hell of a lot of options considering our present time constraint, with all of our 'ready' units lined up stretching from the Baltic Sea to the Bosporus, and with General Chesnokov appearing to be ready to make his move at any moment now. I'm a firm believer in staying with the horse that got you there, so right away I'm thinking of Captain Cleary's 425th Rangers. Cleary did an excellent job of putting this mission together at a moment's notice, coordinating with the Air National Guard, and then dropping the rookie agent of yours safely into General Krause's backyard. Pretty darn amazing, if you ask me. In my estimation, Cleary is a very capable commander, and his troops are absolutely first rate." Bussen thought. "So to answer your question, I would get Captain Cleary on the horn, tell him to muster his best recon patrols, and get that Delaware Air Guard squadron to scramble a minimum of six of their C-130s and see if they can do their magic one more time. What about their coordinates? Do we know exactly where these missiles are?"

"No, sir, I'm afraid we do not. We know which cities, but have no idea where to look for these launch sites. If you figure on drawing a thirty-five-mile perimeter around each of these large metropolitan areas, then you have the proverbial 'needle in a hay stack' situation. We have already started redirecting three of our KH-11 Crystal satellites and need to ask your assistance with any and all of your reconnaissance aircraft to start looking for anything that might resemble a loaded M-5 and/or a twenty-foot shipping container."

"Mr. Agnussi, I'll take the two target coordinates you've given me and contact Captain Cleary right away. At the very least, we can sack Krause's men in Rome and London before he realizes what's going on. If the other six launch teams catch wind of Rome and London going down, they'll go to ground like a bunch of scared rabbits, and then we'll never find them! The key to successfully apprehending these launch crews and ultimately stopping their terrorist assaults is to first separate the lines of communication between the launch crews outside each of the target cities and their field marshal, Krause."

Orders were passed from General Bussen to Captain Cleary. The teams were to take these positions quietly, but at all costs. This was "no holds barred." They were to just get in there and get the job done, quickly and quietly.

Cleary addressed his operations officer and patrol leaders directly.

"We presently have six C-130s at our disposal here at Ramstein, with eight target sites. We will have six flights; Rome is number one, London is two. We know the approximate locations of both of these sites now, but we're waiting for a more detailed reconnaissance report so we can establish a good drop zone close enough to the objective yet out of sight from these Russian launch crews. These first two jumps will take place shortly after sundown.

"Munich and Frankfurt will double up on number three, as well as Brussels and Amsterdam on four, Paris on five, and Zurich on six. Flights three through six will remain static until we are given exact target sites. I don't have a time frame for you at this point, but I will keep you posted."

The company commander continued: "I want two five-man patrols to jump on each of these sites tonight. Prior to deployment, I want each man issued night-vision goggles and a noise-suppressing device for his weapon, be it automatic rifle or sidearm. In each of these five-man teams I want one M60 machinegun, with a suppressor, and one designated sharpshooter to operate the M24 Sniper Weapon System. This person will probably be your most valuable asset if everything goes as planned. We want to avoid a firefight if possible, but if your sniper can't knock 'em all down, we'll have nine other capable troops to help finish the job. We don't know how well these M-5s will be guarded. We assume Krause will want to keep a low profile to remain undetected, so chances are there will not be a full platoon of soldiers, but I can't imagine he would ever let his nukes go out unprotected."

Reflectively, Cleary was grateful for having put his men through a night jump only a little over thirteen hours ago. Like a good coach, he couldn't help but think, *These guys are always sharp, but with just enough rest and with being well-prepared, I know they'll be at the top of their game tonight.*

Agnussi prayed for clear weather. It was their only hope. If the photos from these satellites and high-altitude U-2 reconnaissance aircraft were taken of the tops of the clouds, you could basically kiss their mission good-bye. Weather reports for most of north and central Europe were fairly promising; only the lower southeastern parts of Europe showed any threats of bad weather and partial cloud cover.

Agnussi's next function was to check the status of the newly reprogrammed reconnaissance satellites to determine their exact flight paths. He needed these three KH-11 satellites to fly directly overhead of the remaining six threatened locations. There were only three satellites orbiting the northern hemisphere capable of taking the detailed photographs they required to locate a squad or two of Russian soldiers surrounding a vehicle roughly the size of a small delivery truck. Worse yet, the M-5 could still be concealed in a twenty-foot overseas container. This was the ultimate needle in a haystack.

Three satellites, only four hours of daylight, and six known target sites to locate. The best they could do would be to reprogram the satellites to cover multiple cities in their orbit. Difficult, but not impossible.

In addition to the three state-of-the-art satellites that would soon be following a revised orbit to encompass the six remaining major cities, CICEUCOM mounted a quick, but elaborate air-reconnaissance operation. Everything from the Air Force's high-altitude U-2 spy planes, that were designed for such observations, down to a few old "crop-dusting" Army Cessna O-1 Bird Dogs, taken out of mothballs, would be up and hunting for the mobile launch vehicles. Pretty much anything that could still fly was called into immediate service with red lights flashing and claxtons blaring in bases scattered throughout Europe.

Three programmers hovered over a large map of Europe, deciding on the possible groupings. Satellite 1-Alpha had the most northerly orbit. It could pick up the Amsterdam site, but no others. Although Brussels was not that far in terms of miles, it was almost due south, and these sophisticated flying cameras traveling west to east could not turn on a dime and head north or south. Brussels and Frankfurt were on a close enough line for 2-Bravo/Foxtrot, thus leaving 3-Papa/Mike with the task of picking up Paris and Munich. It was impossible to pick up Zurich on any of these orbits. The best they could do would be to dedicate one of the U-2s and several other lower-altitude observation aircraft to search the Swiss countryside surrounding Zurich.

A special team of Army personnel from the Pentagon, all with extensive combat experience, were assembled to study the topography and environs that encircled the cities within a maximum radius of thirty-five miles. Their main function was to choose what would be the best launch site if *they* were the Russian general. The chief Air Force meteorologist was immediately called in to report on the direction of the prevailing surface winds in each of the six locations to help determine a more probable "upwind" site.

~ * ~

Grinzing, Austria
5:30 p.m.

Chief Schmidt had gotten very busy with a family disturbance that needed his immediate attention. He had prioritized the priest's request to look into the unsightly metal box behind the church and had made it a "back-burner" issue, just now getting around to checking into it.

"Jurgen, I want you and Dieter to go up to Kahlenberg and pay Father Ebersbach a visit. He's complaining that somebody has parked a shipping container behind the church without his permission, so do what you can to find out who's responsible for this thing, and please try to put the good father's mind at ease, okay?"

Chapter Twenty-eight

Southeast of Windsor (thirty-three miles northwest of London)
Saturday, 02 October 1993
1920 Hours

Patrol teams "Charlie" and "Delta" had moved to within about a half "klick" of their objective after a successful night jump in a farmer's clover field about two kilometers away. The terrain in this part of central southern England was mostly rolling meadows and farm land with small patches of wooded areas, interspersed with small towns and villages.

The Russians had set up a perimeter around a wooded area no larger than one-eighth mile square. Sentries were posted around the edge like numbers on a clock. Arial photos of the area from the 56th Rescue Squadron attached to the 48th Fighter Wing out of RAF Lakenheath showed the Charlie and Delta team leaders that the nearest clump of trees was about two hundred meters away. This would be their best approach.

Patrol Leader Staff Sergeant Doug Brandt called up his scout observer and sharpshooter, Private First Class Aaron Pheiffer. Lying on his stomach, Brandt viewed the opposition through night-vision binoculars. He could see four figures dotting the south edge of the wooded circle in front of him. PFC Pheiffer flopped down next to him. The patrol leader handed Pheiffer the binoculars. "How many do you see?"

After a few seconds the PFC replied, "I count four, Sergeant Brandt."

"Can you hit 'em from here?"

"No problem, Sarge."

"I wanna tell you something, Pheiffer. What you see out there are just silhouette targets, like you've knocked down a thousand times before. Nothing more. Understand?"

"I got it, Sarge."

"Can you do this?"

Looking squarely at his patrol leader, Pheiffer nodded and said, "Yes, Sergeant, I can. It's my job."

"Okay, that's what I wanted to hear. Then let's do it."

The guards were in civilian clothing. Staff Sergeant Brandt had been concerned about his shooter. Taking out these unassuming civilian-looking figures could create some major psychological problems for the kid pulling the trigger if he was not in the right frame of mind as he carried out his orders. Brandt was willing to do the dirty work himself if he felt this was going to take a toll on the young man's psyche.

The sharpshooter's weapon was the M24 Sniper Weapon System, the military version of the Remington M700 BDL with silencer, along with a Leupold Mk.4 M3 10X40mm fixed power "Starlight" scope and detachable Harris BRM-S swivel bipod. Except for the camouflage covering, the weapon looked more like a rifle to be used in elite marksman competition rather than a Government Issue.

The powerful night-vision scope brought the targets close enough to read the brand name on a pack of cigarettes. The winds were negligible, and Pheiffer had a clear shot. With four quick pops spaced only seconds apart, the SSG watched the four guards drop to the ground. This cleared a relatively safe passage across the open field and into the wooded area. The patrol leader gave a hand signal for the Delta patrol to move out. He kept a close watch on the movement through the night-vision binoculars. About thirty seconds later, Brandt gave the command for Charlie to go, as he and the sniper moved out with them, taking up the rear.

Regrouped in the cover of the woods, C and D patrols began the critical phase of finding the M-5 and the payload of three XG-777 missiles armed with the tactical nuclear warheads. Fanned out in two groups, they set out to eliminate the terrorist threat created by a rogue Russian general.

It was the assistant Delta Patrol leader who first noticed the small civilian Mercedes cargo van with canvas sides. "Big Dog, I've located a civilian truck to my immediate north, some thirty to forty meters out, two guards standing in front of the truck, and the launcher is just another ten or fifteen beyond that."

"Roger, Rover Two. How's the target look from your position?"

"Good enough; a few trees and some underbrush, but no big deal. It's a pretty easy shot from here. Ah, wait one; I see two more guards flanking the launcher."

"Roger that, Rover Two. You've got the go ahead to take out the two by the truck, and hold your position. I'll bring up the P-man to do the heavy lifting with the launcher group, and Charlie to cover your back. Out."

The D team leader signaled his two point men to take out the two guards nearest the Mercedes truck. Again, only two muffled pops from their silenced M-16s were heard. The only real noise was the sound of one of the guard's rifles hitting the metal bumper as it fell to the ground. Staff Sergeant Brandt wasn't sure how many other guards might still be out on the perimeter of the north side of the small wooded area. He would send out his Charlie patrol to clean up whatever might be left of the Russian guard detachment. Brandt didn't wait to hear back from C patrol if there were any other sentries posted; his path had now been cleared to take his objective, and he wasn't going to wait for anything that might get in the way or change the circumstances.

Staff Sergeant Brandt and PFC Pheiffer moved quickly and silently to some slightly higher ground to their north and west, giving them a better vantage point. As soon as they were both in position, Brandt put the night-vision binoculars to his eyes, as did Pheiffer with the Leupold Starlight scope. Each had a clear view of the launcher that was facing southeast, looking into the cab of the M-5 on an angle.

"Pheiffer, I want you to knock out the guy riding shotgun first, the fire control officer, then hit the driver. We can't take the chance that the FCO might get off one of those missiles if anybody goes down around him."

The shooter acknowledged with the nod.

"And I'll take care of the two guards out front of the M-5. Go when you're ready."

As soon as the words had left the non-com's mouth, the scout observer/sniper let loose two rounds, dropping the fire control officer and driver as they sat comfortably in the cab of the M-5. As soon as Brandt heard the first pop, he too sighted the targets he was responsible for and dispatched them, as well.

The C team had located and eliminated three additional sentries that guarded the turf of their northern perimeter, while Brandt and Pheiffer cautiously moved in to inspect the M-5.

Staff Sergeant Brandt's orders were to radio the "sit-rep" directly back to Captain Cleary just as soon as his mission was completed. Cleary, in turn, would immediately phone in the outcome and complete details to the CICEUCOM, General John Bussen.

In his situation report, Brandt supplied his commander with a detailed account of the equipment they found on site—primarily the vehicles and weapons—plus the number of enemy personnel they had encountered, in what manner they were dug in forming their protective perimeter, and the number of injured or casualties. Along with all of this critical information, Doug Brandt also made note of the radio frequency the launch crew was dialed into to communicate with their headquarters unit. This information would become more valuable than the patrol leader had ever expected.

~ * ~

7:35 p.m.

Almost simultaneously, a very similar assault was underway near the small beach town of Fregene, Italy, some twenty-four miles due west of Rome. Under the cover of a perfectly dark sky, Alpha and Bravo patrols were dropped just a few hundred meters east of a thick line of pine trees that stretched for about four kilometers, running parallel to the beautiful Mediterranean beach only about a half mile to the west. It wasn't until A and B patrols were on the ground and starting to move south toward their objective that the Rome team leader received a hot transmission from Captain Cleary giving him a heads-up on the details from the sit-rep Charlie and Delta had turned in. Hopefully the Russians were not overly creative and would follow the same game plan as they had at the London launch site.

~ * ~

"Sir, I think I might have something here!" shouted Second Lieutenant Nancy Reese, USAF. She had been brought in with several other Air Force personnel as extra sets of analytical eyes. Her military schooling and occupation were Aerial Photo Analysis, with two months of OJT.

An Air Force major hustled over to observe her screen.

"Sir, this is a photo taken through a hole in the clouds from Dragon Lady One, the dedicated U-2 over Zurich, and this is a corresponding picture from an Army OV-1 Mohawk, taken one hour and thirty-seven minutes after the U-2 photo, again from another hole in the clouds and at a slightly different angle and a much lower altitude. These look a lot like the satellite photos we were shown of the Brussels and Frankfurt sites," she said, pointing at the screen with her pencil. "Looks like a military three-quarter-ton truck, and over here we've got what appears to be the mobile rocket launcher with the three rockets sitting right on top, with possible sentries posted here, here, and a few more over here. What do you think, sir?"

"I think you've got a lot of broken-up cloud cover, and that you're dealing with a lot of shadows creating a very hazy and unclear picture of the area," said the major, "but then again, we don't have much of anything else to go on right now." He pondered this for a minute.

"Colonel Houlden!" the major called. "Can you please come over here for a minute, sir? I'd like you to take a look at something." It would be wise to cover his own ass by calling in a higher-ranking officer for his opinion. The second lieutenant explained again what she had interpreted from the photos.

From Colonel Houlden, USAF, to General Bussen at the command post in Stuttgart came the grid coordinates of a site thirty-one miles due south of Zurich. After Bussen had passed along the exact location to Captain Cleary, he cradled the receiver and rocked back in his chair, thinking, *Okay, now let's hope Cleary's Zurich team can be as successful as London and Rome.*

~ * ~

1940 Hours

Krause and his administrative staff had finally finished setting up and had the HQ completely operational. It was an unlikely location for a military headquarters, with a scenic overlook that offered a beautiful panoramic view of the city of Vienna from an elevation of roughly four hundred eighty meters, but it served all of his needs perfectly.

The building adjacent to the historic old church had been a popular tourist destination, complete with a souvenir shop and a rather large restaurant dining area, also with the same impressive view. Krause immediately had the commercial and souvenir items trashed and disposed of. There was no practical use for these trinkets. He arranged his communications center in the dining area, giving him a full view of the city he may or may not have to launch a tactical nuclear warhead against by noon of the next day. This was a tantalizing prospect for him to ponder.

I am lord and master of the land as far as I can see! he silently proclaimed as he stood at the railing on the outdoor observation deck, looking down on Vienna and the stunning surrounding countryside with all of its picturesque vineyards. Krause was already starting to feel the inebriating thrill of victory. By tomorrow this time, his face would be on the front page of every newspaper and every television news report. His work was almost completed. Tomorrow he would have the simple task of communicating with the eight launch crew commanders and telling them to fire or to maintain the "stand down" order presently in place.

As he looked over the city center of Vienna from his safe perch several kilometers upwind, Krause considered that by tomorrow a good portion of this city, so rich with the culture he embraced, could possibly be charred and turned upside down by an attack of three nuclear- tipped missiles. Rather than reconsider the devastating effects this would have on the city, Krause called for his valet. "Make sure my boots and brass are freshly polished and that my personal medals are all in place on my dress uniform. Notify the Vienna State Opera that I will be attending tonight's performance and that I expect a private box or, at the very least, a center- aisle seat near the orchestra." He would enjoy the Vienna Opera one last time.

~ * ~

7:55 p.m.

Time was running short, and options to halt a massacre in Munich were diminishing, as well. In the storage closet of Talbot's small office was a case that resembled an oversized metal suitcase with a carrying handle riveted to the top. This was a listening device that had become more or less outdated and obsolete, only due to its size and bulky shape; the electronics contained inside were perfectly functional and might just be the right tool for the job at hand.

As Talbot hauled the case out of the storage closet, he remembered why he had tucked this piece of equipment out of sight. About six months before, he had broken the long whip antenna that was necessary for clear reception. Talbot cleared the table near the window and opened the hinged aluminum box, then unfolded a twenty inch portable dish antenna, hoping this might possibly work instead of the broken whip. It was worth a shot anyhow; he had nothing to lose. Centering the dish directly in the window, he punched in the radio frequency relayed to him from General Bussen, with the outside chance he might pick up the radio transmissions between

397

the command center, wherever that might be by now, and the Munich launch site.

Talbot picked up various radio transmissions which shared similar frequencies, but nothing remotely close to jargon, even coded jargon, that would be used in a military op such as this, and nothing in Russian. He moved the dish from one side to the other, picking up other transmissions as he did. The unit seemed to be working okay, but he was restricted by the width of the window and some of the surrounding tall structures that interfered with the radio waves without the aid of the exact, factory-installed antenna.

Henry Talbot looked out the window as if he were looking for the radio waves to become visible. He looked across the Mariena Platz at the old church of Saint Peter, or "Alte Peter" as it's known in Munich, and the huge clock at the top of the spire. The clock was about ready to strike eight o'clock. He really didn't need a reminder of how little time was available. Henry Talbot turned away, totally disgusted this expensive piece of equipment was rendered useless because the agency was not able to resupply him with the replacement antenna, something one could buy at Radio Shack for less than ten dollars. "Damn it!" he said, slamming his good hand on the table.

Then it came to him. Talbot folded up the substitute dish antenna and crammed it in the case, fastened the latches, grabbed the handle, and took off for the door. Running diagonally across the Mariena Platz toward Alte Peter, now clutching the oversized suitcase against his chest, he ran as a running back breaking tackles, driving hard for the end zone.

Talbot came to the side door of the church and stopped. For the nominal fee of two Deutsche Marks, visitors can climb the narrow stone and wooden staircase to the observation walkway that forms a rectangle around the top of the steeple. One can view the entire panorama of Munich, from each of the four corners, while elevated ninety-two meters above the city streets.

Out of breath, Talbot set the case down, reached in his pocket, and gave the elderly man selling tickets a fifty DM bill. "Here, take this, and don't sell any more tickets until I come back down. Okay?"

It was perfectly okay with the old man. He hadn't taken in that much all day, and it was only a half hour before he would close the door for the remainder of the day.

Talbot stood at the bottom of the upwardly spiraling stairway with the case once again tucked up across his chest. He wondered how in the hell he would manage to climb these stairs with this extra load without having a heart attack before reaching the top. About a quarter of the way up, he was drenched in perspiration. Nearly halfway up, Talbot became dizzy and began to lose his balance, dropping the case on one of the landings just before he thought he might black out. He stopped, took several deep breaths, and continued to push to the top. Reaching the huge cast iron bells was an encouraging sign; he knew he had to be near the top.

A family of four was taking in the sights and lights of the city from the northeast corner. "Excuse me, please, but the observation deck is closed for the evening. You will have to climb back down immediately!" Talbot said with authority, and down they went without any opposition.

Talbot began at the northeast corner; it was the closest. It took only a minute to set up the equipment and plug in the headset. His theory of rising above the obstructions near the street level had been correct. Talbot was able to pick up conversations on other frequencies much more clearly now, but still nothing panning a ninety-degree area from due north to due east. East to south was no better. At the southwest corner, Talbot struck pay dirt. He listened in on a transmission, in Russian, that made reference to the launch crew and security team closing off the bridge that spanned the gorge over the Isor River, beyond Gruenwald. The missile crew and security team were somewhere on the eastern side of the river. Exactly how far, Talbot didn't know. He did know, however, that it was mostly heavily forested in that area, and it could still be a trick to locate the mobile rockets and crew. He turned off the portable listening device and left it setting right there.

Speed was a lot more important than retrieving any equipment right now. Speed was *everything* right now.

The senior NSA inspector flew down the stairs. He noticed the old man standing and waiting with a large, heavy key ring in hand for his best customer of the day to leave. He sprinted back to his office above the Donsil. Picking up the direct line to the deputy director in Fort Mead, Talbot tried to catch his breath and wished he were in better physical condition.

"Mike, I've got your Munich site." Agnussi was already looking at his detailed map of Bavaria with a red circle around Munich, indicating a thirty-five mile perimeter, and punching in his direct line with General Bussen for a three-way conference call. "I can't pinpoint it, but I can sure get you in the right neighborhood."

It didn't take long. Captain Cleary's E and F patrols were not terribly far, still on the tarmac at Ramstein only two hundred miles away, but they would never in a week's time have been able to find the Russian rocket crew without Hank Talbot.

~ * ~

General Bussen picked up the line with the red light flashing, "Go ahead, Captain Cleary. I hope you have good news to report."

"Sir, based on the *exact* coordinates we were given for Zurich, my team leader reports we have just secured a liquid fertilizer spreader that has broken down on the edge of an alfalfa field along with a maintenance truck with its headlights on, a mechanic, two farmers, and a half dozen sheep. No casualties to report." Just as soon as the last sentence left his mouth, Captain Cronan Cleary regretted the smart-ass remark made to the CICEUCOM. "Sorry, sir. I should not have made that last comment. The fact of the matter, sir, is that we spent our valuable time on a wild goose chase, and those nukes and Russian soldiers are still out there somewhere."

Bussen completely understood Cleary's frustration and let the comment pass. So now it was back to the drawing board to continue to search for the remaining XG-777s, with no lead to their location whatsoever. He also wanted the name of the Air Force colonel who had provided this fine piece of reconnaissance intel.

~ * ~

The complete description and data of the mobile launch sites that had been radioed back from the successful attacks on the London and Rome locations proved to be a godsend for the growing team of aerial photo analysts at the NSA headquarters and the other reconnaissance specialists from the Pentagon. They now knew exactly what they were looking for. Photographs taken earlier, during daylight hours, were steadily coming in from the four Air Force high-altitude U-2 reconnaissance planes.

The photo transmissions, also from earlier in the day, from satellite 1-Alpha had come in clear as a bell, picking up a forty to fifty-mile radius around Amsterdam. Number 2-Bravo/Foxtrot's photos of Brussels and Frankfurt were equally as impressive. Although the equipment on board 3-Papa/Mike was identical to the other two, the weather was deteriorating to the southeast, and the photos being sent back were difficult to analyze. Paris was still fairly clear, and the Munich site had miraculously been located earlier by radio, because it never would have been found by aerial or satellite photography due to the heavy cloud cover over the entire city and surrounding area.

The Frankfurt site was the fourth to be taken out. Cleary's "Golf" and "Hotel" patrols made quick work of the launch site some twenty-eight miles north of the Frankfurt am Main Airport. Armed with the intelligence the first two teams had contributed, the remaining Ranger teams were able to advance with greater speed, and that's precisely what was needed, because the clock seemed to be ticking faster than normal.

Brussels and Paris were located next, almost simultaneously, and then Amsterdam. Although each of the missions was being carried out successfully, there had been three U.S. casualties. The death of American soldiers is always a terrible tragedy, but the price was necessary to save millions from the impending carnage of the nuclear-tipped warheads pointed at the heart of each of these major metropolitan areas.

Only one more site remained. All of the Air Force photo analysts and the Army brass who had been assigned to Paris, Brussels, Amsterdam, and Frankfurt were now all redirected to put their trained eyes on the Zurich photos and all of the accumulated data regarding those surroundings that had been analyzed a thousand times before. With no trace of anything that looked even remotely like an M-5 loaded with three XG-777 missiles or a lone twenty-foot shipping container with a support crew, the general consensus among the ranking officers here was that Zurich might not be the target city after all. There were still plenty of major cities scattered all over Europe that could be potential targets.

Chapter Twenty-nine

Vienna, Austria
Saturday, October 2, 1993
8:30 p.m.

"Mark, look, the message light on the phone is blinking," Laura said as her husband zipped up the back of her black formal evening gown.

"Are you expecting anything?" asked Mark.

"No. Henry Talbot is the only one who knows we're here, but it might be chocolates or champagne or something from Hank. He is thoughtful like that, you know."

"So you think I should call the front desk and check it out?" asked Mark as he fumbled with the phone while he worked at putting in the button studs on his heavily starched tuxedo shirt.

"Yeah, why not? Couldn't hurt," said Laura, as Mark called the operator.

"A message to call our friend Henry in Munich," Bucher said, dialing the number from memory. Talbot answered on the first ring. "Hank, before you ask, the answer is 'No.' I *will not* jump out of any more airplanes and run through the woods in the middle of the night. I am on R&R as you put it," Bucher joked.

"Mark, listen up. You and Laura have got to get out of Vienna!"

"What do you mean? We just got here."

"I mean it's not safe for you there, for two reasons: one, the Russians are looking for *you*. They've circulated a composite drawing of you, and they must want you in the worst way. Two, and this is ultra-confidential because we don't want to cause a panic, but there is a strong possibility that Vienna, among several other major European cities, could come under attack from this nut General Krause tomorrow at noon. I'm not kidding. So you and Laura had better get the hell out of there now! I'm not trying to scare you or anything, but you *do* have the 9mm with you, I presume? You may very well need it now more than ever. Now don't blow this off, Mark. I'm serious as a heart attack. You keep the weapon with you at all times until you're way the hell away from there. I'm telling you this to keep you and Laura alive. She's with you, so therefore she's in danger, too. You had better leave right away! Oh, and don't come back to Munich either for reasons one and two. I would recommend somewhere like Monte Carlo, Nice, or Palma de Mallorca, or a better idea would be to head back home. This is not a good time for a European vacation. Don't ask; just do what I'm telling you to do. Okay?"

"Yeah, if you say so."

"Good. Stay in touch. I've gotta go."

~ * ~

"What was that all about, Mark?" Laura asked.

"Oh, Talbot just wanted to tell us to enjoy the symphony tonight."

"See, I knew it was something nice," Laura said with a smile.

Mark Bucher had promised himself he was not going to frighten his wife anymore. She had been through enough anguish these last few days. *We can leave first thing tomorrow morning, but I'm not going to deprive her, or myself, for that matter, of this evening in Vienna. I'll just explain it to her later,* he thought.

"Hey, you look fantastic!" he said, grabbing her around her slim waist, as she tried to insert the small diamond earrings into her delicate pierced ears.

"Thank you, really, but stop messing around, or we'll be late for the opera," Laura said as she turned back toward the large bathroom mirror and began applying a fresh coat of lip gloss.

Bucher took quick advantage of this time while Laura was still in the bathroom putting on her makeup. He slipped off his tuxedo jacket and dug into the carry-all bag that contained his jacket and jeans along with the Browning 9mm in the nylon shoulder holster and the KA-BAR knife. Feeling more than a little foolish, Bucher once again strapped the knife to his right calf, under his neatly pressed tuxedo trouser leg. He removed the chest strap on the shoulder holster and slipped his arms through the openings and adjusted the load into place. Putting his tuxedo jacket back on, he looked in the full-length mirror to see if the 9mm created much of a bulge under his left armpit. It wasn't too noticeable, just felt pretty bulky. Bucher chuckled to himself. *How crazy is this? I actually look like 007, standing here in fabulous five-star European hotel suite, complete with a loaded semi-automatic pistol under my tuxedo jacket, a concealed knife strapped to my leg, and an absolutely gorgeous woman on my arm.*

He'd always enjoyed reading each of the Ian Fleming and John Gardner spy thrillers and watching the movies, and now, through a series of strange and remarkable happenings, he had actually assumed the role of an international secret agent. He shook his head. He was not moved by the glamour or the intrigue; his first concern now was to stay alive and to protect his wife. He cursed himself for inadvertently putting Laura in a dangerous situation.

Mark looked at his watch and reconsidered his original idea to ignore the advice from Hank Talbot to get the hell out. It was 8:32 p.m. Too late to catch any international flights out. Although the trains ran pretty much around the clock, traveling through the night in territory blanketed by the enemy did not seem like the safest bet either. Better to just stay alert and watch his backside. *We'll be okay for one night.* What had started out as the ultimate adventure and patriotic duty, something that only a handful of nonfiction characters ever actually get to experience, had now become a nightmare.

~ * ~

Mark Bucher was uptight; even he wouldn't deny that accusation, but he was trying his best to keep it bottled up and concealed from Laura for this special evening.

Laura could feel the tenseness in her husband. He was stiff and seemed to be overcompensating for something, when normally he would be extremely excited about going to see a Strauss opera, particularly right here in Vienna. She naturally assumed it had to be related to his conversation with Henry Talbot, but she wasn't going to say anything to him right now; it would have to wait. *Why spoil the charm and elegance of this once-in-a-lifetime evening fit for royalty?*

Knowing the Buchers had "preferred seating" for the opera this evening, the Grand Hotel Wien manager instructed his concierge to arrange their transport to the Vienna State Opera House via one of the famed horse-drawn white hansoms. The Buchers arrived in style, in a luxury coach powered by two fine-looking dapple greys, guided by a driver outfitted in the traditional black boulder hat and short black shoulder cape. Laura did indeed look stunning. Mark wished he had a camera to capture forever this incredible moment.

The tension and worry seemed to fade away like the sun burning off the mist on a foggy morning when the Vienna State Symphonic Orchestra began the overture to Strauss's "Die Fledermaus." Bucher sat back, closed his eyes, and let his mind and body absorb the beautiful music.

Laura Bucher noticed this welcome change in her spouse's demeanor as only one can after twenty years of marriage. Now, subconsciously, she too could relax and enjoy this classical performance and the rest of their romantic evening together.

By intermission, Mark had shed any of the preexisting jitters he had felt after his conversation with Henry Talbot back at the hotel. As the applause died down and the house lights came up, Mark and Laura rose from their seats and entered the mezzanine lobby.

Laura stood along the polished brass railing that formed a large oval overlooking the Grand Lobby, while Mark purchased a couple of glasses of champagne on the opposite side of the mezzanine. Glittering light from the three huge crystal chandeliers illuminated both the mezzanine and the main floor of the lobby. This was a perfect vantage point to do some casual people watching.

Mark returned and handed his wife a chilled glass of Moet & Chandon Imperial. Laura looked fabulous in the warm glow of the gold and crystal chandeliers that provided the perfect backdrop, and the champagne just seemed to taste better in this regal ambiance of the Vienna Opera House. What a beautiful, romantic evening it had turned out to be.

"I wonder who that guy in uniform is down there standing by himself?" Laura said casually, looking down on the Grand Lobby, while Mark leaned with his back to the railing.

There in lesser light, under the recess of the mezzanine opposite their position, was a Russian Army officer with two stars fixed on each of his shoulder boards, a chest full of colorful campaign ribbons, a personal commendation medallion around his neck, and tall riding boots that shined like patent leather.

"Oh, my God!" Bucher said quietly under his breath.

"What is it, Mark?"

Mark took Laura gently by the arm and led her away from the railing. "He, my dear, is the enemy! That is the man I saw briefly this morning." It occurred to him "this morning" seemed about a week ago. "He is the person Henry Talbot is trying so desperately to defeat. I can't tell you much, simply because I don't know very much. What Talbot would call a 'need to know' type of thing."

Laura nodded as if she understood.

"But why is he here in Vienna?" he wondered out loud, *and how and why are they looking for me?*

The house lights dimmed and then brightened twice in succession, alerting the patrons to return to their seats as the production was about to resume.

Mark Bucher sat in his balcony box and began to pan the orchestra boxes with the low power opera glasses. Krause was easy enough to spot, even without the aid of the opera glasses. Bucher was not frightened by Krause's presence, but he was certainly curious and maybe even somewhat captivated. From this distance, in the half-lit balcony of the great opera house, there was no threat to his safety. The house lights dimmed again and the maestro tapped his baton upon the stand and raised his outstretched arms. The music began for Act II.

~ * ~

8:45 p.m.

Chief Schmidt wondered why neither of his two men had responded to a call a couple of hours earlier to tend to a minor traffic accident involving a car and the Number 38 tram. He was forced to take care of the traffic incident, sorting out who was at fault and writing the report.

Not stopping at the station after completing the accident report, Chief Schmidt drove up the winding hillside to make sure Father Ebersbach's mind had been set at ease by his two emissaries. *Hmph!* he thought. *There's the squad car. These guys have decided to make a day of it up here. They probably were invited to the rectory for some homemade strudel and coffee, knowing Father Ebersbach.*

~ * ~

9:00 p.m.

The police chief rang the doorbell of the Josefskirche rectory. No answer. He rang again. Still no answer. He tried the door; it was unlocked. No surprise. He doubted if the old priest ever locked the door. Schmidt called for the priest and then the housekeeper, Mrs. Gerste. No response. He walked through the humble dwellings of the parish priest and saw no one and noticed nothing out of order. The only thing somewhat unusual was a full pot of cold soup on the stove and a loaf of bread sitting on the kitchen table.

The chief walked out of the house and back behind the church to see for himself what the commotion about this cargo container was all about. Sure enough, there it was: a reddish brown box made of corrugated metal about seven meters long and about two and a half meters wide, and about that height, as well, with white letters and numbers painted on it. If the container had not been padlocked, Schmidt would have opened it to inspect the contents.

~ * ~

9:15 p.m.

Chief Schmidt entered the old church from the side entrance. He extended his right hand to the Holy Water font to make the "sign of the cross" and bless himself, a common expression of respect and adoration for a Roman Catholic.

The red and white draped banners suspended high above the main altar as he approached the front of the church reminded him of the historical significance this church held in Austrian history. It was here at this very site that the Polish king Jan Sobieski had knelt down in solemn prayer just prior to leading his army down the mountain and into battle to relieve the city of Vienna from the Turks in 1683. Schmidt wondered how different history might have been if the courageous King Sobieski had *not* stopped to pray and the Turks had been victorious. Robert Schmidt stood in silent prayer for a moment, his head bowed low with sincere reverence.

Opening his eyes, he saw at his feet what appeared to be a smudged trail of blood leading to the sacristy at the left side of the altar. Schmidt slowly drew his gun, an old .32-caliber revolver.

"You can put the gun down, *now!*" The loud voice came from high above and behind him.

Schmidt turned and looked up. There in the choir loft were two men, dressed in plain civilian clothes. One of the men was crouched against a pew with a military rifle cradled on the railing that ran the width of the choir loft.

Chief Schmidt gently laid the revolver down on the marble floor.

"You keep him in your sites until I give you the sign," the Russian officer told the soldier with the rifle while drawing a perfect bead on the Grinzing police chief, his finger lightly touching the trigger, the safety switch off.

It took the Russian officer a minute or so to descend the stairway in the rear of the church and come face to face with Schmidt.

"Unfortunately for you, as it was with the two patrolmen, curiosity seems to have gotten the better of you," said the plainclothes Russian officer.

"Where are my men, and where are the priest and the housekeeper?" demanded Schmidt.

"You'll be joining them soon enough."

Schmidt noted the pistol his adversary gripped tightly at his side. His mind searched for a way out. If he couldn't come up with an idea very soon, he would be as dead as his two colleagues probably were. Suddenly he realized he possessed a valuable tool: his two-way police radio, holstered to his belt. If he could just have a split second to switch the radio on to "transmit," he would virtually broadcast to the dispatcher what was transpiring. No sooner had he realized this than the man in front of him turned his head toward the choir loft and signaled the rifleman to come down.

Schmidt coolly reached back around his left hip and flipped the switch to "transmit." The rifleman, intent on following his leader's command, did not detect the discreet movement.

Lieutenant Gregor Wolfsberger was a veteran law enforcement officer and second in command of the tiny Grinzing police force. He had been sidelined from street duty for the past three weeks because of a pinched nerve in his back. His friends and fellow policemen claimed the injury was due to his overly enthusiastic style of dancing the polka the night of the Saint Joseph's Fellowship Social. Wolfsberger claimed it was brought about by cutting firewood. He didn't mind this temporary assignment as desk sergeant/dispatcher. He actually enjoyed the usually calm and unhurried atmosphere of the police station. Pushing away from the desk to refill his coffee mug, he stopped when the green light came on at the top of the Motorola two-way radio receiver. He did not hear the loud, clear voice of his chief—the customary, "Base, this is Schmidt." Instead, he heard a voice that was not speaking directly into the radio microphone. Wolfsberger shook his head in mild dismay, thinking his boss was starting to get kind of sloppy in his old age. "Can't keep up with this modern technology, eh Robert?" he grumbled as he rose and headed toward the coffeemaker in the adjoining room.

~ * ~

"You know, Mr. Policeman," said the Russian, "you, your fellow policemen, the priest, and the old woman have all done your best to interfere with my job."

"And what exactly is your job, sir? I have no intention of interference, not even knowing what your business is about," Schmidt said, fishing for as much information as he could, hoping to God the message was being picked up on the other end. "I am curious, however, about the shipping container around the back of the church. Do you represent a building contractor or a construction company or something like that?" He hoped he did not sound too incredibly stupid.

"You really want to know, don't you? You, my friend, are too nosy for your own good. That's the problem! Your comrades shared that same problem. Do you want to see what happens to people who do not mind their own business? Come here; I'll show you. Come to think of it, it doesn't actually matter. We're going to have to kill you, too, just the same."

He led Schmidt down into the cellar as the rifleman prodded him in the back with the muzzle of the automatic weapon. Chief Schmidt became ill upon seeing what appeared to be four dead bodies, lined up neatly on the

411

floor, lying in a pool of their combined blood. He could barely hold back the bile in his stomach.

"Why?" he shouted angrily, then suddenly changed to a much calmer tone. "I do have a right to know."

"You have no rights! Shut your mouth!" shouted the Russian officer.

~ * ~

Grinzing, Austria
9:30 p.m.

After ignoring the mostly inaudible chatter on the opposite end of the two-way police radio for several minutes, Lieutenant Wolfsberger suddenly took interest when he heard the familiar voice of his chief cry out in an alarmed tone he had *never* heard from him before.

"Why did you have to kill him? Father Ebersbach has never caused anyone the least bit of harm. You murdered a holy man, and you *will* pay the consequences! You are an animal!"

Wolfsberger heard another party laugh in the background, and then an unfamiliar voice said, "What the hell is *this*?" He heard a loud static pop; then all went silent.

"God in heaven!" Wolfsberger blurted out loud. "What a fool I've been. Schmidt has been trying to alert me all this time. Something terribly wrong is happening up on the hill!"

Wolfsberger sprang to his feet and was out the door. The only vehicle he had access to was the small Tomos motorbike parked in front of the police station. Chief Schmidt had the only handgun on the police force. There was an old double-barreled shotgun locked up in the cabinet, but Schmidt also held the only keys.

Just as well, thought Wolfsberger. *I couldn't control the bike and carry a shotgun at the same time. Better to get to the source of the problem right now than to worry about fire power.*

~ * ~

10:00 p.m.

Wolfsberger was halfway up the road to the church when he noticed a roadblock about one hundred meters directly ahead. *Now this is very strange. What's going on up there?* He geared down, turned the bike around, and headed back down the hill. He needed to gather his thoughts before doing something that might endanger him or the chief and his two cohorts, if they were somehow involved.

Wolfsberger drove the little Tomos APN6 carefully off the road, turned off the headlamp, and proceeded to drive on the grassy strip that separated two large vineyards. The police lieutenant knew the area better than the back of his hand. This is where he had grown up and spent most of his waking hours as a boy playing and later working in and around these vineyards. He could navigate through this area in day or night without a problem. Nothing here had changed in the last century or so, without much exception.

In Kahlenberg, the lights in the restaurant that sat atop the hill overlooking the broad expanse of Vienna and surrounding environs were not the same. Normally the lighting was more or less uniform throughout the dining area, with some soft overhead lighting and individual flickering candle lamps on each of the tables that lined the large picture windows. Now only a few overhead lights were on and no table lamps were lit, although some sections had a blueish glow that could barely be detected from where Wolfsberger had stopped to observe. Gregor Wolfsberger dismounted the bike, put the kickstand in place, and began to climb the remaining part of the hill on foot. He didn't want the bike with the noisy baffle to give away his position.

When he came within fifty meters of the outdoor observation deck, he could see the silhouette of a man with a rifle slung over his shoulder. On the roof of the building he saw another pacing back and forth in the dark.

The structure was built into the hillside. At the east end, the earth virtually wrapped itself around the structure, the ground coming within four or five feet of the top of the lower level, as opposed to the ten or twelve-foot distance between the wide windows above and the steeply sloping hillside on the opposite corner. Ivy covered most of the ground at the base of the building and crept halfway up the foundation.

Wolfsberger was now in a position to get a clear view into what used to be the dining area. He saw several men sitting in front of CRT screens and some in front of what appeared to be radio controls, computers, and other sophisticated electronic equipment. *Looks like some kind of high-tech communications center, but why? Why here? Who are they, and what are they doing here in Kahlenberg?*

The veteran police officer wished he could hear the conversations on the other side of the glass, but that was impossible. He looked for Schmidt, but saw no sign of his boss or his other two fellow policemen.

Wolfsberger backed away from the building, careful not to attract the attention of the man on the roof or the one patrolling the observation deck. Coming around the southeast corner, he saw a large rectangular-shaped object that looked similar to a truck trailer, directly behind the old church. He moved closer for a better look. The doors were open, but in the dark he couldn't tell what the metal container held, if anything at all.

Just before Wolfsberger was able to enter the "box," he stopped dead in his tracks when he heard approaching voices. Taking cover in the dark corridor created by the near proximity of the container to the back wall of Josefskirche, he squatted down and waited in perfect silence. One of the approaching men carried a flashlight. He could not see the men, but he could see the beam from the flashlight dancing haphazardly across the cobblestone surface.

The door nearest him was opened wide, providing his basic cover. If it were moved in either direction, he would be found, no question about it. Wolfsberger heard the metallic squeak from the other door. *Scheisse!* He anticipated being discovered at any second. Through the gap on the hinged door, he could see the light being shined inside and heard someone rustling around inside the container. He then heard the familiar sound of a car or truck door slam shut and the ignition give life to a fairly powerful engine.

Headlights flooded the courtyard area, and the vehicle within the metal box began to pull out. Once out of the box, the man with the flashlight opened the passenger side door and got in. The vehicle drove slowly out of the courtyard.

Wolfsberger could hardly believe what he saw: a military truck with three sleek rockets mounted on its back! He watched it until it stopped only a hundred meters or so away on the adjoining lot that provided parking space for church visitors. Another man with two flashlights was standing at the far end of the parking area, just before the steep downward slope, directing the armed vehicle into place, as a ground crewman would guide an airliner into place at the gate of an airport. The vehicle and its weaponry pointed south toward the capital city of Austria.

The police lieutenant knew this old church as well as he did the rest of the surrounding area. Instinctively, he headed toward the cellar of the church. In his youth, the cellar of Saint Joseph's Church had always intrigued and mystified Gregor Wolfsberger. Dark and musty, with all of the characteristics of a medieval dungeon, it always seemed the ideal spot for anything leaning toward the sinister. As a boy, Wolfsberger and his young friends would sneak into the cellar and play imaginative games of hide and seek, envisioning themselves as early Christians hiding in the catacombs, escaping the wrath of the Roman legions. In their early teens, they found comfort in the solitude of the dank atmosphere of the cellar and indulged themselves in some of the finest product of the Grinzig vineyards.

If Chief Schmidt was in trouble, the cellar would be the logical place to look. But if Schmidt was in the cellar, whoever was holding him there would certainly have locked the cellar doors, wouldn't they? Of course they would, and there was no give to those heavy timber doors. *Ah! But did we ever risk using the cellar doors and getting caught by Father Ebersbach?* he thought. *Of course not!*

There was a large coal chute near the northeast corner of the building. Wolfsberger prayed it was still functional and not bricked up as most of them were when the antiquated coal-burning furnaces were replaced by cleaner, more efficient gas and electric furnaces. "Praise be!" Wolfsberger muttered to himself as he found the secret entrance to his childhood land of imagination. The hinged doors to the chute seemed so much smaller now, compared to back then, and he wondered seriously if he could squeeze through the opening. As he slid the bolt back and opened the metal door, he saw there was at least one low-watt light on in the cellar. Sucking in his stomach, he was able to fit through the coal chute without much problem.

The distance between the opening and the floor was not as far as he had remembered it either. His feet touched the ground, and his head barely cleared the top edge of the chute. Suppressing a cough caused by the dust and mold he had stirred up, Wolfsberger moved quickly toward a single bare light bulb that hung from a floor joist about three quarters of the way down the passageway. It was the musty smell that took him back so many years. The darkened alcoves and cubby holes off to either side of him still retained the eeriness he remembered from his youth.

Nearing the dimly lit area, he slipped on something, falling backward. He extended his arms back to break his fall, and his hands felt the slimy substance that had caused him to slip. Lifting a hand closer to his face, he caught a whiff of the stuff and shrieked. The feel and smell of the blood caused him to vomit immediately. Once back in an upright position, Wolfsberger pulled himself together. He was a cop, he sternly reminded himself, and these things shouldn't bother him so much, plus his back was throbbing with pain. *Shake it off!*

In the darkest corner of the open storage bin, Wolfsberger could make out some horizontal shapes. He feared the worst, and that's exactly what he got. There were the bodies of Father Ebersbach, the housekeeper, and two men dressed in the same navy blue police uniform as his own: his two friends and colleagues. "Dear God!" he repeated softly, over and over. *What is going on?*

416

~ * ~

11:15 p.m.

Focusing again on the problem at hand, Wolfsberger still needed to locate Chief Schmidt. He moved toward the light. Only ten steps away, just around the corner, he saw the chief and another man bound together and tied with thick nylon binding strips to a large timber that supported the floor above.

Their mouths were gagged with strips of cloth. Wolfsberger worked at unknotting the gag around Robert Schmidt's mouth first, nervously rattling off a series of questions. "What in heaven's name is going on here? Are you all right? Who is this man?"

"Thank God you finally showed up." Sensing his second in command's frazzled state, Schmidt said calmly, "First settle down; then I'll explain."

By now, Wolfsberger had taken the cloth gag from Gerhardt Richter's mouth, as well. After taking a deep breath and swallowing hard, Richter blurted, "We have very little time, and the safety of Vienna and all of Europe is in jeopardy. Get these damned bands off my wrists! We all need to get the hell out of here. They have promised to kill us both, and I would guess, knowing General Krause, he would want to schedule this show as a warm-up act to his 'grand finale' before setting off the fireworks across all of Europe."

Quickly, Richter explained who he was and what he was doing there to avoid any questions that could slow down progress. "Now find something—anything—that will cut these bands so we can get out of here," he ordered. "I *need* to stop this mad man!"

Wolfsberger immediately began searching for a sharp object to cut the construction-grade nylon bindings, which were drawn tight with a ratcheted end through a snug opening that locked in place. Most of the cellar was in total darkness. He searched as best as he could in the few small areas where the light from the single bulb could reach. Disgusted and almost in a panic, the police lieutenant came up empty-handed. "Now what?" he asked his chief.

"Go back to the station. In my desk, in the lower left drawer, there is a hunting knife that will cut through these. You'd also better put these gags back in place in case someone comes back down here. Now go, and be quick about it, Gregor!"

Wolfsberger moved as if he were twenty years younger. He found a wooden chair and placed it below the coal chute making the climb back out through the narrow opening with relative ease. After quietly closing the metal door behind him, he began his trip back down the hill to his motorbike as fast as his legs would carry him.

Chapter Thirty

Vienna, Austria
Saturday, October 2, 1993
11:20 p.m.

The audience was on their feet. The orchestra and cast deserved the standing ovation. Snapping back to reality, Mark Bucher watched as the Russian general retrieved his leather-brimmed uniform hat from a valet at the end of the aisle.

"Laura, let's go!" Mark's command was a little too abrupt to suit Mrs. Bucher, breaking the magical spell.

"I thought you were finished with all of this 'cloak and dagger' nonsense! Henry said—"

"I know what Henry said, but I just want to see where this guy is going, that's all."

They rushed down the wide marble staircase, through the Grand Lobby, and out to the Opernring at a pace unlike that of leisurely opera goers, stopping under the canopy of the main entrance. Luckily, not many of the patrons had reached this point yet; most lingered and savored the taste of possibly the best opera company in all of Europe, as Laura had wanted to do.

Too much in the open, thought Bucher as he guided Laura away from the brightly lit curbside. Taxis stood ready for their fares, some already beginning to move out.

At the very opposite end of the taxi queue, also away from the bright lights, Bucher caught a glimpse of the general stepping into a taxi that quickly scooted out into the flow of moderate traffic on the Opernring.

Trying not to appear too hurried with Laura in tow, Mark gave calm instruction to the driver of the first taxi to follow the black Audi taxi at a safe distance. "But don't lose it," he said. Somehow that deeply embedded spirit of adventure had crept to the surface once again.

~ * ~

As soon as Krause arrived back at his HQ, he quickly learned Captain Bakhvalova had apprehended the police chief of the small neighboring town, who had been snooping around, and now held him prisoner along with Richter. But the more unsettling news was that the communications center was unable to raise any of the seven launch crews by radio. "What do you mean we can't reach any of our launch crews?" he asked incredulously. Krause immediately sat down at the center console, the frequency already dialed in, and picked up a microphone headset. "Bengal One, this is Headmaster, do you read me? Come in, Bengal One!" He tried again. Still no reply. Moving on to Bengal Two, Three, Four, and the other remaining location netted the same result. No one was answering the call. *Something must be wrong with the transmitter. Each of the seven radios couldn't be out!*

"Get me the communications officer. Now!"

Ninety seconds later, Lieutenant Charkov reported as ordered. "Why can't we reach any of our launch teams?" demanded Krause. "What seems to be the problem, Lieutenant?"

"Comrade General, I don't know what the problem is. It's as if they have all shut off the power. We first lost contact with Rome and London early in the evening, and then the other five seemed to shut down randomly within the span of a few of hours. I've tried everything. I've even run a cable out to that ORF—Austrian Broadcast Corporation—high frequency tower about four hundred meters down the road, but that didn't solve the problem, either. If that can't reach them, nothing will. The problem definitely appears to be with each of the units individually."

"Do something! Do anything! Just make damn sure you get our communications back up! I want this problem resolved within the hour. Understood?"

Officer Gregor Wolfsberger finally reached the relative safety at the bottom of the hill below the historic Joseph's Church and the now transformed communications headquarters of the new fledgling communist party. He found his abandoned Tomos motorbike and used what energy he had left to kick-start the engine. Without the headlamp, as before, he made his way through the vineyards toward the single road that connected Grinzing to Kahlenberg at the top of the hill overlooking the twinkling lights of Vienna from a distance.

The taxi driver did an excellent job of putting a tail on the black Audi taxi: not too close, but not enough distance to let him slip away. It seemed the driver was enjoying every mile of this fare. He had watched car chases on TV and in movies a hundred times, but had never had the occasion to actually try it for real. They followed the Audi north through the small town of Grinzing and began an upward climb. The driver was able to allow more distance now because, as he explained, "There are really no other turnoffs the Audi can make. This road ends at Kahlen—"

Just then the driver stomped on the brakes, veering off the road to his right, narrowly missing a man on a motorbike who had darted across the road with no headlight on. The man on the bike also swerved to avoid a direct collision, losing control and skidding sideways, scraping the bike and his right shoulder across the pavement.

The driver and Mark Bucher jumped out of the taxi to see if the man on the bike was all right. "Stay put, please," Mark told Laura.

In the beam of the taxi's headlights, it became apparent to Laura the person they had almost struck was in uniform. "Oh, my God, a policeman!"

The police officer sprang to his feet like an animal that had been momentarily stunned. Seeing the motorbike driver appeared to be okay, the taxi driver headed back to his vehicle. Experience as a city taxi driver had taught him that as long as this policeman wasn't badly injured, he didn't want to stick around and be held responsible for this accident.

Before Bucher could ask if he was okay, the policeman began talking franticly. "You must help! Please take me back down to the Grinzig station; it's not that far. You passed it on the way up." He gasped for breath. "There are two men, my chief and another man, being held prisoner up at the church, and there are four dead bodies up there, as well. I have no doubt they will also kill Chief Schmidt and the other man, too, if we don't free them very soon! I need something sharp to cut them free." Still talking fast, Officer Wolfsberger continued: "And the other man mentioned that some general has plans of blowing up Vienna or something."

"Who is this other man? What does he look like?" asked Bucher.

"I think he is a Russian soldier, most likely a high-ranking officer. He's not terribly tall but taller than you, blond hair and average build. He speaks German with a northern dialect— definitely not Austrian."

"Gerhardt Richter," Bucher said under his breath, putting a couple of pieces of this new puzzle together.

In a crisis situation, roles can often be reversed. Halfway up the hill between Grinzing and Khalenberg, the pinnacle overlooking Vienna, the man in a black tuxedo instinctively took charge. The policeman was obviously still shaken by the near collision, along with all he had witnessed in the church cellar and the real threat of what might happen in the very near future.

"Okay, here's the plan," Mark Bucher calmly told the Grinzing policeman. "I've got a knife, and I'll go with you to cut these two men free. Then we'll hightail it back down here to safety. But for right now, sir, please stay right here. Sit down and catch your breath. Relax for a minute, and I'll be right back."

Bucher walked back to the taxi, stuck his head inside the rear passenger-side window, and addressed the driver loudly so Laura could hear. "Please take the lady directly back to the Grand Hotel Wien as quickly as you can."

Turning to Laura in the back seat, he whispered in her ear, "This is *very* important, so listen carefully. Okay? Call Talbot as soon as you get to the room. Tell him I've found the Russian general he's been looking for and that he has Richter and the local chief of police held as prisoners. Also mention there is some kind of threat to the city of Vienna. Tell him the location is the old church in Kahlenberg, just up from Grinzing, and tell him to send some help, *fast!* Got all that?"

"Yeah, I think so."

"Good. As soon as you're off the phone with Talbot, I want you to pack up our things, change into some traveling clothes, and be ready to leave just as soon as I get back. All right?" Mark Bucher extended his body halfway through the window for another farewell kiss and embrace. "I love you, hon," he said as the taxi started to pull away. "I'll be fine. Don't worry."

Laura stared at her husband. Was this a bad dream? Could this really be happening? Was this really Mark? None of this stuff was in the travel brochure. It was all so bizarre. First the incident at the hotel in Munich, and then Mark leaving to attend to some business from which she was still being shielded. Now he had tracked some Russian general to his lair halfway up a dark mountain. *None of this makes any sense!* she thought.

Especially strange to Laura was the fact that her spouse appeared to actually know what he was doing in this crazy situation. He had always been full of surprises in the last twenty years, but this beat all, hands down. Trying to stop him or talk him out of this was out of the question.

"Jesus, I trust in you," she said quietly, with complete sincerity. It was the only prayer she could muster.

The attempts to restart the flooded motorbike were futile. Bucher rolled it into the tall weeds along the side of the road. Wolfsberger and Bucher would make the long trek through the vineyards and up the hillside on foot. Bucher could tell his new colleague was in pain, but he pressed on in spite of it. Gregor Wolfsberger would lead the way up to Josefskirche and the adjoining newly established Russian command post.

Finally at the top, Wolfsberger and Bucher were able to look into the dimly lit communications center near the corner of the building. It didn't take long for Bucher to spot the general, still wearing his dress uniform. Krause stood with his arms folded across his chest and a severe expression on his face as he listened to one of his subordinates who was seated in front of an electronic control panel. The younger officer seemed to speak with a great deal of animation. Bucher and Wolfsberger wished they could hear what they were saying.

They needed to move on, to reach Richter and the police chief, but two sentries blocked their path. It was the only way to get to the far side of the church and the coal chute. The guards were going nowhere. Wolfsberger and Bucher were frozen in place, hunkered down in the ivy and underbrush until the two guards changed their position. After what seemed to be well over an hour, one of the guards checked his watch, said a few words to the other, and both began to walk away.

Wolfsberger and Bucher moved quickly, assuming that two more guards would begin standing this post within minutes. The two men proceeded with great caution, looking for any additional guards who might be walking another post on the other side of the building. All was clear on the east side of the church. They moved down through the coal chute and hustled in the direction of the single bare light bulb. As they approached the stench, Wolfsberger remembered to warn his partner to watch his step as they crossed the dark liquid that had spread across the passageway. Bucher didn't ask; he didn't really want to know. By now the adrenalin was pumping through the rookie NSA operative's veins, and his heart beat like a bass drum.

Somewhere along the line, Mark Bucher's never-ending thirst for adventure had been satisfied and was simultaneously replaced by an urgent call to duty. He was *the* man. There was no one else at this place, at this time, who could prevent the man-made catastrophe that could take place any minute at the whim of this deranged, self-proclaimed leader of the new communist party.

Police Chief Schmidt heard footsteps approaching rapidly: two people, he quickly deduced. He strained to see in the darkness of the passageway. *Ah, thank goodness. It's Gregor and—"*

The tuxedo-clad figure entered the circle of light.

Oh, my God, it's James Bond!

Seeing the astonished look on Schmidt's face, Richter looked in that direction and immediately recognized Bucher as the cut-out who had delivered the satellite control discs and, in return, passed along the microfilm intended for Talbot about seventeen long hours ago.

Who is this guy, anyway? he thought, relieved to see that help was finally at hand, but agreeing their rescuer might be a bit overdressed for the occasion.

Wolfsberger untied the gags as Bucher pushed up his right trouser leg and drew the combat knife with a seven-inch blade to cut the prisoners' thick nylon bindings.

~ * ~

Although venting his anger openly, Krause was realistic and recognized there could very well be a greater threat to his mission than having a glitch in his communications, if that wasn't bad enough. With a look of pure rage in his eyes, Krause yanked an AK-47 from one of the two soldiers standing guard outside the doorway of the communication center.

"Come with me!" he growled. Both soldiers followed.

Stephan Krause was not one to go down without a fight, nor did he believe a wrongdoing should go unpunished. He knew full well he still held a single trump card—the fate of the capital city of Austria—and no one, by God, no one, would take that away from him!

He had postponed the execution of Richter for a more appropriate time. Well, there was not a more fitting time than right now, considered Krause, and he could guarantee the execution would be appropriate for a spy.

Although the policeman had simply shown up at the wrong place at the wrong time, creating a nuisance of himself, he would also bear the brunt of Krause's hostilities.

~ * ~

Before Bucher had begun cutting through the industrial nylon binding, they heard heavy footsteps coming down the stone staircase at the near end of the passageway. Without a word, Wolfsberger and Bucher darted back into darkness. Bucher indicated to Wolfsberger to go, to get to safety. He pointed toward their exit.

No point in both of them being found if Bucher was to be discovered. Bucher took the time to sheath his knife and draw the 9mm Browning High Standard from his shoulder holster, holding it at the ready.

Officer Wolfsberger made his way back to the coal chute. He briefly considered leaving, as the guy in the tuxedo had directed, but chose instead to stay and make his best effort to help free his chief and the other man, regardless of the odds. He cursed silently that he felt so useless without a weapon.

Upon reaching the bottom of the stone steps, Krause began to speak, still some distance from his prisoners. "Mr. Richter and Mr. Policeman, your time is up. I had originally planned a long and drawn out—" Krause stopped mid-sentence as he noticed his captives were no longer gagged. They were still securely bound, but the two pieces of cloth were lying on the floor.

"Well, this is indeed interesting," said Krause, knowing it was physically impossible for either man to have reached his hand to his head or to the other's head and untie the gag. Surveying the setting for a moment, he noticed several dark smears on the floor near the prisoners. They seemed to come from the far end of the passageway. Krause motioned to the armed soldier to follow the bloody tracks to where they originated.

At a quick pace, the soldier shot past Bucher standing perfectly still in his dark alcove. Three or four seconds later, a loud CLANG sounded, like metal against bone. Wolfsberger had taken advantage of the minute or so he'd had in the nearly perfect darkness of his hiding spot below the coal chute to locate a weapon: a simple but effective coal shovel. Wolfsberger's eyes had had time enough to adjust to the darkness, but the soldier, coming directly from under the bare light bulb, was running blind. Wolfsberger could see and hear him coming. He choked up on the handle of the shovel and took a full, square swing from the shoulders with all of his strength, connecting the flat steel surface of the coal shovel to face of the Russian soldier. The sound was horrific, followed by the sound of the man and the rifle hitting the stone surface of the floor.

Bucher did not hesitate. He poked his head out far enough to see the general and one other soldier standing under the light. The general spun around, aiming the automatic rifle in the direction of the noise.

"Drop the rifle! Now, General!" Bucher yelled from the protective cover of darkness.

General Krause responded with three short bursts, spraying the black passageway. Bucher fired a single warning shot well over the heads of the general and the unarmed soldier, still standing in the circle of light. "Drop it, now!" Bucher yelled again.

Krause came back once again with another burst of three or four rounds from the AK-47. When the ricocheting bullets and the deafening echoes stopped, a single shot delivered from the far end of the passageway struck the general in the left shoulder, causing him to spin and fling his weapon sideways, clutching his wound with his right hand.

Wolfsberger had quickly put the opposing force of the two remaining Russians on the defensive by his fast and decisive move to use the rifle of the unconscious soldier to better even the odds.

The unarmed soldier who had been standing near Krause was somewhat stunned by the gunfire and was wiping the blood of his superior officer from his face. He hesitated just for a moment before diving to the floor and scrambling toward the automatic rifle, but it was time enough for Bucher to advance and hover over the outstretched soldier who was only inches from grabbing the stock grip on the AK-47. The Russian sergeant looked up, made eye contact with Bucher and the 9mm, and immediately rejected the idea of taking any further action. By this time, Officer Wolfsberger had made his way back to join the others. In spite of his heroic actions, he was trembling like a leaf in the wind.

General Krause lay quietly in a crumpled heap, his dress uniform blouse soaked in blood.

"Now get us the hell out of here before someone else decides to come down the steps," barked Richter. "Come on, hurry up!"

Bucher holstered the handgun and quickly went to work with the commando knife, cutting through the durable nylon bindings with the razor sharp blade as if he were cutting kite string. Police Chief Robert Schmidt and Major Gerhardt Richter both rubbed their wrists to get back the circulation in their hands.

"Tie this one up, and stuff a rag in his mouth. Quickly!" Richter ordered the police chief, pointing to the soldier now spread-eagle on the ground.

Looking down on the general and then back to Bucher, Richter bent down, picked up the AK-47, handed it to Bucher and said, "Finish him off."

Bucher looked at the major in disbelief. "I can't just kill the man!"

"Yes you can. He *is* the enemy, damn it!" shouted Richter. "And just who the hell are you, anyway?"

Before Bucher could even open his mouth for an abbreviated explanation, the sound of small arms fire could be heard coming from very nearby, probably just outside the main doors of the church. Now the chatter of a larger caliber machine gun was also very clear, returning fire, as well.

~ * ~

The people in the town of Grinzing had never seen such a procession of so many police vehicles of all shapes, sizes, and functions: police squad cars, motorcycles, SWAT Team vans, and even two armored cars equipped with M-60 machine guns in place of the water cannons that were normally mounted on top. Hundreds of blue flashing lights against a faint shimmering of pink in the eastern sky streamed through the narrow main street of the town and up the side of the mountain.

The roadblock halfway between the town of Grinzing and their Kahlenberg objective offered only slight resistance to the convoy of Austrian State Police. The Russians had not anticipated any counter measures of this magnitude. A few wasted shots were fired at the oncoming tank-like armored car before the soldiers dove out of the way as the vehicle smashed through the wooden barricade.

Hearing the shots fired and a garbled radio transmission gave the communication center their first warning that something was in the wind.

Krause's detachment of guards were not without firepower. They had two PKMS 7.62-mm machine guns positioned on the southwest and southeast corners of the observation deck, providing an excellent field of fire. The machine guns held back the onslaught of Austrian police, pinning them down on the road about three hundred meters out. Only the armored cars dared move to find a more advantageous position to return fire.

"We don't have time to debate this issue now!" shouted Richter, yanking the rifle back from Bucher. "I'll do it myself, for God's sake!" Quietly, he added, "…and it won't bother me one bit."

All eyes shifted toward the top of the stairs when they heard the exchange of gunfire, obviously very close by. This was good news, because evidently someone had dispatched the cavalry to save the day, but bad news because the Russian soldiers had just received a wake-up call. Their senses were sharp, alert for anything out of the ordinary, and most importantly, they were looking for immediate guidance and direction from their leader, General Krause.

Footsteps moved quickly overhead in the direction of the stairway. Schmidt, Wolfsberger, and Bucher were already racing back down the passageway. The coal chute was their only exit.

Richter lifted the automatic rifle to his shoulder, took aim at Krause's head, and squeezed the trigger. *Click.* Nothing. "Shit!" exclaimed Richter, extracting the magazine. Out of ammunition. He could now see the black leather boots coming rapidly down the steps. He sure as hell couldn't stand

and fight with an empty weapon. Gerhardt Richter dropped the rifle and sprinted toward what now appeared to be a speck of light.

Wolfsberger, Schmidt, and Bucher had cleared the coal chute and dashed across an open area of about forty meters, vaulted a low stone fence, and took cover among the trees and thick underbrush. They felt relatively safe; they had not seen anyone in their brief trek across the open ground. Hopefully no one had seen them, either, and it was still quite dark in the cover of the surrounding thick vegetation. The three waited and watched for the Russian major. They figured he must be right behind them.

The instant Richter turned to run, Krause was on his feet, having "played opossum." True, General Krause had taken a round to the shoulder, causing him to lose his grip on the AK-47 and causing his body to torque. He did have pain, and he had lost some blood, but neither was severe enough to cause him to lose consciousness. Krause also knew he had spent the last round in his final burst of fire. He had just bet his life on it and won. He *would* have the last say.

Krause reached into the ammo pouch of the soldier tied up on the floor, extracted one full clip, and loaded it into the AK-47 as he ran down the passageway.

"Ah, he's coming now," Wolfsberger said as they watched Richter come through the coal chute and run in a straight line toward them. Even though he couldn't see them, it was the shortest distance to the tree line. Richter had almost reached the low stone wall. A single shot rang out, and the three could clearly make out the contorted expression on the face of Gerhardt Richter just before he fell face first onto the smoothed cobblestones of the courtyard.

They now saw another figure emerge from the coal chute. Krause, standing about chest high out of the opening, laid the rifle down outside and struggled slightly, due to the wounded shoulder, to pull himself out of the chute. Bucher, Schmidt, and Wolfsberger were dumbfounded.

The general picked up the weapon and began to trot toward the front of the building, in the direction of the vehicle with the three slender rockets perched in their launch racks.

Incoming friendly fire was picking up. Some tree branches, slightly above and to the right of the three were ripped apart by machine gun fire. Even friendly fire cannot determine the good guys from the bad.

"We've got to get out of here!" shouted Wolfsberger.

"No!" protested the police chief. "We need to stop this guy and bring him in!"

Bucher waited a moment, trying to evaluate the situation. "Sir," he said, addressing Schmidt, "we are way outnumbered, and just listening to the firefight out there, I'd say we are obviously way out-gunned, as well. It would be suicidal to go after these Russian soldiers with just a rifle and a handgun. I say we first find safety and live to fight another day."

Schmidt nodded his head in agreement.

More machine gun fire seemed to be inching closer.

With a real sense of urgency, Wolfsberbger said, "Come on, let's go! Follow me. I know a safe way to get back down."

Officer Wolfsberger still carried the Russian's automatic rifle. Schmidt was unarmed. Bucher handed Schmidt his 9mm Browning. "Here, you take this. I'm sure you're better qualified at using this than I am."

Schmidt didn't want to admit to this stranger he had never fired a semi-automatic pistol before. He took the weapon.

With Wolfsberger leading the way and Bucher bringing up the rear, they started to make their way through the woods on a gradual downhill slope.

Mark Bucher paused and looked back over his shoulder, just in time to see the general climb into the driver's seat of the rocket-launching vehicle. The two policemen continued to make tracks down the hillside, unaware Bucher was no longer behind them.

Bucher stood and watched. A couple of seconds later, he saw the rack assembly that cradled the rockets raise from a transport position into what he correctly assumed to be a firing position. Now Bucher realized *this* was the whole scheme of things. *This is what Talbot and Richter had originally set out to do, to stop these missiles from being fired.*

Bucher had no idea of the killing power these rockets contained, poised and pointed at the city of Vienna below, but he knew he was the last line of defense before thousands of innocent people were murdered at the hands of a terrorist masked in the cloak of his political agenda.

Letting his instincts take control, Bucher sprinted toward the M-5 rocket launcher. He stopped at the rear of the vehicle to catch his breath and to figure out what to do next. He wished like hell he had not given up the 9mm. *At least I might have been able to persuade this guy to stop, at the point of a gun, but that's no longer an option.* Bucher was committed; there was no turning back now. He shut his eyes for a second, took a couple more deep breaths, and prayed, *Dear God, please help me.* Then he shot around the left side of the M-5 and flung open the driver side door, catching the general completely by surprise. Bucher grabbed Krause by the injured left arm and gave it a fast and powerful downward tug, causing excruciating pain, then punched him straight in the face with everything he had. Bucher stood there flat-footed, expecting a solid hit like that to be a knock-out punch. At the very least, he thought the punch would stun Krause enough that he could drag him out of the vehicle and away from the controls of the deadly missiles, but Krause didn't seem fazed. He simply shook his head as if annoyed by an insect. Only a second later, his eyes filled with rage. *Shit!* thought Bucher.

Sitting high in the driver's seat, Krause leaned back and immediately retaliated with a quick kick to Bucher's chest, knocking all of the air from his lungs and dropping him to the ground, buying a little more time to complete the launch code. The general, now stretched awkwardly across the front seat with his left leg partially over the edge, reached toward the control panel, attempting to continue the launch code. When Bucher got to his feet, he saw a possible opportunity to equalize the fight Krause had been winning, *if* he could just react fast enough.

Only two steps away, he grabbed the open driver side door with both hands and slammed it shut as hard as he could, catching the general's ankle between the door and the metal frame. Bucher could hear the bones crush, followed by a blood curdling scream like he had never heard before.

The Kevlar-plated door rebounded open, and Bucher could see Krause pick up the AK-47 that had been lying on the passenger seat. Bucher lunged for the weapon, but was too late; the butt of the rifle smashed into the side of his head. For the second time within a minute, Bucher struggled to his feet, finding it hard to keep his balance on the verge of losing consciousness. Though his head was splitting, he was coherent enough to recognize the metallic sound of the charging handle and the bolt of the AK sliding forward.

He knew the general was in no shape to come after him with a shattered ankle; he just had to stay out of his limited range of sight. Bucher staggered to the back end of the M-5, within inches of the exhaust nozzles in the tail section of the XG-777 missiles. There were only fifty yards between him and safety, just beyond the low stone fence—a sprint that would take him no more than ten seconds. *Do I run, or do I try to stop this maniac?* The thought lingered for a brief moment.

Mark Bucher knew in his heart what he had to do, but there was a hang-up, a deeply rooted hang-up he couldn't quite pin down. *Can I do this?* It wasn't about his own safety, and he didn't have time to analyze his feelings. He knew these missiles were intended to wipe out the city of Vienna, which now included Laura, along with a population of two million people. Everything was going way too fast.

Three or four seconds later, he heard and felt the vibration of the launch rack moving from right to left. Without stopping to think, Bucher drew the KA-BAR from the scabbard strapped to his leg and charged the cab from the left at a full run. Krause, still in the driver's seat, sat upright holding the AK across his chest, waiting for Bucher's return. He would be ready for him this time.

When Krause heard the approach, he drew the rifle back about shoulder high, poised to give his persistent assailant another taste of the butt end of his weapon. He tried to view his oncoming adversary in the side-view mirror, but the half-open door distorted his view.

Charging from a crouched position, Bucher seemed to appear from nowhere. He sprang up, deflecting a glancing blow from the butt of the rifle with his left arm and driving the blade of the knife sideways into Krause's torso, splitting the ribs and puncturing the left lung. Krause seemed to be in suspended animation; his eyes bulged, and his face froze. After what felt like long minutes but were actually seconds, Krause's body went limp.

Mark Bucher exhaled, withdrew the knife, and started to walk back toward the stone fence. He could not believe what he'd done. He had just taken a human life. He felt sick to his stomach and in his heart. He tried desperately to remember a conversation he'd had with his religion teacher at Aquinas, a priest named Father Anderhalter, about twenty-five years before. It seemed to make a lot of sense at the time. *What was it he told me?*

From behind him came the sound of the powerful electric motor turning the gears of the traverse and elevation mechanism of the M-5, moving the launch rack that contained the three nuclear-tipped XG-777 missiles from right to left. *Wait a minute. Who's operating this thing? It can't be. The general is dead!*

And then it stopped.

It must have been Stephan Krause's determination and unquenchable thirst for power and complete control that had given him the strength to hang on. With a thin stream of blood trickling down from the side of his mouth, and in spite of the terrific pain from all of the injuries he had just endured, he managed to extend his right hand across to the keyboard that sat to the right on the center console nearest the fire control officer's position. He entered the last digit of the five-digit manual override code that controlled the horizontal movement of the launch rack, hesitating as he tried to remember the last five digits to complete the firing sequence.

Seeing the missiles now moving in the direction of the hillside overlooking the city jolted Bucher back to the moment. Still clutching the thick, leather-wrapped handle of the KA-BAR in his right hand and not knowing what to expect, he darted back to the M-5. Whatever it was— *whoever* it was—had to be stopped.

Approaching from the passenger side, Bucher threw open the door to find the general's outstretched body with his fingers systematically striking the keys on the keyboard and lighting numbers on the digital read out. In a split second, Bucher noticed two things: four red lights on the digital display and the High Voltage symbol on the center console directly beneath the flat keyboard control panel.

Krause looked up and into his adversary's eyes as Bucher's right hand came crashing down with every bit of his strength, driving the seven-inch knife blade through the back of the general's hand and through the thin plastic keyboard, making contact with the 220volt power source directly below, literally pinning Krause in place. With the blade of the KA-BAR serving as the conductor, 220 volts surged through the general's body. He gave a short cry, coughed, and jerked with pain one last time.

The stench from the burning flesh was nauseating. Mark Bucher turned away. It was over. He wanted to run, but he couldn't. His legs would not support him. And there was still the risk of being hit by the barrage of bullets that filled the air or of being spotted by the Russian soldiers. It would be better to lay low next to this Army vehicle, reasoning the friendlies would not shoot in the direction of the rockets. He could only wait and listen to the ensuing battle being waged on the opposite side of the rocket launcher.

~ * ~

Once the two armored vehicles with the M-60s were able to negotiate better and safer firing positions, it wasn't long before the Austrian State Police were able to knock out the two Russian machine guns perched on top of the hill. This offered almost free access for the other police vehicles to proceed to their objective unmolested. It was now safe for the police to bring in their SA 341 Gazelle helicopter that had been waiting a mile away for the two big guns to secure the area. The chopper circled the hilltop searching for any Russian soldiers who might have wandered off into the woods once their stronghold had been overrun and it had become obvious theirs was a losing cause.

Bucher noticed the incoming fire had increased considerably. Seconds later, the larger Russian guns became silent, then the fire from below and nearby subsided rapidly until there were no shots at all being exchanged.

The silence was soon replaced by the sound of an approaching helicopter and the distant sound of vehicles coming up the hill. "Thank you, God!" Bucher said quietly.

A loudspeaker was instructing the hostile intruders to lay down their weapons and stand in place. "Do not move, or you *will be* shot."

Bucher got up slowly and watched the area become littered with police vehicles. Police cars with blue flashing lights quickly surrounded the M-5. A police officer with wavy gray hair, bearing some high rank with which Bucher was not familiar, got out of the passenger side of a green Mercedes squad car and walked toward the rocket-launching vehicle. Still dressed in his tuxedo, Bucher felt sure he would not be mistaken as part of the aggressor force. He dusted himself off and faced the approaching uniformed police officer.

"Ah, you must be Mr. Bucher!" the officer said, extending a welcoming hand. "I am Paul Borgsmueller, commander of the Anti-Terrorist Unit of the Austrian State Police. I am *truly* pleased to meet you."

Mark Bucher shook his hand and smiled weakly. There were no words. He looked around at the several dead and wounded Russians, and at others being handcuffed and stuffed into police vans. Bucher was amazed he was walking away from this with nothing more than a splitting headache and a very sore chest. Most important of all, the three missiles were stilled cradled in their elevated rack, and there was the city of Vienna below, unharmed and waking up to a beautiful October morning. Mark felt he must have been dreaming. *How could any of this be real?*

"Mr. Bucher, if you will please come with me. You have performed an extraordinary task, and we are most gratefully indebted to you. My people have the situation under control now, thanks to you. Your American colleagues will be here shortly to secure the missiles."

The driver, a young police sergeant, held open the door to the back seat of the squad car for Bucher. Borgsmeuller came around the other side and joined Bucher in the back seat, giving the driver instructions to "Go."

"We will first get you cleaned up, with a change of clothes and something to eat. You must be extremely tired and hungry," said

Borgsmueller. As they drove down through the town of Grinzing, the police radio chirped and crackled from the dashboard. "Do you possibly need to see a doctor, Mr. Bucher?" asked Borgsmueller.

"No. Thank you, but I really do need to see my wife and let her know I'm okay. And I'm also concerned about the two local policemen that were with me. Could you please check—"

"Excuse me sir," interrupted the driver, glancing in the rearview mirror, "but just a minute ago, the helicopter reported spotting two men in blue police uniforms coming down the east side of the mountain, toward the Hess vineyards."

"That would be them. Could you send someone to assist them? They've had a pretty rough day, as well."

"Of course, sir," said the sergeant, picking up the radio microphone.

Laura Bucher had ample time to take inventory of her feelings as she sat in the sterile and brightly lit-office of Commander Paul Borgsmueller. His staff was extremely courteous and had offered her more coffee or tea to drink than any one person could consume in a week's time.

Twenty minutes ago, the commander's personal administrative assistant had come in, sat by her side, and explained the very basic nature and gravity of her husband's involvement. She closed with the most important information, that he was perfectly fine and that Commander Borgsmueller had located him and they were presently en route back to the office.

Laura was elated and relieved that Mark was safe, and her anger that he would go off and do something so completely crazy like this, leaving her in the dark, was beginning to wear off. She also felt the beginning of a distinct feeling of pride for her husband. She realized, now that some things had been explained to her, that Mark did what he must have felt was his patriotic duty and his responsibility as a true humanitarian. The information she now had, coupled with trust built on twenty years of marriage, helped her fit the pieces together and made things more understandable.

~ * ~

Sitting back, perfectly relaxed, Paul Borgsmueller explained the string of events to Bucher, beginning at around three o'clock that morning. He spoke in a casual tone as if describing the preparations for a picnic in the park. Laura's phone call to Henry Talbot upon returning to the hotel had prompted Talbot—and then General Bussen—to notify Borgsmueller's tactical anti-terrorist unit, headquartered just outside the Vienna International Airport. Bussen realized he could not mobilize Captain Cleary's 425th Rangers faster than the Austrian anti-terrorist unit could reach the objective, fully equipped and ready to put down the threat.

Bucher didn't really care to hear about the details of this event. It was like listening to the post-game show after playing all nine innings. He knew the outcome. He just wanted to be with Laura.

"Is my wife all right? Where is she?" Bucher asked, knowing she must be going through hell for a second time.

"Yes, of course, she's fine; a little nervous, perhaps, but doing very well," Borgsmueller said, understating the facts. "She's at my headquarters right now, waiting for you."

Mark wanted to get cleaned up and change clothes before seeing Laura, to help lessen the impact. The image of her husband in torn and bloodstained formal wear would not be a pretty sight. But stopping to change clothes would take time he was not willing to give at this point.

The reunion was predictable: a most heartfelt embrace and an accompanying kiss with more feeling than a Strauss waltz.

An abbreviated conference call and debriefing was held with Agnussi, Talbot, and General Bussen in Borgsmueller's office, just for the official record. A more detailed accounting would take place at a later time.

"Well, Mr. and Mrs. Bucher, you are certainly free to go," Commander Borgsmueller later told them. "Your luggage is here, and my driver will be happy to deliver you anywhere you wish. Oh, and by the way, when I spoke with your boss, Mr. Talbot, he stated very clearly that you and Mrs. Bucher were welcome to stay and try to *enjoy* Vienna, on the company credit card, of course. Sounds like a good man to work for," he said with sincerity.

Mark and Laura agreed they should go back to the Grand Hotel Wien and stay an extra day or two in Vienna, at least long enough to eat, sleep, and get reacquainted.

Epilogue

TWA flight 821, Vienna to Dulles International
Tuesday, October 4, 1993
8:10 a.m.

The first-class cabin of the TWA 767 was quite comfortable for the return trans-Atlantic flight, compliments of the National Security Agency and Department of Defense.

After a leisurely two days in Vienna, both Laura and Mark were rested and ready to get back to a normal life in St. Louis, after a brief stop in Washington, D.C. Several people in and around the Belt Way wanted to meet this guy, Mark Bucher.

Just prior to leaving Vienna, the Buchers had received a telegram from Deputy Director Mike Agnussi at the National Security Agency headquarters in Fort George G. Meade, Maryland, inviting them to a private reception to be held in their honor tomorrow evening, as a small token of the nation's appreciation.

Captain Cronan Cleary, representing Company F (RANGER), 425th Infantry, would also receive a Presidential Unit Citation for his unit's service.

Unfortunately, the president, vice president, and secretary of defense all claimed to have prior commitments.

Realizing the importance of the mission taken on by a lone, patriotic civilian called to duty, Missouri Senator Tim Murphy and Congressman Frank Megargel from Missouri's Second District, serving as chairman of the House Committee on Armed Services, both agreed it would be a great honor to personally thank and congratulate the most recent hero from their state of Missouri.

No military band would greet them at the airport as they stepped off the plane; no interviews or media coverage would take place. In fact, the NSA could not even publicly acknowledge that Mark A. Bucher had had any part in the collapsed coup attempt that threatened millions of lives across the girth of Europe while they slept. Mark didn't have a problem with this. He was actually quite relieved.

~ * ~

"Mike, this is Hank."

"Why did I assume I was going to get to sleep until maybe five-thirty this morning?" said the deputy director of the NSA before even opening his eyes.

"Have you read your faxes yet?"

"Hank, it's oh five hundred. Think about the context clues here. You woke me up from a much-needed deep sleep. It's almost five o'clock, and no one would dare wake me with a fax unless we were being invaded by the ChiComs on the coast of California this morning. So your answer would be...no! I have not read any of my faxes yet, but I'm sure I'm about ready to find out what has taken place while I slept."

"Yep, you're right. You might call it a preempted 'I told you so.' Our link with the Russian wire service reads as follows: 'Yeltsin's troops are in the process of putting down an attempted coup d'état.' It goes on, 'Moscow: Russian "White House" attacked...troops faithful to Boris Yeltsin are holding off an attack believed to be spearheaded by General Aleksey Chesnokov,' etcetera, etcetera. So I guess what you were telling me about assets being spread so thin with General Chesnokov making waves in the political arena was not really an exaggeration after all. Could it be we were both right about these two lunatic generals?"

"Yeah, we were both right. But there was only one 'lunatic general,' and that was Krause. He was willing to murder millions of Europeans just for his own personal gain, just to be in control of this 'new order' communism. Chesnokov, on the other hand, was only interested in knocking out Yeltsin and anybody who got in the way, not the destruction of eight major European cities. I think Chesnokov really bumped up his campaign to oust Mr. Yeltsin once he caught wind that his underling, General Krause, had not only been stopped, but eliminated. Maybe this was the extra momentum he was looking for. I don't know." Agnussi paused briefly, thinking about his last statement. "Have you seen any print on Vienna or on the taking out of trash in the other seven cities?"

"No, Mike, not a word on this side."

"Not on this side either; knock on wood."

"You know, one has to wonder," Talbot said, thinking out loud, "if someone or some clandestine organization might actually have been involved in taking some of the sting out of Chesnokov's strike on Yeltsin. You have to wonder why all of Aleksey's troops didn't just mow down Yeltsin's faithful and leave the Russian White House in a pile of rubble."

Agnussi smiled, but did not respond to Talbot's hypothetical question. *One doesn't need to wonder when one knows.*

"Sure wish I could be there at your shindig for Bucher tomorrow night, but somebody has to mind the store. Please tell Mark and Laura I said hello, and extend my sincere thanks for a job well done. Oh, and you can also tell Bucher that if he's ever interested in going to work for me full-time, all he has to do is call."

"Good luck getting that one past Mrs. Bucher, but I will certainly relay your message, Hank."

~ * ~

Mark Bucher stared out of the small rectangular window at the steel blue North Atlantic about thirty-five thousand feet below. Laura had dozed off and pulled the navy blue airline blanket up over her head, blocking the bright sunlight that poured into the cabin. She refused to wear those silly looking blinders they gave you in first class. Mark wished he could sleep. His mind or, more accurately, his conscience was struggling with the events that had taken place over the last few days, specifically Sunday morning.

He clearly understood, after his teleconference debriefing with Mike Agnussi, Henry Talbot, and General Bussen, the magnitude of his service. Each one of them, in their own words, had told him he was truly a hero. Of course this all sounded great, and he appreciated all of the praise, but…now he could not help but see the contorted face of the Russian general every time he closed his eyes. The tape played in his mind, over and over and over again, starting with the moment he drove the knife into the general's side, then through the back of the general's hand, followed by a short scream and the death rattle. Then it would start all over again.

"Can't sleep?" asked Laura, peering out from under the blanket.

Bucher explained the problem, skipping the gory details; no point transferring his nightmare over to her. He could not believe he had actually killed someone! Were there other measures he could have taken to stop that man from making the last keystroke in that launch sequence? Why him? The thoughts filled his head, as if there was no room for anything else.

Mark stopped speaking as the flight attendant came by to offer tea or coffee in small white china cups with the red TWA logo outlined in metallic gold. Laura resumed the conversation once she had moved on.

In a stern tone, which took Mark by surprise, Laura said, "From what I understand from my conversation with Henry Talbot, after they located you, you must have had to really reach back for some kind of extra strength or courage to see this thing through to the end, to go the distance to stop this bad guy dead in his tracks." She immediately regretted her choice of words, but quickly recovered. "You did something no one else was able to do. You didn't even think you were capable of doing such a thing, did you?"

Mark shook his head deliberately.

"Call me crazy, but I don't think you were alone."

Mark raised a curious single eyebrow.

"I think—rather I should say, I *know*—the good Lord was with you all the way. You directly saved the city of Vienna from a holocaust, and you directly or indirectly made it possible for seven other teams of trained soldiers to stop similar catastrophes all across Europe. Let's face it, Mark, as capable a guy as you have proven yourself to be, you could not have done all that by yourself. I think God chose *you* to be His hand in stopping this unspeakable threat. You were at the *right* place at the *right* time. Not the other way around."

Laura paused a moment to let her words sink in. "You would feel guilty about taking the life of any living, breathing being. I can understand that, and that's one of the reasons I love you so much. You were doing exactly what you were called upon to do. You enabled several million people to live and restored peace, at least to this part of the world. So with that in mind, don't be too hard on yourself."

Finally, with a loving smile and a much lighter tone, Laura said, "Mark, I am *very* proud of you, but the next time you're called on 'a mission from God,' check with me first, would you, please?"

Mark smiled and drew his wife closer to him. He rested his head against the window, and Laura laid her head on his chest. They both slept in dreamless comfort for the next three thousand miles

.

About the Author

Photo by Jackie O'Rouke

The author is a graduate of Western Illinois University, earning a Bachelor of Arts degree. Bob Rothermich proudly served in the U.S. Army National Guard and presently follows a career in international sales and exporting. He enjoys distance running and has successfully completed several marathons. Rothermich is a member of the Catholic Writers of St. Louis and resides with his wife, Linda, in St. Charles County, Missouri.